By
R.J. Linteau

Kravitz and Sons LLC
1301 Farmville Blvd, Suite 104
Greenville, NC 27834

Published by Kravitz and Sons LLC.

ISBN: 979-8-89639-237-8 (sc)
ISBN: 979-8-89639-238-5 (e)
Library of Congress Control Number: 2025907345

Dedicated to all the friends that I made from 1966 to 1972 at
the University of Detroit, and to the great City of Detroit.

Many thanks to Kay Olsen, my editor. You rein in my bad ideas, celebrate my good ones, and are my writing conscience.

I offer my continued thanks to all my readers who have enjoyed my first three books.

<u>Novels:</u>

The Architect
The Black Orchestra
Voudo Island

<u>Screenplays:</u>

The White Rose
Second Trumpet

Greenville, North Carolina

"If I went to work in a factory the first thing I'd do
is join a union."

Franklin D. Roosevelt
President of the United States

ANGUS DRUMMOND

1887 / 1937

CHAPTER 1

1887
Aberdeen, Scotland

Callum Drummond walked into the stable where the odor of horse manure and moldy hay fouled the air. A setting sun glowed orange red behind his hard, muscular frame and cast a long and large shadow over the uneven wood floorboards. His young son, Angus, completed his chores, and shoveled the last of the horse droppings into a pail. It was April 29, 1887, and warmer weather had finally come to the County of Aberdeenshire.

"Angus, the Earl and her Ladyship will ride the bicycles tomorrow. The weather should be pleasant. Make sure they are in good working order. Do not forget to grease the chains."

"Yes, Da, I'll do it now."

"Your mother wants me to the house straight-away. Maisy's taken ill so you'll need to walk home. Be there before dark."

Eight-year-old Angus Keir Drummond, wondered what new ailment had now befallen his sweet, sickly sister. It didn't matter at that moment; he needed to tend to the bicycles.

His father was an experienced equestrian and looked after the horses and stables at Leith Hall for Lord Edward, 5th Earl of Aberdeen. Rose Drummond, Callum's wife of ten years, was a chambermaid in the great house. The Earl was aloof, demanding and often cruel to those in his employ; he treated them as chattel. A miser, he paid his staff barely enough to survive, but with little work available in 1887, it was better than starvation. The Drummonds did not live on the grounds of the estate like the houseman, gardener, or gamekeeper, but in a two-room weaver's cottage over a kilometer south in the neighboring hamlet of Portlethen. The town was poor, but the Drummonds were hard-working; the whole family worked, even Maisy when she wasn't ill with a fever.

Through his father's influence, the Earl hired young Angus to clean the stables for five pence a week, and he was allowed to keep two coins. In one corner of the stables, the Leith clan kept several bicycles that they rode about the grounds and into town. Angus kept them in good working order, but had strict instructions from his father never to ride them, as the earl instructed upon hiring the young lad. But the simple conveyances fascinated young Angus.

The stocky boy with deep red hair put up the broom and carried out the last bucket of manure, emptying it into the pile behind the barn. He washed his hands under the frigid water of the pump, filled a pail, and fetched a clean rag. The bicycles, stored along with the grease can in a small pen beside the tack room, leaned against rough, wooden walls. A wistful sigh escaped his lips as he looked at their shiny black frames, thick white-wall tires, and the woven wicker baskets. The bells on the handlebars jingled as he moved the bikes into an open area of the barn. He reached into the bucket, wrung out the rag, and proceeded to clean the bodywork, the forks, then the wheels and spokes. The boy wiped the seats and baskets, and last, put his hand into the can of grease and applied it liberally to the chains, wiping off the excess so her ladyship's jodh purs would not be ruined. He studied the two chain wheels, the larger at the front attached to the pedals and the smaller at the back, the movement of the continuous chain forcing the rear wheel to turn. The front chain wheel provided the power.

Such a marvelous invention, simple but amazin' in how it all works, the boy thought with wisdom beyond his years.

He'd watch the lord and lady ride. It looked easy enough. He thought of his father's admonishment, but his Da had gone home. There was no one around. On Friday, the gardener and gamekeeper were at the pub, already half-drunk. Angus took one of the bicycles out to the gravel path that led to the manor's main drive. He lifted his leg over the top rail and sat on the seat. He set his left foot onto the pedal — easy enough. He pushed down on it as he had seen the earl do before lifting his right foot just in time to catch the other pedal on its downward movement. He pushed down against it. The bicycle lurched forward. Angus pushed down again on the opposite pedal. He realized he was moving forward, the conveyance wobbling from side to side, the novice rider unsteady. The front wheel and handlebars jerked left to right. Panicked, he jumped off the bicycle as it toppled over. He looked at the bicycle. *No harm done*, he thought. *Try again.*

Angus climbed back on, determined to conquer the machine and emboldened by the brief, exhilarating ride. He repeated the downward stroke of the left pedal, faster this time, then followed with a faster right foot the same way. Two rotations turned to three, then four, and five, more as his strong legs moved the bicycle forward. He pedaled faster, the machine gaining speed, the young boy gaining confidence with each turn of the chain wheel. He looked down at his feet and the front wheel. He felt the cool afternoon air on his face, his body alive with this new sensation. He moved but he wasn't walking. He looked up briefly to see that he was off the gravel road. He jerked the handlebar, almost losing his balance, but returned to the path. Angus pedaled faster mesmerized by the chain circling the wheel with greater velocity. The wonder!

The gravel road below him was a blur. He rode faster, and suddenly, gray gravel turned to grass. He looked up to imminent disaster. There was no jumping this time as the front wheel slammed into the trunk of an ancient oak. A horrible screech of metal filled the air. Angus flew off and missed the tree by a few inches. He landed hard on his chest and his head bounced off the soft ground. Unconscious for a moment, he opened his eyes, blinked twice and felt warm blood flow from his nose. The expanse of the estate spun around him. Angus caught a needed breath of air, focused, shook his head and then sat up and saw the shiny black bicycle shattered by the mighty tree; its front wheel mangled; the wicker basket, silver bell, and handlebar destroyed. The boy's heart sank; momentarily he thought it might even stop beating.

In the distance, he heard hooves pounding the ground. They beat faster and louder. Angus got up, his head foggy, his legs like rubber. He had to get the bicycle back to the barn and hide it. There were three more available for the Earl's ride tomorrow. He could fix this one afterwards. He looked up. It was the Earl on horseback, looking down at the mangled machine.

"What in God's name have you done, boy?"

"Nothing, your Lordship." He searched his mind for an adequate excuse. "I, I was, well, sir, I was just trying the bicycle out. Making sure I had not added too much grease to the chain. I guess I hit the tree."

"You guess? You've destroyed this bicycle."

"But sir, I can fix "

Lord Leith pulled on the reins of his horse and came astride Angus and began to whip him with his riding crop.

Angus cried out and put his arms up to shield his face from the sting of the leather whip.

"Stop it! You're hurting me!"

The earl continued his thrashing, shouted, "Insolent lad! I'll not stop and you'll be paying for a new bicycle you little bastard! When you have done that, you're dismissed from my service. Now take it back to the stable and get home. Tell your father I'll want to see him first thing in the morning."

The boy glared at his master, saying nothing.

"Have you nothing to say, you insolent child?"

Angus wiped the tears from his eyes, "Yes, M'lord. I'm very sorry, M'lord."

"Yes, you're sure to be more than sorry tomorrow."

Angus turned and walked toward the wreck. "You bloody asshole," he muttered to himself.

His father's belt stung more than he ever remembered. Angus had been whipped before, but not like this. Tears flowed freely and he screamed with each strike.

"Stop, Da, please stop!"

His mother, crying by the fireplace, wiped her tearing eyes with her apron.

"I've been denied a weeks' wages because of your foolishness. Your ma will probably be dismissed later today. We'll be destitute. I told you to never ride the bicycles!"

"Stop, Callum, stop! He's just a boy. He was curious and wanted to ride it, for the love a' Jesus. If you want to be angry, be angry with our bastard employer."

Angus felt the same anger. With each hit of his father's belt, his hatred of Lord Leith grew. *Bastard. Yes, you're an*

*asshole and a bastard and someday… someday, I'll get even.
I'll be better 'n richer than you!*

Later that night, very late, Rose came home. She had not
been dismissed due to the pleading of the head housemaid.
But she would also be docked two days pay for her son's
brief, but grand adventure.

CHAPTER 2

1891
Portlethen, Scotland

Edward Leith managed his steed across the wide stream on the grounds of his vast estate. The stallion picked his way carefully along the rocky bottom of moss-covered stones. The horse stumbled on a large rock. Startled, Leith pulled up the reins, and the beast steadied. The current was strong, and it took great effort to control the horse. It stumbled again, almost causing the earl to fall out of the saddle. He began to breathe hard and pulled again on the reins but his arm was suddenly numb. He tried again with no luck. Winded by the effort, he began to gasp and struggled for air. Then a deep, searing pain spread through his chest; he let out a cry of panic and anguish. He swayed in the saddle and fell off his horse into the cold, rushing water that carried his lifeless body to an inlet one hundred yards from the fall.

The cost of maintaining a 1,500-acre estate and a 37-room castle, despite, or perhaps because of, the earl's parsimonious ways, had been too much to bear. His only son, Andrew, became the 6th Earl, but could not right the floundering ship. Within two years, the spend-thrift playboy frittered away all his inheritance and was forced to sell Leith Hall. The staff dismissed, the manor house shuttered, and the furniture covered, the estate was foreclosed upon and given over to a barrister to find a new owner. But there were no buyers and the manor fell into disrepair, a victim of time, neglect, and the harsh Scottish weather.

"Da, why must we leave?" Angus Drummond, now 12, looked at his father, the once formidable man's shoulders stooped over, his hair turned white in only a year, the hands ruddy and thick, holding the reins of the horses pulling the wagon. The eyes were still sharp, but there was a sadness in them.

"There's no future here, boy, there's no money. That fool son, Andrew, squandered his inheritance and we are paying the price. America is the future, laddie. If not for me and your ma, for you."

"When will we go?"

"Soon. As soon as we save a bit more and sell all that we have what's worth sellin'."

Angus was silent. The thought of leaving Scotland was exciting and terrifying at the same time. He hated the dreary weather, the ever present rain, the smoke from the factories and the soot from the coal mines. But it was still his home and he knew little of that distant place called America.

Callum Drummond snapped the reins to speed the horses as they left the small village of Portlethen. A local stone mason had hired him to transport rocks to the construction site of a wall alongside the road to Aberdeen. The mason wanted Callum for his knowledge of the Clydesdales. They were huge, powerful, but stubborn beasts, the only animals strong enough to pull the heavy stone-laden wagons.

Once they arrived, Angus would help unload the rocks. It was hard work, and his strength increased with each day's work, along with the blisters and scars on his hands.

His father guided the horses down the rutted lane and said nothing. After what seemed to Angus an eternity of silence, the boy spoke.

"I miss Maisy."

"We all do, lad. She was kind and gentle, but frail. The fever finally kill… sent her to heaven." Callum's eyes moistened at the thought of his youngest child, consumed by a disease that no one could name, her small body wracked and burning with pain. All their savings were spent on her care. The bad luck seemed to go on endlessly. The Earl dead, then his son bankrupt, his job and Rose's gone. And then the fever finally took his darling Maisy. It was all too much for a sane man to handle. He looked into the distance, to the West. America would surely offer a fresh start and the hope for a better future for his family.

Father and son rounded a bend in the road and approached the work site. Masons slowly built the wall up to a meter high, large stones laid out on either side to allow for final selection and the best fit. Various infill rocks of other sizes lay on the edge of the road. Approaching, Callum was about to pull on the reins to slow the team when he heard the rumble, a low growl, a sound he had not heard before. Angus looked toward the noise coming from down the lane. Hurtling at them was a strange contraption, a wagon without horses. The two front wheels were smaller than the rear; there was a small front seat and a larger carriage seat. Upon it was Andrew Leith, steering with a horizontal wheel and a vertical lever. He wore a leather coat, goggles, a cap, and gloves. He was grinning like a man possessed.

The automobile sputtered and then backfired as it approached the wagon at the amazing speed of twelve miles an hour. The Clydesdales reacted with a combination of fear, then anger. Callum pulled back on the reins, but it was no good. The team, acting as one, reared up, quickened their pace, and headed toward the construction site. The front wheel of the dray hit a small rock at the edge of the road causing the wagon to veer toward the work site and the greater assemblage of stones. The wagon hit one rock after the other, the wheels cracking, splinters of wood flying in every direction. The horses' whinnied and bucked, angry. The horseless carriage sped by, the Earl ambivalent to the chaos it was causing.

Callum was barely able to control the horses and the wagon any longer; the front wheel hit the largest stone alongside the wall, and it collapsed into twisted metal and broken shards of wood.

"Jump!" he yelled. Angus needed no urging as the wagon rolled over. He leapt onto the dirt road, landing hard, but unhurt. However, Callum had nowhere to jump. He tried to remain on the seat, bracing his feet against the buckboard for a certain collision into the wall, and lost hold of the reins. The horses, in full fury, released from their master's hold, tried to go off in different directions, causing the wagon to lurch, turn, and then crash into the bulwark, stones flying. Callum flew over the wagon.

Angus got up and ran to the wreck. He stopped, unable to go further. His father's body was on top of the wall; his life's blood slipping away from a great, gaping head wound, his neck bent at an ungodly angle. Angus tried to scream but no sound would come.

CHAPTER 3

1937
Detroit, Michigan

Forty-six years had passed. Angus Drummond opened his eyes, looked around the large library and sighed. *What is the point of this sad reminiscence,* he thought. The image of his father, the man's life slipping away, his blood covering his face and dripping onto the stone wall, was as vivid 46 years later as it was on that miserable day. He looked at the sideboard and the crystal decanters.

To hell with the doctor's admonishments, he thought. He placed several ice cubes in his glass and poured a double scotch.

"Alright then, let's get this over with," he muttered, and eased into a big leather chair. He closed his eyes. Though the past was the past, for Drummond it was a sore that had never healed. So he re-lived it, not often, but often enough. Enough to feel the pain of his great loss. That day was the saddest day of his life, but also the day when he knew what he would do from then on, and it involved that magnificent vehicle that came at him, that horseless carriage, that motor car. He loved them, even though one had been responsible for his father's death. It didn't matter. Angus Drummond would someday build auto-mobiles, fine, shiny automobiles with engines as powerful as the Clydesdales.

After his father's funeral, thoughts of America were buried by the necessity of getting by every day. Besides, there wasn't enough money for passage for two people, even in third-class steerage. After several months, the general economy improved and his mother found work as a housekeeper for another lord and lady, and Angus became an apprentice at a machine shop, where he made small parts in a make-shift forge and fixed small engines. The work ignited his passion for engineering, and his diligence was rewarded with knowledge and decent pay. He began to save for America while they lived on his mother's meager earnings.

In 1893, the Long Depression came, and his mother lost her job again, but it was of little consequence. Angus had put away enough money to travel to the New World. Rose sold her wedding ring along with several other pieces of heirloom jewelry passed down to her over the years.

"Angus, this is such a busy, crowded place. I've no way of knowin' where to find the White Star Line's offices."

"Go ask the agent at the counter, over there. I'll carry our bags."

The two unseasoned travelers made their way though the throng of humanity that rustled through Liverpool's great train station. Rose Drummond moved to the back of the line at the Inquiry Counter.

"Ma, let me see the address the agent gave us."

"Where did I put it?"

"Try your purse."

"Oh yes, next to the Emigration papers."

His mother's hand shook as she removed the slip of paper. She handed it to her young son. Momentarily they were at the front of the line.

"How can I be of service, madam?"

"The White Star Line… "

"What about it?"

Rose said nothing, looked around the vast space, frozen.

"Maam?"

Angus moved in front of his mother and handed the piece of paper to the agent.

"Sir, how do I get to this address?"

"Oh, yes. Let me write the directions down for you. It's not far. But with your bags, you might want to engage a carriage."

"We'll walk, thank you."

With quick scratches of a fountain pen on thick parchment, the agent drew a map and wrote down street names.

"Here you are lad. Help your mum now. She seems a wee bit flustered. Go through that door and turn right," the agent said and pointed toward the main entrance. "Be a brave boy then. And watch out for pickpockets."

"Thank you, kind sir."

Angus handed his suitcase to his mother and took her hand. "Come Ma, let's go get our tickets for America."

Rose and Angus made their way down busy streets, searching for signs that matched the intersections sketched by the agent. The boy clutched his mother's hand, but held onto his mother's carpetbag more tightly as it contained all their meager funds. He was not about to have it snatched from his hand, strong and scarred from lifting rocks and operating a small smelter. Down the street, a dirty, large man eyed the two, sensing their anxiety. He walked quickly toward them.

"G'day, missus. Can I be of service to you and the boy?"

Angus spoke. "We're fine, sir. Leave us be."

"For a quid, I'll take you to wherever it is you're wantin' to go."

"I said we're fine. Let us pass."

The man looked at Rose closely, a twisted smile forming on his pock-marked face. "You're a pretty one. Lose the boy and I'll pay you for your treasure down there."

Fear gripped Angus. Then he reacted and kicked the man in the balls, and his fist delivered with a hard blow to the stomach. The man dropped like a rock. Rose, startled and confused, began to cry.

"Come on, Ma, I see the White Star sign down the street."

The two travelers quickly walked into the safe confines of the offices of the great White Star Line. Angus strode to an open window.

"Good day, sir. I want two tickets to America. Your agent in Aberdeen told us that a ship's goin' there and leaves in two days."

"Aye, the *Teutonic*. She's a newer ship, and most lovely inside. What kind of accommodations do you want?"

"Well two beds and meals… "

"I meant saloon, cabin or third class?"

"My ma and I have about twenty pounds. What class will that buy us?

"Third class. Seven pounds, three pence each."

"Well, I guess that's how we'll be goin' then."

"Gets you to the promised land in the same time as the fancy people in first class — six days."

The *Teutonic* carried 300 passengers in first-class and 1,000 passengers in third-class. Completing the ship's manifest were 100 head of cattle housed forward on the deck below steerage.

Third-class passengers entered through double iron doors slightly above the dock and after a long queue, they entered a cramped lounge, situated aft, directly above the engine room. From a desk, a purser and chief steward assigned beds, or cabins for families. Though clean, it was redolent with the previous voyages' odors of humanity, grease, and coal. It was warm and the air stale. The passengers were forbidden to open the portholes, the steerage deck so low in the water as to invite the sea to come roaring in, even in the slightest inclement weather. With the portholes closed the stench of cow dung from the deck below passed up through the forward staircase back to steerage.

Sleeping quarters were large cabins holding 20 unfortunate passengers. Fresh straw mattresses were stacked three high. The experienced passengers sought out the top bunks, so in rough seas, they would not receive an unwanted bath of vomit from above. Women, men, and families were segregated in different cabins and at 14 years old, Angus had to sleep with the male passengers, while his mother was in a cabin for the single and married women. They would be reunited each morning at breakfast, where they ate warm oatmeal, sausages and bread, the boy happy to be reunited with his mother. At night more bread and a potato-laden stew appeared with tough pieces of meat and some carrots or beans. For most, it was a feast, for they had escaped poverty and near famine.

During the first three days, Angus sat outside on the cramped deck space, huddled with other third-class passengers. He watched in awe at the power of the endless

Atlantic Ocean, with its dark water and great waves four to six feet high. His mother preferred the confines of the main lounge, the hot, stale air taking a toll on her lungs. Each day he would coax his mother outside, but after fifteen minutes in the cold, windy weather, watching the menacing sea, she retreated to the lower deck.

At night, Drummond sat in a corner of the men's common room while they played cards and drank until they could not recognize a jack from a king. Then the boxing matches began, and the contestants beat one another to a bloody pulp, as loud wagers were made. Angus took a keen interest and realized he had picked out the winner of each bout. On the third night, he laid down a bet with a bit of the precious money they had left over. He won. He bet on the next match, and won again. He continued until the end of the fights, winning all but one match. A large Irishman noticed Drummond's fistful of bank notes and decided to separate him from his winnings. The man grabbed Angus. The boy struggled away, kicking the big man in the groin. To follow, he landed a roundhouse punch to the jaw, which drew the approval of several other Scotsmen, who quickly surrounded the boy in a defensive circle. He was not bothered again.

On the last night, Angus thought about his successful encounters with men much bigger than him. He decided to box himself. Paired against a small Irishman, Angus gave $10.00 to a fellow Scot to bet it on him. The match was long and bloody. After five rounds, Angus had a cut above his eye and had won. He put $97.00 into his trouser pocket.

On the third day of the six-day crossing, the *Teutonic* was beset by foul weather and gale force winds. The engine's constant vibration and rumble, and the propeller shafts' groans, added to the passenger's misery. The Atlantic tossed the ship, less than 10,000 tons and 582 feet in length, like a child's toy boat in a bathtub. With every wave and swell, the constant heaving and rolling afflicted the passengers. On embarkation, they had been given tin-ware plates, eating utensils, and pails. After a day or two of rough seas, they realized purpose of the pails.

No one dared venture outside for fear of ending up in the icy-cold Atlantic. No one, but a stocky, red-haired fourteen-year-old boy. Topside was better than down below. At least the air was fresh and cold and he loved the hard rain on his face. With a well-worn bar of soap, he stripped to the waist and washed his body and hair, letting the rain and wind do the rest. He rid himself of lice and days of stink. He lifted his trousers, removed his shoes and secured them around his neck with the laces, and rubbed his skin clean. Once again, he tried to get his mother to come outside, promising to hold her tight in the face of the winds, but she refused. She preferred the lounge, packed full of immigrants, and the air foul with the lack of bathing.

On that gray, blustery day, Angus inhaled another mouthful of the swirling soot from the twin smokestacks, belching smoke from engines working at full throttle. He knew that he could not stay outside long for fear of freezing or drowning and now that he had washed himself, decided a visit to the engine room was in order. An inquiry to the steward was rebuked with a laugh and a quick dismissal: "Passengers are not allowed in the boiler rooms, laddie!"

Undeterred, Angus located a stairwell with a closed gate and a sign: "No Admittance–Crew Only." Though it appeared locked, Angus shook the chain until it opened into two strands; the lock had not been secured. He removed the chain, opened the accordion gate, and quickly descended a flight of steep iron stairs. He could feel heat build in waves as he climbed down further. Finally, deep in the ship's bowels, he found a narrow passageway leading aft some thirty feet to an oval-shaped door, the door-sill a foot above the floor. Another sign posted on the sooty gray-white hatchway starkly stated: "DANGER."

Undeterred, Angus grasped the wheel in the center of the door, turned it intuitively counterclockwise as if he had done such a thing many times before. It separated slightly from the bulkhead with a groan, and a blast of hot air pummeled his face with a fiery fist, heavy with the smell of industry. He pushed the door to the bulkhead and his eyes opened wide. Before him was a line of sweat-soaked bodies stripped to the waist, their wet skin covered in soot. Massive men with mountainous biceps shoveled great bucketsful of coal into boilers spewing fire and fumes. He slithered by the men, knowing full well that he wasn't allowed within this fiery pit. The main engine room had to be beyond these great coal furnaces that heated water, turning it into steam to power the ship's engines.

If he could only get by the stokers… he walked quickly; the last one in line rose up and saw him. He dropped his shovel and grabbed the boy by the scruff of the neck.

"What's this? A bilge rat? And where an' you thinkin' you'd be goin' boyo?"

"I just want to see the engine room, mister. Nothing more."

"Come with me then!" The hard-muscled man dragged Angus by the neck who struggled to get free past the boiler room and into the three-deck-high engine room. Great iron pistons, shining with grease, pushed down and returned upward in a smooth, continuous motion. The room was an orderly confusion of brass pipes aligned in rows going in every direction. Beyond the engines, Angus could see to the very rear of the steamship, two round shafts that terminated at a large black wall, the rotating propellers beyond the hull. He stood in awe of this great temple of the machine age.

Angus was taken to a large steel-grated deck, the bridge of the engine room, enclosed by a black iron railing, stairs leading up and down, fore and aft. In this area, polished brass gauges monitored the rotation of the engines, the water temperature, the steam pressure, the ship's speed, and other crucial barometers. They were all arranged at various levels, visible by the ship's engineers at any time. This was the beating heart of the vessel.

The stoker grabbed the prostrate boy's hair and jerked his head up. An imposing man in a black uniform stood before him, his sleeve bearing three gold braids trimmed in purple. There was a grim look on his face.

"Who's this then?"

"I don't know, Chief, beggin' your pardon. A stowaway, maybe?"

Angus kicked backward, hitting the shin of his captor. He tried to free himself from the man's grasp, which only became tighter.

"Owww, you little shit! I should throw you overboard now!"

"I'm not a stowaway. I'm in third-class with my ma. I only wanted to see the engine room. Let go o' me!"

A small smile broke on the Chief's face. "Well, now, you've seen it. Go back to your mother. And don't come back here again or you'll be in the brig for the rest of the trip."

"Can't be any worse than steerage. And I'm not done looking at things, sir."

"Cheeky lad, eh? I guess you might have a point about your accommodations. What do you mean, son, you want to look at things?"

"Well, sir, I've worked on small engines, but this is, well, it's magnificent!"

"Indeed, it is." The second engineer looked at the stoker. "Mr. Callahan, you may go back to your shovel. I'll deal with the boy."

"Ay, sir." Callahan frowned and sulked away. He hoped to garner a small reward for capturing the intruder.

"What's your name, lad?"

"Angus, sir. Angus Drummond. I'm going to America."

"Indeed, we all are if we can pass this storm. The engines are working hard to compensate."

"I saw the heavy smoke billowing out of the smokestacks, sir."

"You were on deck on a day like this?"

"Better than being inside."

"You're inside now…"

"But this is different. You've got great furnaces boiling the water, makin' steam. The steam gets pushed into those big chambers, and the built-up pressure causes the energy to move the pistons there up and down. That makes the shafts turn, and the propellers move the ship forward. Anyway, me thinks it's something like that, sir."

The second engineer looked at the youth before him, amazed. "You're a smart lad you are young Angus. Come back tomorrow at eight in the mornin'. I think I can use an assistant. I'll teach you more about engines; and there may be a silver dollar or two in it to boot."

"Yes, sir. I mean, aye, aye, sir, Chief…?"

"Second Chief. Name's Fitzhugh. James Fitzhugh."

"Pleased to make your acquaintance, sir."

"The pleasure's all mine, Master Drummond. All mine."

Chapter 4

RMS Teutonic

Rose Drummond began to cough incessantly on the fifth day of the voyage. She took to her bed, the now moldy, rotting straw making things worse. Poultices of mustard plaster on her chest did little to ease the cough. Then she began to spit blood. Chief Fitzhugh let Angus leave the engine room and tend to his mother. But he knew what ailed her; it was commonplace for such passengers. The ship's doctor was summoned. A cursory exam diagnosed the disease… tuberculosis. It was the most common ailment contracted among people traveling in steerage.

But the full impact of the disease was worse. Rose Drummond would be denied entry to the United States. Angus didn't know what to do; he could not leave his mother, but they could not return to Scotland.

"Ma, I'm told they have fine doctors at Ellis Island, at the hospital. They'll get you well, and we'll be off to our grand adventure in America."

"I'm thinking the adventure will be yours, my son. I'm dying."

"Don't say that! Don't even think that. We lost Da, and I'm not about to lose you."

"It's all right Angus; your father's waiting for me up there in heaven." A bony finger pointed upward.

"Just rest, Ma. Just rest."

Two days later, the ship docked. Rose Drummond, ashen and hardly breathing, was taken off the *Teutonic* on a stretcher by two white-jacketed orderlies, her son beside her. Two American silver dollars and a roll of foreign currency, almost $100, were safely tucked away in his suitcase. More valuable though was the name, address and note of recommendation that Chief Fitzhugh gave Angus for his brother-in-law, a foreman at a steel mill in Bethlehem, Pennsylvania.

At Ellis Island's hospital, Rose Drummond received a minimum of care. A perfunctory exam told the doctors that she would not live out the week, and all they could do was make her comfortable. After two days of attempts to feed his mother some hot broth and bread, to take deep breaths, to open her eyes, Angus watched his mother take her last breath. Angus sobbed more than he'd ever done, the boy hugging her lifeless body, crying deep sobs of grief. He had lost everyone he loved, and the grief was unbearable.

Because he was now an orphan, Immigration sent a telegram to his nearest relation, an uncle in Aberdeen. The uncle replied that Angus was not needed and could not be cared for back in Scotland, which was a great relief to the boy, as he never wished to return to that sad, miserable place. But what then? Where would he go? Who would care for him?

The matron looked down at her young charge. "Come with me."

"Where are we goin'?" Angus stared at the lady, her face hard and uncaring.

"Where I say. You're an orphan now, so where do you think?" The fearsome woman grabbed him by the arm. He tried to wrestle free, but her grip, as strong as the stoker on the ship, only increased.

"Lad, you're going to a school for boys without parents. An orphanage. They take your kind in, God knows why."

"My kind?"

"Yes, Irish immigrants. You're over-running New York, coming in by the thousands. You'll ruin our fair city. You're a plague of locusts, takin' over everything and everyone!"

Angus tried once more to free himself from the clench of her thick hand. He might have succeeded, but at that moment of uncertainty and fear, his heart wasn't in it. It beat hard with a greater fear of the unknown.

"I'm a Scot. I'm from Aberdeen, Scotland, you witch! Let go a' me!"

The warder spun Angus around and slapped him hard across the face. "Watch your tongue, you impudent little shit. Now, move along. We've a ferry to catch."

"Here's another foreigner for you, Brother Jonathan. This one's a handful. Be careful. He might be a runner."

The tall, muscular cleric with dark eyes and black hair looked down at the boy, thrown at his feet by the Immigration agent.

"Thank you, Miss Rutledge. I think I can handle him. Stand up, lad. What's your name?"

"Angus. Angus Drummond. From Scotland!" The boy glared at Miss Rutledge.

"A fine name. And I can certainly tell where you're from by that accent. Welcome to your new home. You're at Saint Anselm's School for Boys."

The long dormitory was quiet now except for the sounds of sleep — a slight snore, a deep breath, a low whistle. Yellow light from gas streetlamps outside invaded through tall windows and created a backdrop of uneasy, moving shadows. Earlier, those shadows were real boys who snuck up on Angus sulking in his bed, dragged him to the center of the large room and proceeded to give him a ritual beat down, an initiation for a new charge. It was a tradition at St. Anselm's, and the brother's tacitly approved of the hazing, for to survive in New York, you had to be tough. Though he fought back valiantly, there were too many boys, a few older and stronger than him. He took the punishment in a fetal position, refusing to cry.

The confident boy who had negotiated the backstreets of Liverpool to find the White Star shipping office; who had boxed victoriously on board the *Teutonic*... had vanished. Angus shivered in his bed, though the night was warm. Tears welled up in his eyes. He turned, and cried deeply into his pillow until he caught his breath, inhaled, sat up and took in the shadowy space. It was all too much to handle, so he lay back down and covered himself with his blanket to shut out the new world. A world hard and mean, and unforgiving. And Angus Drummond was all alone in it.

You have a new home, Angus — America. It's where your Da and Mum wanted you to be. Make the most of it. Make the most of yourself. Don't let the bastards take you down.

Initially, Angus kept to himself, because of the initiation, partly out of childhood shyness, and mostly as a defense. During the first week, at night, he checked his suitcase under the bed and counted his small fortune, and kissed the photo of his mother and father before locking it with a key, safe on a leather woggle around his neck.

Brutus, the oldest orphan at St. Anselm's, whose bed was across the main aisle from Angus, took note of the late night occurrence. As his name implied, he was the school bully, and at almost sixteen years, the biggest and strongest boy at the school. Soon, on his birthday, he would be released into the streets of New York, to join a gang to rob and terrorize the city with other Irish thugs.

One evening before curfew, Brutus asked Angus what was so special about the key around his neck.

"Nothing that you should be concerned about."

"I want that key, you faggot. I know what it opens. Your kit will be mine. And you can't stop me. You're a sissy and cried like a baby the first night. I heard you."

"I've no fight with you. Leave me be."

"Are ya deaf? Gimme that key!" Brutus reached out to rip the key from Angus' neck.

Angus grabbed the imposing boy's extended arm and quickly put him in a half-nelson. He kneed him from behind; a cry of pain summoned other boys to watch. Angus held Brutus immobile. "I said, leave me be or I'll break your arm."

Brutus struggled to free himself. He kicked Angus like a mad donkey, and freed himself, turned round to face his prey.

"You want a fight, then?"

"No, I want to be left alone. You'll not have my belongings."

"I will!" Brutus raised his fists and moved in to the kill.

But Angus he had not used his most powerful weapon — his boxing skill. Within a minute, Angus dropped the would-be thief like a rock with a solid right hook, an upper cut, and blows to the ribcage. The bully's head hit the iron bed rail. He rolled on the floor, blood flowing from a significant gash. Angus reeled back in horror; memories of his father dead on the stone wall flooded his mind.

"Damn you to hell, Brutus!"

Two brothers entered the dormitory and found the large boy, bleeding and unconscious.

Six stitches were required to close the wound, and for his major infraction of the rules, Angus spent a week in solitary.

The weeks and months passed. Angus grew more comfortable with his surroundings, he found he was a natural-born leader, and made friends easily. He returned two-fold the teasing and barbs that were natural among teenage boys.

His shock of red hair, the easy smile, and Scottish accent attracted the other boys who called him "Brick," a nickname earned from his stocky, muscular physique and the beating he had given Brutus.

Life at St. Anselm's School for Boys was rigorous, but the brothers were good men who cared about their charges. For the next two years his entire world would be a relentless and demanding education. The Christian Brothers realized that Angus was bright and eager to learn, and advanced him quickly from sixth to ninth grade. He excelled at mathematics, physics, technical drafting, and shop, where he wanted to work on anything mechanical. In the gym, he honed his boxing skills.

He loved to read, and especially liked Charles Dickens's *Oliver Twist*, James Fennimore Cooper's *Last of the Mohicans*, and a short story, the *Adventures of Sherlock Holmes*, by Arthur Conan Doyle, followed by other books about the great detective.

On the morning of his sixteenth birthday Drummond was summoned to the headmaster's office.

"Angus, today is your sixteenth birthday. You can leave St. Anselm's if you choose, or stay on one more year. What would you like to do?"

"If'n it's all the same, Brother Jonathan, I need to leave."

"Ready to face the world outside, then?"

"I have to face it sometime."

"Tis true. What are your plans?"

"I'm going to a place called Bethlehem in Pennsylvania. There might be a job there for me."

"I see. Work in the steel mill?"

"Yes, I hope so. But I want to build machines. Things that move. Have you seen those new horseless carriages on the street, Brother?"

"Yes, they're marvelous."

"Aye, they are."

On foot, he made his way to Bethlehem, Pennsylvania, hitching rides when a carriage would stop and pick up the ragamuffin boy. After a week of travel, he reached the great industrial town. The smoke seemed to blot out the sky. It was an ugly, foul place, and it reminded him of the mines and factories of Aberdeen. But the town burst with the raw energy of the industrial age. The note from the chief engineer had its desired effect. He went to work at the Bethlehem Iron Company.

The job in the steel mill was as hard as anything he had ever encountered in his brief existence on God's earth. He worked six days a week, twelve hours a day; the work was hot, dismal, and dangerous. He and two other men guided hot ingots along the conveyor belt until they were out of the furnace, and then lowered great metal jaws onto the iron. Fastened, the jaws moved the bar onto an adjacent set of rollers for the same trip in the opposite direction until the metal had reached its intended thickness. His body became rigid and muscular, just like the steel he forged from the Bessemer furnaces.

A grim, two-story boarding house provided simple accommodations for two dollars a week — a hard bed, a chair, a washbasin, and facilities down the hall. The rent included dinner with ten other boarders, served by a gruff woman who couldn't cook. Occasionally, he would walk to a nearby hotel for a feast of roast beef and apple pie`a la mode. Beyond that extravagance, and an occasional bottle of scotch, he saved every dollar and dime he could.

One rainy Saturday evening, after yet another unappealing dinner, he and several other boarders who worked in the steel mill, visited a local fight club. He watched the fighters carefully but did not bet. He returned the next week, scrutinized many of the same pugilists, remembered their techniques, and noted the toughest brawlers. The following week, he went back and placed wagers, modest at first, but in larger amounts and with the same success as he had on the ocean crossing. His winnings became substantial, so he opened a savings account at the local bank.

The fight club was crowded, the air thick with smoke from cigars and cigarettes. Bottles of Irish and Scotch whisky were passed around. Two fighters in the ring seemed determined to beat one another into oblivion, as blood flowed freely from cut eyebrows and torn lips. Angus yelled at the fighter he had bet on.

"Finish him! Finish him!" Drummond screamed; he had bet five dollars on the man, almost a week's pay.

This time the object of Drummond's wager didn't comply. A solid uppercut against the ropes sent him sprawling and unconscious to the mat and a certain ten count. Angus ripped his chit in disgust.

"Why don't you get in the ring?" Sean Murphy, a fellow boarder, yelled at Angus above the cheers for the winner of the bout.

"I'm don' want to ruin me good looks."

"Fighters make ten dollars to show up. If they win, fifteen. I could teach ya."

"Why don't you box, then?"

"I did, back in Dublin, but I lost an eye. Quit, because this world's got no use for blind people. But I can teach you. Gimme three dollars for each match and I'll be your corner man."

"Will I win?"

"Ifn' you do as I tell ya."

"What about me mug?"

"I'll teach you footwork, dancing. I bet you already know how to hit, but we'll work on that, too."

"I learned a little in New York."

"Show me."

Drummond put up his fists and circled Murphy, taking a few jabs that didn't land. He moved in and never saw the hard uppercut from his new friend. Angus fell, sat up and shook his head. "You got a deal, Murphy. When do we start?"

"Monday night after the shift."

"I'll be a wee bit tired, but I need the money. I'm not workin' in the mill forever. I have bigger plans."

"Drummond, you'll be the death of me. We've been here since seven and it's now eleven o'clock. We have work tomorrow, remember?"

"Murphy, my first fight's Saturday night. I want to be ready."

"Angus, I taught ya footwork, keepin' your hands up, jabbin', and now you got a solid right hook and a good uppercut. I think you're ready."

"Good then, we'll call it a night in another half-hour."

"Sweet Jesus, Angus!"

The following Saturday night, Angus made fifteen dollars, and thirty more from bets he and Murphy placed. Over the next nine months, he won often. There were only two losses: split decisions, not knockouts. And his handsome face was intact, save for a small scar above his eye and he sported a short red beard.

After two years, Drummond's savings account contained a substantial amount of money, over $4,000. Now a man of 18, he quit the foundry that he thought of as hell-on-earth and bought a train ticket to Detroit, Michigan. He knew little about the growing city, but knew that a few carriage companies and several automobile manufacturers were there. If automobiles were going to be built, Detroit seemed poised to build them. And any place was better than Bethlehem, PA.

CHAPTER 5

1897

Detroit, Michigan

The Baltimore and Ohio locomotive slowed to a crawl as it pulled nine Pullman cars onto one of six terminus tracks that comprised the rail yard of Union Depot. The station, located at the corner of Third Avenue and Fort Street, connected Detroit with the rest of America. The imposing red sandstone edifice had been completed just a few years earlier. The boarding platforms led to a good-sized greeting room and into an immense waiting hall several stories high. With the gawky stare of a newcomer, Angus Drummond turned and took in the size of this first introduction to his new city, a bustling center of transportation. He removed a piece of paper from his pocket given to him by a fellow passenger, a businessman on the train.

"What's your game, son?" asked the well-dressed man to the handsome young fellow across from him in the same compartment as the train chugged into the Pennsylvania night.

"I'm a boxer, a prize fighter," was the reply. "And I'm looking for lodging in Detroit."

"Go to the YMCA, then."

"What's that?"

"Young Men's Christian Association. It's a hotel, but they have a gym too. I'll write down the address."

"I thank you, sir."

The man listened to the reply. "You're a Scot, aren't you?"

"Aye. Angus Drummond."

"And you box?"

"In my free time. It pays good money. But what I really want to do is build the motor carriages."

"Now, doesn't everyone? They'll never be a success. But bicycles — that's the ticket. Name's McVicar, Donald D. McVicar. I'm about to open a shop in the city, McVicar Bicycle Sales & Repair."

"Are you now? I just happen to know something about them. A great deal, actually."

"Can you repair the cycles?"

"Aye, I surely can."

"You get settled at the 'Y' and then come see me. The shop is located at the corner of Woodward and Clairmount. I open the business next week; I believe I could use a hard-working Scot."

"Aye, I will come and see you. You can be sure of that."

Angus walked out of the station and rain was coming down hard. He glanced down at the note: *YMCA-Grand and Griswold*; he had no idea where that was. The ominous gray sky framed the deep-red silhouette of the great clock tower above the station hall, the dominant feature of the handsome and rugged Romanesque structure. The rain pelted his face, and he moved back under the awning. Hansom cabs lined up along the street. He knew they would be expensive, but his worldly possessions had grown to include a large suitcase and the small one brought from Scotland. Now was not the time to save a quarter-dollar. He tucked the note into his side pocket, and got in line with others waiting for a carriage.

Two days later, after Angus had paid for a month's lodging at the Y, and joined a large gym with a boxing ring on Gratiot Avenue, he was hired by Mr. McVicar for a dollar a day. Business was brisk for sales but not for repairs, so young Angus began to busy himself in the front of the shop. He assembled bicycles, arranged them in neat rows, and ensured they were dust free and shiny, well-oiled and ready for use.

He spent some of his savings on a good tweed suit, two white shirts, and several bow ties. His handsome, deep russet hair, green eyes, and strong, muscular physique impressed customers, and his winning smile elicited trust. Never shy, the natural salesman rarely missed ringing up a sale. Angus always greeted new customers at the front door, never waiting for the bell to ring.

"Good morning. May I be of some assistance to you fine folks?"

"Yes, we are interested in purchasing two bicycles."

"Aye, I can surely help with that. We carry several brands, but I highly recommend those of the Wright Cycle Company. They make the best by far. Two brothers, Orville and Wilbur, make them in Dayton, Ohio."

"Well then, let's look at what you have."

"They make two models, the Van Cleve and the less costly St. Clair. But I assure you, both are fine conveyances."

"What are the prices and the differences between them?"

"Yes, well, Mister… "

"Brooks. John Brooks."

"A pleasure. And Missus… "

"Elvira."

"Angus Drummond at your service. Now, the Van Cleve model comes in either a 22" or 24" frame and has, as standard features, coaster brakes, a one-piece crank, star sprockets, white wall tires… "

Mr. Brooks interrupted. "Yes, but is the bicycle easy to ride, Mr. Drummond?"

"Oh my, it certainly is!" He quickly thought of his first time on Lord Leith's bicycle and shook his head slightly.

"And the price?"

"Today we have a special. It is $50.00, including a year of service and a free bag of tools. The cheaper, I mean the less expensive St. Clair is only $42.50."

And so it went. Bicycles were all the rage, and despite their cost, everyone wanted one. After three weeks in the front of the shop, Angus sold 57 bicycles, most of which were the top-of-the-line Wright Cycle. McVicar promoted him to sales manager with an increase of another dollar a day.

"Sir, I would like to go on a commission basis."

"Commission?" McVicar stared in disbelief at his young protégé. He had just doubled the boy's salary.

"With all due respect, Mr. McVicar, I see the invoices from Dayton. You pay $26.00 for a Van Cleve. Your overhead for the shop is another $13.00. Your profit, if I've done my sums correctly, is $11.00, and that's on the 'sale' price."

"My overhead is $12.00 as I've just given you a raise and a handsome one to boot."

"Sir, I request a commission of two dollars on every sale of the Wright Cycles and a dollar on the others, and I want my two dollars a day salary."

"You're a bold lad. I just doubled your salary!"

"They make five dollars a day in the auto factories."

"And work you to death, too."

"I want a commission."

"Sorry, I won't do commissions."

"I'll turn in my notice, then." Angus crossed his arms, widened his stance, and said no more.

A minute passed. Mr. McVicar looked up at the ceiling, around the shop, and rubbed his hand through his gray beard. He stared hard at the upstart boy, who stared right back.

"I'll give you a raise to three dollars a day, no more."

"Five, like in the plants."

"Oh, for the love of Jesus, four, but no commissions. And only because you're my best salesman."

Angus nodded.

The following year, Angus made $1,248 selling bicycles and $1,115 in boxing matches. But he wasn't happy. Drummond wanted more.

CHAPTER 6

1899
Detroit, Michigan

Angus was distraught.

"What are you goin' ta doo?" his friend asked.

"I guess I need to enter more fights. I almost made as much last year on them as I did sellin' the bicycles, Jack."

John Bullard met Angus in a sparring match at the Gratiot Avenue Gym. Jack, as his parents called him, was a year younger than Angus, a bit shorter in height, and boxed in the lightweight division. They became close friends despite their differences. Jack neither drank nor smoked. Angus had a weakness for Scotch whisky and enjoyed a good cigar. Though frugal, he was not about to become a miser like Lord Leith and live an unhappy, parsimonious life.

Business was good at McVicar's, so Angus hired the young Irishman to fix bicycles at the shop while he met with the increasing influx of customers. John Patrick Bullard's ancestors lived near Ulster, the center of Irish Protestantism. His grandfather made his way to Georgia to Gilmer County, at the foothills of the Appalachian Mountains in 1850, a victim of the Great Famine in Ireland. Jack was one of eight siblings and grew up poor, as his father farmed ten acres of rocky land. Young Bullard was proud and full of prejudice against the Negroes who had arrived as slaves in the early

1700s, and the newly immigrated Catholic Irish fleeing the second famine of 1879.

He was 'Black Irish,' with black hair, dark coal-like eyes, and brown skin, but it had nothing to do with the myth of Spanish explorers being shipwrecked along the Irish coast. His grandfather, Shamus had bedded a Cherokee Indian woman. Jack was tough but not very smart, but he would do anything for Angus Drummond. He knew his friend would be a success and if he hitched his star to the young Scot, he would be too.

"I'll never be able to save enough money to buy the bicycle shop from Mr. McVicar," Angus said and took a sip of his whisky.

"Angus, this might be your answer. Look what I found on the bulletin board at the gym today." Bullard passed the handbill to his friend. "It says a big night of boxing is coming up at the Olympia. The under-card is going to feature amateurs against professionals. Pays $100 a match to the amateur, but a grand if you win, Angus."

"Fine. And I'll still be well short of what I need to buy the shop. And a professional? I don't know. Any one a' them blokes could pound me brains out."

"I've seen you fight. Hell, I've fought you. You're betterin' most of those monkeys who call themselves pros."

Angus looked hard at the handbill. "Maybe it could work."

"What could work?"

"I'll need your help. Will you be my corner man?"

"You know I will, in a heartbeat. And there'll be no quittin' on my stool just 'cus you're bleedin' a wee bit."

"I'll need your help before the match, too."

"How? Taping your hands and wiping your brow?"

"That for sure, and you could also place wagers. Bet on me."

"I would, but I've no money."

"No, you'll have mine. I'll give you the lion's share of every red cent I've saved."

"Oh, that's a wonderful idea. What if you lose?"

"I can't lose. I won't lose."

"How much we talkin' about?"

"I have $5,974.00, last count."

Jack whistled. "That's a fine sum. Could you perhaps be a little more exact?"

"I go to the bank every week and ask for an accountin'."

"Aye. I see. It says the under-card matches begin at six. There won't be many people in that big arena, and they generally won't be bettin' on the pointless matches of a professional against a green amateur. There are no odds to be had." Bullard had a point,

"Let me see what I can do about that. I'll give you $5,000, and you place the bets. If I lose, I'll still be able to pay me rent and buy groceries."

"Aye, and your scotch, too."

"I'll need it if I lose."

"Well train hard. I'll be your sparring partner; you won't lose." Bullard made a fist and gently hit Angus on the cheek.

"It says here the main event is Jack Johnson against Klondike Haynes. They call him the 'Black Hercules.' Two Negroes battlin' it out."

"I can't believe that two niggers are the main event." Bullard shook his head.

"Jacky, a fighter's a fighter. What difference does it make if a man is white, brown, or even green? We all bleed red. Anyway, I'd like to see that match."

"You will, if your eyes ain't shut from the fight. But we need a sportin' name for you. Somethin' that will inspire fear."

"Jacky, you been sippin' me whisky? You're daft."

"Dead serious, I am. All the greats have fightin' names."

"Yeah, they're all named 'Kid this' or 'Kid that.'"

Bullard looked around the rear of the bicycle shop. He stared over at the large workbench. "I know! Angus "The Vice" Drummond."

Angus laughed and finished his drink. "You're off your rocker, Jacky Bullard." He quickly surveyed the shop. "Okay, how about Angus "The Anvil" Drummond?"

"Perfect! You can't lose with that moniker!"

The next day, Angus handed over ten dollars and signed up to box against a professional in the welterweight division. He had one month to prepare for the fight. There would be two seven-round matches in his weight class. He would fight "Kid" McPartland or, worse, an up-and-coming contender named "New York" Tommy O'Brien. He wouldn't know his opponent until the day of the fight.

First, he needed to ensure that there would be higher attendance at his match. He visited the event's promoter, noted at the bottom of the handbill.

"Is Mr. Choynski in?" Angus looked around the office located just off of the rafters of the giant Olympia arena. It was full of cigar smoke and void of windows. The receptionist was a well-dressed Negro lady.

"May I tell him who is calling this morning?"

"You may. I'm Angus 'The Anvil' Drummond. Prizefighter, welterweight class."

The woman raised her eyebrow. "He may be accepting callers this morning, but he's very busy." She got up from behind the desk and entered a door that said "Private."

Momentarily, she returned. "Mr. Choynski will see you. You have five minutes."

Angus took a deep breath and smiled at the secretary. "You're very kind. My thanks to you."

The office was windowless too, dimly lit, a drab place to conduct business. Choynski sat behind a large desk as if it were a barricade. The fight promoter puffed away on a large cigar as he checked the horse racing forms. The smoke from Choynski's stogy wafted around in thin clouds and floated upwards to the ceiling. He didn't get up, but Drummond could see that the middle-aged man possessed a prize-fighter's body. It was thick and solid, but the man's hair was thin, almost gone, and his eyes showed little passion.

"Who the hell is "Anvil" Drummond?"

"Amateur boxer, sir. Soon to turn professional. I'm signed up for the matches next month at the Olympia."

"So, you've signed up. You're on the under-card. You're entertainment. You'll be a bloody pulp after a pro gets done with you. That's what the spectators pay to see… blood."

"I don't think so. I'll be winnin' my match."

The fight promoter sized up the well-dressed young man, eyebrows raised in surprise. "Really? Against "Kid" McPartland?"

"I don't want to fight him; I want to fight "New York" Tommy O'Brien."

"He's sure to make mincemeat of you. He's a contender. Got a title match in a coupla months."

"It's him I'll fight, and not in the under-card, but in the first fight of the main events."

"You got some stones, boy. Must be that red hair."

"No, I got a bone to pick with that bastard, O'Brien."

"Really? I'm listin'."

"He was engaged to my sister, Mary. The date for the grand affair was all set. One evening, she went to call on him to discuss the final arrangements of the nuptials and found him in bed fuckin' another woman. Later, Mary found out she was expecting. It was a scandal to be sure; the wedding called-off, and my sister humiliated. I'm needin' to set things straight. You see, it's me who'll be makin' hamburger out of Mr. "New York" Tommy O'Brien. And I want more than a few early freeloaders witnessing it."

Choynski rubbed his chin, puffed on his cigar, and slowly smiled. "Anvil" Drummond, huh? What kind of fighter are you now?" His brain swirled with ideas about how to use the heart-wrenching story to draw the crowds.

"Out-fighter, counter-puncher. I don't like me pretty face gettin' hit. Oh, I'll want $500 to be fightin' in the main event and $1,500 if I win."

"Stones, all right; you got 'em. Okay, that should be a good match. O'Brien's a brawler, a swarmer. He'll be coming right after you."

"I know."

"You'll be the first match at 8 PM. But it will be ten rounds, not seven. How's your stamina?"

"I wouldn't bet against me, Mr. Choynski."

CHAPTER 7

Olympia Arena was half-full by 7:30. The raucous crowd grew steadily. Bookies, well-dressed men with notepads and pencils, collected money and wrote down the wagers, handed the chit back to the bettor for future collection if successful. Technically, it was illegal, but no one cared or tried to stop it. Most of the bets were on the main event between Jack Johnson and Klondike Haynes, where Johnson was slightly favored to win in a split decision.

In the locker room, Jack Bullard taped the hands of Drummond, giving Angus instructions.

"I checked this O'Brien fella out. He's just a street brawler. Got a good punch but no finesse if you take my meanin'."

"I do. Choynski said the same about the man. Their kind can be dangerous, though. They don't exactly play by the Marquis a' Queensberry rules."

"He's won the last four fights by knockouts in the early rounds. So he's sure not to have trained too much worryin' about the likes a' you."

"Aye, no stamina. Got to keep me self in the match 'til the late rounds."

"Right. Do a little dancin'. And when do you want me bettin' on "Mister sure-thing Anvil" Drummond?"

"Wait until the fightin' starts. Leave the corner and work the room. I'll try to improve your chances after a few rounds. Make a few wagers, but don't bet it all."

"If ya don't mind me askin', how'd you get on the main card and with O'Brien to boot? Brawler or not, he's a contender."

"Back in the old country, what were the best fights: roundabouts in the pubs or the ones in the streets where two men were truly hatin' each other?"

"That's easy. The last one where the fellas' blood was up."

"Exactly. And that's what I told the promoter. Who's fightin' out there now?"

"It's the last of the under-card. "Kid" McPartland's beatin' up on some Pollack. But the fella seems happy enough; he's makin' a hun'red dollars."

"I guess we better go, then. What's it like?"

"You'll see soon enough. Let me check the tape one last time."

Drummond shook his head. "One last time?"

The fighter and his corner man walked out of the locker room, Drummond wearing an old flannel robe. They walked down a long series of corridors and entered the arena. When he visited Mr. Choynski, the arena was dark. He could sense that it was a big space but could not appreciate the scale of it. As they exited the vomitory, Angus "The Anvil" was stunned by its immense size. The vast arena was five stories high, with seats and benches for 5,000 people and more seating on the floor for the prizefights. Great gas lamps hung from the rafters, aflame with conical shields that dispersed the light and illuminated the torpid space, redolent with body odor, whisky, and cigar smoke. At the center was the finest boxing ring Angus had ever seen.

"Jesus, Mary, and Joseph! What have I gotten myself into?" Angus looked toward the ring, momentarily frozen with fear. The referee held up "Kid" McPartland's arm in the air, the crowd roaring and clapping.

"Come on, let's get up there. We're up next." Jack said, pushing through the crowd who gawked and laughed at the lightweight, the plain flannel robe around his shoulders. Some chanted, "Blood, blood!"

As they arrived at their corner of the ring, two men, one with a white coat and stethoscope around his neck, carried the defeated fighter on a stretcher out of the arena. Drummond looked at his face. It was bloody, swollen, and bruised, the eyes shut. He moaned something in Polish and made the sign of the cross.

"That lad's a punk. I seen him at the gym once or twice. Anvil, you got scores more fights, winnin' fights, under your belt than the likes a' him."

"I guess it's a wee bit late to change me mind."

"A wee bit. Here, take a swig a' courage."

Angus did as instructed and gagged on the whisky as the ring announcer lifted his megaphone and began to speak. Angus heard none of it. The quick drink made his head swim; the thick, smoky air made every breath a chore. He looked across the ring. "New York" Tommy O'Brien was pacing around the small square, arms uplifted, a silk dressing gown embroidered with scenes of New York's Lower East Side. It accentuated his hard, lightweight frame. He stared in the direction of Angus and snarled.

The crowd roared at his opponent's introduction. He barely heard his name but stood up and bowed to the masses. Boo's and catcalls followed.

"Ignore the bastards, Angus. Remember, the bigger they are, the harder they fall."

"After the bell rings, go out an' bet a third. Get the best odds possible."

"A hundred to one shouldn't be too difficult."

The bell rang. Angus got up and headed toward his opponent and his destiny. His last thought was, *Oh, Lord, the man's a sturdy big beast, and he's a comin' right at me.*

The bell rang. Round 3 was over. Drummond returned to his corner, his nose ajar, one eye bleeding and swollen.

"How are the odds?"

"I'm getting up to 20 to 1, and you're losing if that's what you been hopin' for."

"It is, for now. Those are good odds. Bet the rest after the bell. By then, you'll get better odds. I think the bloke fractured me nose!"

"Yes, and your eye ain't so good either, boyo. You need it to see Mr. O'Brien. Now be still; I'll put some grease on it."

"Grease?"

"Sure. Axle grease from the shop. It's better than any apothecary ointment. It'll stanch the blood good. How're the legs?"

"Grand. Did you see him after I landed me jabs?"

"I did. I be thinkin' you got him worried. Just keep dancin' around, and when he moves in, try an upper cut. I'm seeing an openin' there when he moves his arms out a wee bit."

"Aye, I saw that, too."

Dammit, man, stand still! a frustrated Tommy O'Brien thought.

O'Brien, winded, moved in again, hoping to corral his wily prey. It was Round 7, and the little Scottish pugilist had still not fallen. O'Brien had landed more blows to the right eye, which was now swollen shut. Drummond's bottom lip was cut, and blood flowed down his chin. The spectators were wild with their lust for more carnage.

Yet the atmosphere in the arena had changed. Chants of "Anvil," "Anvil," rang throughout the hall. With each round, Drummond landed more solid blows, jabs, and even several left hooks. The bell rang, and Round 7 was in the books. A startled and angry O'Brien retreated to his corner to re-group. The Scotsman was an amateur, yet O'Brien's corner man had told him that the judges had scored three of the first six rounds for Angus. It was time to end this and go home. He was sure he had won the last one; he had gotten Drummond on the ropes and scored at least a half-dozen punches to the ribs. He could see the Scot's legs wobble. But he had not fallen, and O'Brien was tiring fast. His arms were slack appendages, his legs felt like lead weights. *This next round has got to be the last,* he thought.

Across the ring, Jack staunched a multitude of cuts.

"Angus, let me throw in the towel. I'm running out of axle grease, for Christ's sake." Jack was worried for his friend. Even if he won the match, the blows would so rattle his head, he would never be able ride a bicycle much less run a bicycle shop.

"I thought you said you wouldn't let me quit."

"Aye, for a few nicks but you're takin' a bloody poundin' out there."

"I'm well aware. Pour some whisky on my cut."

"Why?"

"Do it. And give me more water."

His corner man did as instructed. The cut burned as the whisky flowed over it. Drummond licked at the whisky; it, and the cold water sponged on his red hair revived him.

At the bell, Round 8 began. O'Brien didn't wait. He closed in for the kill immediately, but Drummond fended him off for most of the round, scoring a few harmless blows. The restless crowd booed. They wanted to see a prize fight, not a dancing contest. O'Brien moved in again. This time Drummond let his arms down just enough for a vicious right cross to his face, followed by an uppercut to the chin. Drummond fell like a Braemar stone onto the center of the ring.

"1, 2, 3… "

Bullard screamed from the corner. "Sweet Jesus, Angus, get up!"

"4, 5, 6..."

Angus saw his mother on her deathbed, his father's lifeless body on the stone wall, and Maisy's casket lowered into the ground. He shook his head.

"7, 8… " The referee counted slowly.

He got up on one knee and raised his arm to signal the official to stop counting. The referee checked Drummond and determined him fit for more of a beating. The instructions to him from Mr. Choynski were brief and to the point. Let the crowd have their blood sport. Allow O'Brien to chew up

Anvil Drummond and spit him out. The little Scot upstart would have his comeuppance.

Anvil Drummond got up slowly and retreated to his corner, his head a fog, the arena spinning around him. He saw a blur of a man coming straight at him. He closed his good eye, ready for the end.

The bell rang.

O'Brien stopped inches from Angus and turned to the referee. "Can you not count to ten, you moron!?"

"What did you say, boyo?"

"You heard me. The fight should be over. You fuckin' stopped countin', and it was a slow count at best. Let me help you out: nine, ten. Over. The fuckin' fight should be over!"

"Get back to your corner, O'Brien, or I'll award the round to Drummond. The fight's over when I says it's over."

O'Brien fumed and sulked back to his stool. This charade should be done. He waved off the sponge, took out his mouth guard, took a drink of water, and spit it into a bucket. He realized he was gasping for air, his legs rubbery and on fire.

"Gimme the lead weight," O'Brien told his corner man.

"Tommy, boy, no. He's an amateur, for Christ's sake."

O'Brien glared, and the corner man removed the glove, his back covering the motion from the referee. He inserted a small bar into the right mitt and slipped it back on.

Across the ring, Jack Bullard tended to his fighter.

"Since I can't convince you to quit, would you like to tell me what you're plannin' to do? You can't take much more."

"I'm changing me game. You wait an' see. Whisky."

Bullard handed the pint to his fighter without argument, who took a hard pull. He swallowed a good bit and spat out the rest onto his glove, rubbing the wet leather over his eye.

It burned and he winced at the sting but he felt alive and more confident than ever.

The bell rang. Drummond sprang from his stool and headed straight for O'Brien, who had barely stood up, still breathing hard, his legs unresponsive. He took one step into the ring when Drummond attacked his ribcage. Drummond's hands were like the pistons of a two-stroke engine, pounding relentlessly, one hand followed by the other. O'Brien staggered back toward his corner. Anvil continued to attack and saw his opening. "New York" Tommy reached for the ropes but his hands never found them. Drummond quickly shifted from the ribcage to the face. An uppercut, then a right cross, and another uppercut, none as powerful as anything Drummond had delivered previously but lethal in their trifecta. It was all that was necessary. O'Brien's head rotated like a broken doll, blood spurted out his mouth, and he fell. Angus backed up. O'Brien landed on his knees, tried to steady himself, and just as the Scot was preparing a final punch, fell prostrate onto the ring.

The referee counted quickly: "1, 2, 3, 4, 5, 6, 7, and 8… and 9, 10! Yer out, ya moron!" He smiled broadly and lifted Drummond's arm into the air.

CHAPTER 8

The winnings from bets that night were over $14,000. Drummond had received another $1,500 for beating Tommy O'Brien, and tripled his savings account. Mr. Choynski offered him a handsome contract to turn professional, but Angus the "Anvil" told him he was retired. He insisted that Jack take $2,000, but he refused. His friend had taken all of the beatings, and had a broken nose to show for it. Finally, the two friends agreed on a compromise: $1,000 and Jack Bullard would work for Drummond forever, in whatever capacity needed, and always at a handsome salary.

Purchasing the bicycle shop was another matter. Though Angus had offered $10,000, McVicar was not interested. He made a handsome living selling the basic transportation. Fate intervened a year after Drummond's offer, as Angus pondered his next move. Angus was in the back of the shop to check on a repair when Donald McVicar suffered a massive stroke as he demonstrated how to ride the Van Cleve bicycle to a well-dressed woman who had caught his eye. The crashing of numerous cycles and the woman's scream brought Angus running to the front of the store. He sent Jack to fetch an ambulance straight away.

"Nod if you can hear me, Mr. McVicar."

McVicar nodded slightly from his hospital bed, his face and cheeks drooped on one side. A thin string of glistening spittle hung from his chin.

"Now, I'm not wantin' to take advantage of your situation, but some time has passed from me initial offer, and sales are slowin' down a wee bit. I'll offer you $8,000 for the business, which will pay for a nice sanitarium in the Upper Peninsula that will care for you."

McVicar stared at the ceiling and tried to mouth some words. Angus thought he heard "bastard," but couldn't be sure.

"It's the best arrangement, sir. Truly, it is."

With all of his strength, McVicar spoke. "Deal."

Under Drummond's ownership, the shop thrived. A shop manager and new salesmen took over his duties. Sales continued to increase as he advertised in the *Detroit Free Press* and *Detroit News* and offered bicycles at lower prices than the competition. He was selling over 200 bicycles every month.

Drummond turned a large part of the repair shop in the back of the bicycle store into a machine shop and rented the space next to the store. He took out his first bank loan and purchased $50,000 worth of equipment: milling machines, lathes, a three-way drill press, an eight-spindle press, grinders — everything necessary to build a 2-cylinder, overhead-valve engine. An assembly line was set up, five machinists hired, and quickly, the fledgling business turned out fifteen engines a day. He sold them to the Maxwell Car Company, and other auto manufacturers soon noticed. Drummond bought an adjacent building across the rear alley for a small foundry and parts production and sold the engines to many small startup companies that flourished in the Midwest's burgeoning auto industry. He could not keep up with the demand.

Then, Angus did something very unusual. He went to work on the assembly line at Ford Motor Company on Piquette Avenue for five dollars a day. After his shift, he changed into a suit and pretended to be a supervisor and explored other areas of the plant. At night, in his small apartment on Woodward Avenue, Drummond wrote copious notes and sketched diagrams of the assembly line, the chassis and engine works, the parts department, the paint booths, and final assembly. After six weeks, Henry Ford had taught him all he needed and he gave notice.

Angus now had a first-hand understanding of the manufacturing process. But he had become aware of something else from the experience. His time on the "line" was hard, monotonous, and demeaning. He was a cog in the wheel of production, nothing less, nothing more. It troubled him, but he could not see any other solution. The assembly line was the new way cars were being made, and as long as he owned the means of creation, it didn't matter whether the workers liked it or not; he would be the boss.

In 1910, Angus Drummond sold the bicycle shop for $25,000. With three investors, fellow members of the St. Andrew's Society, a local fraternal organization of emigrated Scots, he bought a 75,000 square-foot building in Hamtramck and incorporated Drummond Engine Company. In 1912, he manufactured over 10,000 four-cylinder engines as he worked on perfecting a six-cylinder version. By then he was a millionaire and bought out his original investors. But it wasn't enough. Angus Drummond wanted to manufacture a car — the best car Detroit had ever seen. It would happen four years later with the help of Maxwell Motors.

"Mr. Drummond, we have a small problem." Archie McLagan, the company's first comptroller held a sheaf of papers in his hand. He feared his tenure at the new company would be short-lived with the bad news he had.

"Archie, I told you to call me Angus. We're a small company. Now, what is it?"

"We've been shipping engines to Maxwell Motors every week for three months. But we've not been paid a dollar by them during that whole time."

"I see. What's the tally?"

"One hundred eighty thousand dollars, sir."

"I think I'd best visit Mr. Maxwell for a set to."

The next day, Drummond made an offer to Jonathan Maxwell. If Maxwell couldn't bring his accounts current in 30 days, Drummond would buy the company for sixty cents on the dollar. A month later, in the fall of 1916, Angus Drummond owned an automobile company. It included a large manufacturing complex in Highland Park, one he had coveted for several years. Soon, a large sign appeared at the top of the main building on Woodward Avenue: Drummond Motorcar Corporation. The plant was modernized based on the operations he witnessed at the Ford plant. He re-tooled the space and created an assembly line that could produce 250 automobiles a day.

But it was not to be just any automobile. For months, he toiled on a new design, a new look, much different than the Ford or Maxwell autos, which he considered unimaginative and humdrum. The result was the Drummond, which debuted in 1918. It sold for an affordable $725, a bit more expensive than Maxwell Mascotte, but with a new, more powerful straight-6-cylinder, 75-horsepower engine. Additionally, it possessed a more elegant appearance, came in three colors, was as reliable as a Swiss watch, and as tough as 'Anvil' Drummond the boxer.

Sales boomed. Two years later he renamed his company Republic Motors Corporation and bought a thirty-acre tract of land in Hamtramck to build a great manufacturing city to imagine, design and build multiple models of automobiles. Work commenced immediately on the Republic Motors Factory complex, second only in size to Ford's River Rouge plant. By 1920, forty-one-year-old Angus Drummond was on his way to becoming one of the wealthiest men in America.

CHAPTER 9

1937
Detroit, Michigan

In 1915, a buyer for the Leith estate in Aberdeen, Scotland finally came forward. The man, an upstart automobile manufacturer, bought Leith Hall and its grounds for a paltry $16,000. He was building a mansion for his growing family in a new upper-class neighborhood east of Detroit — Grosse Pointe Shores. He wanted a great Scottish manor, not a new building that looked like one. And he knew where he could find it. And though there were granite boulders from the Upper Peninsula readily available for the foundations, the buyer had the manor taken down stone by stone into the ground, and shipped to America. And in a prominent location of his new eight-car garage were three restored shiny, black bicycles.

The well-dressed man, not tall at 5'-9", his build still as hard and sturdy as the prize fighter he once was, looked with deep-green eyes out the divided-lite bay window to the rear terrace, through the gardens, over the expanse of a lush emerald-green fescue lawn, to the dark-blue water of Lake St. Clair. A freighter made its way down the wide waterway. He knew that the ship, its hull deep in the water, was loaded with iron ore, bound for the docks at River Rouge on the Detroit River.

Steel for my cars, steel for hundreds of my cars, he thought with satisfaction and comfort. He turned and went over to a mahogany sideboard and a crystal decanter, refilled his Baccarat glass with 18-year-old scotch, put it to his nose, and inhaled the scent of his native Scotland — the peat and oak, the hint of ever-green trees by the clear water of mountain streams, the mossy ferns, and craggy hills, and took a drink. He looked around the library, his refuge from the world of commerce. It was his favorite room, paneled in carved, polished English oak. His sanctuary was surrounded by bookcases, Corinthian columns between them with their ornate capitals. Marble busts of the great medieval Scottish kings beginning with Robert the Bruce were carved into the entablature above the capitals. The ceiling was coffered with gold leaf beams, and in the center, a twelve-foot square mural depicted William Wallace defeating the English at Sterling Bridge in 1297.

Angus Keir Drummond, now 58 years old, president and chief executive officer of Republic Motors Corporation, let out a sigh, the wisp of a smile slipped across his mouth. The great mansion signified everything he had worked for in the last 42 years. Angus lifted the glass. It touched his lips; a trimmed red beard softened with the gray of late middle age framed his mouth.

"Here's to you, Lord Edward Leith, you bastard. I hope you're burning in hell. But I do thank you for your castle."

He looked down at his large mahogany desk and smiled. The rendering for Republic Motor's newest automobile lay before him — the Epoch. Its lines were sleek, unlike the conservative, dowdy chassis' of his competitors, Ford and Chrysler. No more right angles and black paint, but aerodynamic curves and new vibrant colors, like blazing dark red. And a powerful V-8 engine to take its owner anywhere, fast.

I've survived the depression, and now, you, Mr. Epoch, will bring me greater success. Drummond sipped his scotch, and toasted to the view out the window, the freighter gone, and the daylight fading.

I should check on Fiona. He looked at his drink; still half full. *Yes, in a minute.*

Angus stood at the window, several of the individual panes embellished with ornate stained glass. He cherished the view out the clear glass. Now there was no one in the house to enjoy them. Nineteen years earlier, the mansion rebuilt and grand, he watched from this same spot as his darling Fiona played hide n' seek on the lawn with his four children, running like a sprite to find them hidden behind the tall elms or the topiary. She laughed her infectious laugh at the antics of her offspring, and when she caught one, she would hug and kiss them until they pulled away, only to hide again. Close by was the Irish nanny, Miss Maggie, to tend afterward to the brood of children. Now they were grown, and it was just his beloved wife and young Wallace, now twenty-one, living in the great manor house.

As he continued to peer out, he remembered the first time he had met Fiona. Only 25, owner of a successful bicycle shop, he was an entrepreneur and a successful businessman. She was just 19, a student at St. Mary's Academy in northwest Detroit.

It was 1904; the St. Andrew's Society had begun to admit women into their ranks. Fiona Stewart was one of the first to enroll. Her parents, John and Moira, immigrants from Glasgow, wanted only the best for their only child and enrolled her at St. Mary's Academy, to study to become a Christian lady of letters, refinement, and hopefully a future member of high society. Fiona had other dreams — she wanted to be a teacher.

Fiona walked into the clubroom. The maître d' advised her that she had mistakenly breached a male preserve. She tilted her head up to meet his gaze and questioned, with coy words and a wry smile, why women weren't welcome.

Angus overheard bits of the conversation, then moved closer. He walked up, introduced himself, and told the maître d' she was his guest. Together, her hand on his arm, they entered the inner sanctum, and were seated at a small table with two chairs in the far corner of the room, away from the stares and crude comments of the male members. He ordered a scotch, and she nodded, asking for one as well.

Immediately smitten by this fiery, independent woman, his eyes watched as she enjoyed her whisky. She had not ordered it to merely impress him. She lowered her eyes and blushed after catching him looking at her.

She laughed. "What is the matter? Have you never seen a girl drink whisky before?"

"No, I suppose not. Is it to your liking?"

"Aye. It's scotch, and I'm Scottish, after all." She laughed again.

As the evening went on, she could not believe her good fortune at meeting such a handsome, polite, and industrious young man. When he spoke about his shop and his plans to build automobiles, she heard the excitement in his voice. Carried away by his enthusiasm, she felt comfortable and thrilled with his drive and optimism. And she thought the scar above his eye and the crook in his nose made him look distinguished, maybe slightly dangerous.

An ardent suitor, Angus devoted thought and energy to pursuing Fiona. They rode Van Cleve bicycles around Belle Isle Park and had a picnic lunch along the Detroit River. He took her to Jacoby's for wiener schnitzel and German beer, and they sang German songs with the rest of the patrons.

With her parents in tow as chaperones, they traveled on a lake steamer to Mackinaw Island and stayed two nights at the Grand Hotel. Fiona occupied a two-room suite with her parents. In the evening, they dined in the hotel restaurant on roast turkey, prime rib of beef, and Fiona's favorite, crab croquettes. Though Fiona's father was a prosperous, well-respected surgeon at Grace Hospital, Angus convinced him, with humility and pride, to accept the trip as a gift.

After dinner, they sat on the front porch in rocking chairs and watched the amazing array of stars intermingle with the planets in the night sky. Afterward, during a carriage ride around the small island, Angus proposed to Fiona. She said yes without hesitation.

In 1908, Fiona gave birth to their first child, a daughter, who they named Olivia. Three years later, twin girls Freya and Jane blessed their lives. Then there was the birth of a baby boy named Robert, who died after a day in 1913. The couple abandoned plans of any more children, and Angus gave up his dream of a son to take over his growing empire. But they were surprised in 1915 when Fiona realized she was again pregnant. In 1916, she gave birth to a fine, healthy child. They named the baby boy Wallace after the great hero of Scotland's independence, William Wallace. Angus doted on the child, as did Fiona. He loved and played with model cars, trucks, and fire engines from the earliest age.

During those happier times twenty-one years ago, Angus believed that young Wallace would grow into the same man that he was — hard-working, industrious, and proud. Later, when the lad was seven, his son often showed him drawings of cars that he had designed.

"Look, Father, at my newest invention! It's a sports car. I'm calling it the Zenith!"

"Very handsome, son. It looks very fast. Perhaps, however, we should call it, let's see, how about the Zodiac? The Zodiac consists of all the stars in our solar system. Besides, I believe the word Zenith is already taken. You have a Zenith radio in your room, do you not?"

"Zodiac. That sounds great. Can I help you make this car?"

"Of course, you can. But you must study hard, attend university, and learn mechanical engineering."

"Yes, Father."

There was a knock on the library door. Angus shook out the old memories, and finished the Macallan, warmed by his hand.

The large door opened, and Jack Bullard entered. "Angus, you wanted to see me?"

"Jacky, come in; help yourself to a drink."

"Now, you know I'm on duty."

"Right. It isn't quite five o'clock yet."

"Beggin' your pardon, but you know I don't partake."

Drummond chuckled. "My da told me to never fully trust a man who doesn't take a wee drink now and then. So, I must keep tempting you."

"As you have for years. But I never liked that foul swill."

"Many a Scot will disagree with you, but that's why you're the head of security for what, going on seven years? The year after the market crash."

"It's now called the Service Department, but, that's right, six and a half. What can I help with today, Angus?"

"It's Wednesday and Wallace told Blackburn to ready the Zodiac convertible for him for tonight."

"I'm sure Blackburn will have it cleaned and ready for his escapades." Bullard referred to the senior chauffeur and mechanic who kept Angus Drummond's collection of fifteen automobiles in top working order. In 1929, just before the stock market crash, the garage was enlarged to hold up to twenty cars. Soon, there would be another addition, Republic's newest car, the luxury Epoch.

"It's not the Zodiac I'm worried about." Angus looked back out the window and frowned. The late afternoon light was casting long shadows from the tall elms.

"I know. The usual?"

"Yes, but I need you to assign a new man. Wallace can spot a tail better than a Scotland Yard detective."

"Yes, he surely can."

"What are the lad's favorite hangouts these days? Club Three Sixes, or is it the Painted Lady Lounge?"

"Amongst others. Lately, he's been heading to Club Paradise for the Negro jazz. Last week, my man saw him kissing a young Negro woman, one of the dancers, and buying her drinks."

Drummond returned to the sideboard and poured another drink, a stout one this time. He dropped in two large cubes of ice. "I had such high hopes… "

"There's more, I'm sorry to tell ya."

"Mother Mary, now what?"

"He was stopped for speeding on Gratiot Avenue, 90 in a 40."

Angus smiled. "I didn't know that old V-6 could hit 90. Was he ticketed?"

"Warning. His last name jumped off his license. It was also the same officer who stopped him before. Lucky break."

"He should have hauled his ass to jail and taught Wallace a much needed lesson. Was he drunk?"

"No, it was early; he was on his way to the clubs."

"Lucky kid. I'll call the commissioner and apologize."

"This is the fifth time. Your regrets are wearin' thin on Commissioner Reilly, I'm sure."

"That boy will be the death of me if he doesn't kill himself first."

"Angus, he's only 21, sowin' his wild oats, is all."

"Yes, 21. At 21, I owned the most successful bicycle shop in Detroit. He's a freeloader, dismissed by the University of Detroit after one year, sure as hell fucking Negro whores, sleeping under my roof and living off the sugar tit of me wealth. He's not been to the factory in days."

"You know he loves cars, boss. Maybe more 'an you do. And that's sayin' a lot, my friend. It's the factory he's not fond of."

"He drinks too much."

Bullock raised an eyebrow and smiled. "I'll be going then, Angus."

TOBIAS WOODSON

1937

CHAPTER 10

1937
Tallula, Mississippi

A threadbare cotton shirt barely shielded his back from the morning sun. It was no hotter than usual on this June day, but to Tobias Woodson, it seemed like an inferno. He told himself it was just his mind, his restless, unhappy mind. Dreams and fantasies of freedom had been part of his life for as long as he could remember, but when he turned 18 last month, they became as common as a heartbeat. *Are you gonna pick cotton all your life, Woodson? You gonna work for the man? You a free man, but you still be a slave in so many ways. There got to be mo' to life. Got to be.*

His daddy, Thurgood, and his momma, Leonie, had worked the fields all their lives on the big plantation, Long Moss. They were born free, but their parents had been slaves, the property of the Buchanan family. After the Civil War, the mistress, a kind woman by the name of Eugenia Buchanan, an impoverished widow, pleaded with them and others to stay and help with the farm. They knew no other way of life; without any other choices, they stayed and picked the cotton for paltry wages and help re-build the plantation. And so did their children, for the South offered little opportunity for the Negro.

Tobias was born in 1919, the fourth of six children. Now, his parents were too old for the fields, and he and his two sisters worked for a dollar a day and sleeping quarters of their own, a two-room shack. Down the road from the humble abode, Thurgood fiddled with his prize possession, a 1927 Ford pickup. When he first bought it, it barely ran. The old man had the truck spinning like a top a year later. Tobias was fascinated with the motor, pistons, spark plugs, wires, radiator, and a big fan behind the grille that kept the engine cool. He didn't know how it all worked, but over time, his father taught him the rudiments of the internal combustion engine. Someday, he would have his own truck. And he knew which one it would be: a Toiler-75 built by Republic Motors.

He bent over, filling his fourth sack of cotton. Rumor had it that there would soon be machines to do the picking. He couldn't understand how a machine could do this work, but he knew that an engine had horsepower and could do the work of 100 men if it was attached to a drive train and pulleys as he had seen the big tractors at the modern farms on the way to Tallula.

As he worked, he heard the smooth rumble of a motor in the distance. He stood to watch Eugenia Buchanan's daughter, Beatrice, coming toward them in her shiny, black coupe. Beatrice was cold and distant, unlike her mother, but she came out to the fields every Wednesday morning to lead them in prayer. After reading a bible verse, she told the 30 or so workers that after God, she, Beatrice Buchanan, was their sole protector. True happiness lay in the next world, not in this.

Today, the message was different. In the last year, she had lost six good, strong men who decided to leave the fields for work up north in the great factories. She told the workers they were indentured and could never leave her employ. She told them not even to try to head north. In the north, people hated the Negro. But here, at Long Moss, she loved them and would take care of them forever. Tobias stood up straight and took a drink while she spoke; his eyes, narrow slits, stared hard with hatred as he listened to the uncompromising words. He had heard the term "indentured" many times before. His daddy told him it meant you were now half a slave. The missus had no right to say he was indentured. He would leave by his own choosing and in his own good time.

Tobias ignored her sermon and walked around to her fine car. With a fifth-grade education, he had learned his letters and could sound out most words. The words on the hood spelled "Zodiac." He didn't know what that meant, but if someone could make such a fine car, he would like to help in the making of it. He looked back at Miss Buchanan. She had opened her Bible and was reading a verse from the Old Testament, about someone smiting another person and getting justice — an eye for an eye, a tooth for a tooth. He shook his head.

His six-three frame loomed over the hood of the car. He had thick shoulders and a muscular neck, his biceps hard and large. His strong body was the byproduct of years of toil in the fields and six months at a youth detention camp, working on a new paved two-lane state road. The sentence was handed down by an un-compromising White judge who took no mercy on a 15-year-old Black boy who had shoplifted a handful of licorice whips. The chain gang was brutal, but it made him strong, and when he got out, he treasured his freedom. Woodson walked around the car once more back to the hood; he had to see what was underneath. He reached under the cowling, found the latch, eased it to one side, and lifted it. And Tobias was not disappointed. The engine was a straight V-6 with a dusty chrome cover over the cylinder head. The wires were black, the engine block gray. He stared at the wonder, not touching anything.

"What are you doing, Tobias?" The missus' voice carried the hint of a reprimand.

"Sorry, ma'am, I jus' wanted to see what the engine be like on this here beautiful automobile."

"What do you even know about cars, boy?"

"Oh, I knows plenty, ma'am. My daddy taught me."

"I see. Well, now you've seen it. Put the hood down and get back to work. And don't be entertaining thoughts of working in a factory. You have plenty of work to do here." Beatrice's tone was arrogant, and demeaning.

"I be a free man…," Tobias muttered under his breath.

"What did you say, boy?"

"Nothin', ma'am. I best get back to my pickin'."

"Yes, you had better." Tobias's employer stepped up onto the running board of the Zodiac, slid onto the dark brown leather seat, started the car, engaged the clutch, and drove away. Engulfed in the dust from her tires, Tobias returned to his half-filled sack of cotton.

The day wore on, and the heat rose from the dirt like steam from a radiator. He bent down and picked a few more tufts of cotton, pricking his finger on the last boll. *Shit, boy,* he thought, *you need to be done wit dis kinda work.* He stood up and went to the edge of the field to the water bucket. He heard a deep rumble. As he took a drink, it grew louder and began to drown out the field hands singing "Swing Low, Sweet Chariot." A Magnolia Transit bus clipped along the dirt road, and kicked up plumes of dust. He shook his head, his dark eyes staring at the large vehicle. *Where they be headin'?* He sucked the blood from his finger and watched the bus disappear into the trees down the road. At that moment, Tobias decided that there was another life for him, not picking cotton, but one that involved automobiles. He knew they made the cars in a city called Detroit; he had looked the town up in the *Goode's School Atlas* his daddy owned. It was far away from Tallula, almost a thousand miles. He'd save his money, buy a ticket north, and go there. The mistress would not tell him how to live his life. Tobias returned to his tow sack, and bent down again to pick another white, fluffy boll. Now, the sun didn't seem so hot.

CHAPTER 11

"Pops, I gots to go. I can't pick cotton no more." Tobias watched his father remove a spark plug, clean the tip with a file, and hand it to him.

"Missus won't let you leave. She won't."

"Daddy, I ain't no slave. I ain't indentured."

"No, son, you's be free. But she already lost too many workers. Tell her you leaving, she won't stand for it."

"I hear they be makin' a lot of money in the factories."

Thurgood removed another spark plug, cleaned it, and shook his head. "Where you get these crazy ideas? Me and your momma need you here. We gettin' old. And you jus' turnin' 18."

"Yeah, I be a man now. The others will look after you. I be sendin' money back to y'all so you can live better."

Thurgood straightened up and looked at his son. "We be livin' jus fine, thanks all the same."

"I didn' mean no disrespect, suh."

"I know." Thurgood was quiet for a moment as he put each spark plug back into the engine.

"I ain't pickin' cotton no mo'… " Tobias said in a barely audible voice.

They worked quietly for a while. Thurgood finally let out a sigh and spoke. "Son, I see you got your heart set on leavin'."

"I do. Daddy, I got to go north."

"Maybe I jus' be jealous. You finish workin' the week. On Sunday mornin', I'll drive you to Jackson."

"I need to tell the missus I'm quittin'."

"Don't breathe a word of it to her or no one. I tole you she won't let you go."

"What can she do?"

"Never you mind. Jus' do your job 'til Sadderday sunset. Get your wages, and then we'll leave."

"What does I do when I get to Jackson?"

"The Greyhound bus be leavin' there going to Memphis. At Memphis, you change to one for Detroit. They will make announcements and have doors headin' for each bus. You smart; use your wits. The trip take you one an' a half day. But then you'll be in Detroit. Find the Second Baptist Church on Monroe Street near downtown. Church used to be a stop on the Underground Railroad. Pastor Bradby set you up right, and helps you find a place to live with a nice family in the Black Bottom neighborhood. It's where our folks live. The Republic Motors factory be jus' up the road north in Hamtramck. That's where you wants to work, right?"

Tobias looked at his father in astonishment. "How you know all that, old man?"

"I had dreams, too, boy. Remember when I was gone for three year?"

Tobias nodded.

"All right, I never tole you this, but when you was nine, I made it up to Detroit. I got me a good job in the Ford factory an' made me six dollar ever' day. You think we got a nice house and this old pickup on cotton pickin' money?" Thurgood smiled and put his hand on Tobias' shoulder, squeezing it.

"I always wondered, Daddy. Why'd you come back?"

"The depression, son. I lost my job in '30. And I missed your ma, the other kids, and you so much I woulda come back anyways. Then all my dreams died in the cotton field. So, you go live them now. You live them for me." The senior Woodson put down his wrench and walked back into his painted clapboard four-room house. He returned with an envelope in hand.

"What's that, Pops?"

"It cost money to ride the bus, son. And Detroit be an expensive place for livin'." He handed the envelope to Tobias and hugged him.

Thursday and Friday passed quietly but slowly. Tobias picked the cotton bolls furiously as if working faster would make the day end sooner. *Will sundown Sadderday ever come?*

As he picked, he thought of Jackson, the capital of Mississippi. He had been there once, when he was ten, to attend the funeral of his aunt, his mother's sister. Tobias was more interested in the buildings and the cars than the three-hour service that followed. He thought of the fine bus that would take him to Memphis, then Detroit. If Jackson was a big town, Memphis must be even grander, high on the banks overlooking the great Mississippi River. He wondered if the Black city folk who lived there wore fine clothes and sported fancy hats. He knew they had Negro music, the Blues, and he wanted to hear it live, not on the old radio in his folk's house, the signal fading in and out.

At night, the day's work done, he read a worn book his father gave him, *The History of the Automobile,* as best he could. There were lots of big words he didn't understand. He continued to study the Atlas and memorized the map of Detroit. Just east of the city's center, below a big boulevard named Gratiot Avenue, it noted a neighborhood — Black Bottom.

That be my new home soon, Tobias thought.

Friday morning, Tobias was in the field early, and around eight, Beatrice Buchanan drove up in her shiny black Zodiac and slowed down near the workers assembled around the water bucket and a basket of biscuits. Friday morning was Bible reading and sermon time. The car came to a stop. She got out, Bible in hand, and before she could open it, one of his friends went up to her and spoke. His friend, Marcus, seemed nervous. The mistress of Long Moss listened intently, and a frown lined her face. She closed the holy book, shook her head, shook her finger at the boy, and pointed to the fields. He twisted the large straw hat he held, mashing it, and let it drop to the ground. He raised his hands into a prayer shape against his lips, pleading. It was all for nothing. The rigid woman called Marcus an uppity nigger, climbed back in the automobile, and drove off, the Bible verse and homily unspoken.

Thurgood Woodson entered the shack and went over to his sleeping son. He whispered in a low, but strong voice.

"Wake up, boy, wake up now."

Tobias opened his eyes, focused, and saw his father. "What, what time is it, suh?"

"Round 1 AM, son. Get up, get packed. Pack your best clothes and a pair a' overalls. We be leaving for Jackson." There was fear and agitation in Thurgood's voice.

"Why? It's just Friday night; it ain't Sunday yet. I needs to say goodbye to Mama."

"She's up, fixin' you some food for the bus ride. We need to get you far away from here."

"Why?"

"You know Marcus? He your friend, right?"

"Yeah, I know him since we straplin's. He had words with the missus in the field today. Why?"

"He's dead. Me and some other fellas just cut him down from that oak tree down the road. He was lynched."

"What, Marcus? Why?" Tobias struggled to process the news.

"A sign was hung round his neck, say, 'Indentured.'"

"Indentured?"

"It be a message from Miss Buchanan. It mean don't even think of leavin' Long Moss. Pack quick now, your best Sunday clothes and such. I'm takin' you to Jackson tonight. Get you on that bus before she ever know you gone."

"My pay… "

"Don' worry about no six dollar, son. I gave you a hundred. It's plenty for your trip."

"Daddy, I scared."

"So am I, son."

CHAPTER 12

"Listen hard, son. Listen good."

"Yeah, Pops, I listenin'."

"You get to Jackson, I don't know what time the bus leaves for Memphis. Sit in the waitin' room and mind your bidness. You want, they got a lunch counter and you can get a nice meal. Sit where it say 'Colored.' You know how to spell colored, boy?

"Yeah, Daddy…. Color… "

"Ok, good. You sit in the white section, you be in big trouble."

"Okay."

"Where you put the money I gave you?"

"In my pocket."

"Shit, boy, you ever hear of pickpockets? You need to be on your toes ever' minute. This ain't no plantation. Put your money inside your shirt, held tight by your belt."

"All right."

"You pack that book I gave you on automobiles?"

"I did."

"You needs to learn to read good."

"I know how to read."

"You need to read better."

"I also got the readers to study up."

"Good. Lots of educated peoples up north. And keepin' your nose in a book on the bus best way to avoid trouble. We can even buy a magazine or two at the station. Practice your readin'. A few cents on magazines ain't gonna make much difference."

Tobias was silent; the headlights of the Ford pickup showed the way down the two-lane macadam road. He knew Jackson couldn't be far off. The sun rose in the distance, a pink wash hugging the horizon. He began to question his decision to leave.

"Daddy, maybe we should head back to Tallula. This ain't such a good idea."

"No, son, it is a good idea. Your idea, your dreams, jus' like they was mine. Now listen. I gots more to tell you. Once you get to Memphis, the station be bigger than anything you ever seen. You need directions, ask one of our kind. But be careful. Watch out for fancy-dressed niggas wantin' to do you a favor. They spot a hayseed a mile away."

"What's a hayseed?"

"That be you. Fresh off the farm. Gullible. Trustin' ever'one. Don't trust no one, 'cept maybe some nice ol' Negro lady, if there be any. Now, how you spell Detroit?"

"D-E-T-O-"

"No. Again"

"I gots it. D-E-T-R-O-I-T."

"Good. Look up on the big sign says departures. You don' need to spell it jus' look for the sign starts with a 'D'. The other say arrivals, starts with an 'A'. You jus' arrived but you wants to leave. Departures means leave. Look for Detroit and the gate number and time."

"Okay, find the sign and go to the gate before the bus leaves."

"You catchin' on. Now they's a big bathroom there in Memphis. They gots showers."

"Showers?"

Thurgood shook his head. Maybe his son was too young to leave. But there was no going back to Tallula.

"A place where water falls on yo' head an' you get clean. They have them there for color folk for jus' twenty-five cent. Make sure you go to the one say 'Colored.' You use the soap and get washed up. Smell good when you get to Detroit. After, get a good meal at the restaurant. Maybe cost a dolla' or mo', I don' know. Was jus' fif'y cent years ago."

"Sho is a lot to remember, Pops."

"You be fine. Jus' mind yo' own bidness. And don' get into no dice games. They cheat. You lose your money, you be in a fix. Promise me."

"I promise."

"You got the address of Second Baptist and Pastor Bradby?"

"Yes, suh."

"Don't forget the sack of fried chicken and biscuits your momma gave you when she say goodbye. It broke her heart to see you go, but she be fine after a while. Buy you a cold drink at the station."

The sky's pink hue began to change to rays of gold, that criss-crossed a deep blue morning sky. Buildings appeared and grew more frequent; before long there was no space between the structures, short or tall. As they grew closer

Tobias could no longer see the building parapets through the truck's window. His father made turns onto wider streets, and crossed several railroad tracks. A large, single-story structure appeared where several buses were parked at an angle under a lighted canopy. Each berth had a number over the canopy. Thurgood drove to the other side of the building into the parking lot. His stomach churned. He worried for his son and knew it might be the last time he'd ever see him. He held back tears but his son deserved a better life than picking cotton like a damned slave.

"Let's get you inside an' get you a ticket."

"I better do it myself, Pops. Got to start sometime."

"You be startin' soon 'nough. Plus, I gots more to tell you, and it's a hard tellin'."

The interior of the bus station was brightly lit with industrial fixtures holding 250-watt incandescent lights in big metal bowls. It gave the space a harshness that was not welcoming, although it was good for security. The walls were painted high-gloss beige above glazed blocks in the same color. The only redeeming architectural feature was the dark wood beams of the ceiling, overlaid with a gold stenciled pattern of squares and triangles. Spider webs and a thin layer of dust betrayed a lack of maintenance. Across from the boarding doors, a newspaper stand and a sundry shop book-ended the long, main ticket counter, all of it a single element curved at the ends, a nod to 1920's Art Deco design that was absent everywhere else. Behind the counter large chalkboards noted the departures and arrivals of buses, and impromptu paper notices surrounded them, added over the years, that stated new rules, regulations, and admonishments.

Thurgood motioned Tobias toward the ticket counter and stood behind him, giving him a nudge when the clerk, wearing pince-nez glasses and silk armbands above his elbows, looked up with disinterest.

"Ahhh… I like a bus ticket to Detroit, suh."

"We don't have any buses to Detroit, boy."

Tobias turned and looked at his father, who moved to the counter.

"Beggin' your pardon, suh, a ticket to Memphis be fine, then another to Detroit from there."

"Why didn't the boy say that to begin with?"

"He new to travel, suh."

The man reached into his top drawer and pulled out a yellow and a green ticket, wrote words on them and reached for a large stamp, then pounded each with a date, 'Good until June 1938.'

"$7.50 for the Memphis ticket, and $10.75 for the one to Detroit. Cash only. Bus to Memphis boards in an hour. Not sure when the bus for Detroit will leave. Ask there. Understand?"

"Yes, suh." Thurgood looked at Tobias and whispered, "Pay the man."

Tobias reached deep into his shirt, and fumbled around for the envelope. Finally removing it, he quickly tried to add the two sums in his head, and beads of sweat formed on his forehead. He began to turn and leave, but his father grabbed his arm, whispering again, "Give the man $20.00, son. It's all right. You be fine."

Tobias slid a twenty-dollar bill under the glass. The clerk reached into another drawer, counted out $1.75, and slid it back with the tickets.

"Yellow ticket is for Memphis. Green gets you on the bus to Detroit. You lose the ticket, there's no refund. Bus to Memphis boards at gate three."

"Thank you, suh."

"Oh, by the way, the bus to Memphis has a Colored section. Make sure you sit there. One to Detroit don't care where you sit, boy."

CHAPTER 13

Tobias and Thurgood sat at the Greyhound Bus Station's luncheonette counter under the 'Colored' sign. Regardless of the sign, the food was the same for all the patrons. Tobias wiped his mouth with the paper napkin.

"That sure was good, Pa."

"I guess your ma don't feed you enough. You had four fried eggs, six pieces of bacon, and biscuits with gravy. At that rate, you'll be outta money before you get to Detroit."

"I was hungry… "

"It's all right. You got a long journey ahead; you needs your strength."

"Daddy, you said you wanted to tell me somethin' important."

"Oh yeah, I almos' forgot. Son, I'm not a smart man… "

"Yeah, you are."

"Hush, what I gots to say ain't advice. It's a way to look at the world. On the farm, you got soft things. Soft dirt, soft bolls a' cotton, soft rain. You got a constant sun and most times, blue sky. You knows ever'one and ever'one know you. They're all like kin, all of 'um, takin' care of you. 'Cept Miss Buchanan. She say she care, but she only care that you keep working for her."

"All right, I think I knows all that."

"Whats you don't know is what you're gonna know soon enough. Look at the people around here. You don't know them, they don't know you. They don't want to know you. You a nobody to them. They minding their own bidness. There ain't no soft soil, no soft rain. There be nothin' but bricks and steel and concrete. It's all buildings, some bigger than you can imagine. Ever once in a while there be a little patch of green called a park. From there you might see the sky. But the people, they hard. Been made hard by the hard buildings, the hard things and the hard people around them. The city makes people hard. You gonna survive, you have to become hard, too. Unnerstan'?"

"I guess… "

"All's I'm a sayin' is that if you gonna survive in Detroit, you got to become tough. Be more doubtin', suspicious of some people. Not mean, but I don't know, hard as a rock. Lots a' people lie, tell you what you want to hear."

"People gonna lie to me?" Tobias finished his cup of coffee, more confused than ever.

"Depends. Not always. Jus don' believe ever'thing ever'one tells you. Keep your guard up, like when you was in youth detention. You learned when people be talkin' bullshit. You knew if they wanted to take advantage."

Tobias thought back to that awful time and began to understand what his father meant.

"I get it. The city world ain't like the country world. It's not as nice, so I's got to be strong. Maybe a little bad."

"Yeah bad, but bad only if necessary. You'll be all right once you get to Detroit and find Pastor Bradby at the Second Baptist Church."

"All right, Pops. But I's scared. I couldn' even buy my own ticket."

"That be because the counter man knew you was country. He knew what you meant; he jus' hate our kind. You be fine."

The loudspeaker crackled. "Your attention, please. Dixie Greyhound's Coach to Memphis is now boarding at Gate 3. Departing in 15 minutes. All aboard."

"That's me. I bes' be goin' now."

"Tobias, one more thing. Take this." Thurgood reached into his pocket and pulled out a switchblade. "I had this in Detroit. Never had to use it, but you keep it now. Use it only if yo' life be in danger. Put it inside your boot."

Tobias looked at the hefty five-inch weapon. He was frightened. "Pa… "

"It be all right, you won't be needin' it. Let's get you some magazines for the ride. When you get to Detroit, have Pastor Bradby write me and your ma, tellin' us you doin' good. I think they makin' maybe ten dollar a day in the factory now."

"Ten dollars a day? I guess I better get on that bus."

"I think so. It's what you needs to do, son."

Thurgood got up, put money on the counter for their breakfast, and watched as tears formed in his son's eyes. He picked up the suitcase, put his arm on Tobias' shoulder, and they went over to the newsstand full of magazines, comic books, and newspapers. Tobias seemed confused. Thurgood reached for a *True Detectives* comic book.

"No, Pa, no comic books. I be a man now." He looked at the rack and picked up *Popular Mechanics*, and then looked some more. On the top row, there was a *LOOK* magazine. He took it in his hands and nodded approval. On the cover, a smiling Franklin D. Roosevelt, President of the United States, held a baby. To the right on the cover, another photo of Fred Astaire and Ginger Rogers dancing.

"If I goin' into the big world, I better start readin' about it, and know abouts it."

"Good idea, son, even if it be about dancin' movie stars." Thurgood chuckled.

The loudspeaker said: "Dixie-Greyhound to Memphis, now boarding at Gate 3."

Tobias looked at the two magazines, closed his eyes as he added the sums, and went up to the clerk. "I think this be, I mean, this is right." He handed her fifty cents.

"Yes, it is. Thank you. Have a nice trip."

Tobias smiled, picked up his suitcase, and walked briskly to Gate 3. Thurgood followed behind, catching up to his son who was already in line. He turned and faced him.

"I'm proud of you, Tobias, very proud. I love you."

Tears streamed down the boy's face. "I love you too, Pops. I'll write, be sure of that. I brought those McGuffy Readers, level three and four, with me. I'll study them on the bus, along with readin' the magazines."

"An' think about your Momma when you eat the chicken and biscuits she made. Damn, we forgot to buy you a soda pop. Get on the bus, open the window. I'll go get you one."

"It's okay, I can do without."

But Thurgood had already jogged off to the sundry shop, and Tobias got on the bus, handed the yellow ticket to the driver, and made his way to the rear, beyond the sign that said 'Colored.' He found a window seat and looked at the configuration of the window. There were two latches. He put his hands on them and squeezed. The window slid down, and Tobias smiled. He looked out and saw his father running up to the window, two bottles of Dr. Pepper in his hand. Tobias reached out and grabbed them and saw that his father was crying. The bus began to back up, and soon it was out of its berth. It slowly moved forward, and Tobias felt the gears shift. He stuck his head out the window.

"I love you, Pops. Tell Mama I love her, too."

"I will, son, I will. I loves you, too."

And in a moment, the bus was around the corner and out of sight.

CHAPTER 14

Memphis, Tennessee

It was past noon when the Dixie-Greyhound bus pulled into the imposing Memphis station, a harsh tan and red brick building. Tobias hurriedly finished the chicken and biscuits and washed them down with a bottle of Dr. Pepper. He had no idea when the bus would arrive at the station. He opened his lunch as the last of the cotton fields passed by his window. Architecture of brick, stone and glass pierced the horizon, high above the landscape — buildings taller than any he'd ever seen. He wiped a thin line of sweat from his hairline and loosened his belt. His stomach rumbled with an uncomfortable flutter of fear. He took a deep breath, pulled his suitcase from the overhead rack, and put his magazines and the unopened bottle inside.

The bus pulled into Gate 2 at 525 North Main Street, and Tobias waited as the white passengers got off. Then he and several other blacks moved forward and stepped off onto the concrete sidewalk. The area was full of people, jostling and pushing in the noontime bustle. He nervously looked around and saw the sign: "Colored Waiting Room." He exhaled, walked to the door, and went in. To his relief, it was not nearly as busy as the boarding area. He didn't notice two Black men leaning against the brick wall, sharply attired. But they took note of the big Negro boy dressed in country clothes; they nodded to one another, smiled, and entered the waiting room through another door.

As his father had instructed, he looked for a sign that said "Departures." He studied it carefully. He saw towns and cities like Pittsburgh and Chicago listed even Jackson, Mississippi, but not Detroit. The Jackson bus was leaving in an hour, and Tobias really wanted to board it and go back home. His free hand shook, and his stomach roiled with nerves and uncertainty. This adventure was probably a bad idea, the dream of an idealistic boy. He surveyed the room, larger than the entire bus station in Jackson. In the center was a circular counter attended to by two older Black men. Above, the words said "Information." Thinking hard, he remembered this word from his McGuffey Reader. It meant knowledge, something of value told to another person. He walked up to the counter.

"Scuse, me suh… "

"Hello, young fella. How can I help you today?"

Unlike the agent in Jackson, the Negro counterman was pleasant, and smiled at him.

"What's time the bus leave for Detroit, suh?"

"Detroit? Son, I was just about to take my chalk and add that city. Board only notates buses leavin' within four hours. No room fo' more. Bus leaves for Detroit at five o'clock. Travel all night, takes 15 hour. Be there tomorrow morning. You got a ticket?"

"Yes, suh."

"Lemme see it."

Tobias reached into his inside pocket of his old denim coat and pulled out the green stamped ticket. He handed it to the agent, who looked keenly at it.

"You good as gold, son. Bus boards startin' at 4:30. You don't want to miss it unless you want to spend the night on Beale Street listenin' to music and chattin' up the ladies." The agent smiled broadly, a gold front tooth glinting.

Tobias failed to pick up the man's meaning. "I heard about that street. Is it near here?"

"Just four blocks south. You have plenty o' time and you can walk down there. They play music all day in the joints."

Tobias looked down at his suitcase.

"You can check that at the cloakroom over there," the agent said, nodding over his shoulder.

"My daddy said there be showers here for a quarter. Where they be?"

"Your daddy must a come through here long time ago. They're fifty-cent now. Go into the bathroom and pay the attendant. He'll give you some soap. You a smart boy, wantin' to get all gussied up for the ladies on Beale." The man smiled again, and winked. Tobias now understood the drift of the conversation.

"I jus' want to get clean for the long trip, suh. Thank you for your info… ma… tion."

"You be very welcome Mr. …"

"Tobias. Tobias Woodson."

"Don't be late for that bus, Tobias. Remember it boards startin' 4:30."

The well-dressed Black men sat on a bench and watched a tall young boy check his suitcase and go into the bathroom. When he came out, he returned to the Information counter and talked to the same man as before. They saw the boy nod his head, take a piece of paper the man had scribbled on, and head for the south exit. After a moment, they followed him out the same door, keeping their distance.

Though the day was hot, Tobias kept his jacket on. The tight-fitted coat gave him a sense of security and a memory of home. With each step, he felt a greater sense of calm. His quick steps grew slower, his gait sure-footed and normal, not the forced hurry of a frightened boy. Rather than a defeated slump, his spine straightened, and his broad shoulders held an air of confidence. He unbuttoned his coat as the day grew warmer, and his mood brightened.

At the corner, he looked up at the street signs, first Union St., then Gayoso, and then Peabody Place. It was just as the man at the bus station had written down. He could hear distant music, looked at the paper, and saw that Beale Street was only another block away. He looked around at all the buildings, the people on busy Third Street, white and black walking by, serious or smiling, and minding their business. No one paid attention to him.

Then it struck him. He was free. No longer at Long Moss, almost indentured, where the foreman told him where to go to pick the cotton, when to rest, when to quit. The sun was hot, but now he welcomed its warmth. His muscles relaxed; he was no longer anxious as he walked toward Beale Street... a free man, a new man, making his own choices. He had made it to Memphis on the bus. In a few hours he would be on his way to Detroit to do what he wanted to do, make automobiles, make money, and make a good life, a life of freedom. He smiled at the thought, savored the feeling and turned left at the corner of Beale, heading toward the sweet sounds, the home of Negro music — the Blues. A hundred feet back, the two men followed.

The signs were plentiful and confusing. "Tonight: Howlin' Wolf" at P. Wee's Saloon; at the Old Daisy, "Bessie Smith & Ethel Waters"; on the great marquee above the Palace

Theatre, "Special Performance, One Night Only — Charlie Patton;" and at the Monarch Club, "Today at 2 PM: Robert Johnson and Memphis Minnie."

On the sidewalk were sharp-dressed Negroes and White folk in overalls and muslin shirts. Black boys made music from jugs, blew kazoos, and strummed washboards with spoons or knuckles, singing lively tunes. Others tap danced, a hat with bills and coins placed at their feet. Heavenly-scented, beautiful women stood in doorways blowing kisses at strangers or whistled out from windows above the street showing their wares. It was a cacophony of humanity the likes of which Tobias had never seen in Tallula.

"Hey, baby boy, you want some suga'? Only a dolla'. I'll make a man outta you."

Tobias shook his head, smiled, and walked on. He rolled his tongue around in his mouth but couldn't gather any spit. The sun didn't seem as hot as it did in Long Moss, but the walk and his nerves dried out his mouth just the same. Maybe he could buy a beer in one of the joints? He had snuck a glass once when he was thirteen at his aunt's wake in Jackson. His mother scolded him while his uncle only laughed. The brew made him feel funny and light-headed.

"Hello there, my friend. How are you doing on this fine day?"

Tobias turned. The two Black men were smiling broadly at him. They wore fine clothes; one sported a white boater, the other a wide-brimmed fedora with a prominent red feather.

"I be fine, thank you." Tobias was wary, but the two men looked very well-to-do, and one spoke perfect English without any accent.

"Allow me to introduce ourselves. My name is Rivers Johnson, and this gentleman is Bluffton Jones. We call him Bluff. Together, we are both the River and the Bluff. We are part of the welcoming committee for the City of Memphis, unofficially, that is. Are you visiting from out of town?"

Tobias was uncertain how to answer. "Yes, sir, I be visitin' only for a little while."

"I would wager you are thirsty from your long trip. Allow me to buy you a beverage."

"Thanks, suh, but you don't need to buy me no drink. I got's money." As quickly as the words left his mouth, Tobias realized he had said too much.

"I'm sure you do. But as part of the Chamber of Commerce, we must spend some of our funds on visitors. Allow me, right this way." He dipped forward from the waist while his right hand waved across the front of his body, his arm outstretched, and a forefinger pointed in the direction of the Monarch Club.

"Are you familiar with Memphis Minnie? She's singing right now inside. She has a fine voice, and it's pleasant inside. The establishment has many ceiling fans." Rivers took Tobias firmly by the arm, and they entered the saloon, the boy reluctant to resist. He was thirsty, and a cool drink would be nice.

Even at 2 PM, the Monarch Club was busy with patrons lined up at the long bar, a painting of a naked woman above many bottles of gin, rye, and bourbon. Others sat at tables and focused on a small bandstand at the rear. The fans above swirled the cigar and cigarette smoke throughout the dark-paneled room covered with etched mirrors surrounded by mahogany paneling; huge brass chandeliers hung from the stamped metal ceiling. At the microphone, Memphis Minnie, in a yellow chiffon dress, had just finished singing "Kissing in the Dark." She smiled in appreciation of the scattered applause and began to light into one of her favorites, "If You See My Rooster."

Rivers found space at the bar, and a stein of beer was quickly in Tobias' hand. He grinned at the beer, gawked around the room, and diverted his eyes from the painting above the bar.

"A toast to your trip and to Memphis, home of the Blues."

Tobias did not know what a toast was, but when he saw the two raised glasses, he lifted his and slowly touched the mugs. "You sur' be kind here in Memphis."

"Southern hospitality. I'm sorry. What handle do you go by?"

"Suh?"

"My apologies. Your name. You haven't told us your name."

"Oh, I'm Tobias Woodson."

"Where you headed for, Tobias?"

"Detroit, to make automobiles." Tobias felt uncomfortable, telling too much. He remembered his daddy's lecture on the hard city. The beer did taste good, though.

Rivers nodded to Bluff and winked.

"An excellent choice, Tobias. You will thrive there. Ah, I see that your beer is disappearing quickly. Let me order another, and I'll tell you about the Peabody Hotel. A visit to our fair city must include a stop there."

"I never been to a hotel. It nice?" Tobias finished his beer, light-headed on an empty stomach; the fried chicken lunch eaten three hours earlier.

"The finest hotel in America. They even have ducks swimming in the fountain in the lobby."

"I ain't seen anythin' like this. What a beautiful place. And look at 'dem ducks in the pool."

"Tobias, friend, what time is your bus to Detroit?"

"Five, but I needs to be there by 4:30. I don't feel so good."

"Perhaps you overindulged. Five beers, my, my. Not to worry. Bluff and I know a shortcut. We'll get you to the bus station in plenty of time."

As the two led him out, through his fogged brain, he wondered how his new friends knew he was going by bus, not the train, or by car to Detroit. His daddy's words penetrated through his pounding head: *Watch out for fancy-dressed niggas wantin' to do you a favor.*

"If it's all the same, I jus' get there myself. Thank you for your kindness."

Bluff grabbed Tobias' arm and River the other, this time hard. "Oh, it's no problem at all. Come now." The two directed Tobias down an unfamiliar corridor, into the hotel kitchen, and into a rear alley.

"Let go a me! This ain't no street!"

The alley was narrow, and little afternoon light crept through between the hotel walls and its neighboring buildings. It was a mess of empty boxes and crates, large trash bins, and garbage cans, that reeked in the summer heat. The two men cornered Tobias between two trash containers.

Rivers reached into his coat pocket and in an instant, a shiny steel blade was at Woodson's throat. "Nigga boy, give us all your money, and you'll be free to go." Bluff punched him in the stomach, and he doubled over, throwing up his beer.

Be bad, but only if necessary.

Rivers righted Tobias, and the knife was at his throat again. He stuck the point into Woodson's bulging neck, and the boy could feel warm blood on his skin.

"Be quick, now. We know you got money. Give it to us an' you can go. Bluff, hit the Nigga again to make him pay better attention."

Tobias took a deep breath, and Jones hit him again with full force. Woodson gasped for breath.

"Don'ts hit me no mor'. I gots money; it be here in my boot. Move that blade, so I kin reach down and get it."

Rivers lowered the blade, and Tobias slowly reached into his boot feeling for the knife and the button to unleash the blade. Sobriety came quick as the adrenaline coursed through his quivering body. The blade opened as his knife left the boot, and Tobias swung it wildly.

Blood flew everywhere. Rivers grabbed his throat where the five-inch blade had severed the carotid artery. He dropped to the ground; his knife fell to the stone pavement. Bluff looked down in shock, turned, yelled an epithet, and ran, knocking over several garbage cans.

Tobias screamed, but no one heard him except the alley's rats. He looked at the bloody knife in his hand, held it for a moment in shock, then dropped the switchblade, and staggered down the alley. Stumbling over some wooden fruit crates, he regained his footing and began to run. At the end of the alley, he stopped. His jacket was splattered with Rivers' blood, and his shirt and collar were red from the cut Johnson had made. He emptied the pockets, stuck his bus ticket into his trousers, and took off the bloody coat. He opened a metal garbage can, dropped it in, and turned the corner onto Third Avenue. He recognized the thoroughfare from earlier and walked briskly toward the bus station. A clock inside Pantaze's Drug Store told him it was 4:15. He needed to get to the showers at the terminal and get on the bus. Forget dinner. Tobias Woodson had no appetite anyway.

Chapter 15

Detroit, Michigan

Tobias dare not stay overnight in the bus station. As the bus to Detroit departed, he thought he heard police sirens and peeked out the window. At stoplights, he was certain the bus would be pulled over and searched.

Once back at the terminal, the attendant barely looked up from his newspaper as he collected the half dollar and handed over some soap and a towel. In the bathroom Tobias saw blood on his face and hands and quickly stepped into a shower stall. He washed every inch of his body, got out and dried. He staunched the cut with his dirty shirt and put on his clean one. Then he saw it. There were red stains on the towel. He wrapped the ruined shirt in the towel and shoved both as deeply as he could in the half-filled trash can and walked quickly out of the restroom and directly onto the bus. It was 4:55.

The trip to Detroit was a journey of guilt, depression, and fear. Though there wasn't a Colored section in the back of the bus, Tobias sat in the second to the last seat, at times in the fetal position, shaking. He had killed a man. Yes, it was self-defense, but it felt like murder. A white jury would agree. He'd be lynched, or at best, sent to prison and a chain gang for the rest of his life. He wished his daddy were next to him to offer comfort and advice. He wished he was on the bus returning to Jackson, but there wasn't one until the next morning. Most of all, he wished he could have that split second back when he slashed the air with that knife and killed Rivers Johnson.

At eleven o'clock, the bus pulled into a parking lot with a large restaurant. They were just outside Bowling Green, Kentucky. The driver announced a 45-minute rest stop. As the miles went by, the fear dissipated, but not the guilt. Pastor Bradby would have some solution. After all, Rivers Johnson was a con man and a thief who had put a knife to his throat and cut him. Bluff, his accomplice, had gut punched him so hard his stomach still hurt. Yes, using his knife was self-defense. But try to prove that with no witnesses. He was smart to get on the bus.

Famished and hung-over he devoured chicken fried steak covered in gravy, mashed potatoes, and green beans, washed down with sweet tea. A passenger he recognized from the bus, a Black woman, came up to his table.

"Hello. I saw you in the back. We can sit anywhere we want. Are you all right?"

"I be fine. I'm new to travlin'. Bus motion maybe make me a little sick. Now that I got some vittles in me, I feel better."

"I'm going to visit my son in Detroit. I think he's just a little older than you. He works at Ford Motor Company in the foundry. It's very hard work but it pays well."

"I hopes to work making cars, too. Republic Motors. But Detroit sur' is a long way from Mississippi."

"Oh, my yes. Well, good luck, young man. I'll pray for you."

"Thank you, ma'am."

As Tobias dug into a piece of apple pie, he thought, *I be needin' a lot of prayers.*

The sun was full up as the Greyhound bus pulled into the blue-enamel paneled Art Deco station in Detroit. Tobias had slept through another rest stop in Fort Wayne, though the sleep was fitful and troubled.

As he got off the bus, a middle-aged black man approached him.

"Are you Tobias Woodson?"

Fear struck Tobias. "You be the police?"

"My goodness, no. Why would you think that? I'm Reverend Bradby, Robert Bradby. Your father sent a telegram saying you were coming. He said you were tall, muscular, and handsome. I guessed that you might be Tobias."

"I am. I'm sorry, Pastor. It's good to meet you. Thank you fo' takin' me in."

"It's my pleasure. Your daddy is a fine man. I was happy to help him some years ago, and I'm happy to get you settled in your new hometown. I understand that you want to work at Republic Motors."

"I do, suh."

"Well, I know a man there. He owes me a favor."

 CHAPTER 16

Homicide detective Lucas Smith and his assigned recruit, Samuel Melton, got up from the table by the window of Joe's Diner on Beale Street. Smith headed for the door, two quarters left on the table.

"Aren't you going to pay the bill, Detective?"

"What, Melton?"

"The bill. Dinner cost $2.75."

"We're the police. Breakfast, lunch, dinner, it's always on the house."

"Really?"

"Melton, you got a lot to learn."

As soon as they got back to the black and white the two-way radio was buzzing: *"Screams reported from behind the Peabody in the vicinity of the alley."*

Smith took the handheld, and pressed the button on the side. "Unit 509. We'll take it."

Detective Smith looked down at the body of a man with his throat cut open. The dead man's skin was as ashen brown as the mud along the banks of the Mississippi, the cut as deep as the river, and a stream of drying blood trailed into the gutter. There were two knives on the ground, but only one covered in blood. Rookie officer Samuel Melton stared wide-eyed at the corpse.

"Excuse me, Detective, but I'm going to be sick." As the last word left his mouth, he ran to a garbage can and threw up. Unfortunately, he didn't have time to remove the lid.

Rookies; you'd think they've never seen a dead body, or blood before, thought Smith. It was Melton's first week on the job, assigned to the detective to see the seamier side of police work. So far, the new cop was not impressed.

"Well, if it isn't my old friend, Rivers."

"Who?" Officer Melton wiped his mouth with his handkerchief and threw it on top of the filthy can and returned to the crime scene.

"This is Rivers Johnson. Been trying to nail him for months. He and his associate, Bluffton Jones, prey on Negro folk getting off the Greyhound buses, less often at the railroad station. They pretend to be part of a Memphis Chamber of Commerce welcoming committee. They buy them drinks, get them drunk, or get 'em laid by some whore who gets a cut of the money they rob from the poor bastards. Most are country folk, gullible, and new to the city. What boils my blood is these two sweet-talking niggas prey on their own kind. I guess he finally got his comeuppance."

"Where do you think the other guy is now, that Bluff… Jones?"

"I expect he's probably skedaddled his way out of town. Off to a new city and a new grift."

"Grift?"

"Geesus, Melton, a grifter, a scam artist, one who uses a ruse, or an elaborate scheme to bilk people out of their money, except in this case, it's nothing but simple robbery in the end.

If you're done being sick, Melton, check the other trash cans and see what you can find."

Smith removed two unused brown lunch bags from his coat and placed a knife in each one. The bloody one was old, an antique. Rivers' blade looked familiar; he probably bought it at Schwartz's, the local mercantile store. He touched the flesh of the dead man. Not warm, but not yet cold.

"Detective, look!" Melton hurried back to where Smith was looking for other evidence. "I found this coat in the trash can at the end of the alley. There's blood on it."

Smith carefully took the garment from the rookie officer and studied it.

"Kaufman's Department Store, Jackson, Miss. The killer must have been wearing it when he did the deed. Probably a local boy from Mississippi headed north to work in the factories."

"There's our evidence, sir."

"You know how many coats like this have been sold by Jacobsen's? And this one's old, threadbare, probably handed down to the person who wore it."

"We should check the bus station, then. Look for a man who fits this coat."

"Why? He's probably on a bus north and out of our jurisdiction."

"But, sir, justice must be served."

Smith looked down at Rivers Johnson, the white boater beside the body, blood creeping within an inch of it. He picked up the hat, placed it over his heart, and smiled.

"Lucas, I believe that it already has."

The detective wiped the inside brim of the boater and placed the hat gently on his head. It fit perfectly. He smiled.

Melton, sighed, slowly shook his head, but said nothing as he stared at the detective.

CHAPTER 17

Tobias nervously walked into the employment office pointed out by Reverend Bradby, who said he would remain outside. Woodson had not summoned the courage to tell the pastor what had happened in Memphis and, with several days passed, did not think he could ever garner the mettle to do so. It would be a secret he would have to keep, probably forever.

"Can I help you?" A matronly clerk met Woodson at the counter.

"I'm here to ask for a job."

"In the factory?"

"Yessum. Here at Republic."

"We're not hiring."

"Ah, I see. But Pastor Bradby said to asks for Mr. Donnelly."

"I see. Name?"

"Ah, Woodson."

"Fill this out. I'll see if he's in." The woman was matter-of-fact, with no emotion. She knew the chances of a Black boy being hired were slim.

Tobias took the clipboard, a pencil, and sat down.

First name. *First name?*

He stopped, ready to write down "Tobias," a sharpened pencil poised over the form.

If the police goin' to look for me, and somehow find out my real name from that man at the bus station, or from that Bluff fella who punched me, they'd be lookin' for Tobias. He looked hard at the sheet of paper.

Tobias wrote "George."

Perspiring, he filled out the rest of the form as best he could, handed the application back, and sat down. Minutes passed but it seemed like hours.

"George Woodson?" A tall Irishman, cigarette in his mouth, called out into the waiting room of Republic Motors' employment office.

"That be me, suh." Tobias stood up and walked toward the man with the clipboard. Woodson wore his best clothes — pressed wool pants that Bradby had given him and a blue flannel shirt.

The director of employment did not extend his hand. "I'm Mickey Donnelly. Come on back."

Pastor Bradby reminded Tobias to make eye contact and shake hands firmly. Tobias tried to look Donnelly in the eye, but the man had already walked away. He went through a low swinging gate and followed the director to his office, all glass above wood wainscot-paneled walls.

"Where you from, George?" Donnelly did not offer Woodson a chair, although there were two.

"Mississippi, suh. Tallula. It's a small town."

"Ever worked in a factory, boy?"

"No, suh, just the farm. But my daddy taught me a lot about cars. He used to work here in Detroit."

"Does he own an automobile?"

"Yes, suh, he do. A Ford pickup. I worked on it some with him. I been studying 'dem in books and magazines."

"Can you read and write?"

"Yes, suh, I do pretty good, suh. I practice ever' day."

Donnelly lit another Lucky Strike and blew the smoke into the air. "I owe Pastor Bradby a favor; that's the only reason you're here. We don't hire many Negroes. It upsets the white boys. But he speaks highly of you, and you look like a strong, young buck. And you're in luck, boy, a job just opened up."

Tobias was uneasy. He hoped the insults would be left behind in Mississippi, but 'boy' and 'young buck' had traveled north with him.

"Suh, I'm hoping to get any kind a job here at Republic. It be my dream."

"Did you see all the men milling about the gate when you came in? It's their dream, too. So, yes, I'll hire you. Like I said, I owe the minister a favor. But you screw up or don't keep up, anyone of them boys be happy to take your place. You'll work in the foundry. It's small; we're not Ford, and the work is hard."

"I cans handle hard work, suh."

"Good. Report back here tomorrow. And on your way back through the office, see Miss Bessie. She has paperwork for you to fill out. You *can* fill out paperwork?"

"I think so, suh."

"Good. Goodbye then."

"Suh?"

"Yes, George?"

"What the job pay, suh, if you don't mind me askin'?"

"$5.70 a day."

"Suh, 'scuse me but my daddy worked at Ford long time ago and made six dollar. He said I'd probably be makin' eight, maybe ten dollar a day."

"Well, your daddy told you wrong. That was true back in 1928, but we're just now getting out of the Depression. So, if the pay rate isn't to your liking, like I said, there's boys waiting outside be happy to make it."

"No, suh, that be fine. I'm sorry to cause a fuss."

"No fuss at all. And Woodson, if you want, you can work six days a week and make an additional days' pay."

"Uh, that be jus' fine, Mr. Donnelly. I sure do thank you."

JACOB HOFFMAN

1937

CHAPTER 18

1937
Stuttgart, Germany

The morning light streamed through the large windows of the modern, Bauhaus-designed engineering building of Daimler-Benz Autowerks. Jacob Hoffman sat at his gray metal desk in a corner office with a drafting table, file cabinet, and shelves that held prototypes of differential gears, crankshafts, clutch-disks, shift levers, and a myriad of other parts of an automobile's transmission.

The diminutive man pushed his wire-rimmed glasses up on a prominent nose. He worked his slide-rule with deft precision and wrote down numbers on a yellow legal pad. A crystal ashtray cradled his unlit pipe, and a china cup contained lukewarm coffee.

The morning copy of the Grafinger Zeitung newspaper lay in the trash can; Jacob was disgusted by its latest anti-Semitic rants on the editorial page. His work on an improved transmission for the Model S Mercedes took his mind off the worsening situation for the Jewish people in Germany.

He looked up from his work at the sound of a polite knock on the door. Conrad Schmidt, vice president of the engineering department and Jacob's boss, entered.

"Good morning, Jacob. How are you?"

"Fine, well, almost fine." Hoffman looked down at the trash can.

"How is your progress on the new transmission?"

"Almost there. We should be able to cast a mock-up by next week. I think I've found the problem in the gear ratios. Just a little tweak is all that is necessary."

The young assistant director of engineering had no trouble solving most technical issues. He was one of Schmidt's best and brightest employees. And he was only 29 years old, though he looked barely older than a university student with his slight build and shaggy brown hair that touched his shirt collar.

The older man, a sturdy Bavarian with thinning blond hair and a moustache, stood silent.

"So, to what do I owe the pleasure this fine day, boss?"

"Jacob, this is difficult for me. Very difficult."

"What is difficult?"

"I have to let you go."

"Go? You mean I'm fired?"

"I'm afraid I have no choice."

Jacob pushed his glasses up and rubbed the bridge of his nose. He put his head down, and took a deep breath. When he looked up at Schmidt, his face was red with anger.

"Yes, you do have a choice."

"I don't."

"Is it because I'm Jewish?"

"The Law is the law."

"What law?"

"The Law for the Restoration of Civil Service, that law."

"It was enacted in 1933, and I'm not working in civil service. I work for a private company."

"A private company that does significant business with the Reich. We are getting a lot of pressure. You are more than seventy-five percent Jewish. You are no longer a German citizen but a state subject. And as such, you can no longer hold a professional job."

Jacob shook his head. "I cannot believe this. I have been a good and loyal employee of Daimler-Benz since graduation. Over seven years."

"Yes, and you have achieved great things. But I have a directive from the top. All Jews are being dismissed. Let me tell you, it will throw a monkey wrench into our research and development sector."

"Fuck your sector! What am I to do? Become a chauffeur for a high-ranking Nazi engineer?"

"You'll get two weeks' severance pay. It's the best I could do. They wanted to give you nothing, but I insisted. Your last day is Wednesday. Jorgen will be taking over your research. Make sure he has all your notes."

"Screw you, and screw Jorgen!"

"Watch your tongue, Jew. Your severance can disappear in an instant. Good day."

Jacob stared at his boss as he walked away. Schmidt passed another supervisor; they both raised their right arms, hands extended, and he heard them say a crisp, "Heil Hitler!"

CHAPTER 19

Summer, 1937
Southampton, England

Jacob Hoffman stood in awe of the great ocean liner. The white hull blinded him in the afternoon light; its three ochre smokestacks reached to the sky, their tops obscured by the pier's roof. He looked down the quay; there was no end to the massive steamship. The sight of the *Empress of Britain* moored dockside, the chaos of activity swirling around it, made him forget his exhaustion from the long journey from Germany. In tow on the grueling trip were his wife, Hannah, and their seven-year-old son, Tomasz.

Shortly after graduation from the Technical University of Berlin in 1929, Jacob married a wispy, some thought homely girl, Hannah, studying to be a nurse. They had a son, and after Jacob garnered several promotions, finally to assistant director, the family moved into a new apartment in Stuttgart. Then in 1933, the Nazi Party came to power.

At first, life did not change for the Hoffmans under National Socialist rule. But anti-Semitism grew. In 1935, the Nuremberg Laws were passed, although not fully implemented until after the 1936 Olympics. In 1937, dismissed from Daimler, Jacob found work in a grocery store owned by a family friend, a Christian. Every day forward, life grew grimmer.

The German government wanted to eliminate the Hoffman family and all Jews. One evening, the Gestapo paid a visit to their apartment, looked around, took notes, and said another German family wanted the flat. They were given a month to vacate, and strongly encouraged to leave the country. All they had to do was hand over all their belongings and eighty percent of their savings to the government, and a visa could be forthcoming. But nothing was guaranteed. With the assistance of a friend in Daimler's personnel department, he secured the proper passports and exit papers that allowed them to leave the country with only enough Reichsmarks to travel. But to where?

Jacob immediately thought of his uncle Max Hoffman, successful and content in America. He wrote to him. The reply came within two weeks; go to the American Embassy and apply for a special visa, emphasizing his degree and technical experience. Max would go to the Immigration office in Detroit, where he had a friend, and see what he could do. By good fortune, the friend, a Jew, had helped others in the same predicament. He wired the embassy in Berlin, and vouched for Jacob Hoffman. Jacob secured the precious visa for his family to come to the United States. And so, their long, frightening exodus began.

First, the Hoffman's traveled from Stuttgart by train to Cologne, then on several buses to Antwerp on the North Sea. From there, they sailed on a small packet boat to Liverpool. Another train took them to the great port of Southampton, where all manner of steamships, some grandiose in scale and magnificence, departed for America and Canada. The trip took six days and would cost them most of their money.

"Look, Tomasz, look at the great ship. It is truly an empress. Soon we will be on our way to our new home in America, to Detroit, Michigan." Jacob lifted the boy so he could see above the jostling crowd, and kissed his son softly on the cheek.

"Papa, are there going to be any other children on the boat?"

"Oh, yes, I am quite sure. But it is a ship, not a boat. A boat goes on a ship, not the other way around."

"Yes, Papa, it is a big boat."

Jacob laughed and kissed his son again. "And we have our own cabin… on the, ah, ship, and you will have your own bed."

Hannah squeezed Jacob's hand, a weak smile across her face. Then the smile turned downward, and she began to cry, soft sobs of uncertainty, even fear.

"Hannah, my love, you know this is for the best. Uncle Max said there is plenty of work at the factory. And they need engineers." He gently kissed his wife's cheeks, wiping the tears with his fingers.

Despite Jacob's assurances, Hannah Hoffman had no idea what the upcoming ocean voyage would be like. Once they arrived in Quebec City, they still had another long train trip to this strange place called Detroit, Michigan. She hoped it would be worth it. Her husband's uncle and his wife, whom she didn't know, lived outside the city in a village, Hamtramck. He worked on the assembly line at a giant automobile plant called Republic Motors. He promised his nephew that there would be a job for him. The Hoffman family could stay with them until they got on their feet.

"No more tears now; this is our big day. We are going to the United States. Here, hold onto Tomasz; it's time to board."

Jacob handed his son to Hannah, picked up their suitcases, and moved into and through the throngs of passengers with his wife and son behind him. Hannah held Tomasz tightly by her side. The great pier smelled of coal and oil, wool and tobacco, sweat and humanity. Occasionally, there was the scent of perfume and talcum powder. They passed the gangplank for first class, an orderly affair in contrast to the rest of the scene, then past second class, and finally, they arrived at the embarkation desk for third class. People elbowed and jostled one another to get to the front of the line. Jacob pushed hard; Hannah and Tomasz followed while Jacob's slim body pushed through the queue. At the agent's desk, he reached into his coat pocket and handed thick paper tickets, their precious visas, and passports to a burly, wide-shouldered employee. The man arched his bushy eyebrows and twirled his handlebar mustache, then looked intently at the exhausted travelers. He perused the documents carefully, nodded at the stamp on the German exit visas "Jüdisch, Wiedereinreise nicht gestattet,"* and finally said: "Welcome aboard, Mr. Hoffman. Have a fine voyage, and welcome to Canada."

* Jewish, No re-entry permitted.

Jacob looked out toward the fading lights of Southampton. The wind picked up as the ship headed toward the open sea, but the air was cool and welcome. His 5'-7" frame stood at the railing of the aft deck, the only outside space afforded the 400 or so third-class passengers. His chiseled face was softened by pale blue eyes that took in the view. Despite the long journey and the adversity, he was confident he had made the right decision for his family. He had studied everything possible about the American auto industry, and was sure that a good position in the engineering department awaited him in Detroit.

He turned and headed for the door and the stairwell down to their humble third-class cabin. It was time to clean up before supper in the dining room. Tomasz would be excited. The meal was sure to be a feast.

CHAPTER 20

Hamtramck, Michigan

"Next is Jacob Hoffman. He's a well-qualified engineer with seven years' experience at Daimler-Benz."

Mickey Donnelly took a drag on his Lucky Strike, and sighed. He was tired of defending every new hire to Jack Bullard, head of Special Services. Mickey did the hiring and firing, but in the last year, Jack Bullard had begun to take a keen interest in who Donnelly employed. And Bullard was Angus Drummond's best friend and confidant, in charge of security, and he outranked him in the pecking order at Republic Motors. Bullard had been with Drummond since the days at the bicycle shop, as all the key employees knew of the legendary history of Republic's humble beginnings. Bottom line: you didn't fuck with the head of Special Services.

Bullard looked down at the file folder containing a single sheet that was the compendium of the life of Jacob Ashkenazi Hoffman. His fingers tapped on his gray metal desk.

Donnelly inhaled again, the smoke poured from his mouth with his words. "So, what's the problem, Jack? I say welcome to the Promised Land, Mr. Hoffman. He got one of our precious American visas allowing him into this country. And Mr. Drummond needs bodies for the engineering department. The technical kinks with the Epoch's transmission have got to be worked out."

"Mickey, here's the problem. Hoffman's uncle is Max Hoffman. He recommended Jacob; it's right here on the form."

"So? They're blood; that makes sense. I know Max; he's a hard worker."

"Max Hoffman is a Jew, an agitator, and a pro-union man. My people have been keeping tabs on him. He attends every Union organization meeting they have. Hell, he's probably a Communist since he's also a Jew. They won't be happy until they take over this country."

"Jews are regular people like you and me. Why don't you lay off of 'em? "

"They're trouble for Germany and they'll be trouble for us. Just look at all the Union agitation we have going on."

"You know as well as I do that unionization is coming. It's only a matter of time. Many of our workers attend those meetings since they can't discuss a union on the factory floor."

"Mr. Drummond will never unionize. You know that. I know that. And he doesn't need any more agitators."

"Jacob isn't labor; he's management material. He was an assistant director at Daimler, for Christ's sake. And those Germans are smart engineers."

"Jacob lists the same address as Max, so his family is probably stayin' there until they get on their feet." Bullard shook his head and continued to tap his fingers on the desk. "Birds of a feather."

"Jack, we need good people, and Drummond told me to hire them. This man is well qualified. Not everyone is a fuckin' socialist."

"Take it from me. He's a damn Jew, and I bet, a union man. You know, Henry Ford was right on target about them people. Have you read *The International Jew*?"

"No. Don't want to. It's all bullshit. I'm going to hire him, anyway."

"To do what?"

"Work in engineering, of course. Look at his sheet. He headed up the transmission group at Daimler. If we don't iron out the problems with the Epoch's gear shift, there won't be any Epochs to sell next year."

"He won't be working in any engineerin' office at Republic. Put him on the line. He won't last more an' two weeks. If he lasts, we can reconsider. Hell, if he were in Germany that would be his lot. Now, who's next?"

You prejudiced Irish son-of-a-bitch. Go fuck yourself! Donnelly frowned, put out his cigarette, and reached for another file.

Chapter 21

Max and Isabel Hoffman lived on the second floor of a duplex on Charest Street, two blocks off Joseph Campeau Avenue and a dozen blocks from the Republic Motors manufacturing plant. The flat contained three bedrooms, one bath, a living room, and a good-sized kitchen with a center table where the family ate. They had two girls, ages nine and seven, who occupied the second bedroom. The third and smallest bedroom was now the home of Jacob Hoffman and his family. The cramped quarters were in stark contrast to their spacious apartment in Stuttgart on the Koningstrasse, which over-looked a large park. But now they were free from Nazi oppression and persecution.

Max Hoffman was a talented machinist. However, he kept a profound secret. He was a member of the Communist Party.

After fighting in the Great War, the harsh Allied terms imposed on Germany at the Treaty of Versailles left him a bitter man. He became a victim of Germany's anemic and financially burdened economy in the early twenties, beset by hyperinflation and food shortages. He attended party meetings and agreed with many tenets of the Marxist philosophy. One night, after too many beers, he joined the party, even if it meant he could never secure another job. It was true, so in 1925, Max Hoffman left Germany for the United States.

He hoped to find work in Detroit, where America made its cars. Lured by the seven-dollar-a-day wage, he went to work at Ford. In 1931, he was laid off, even though he was part of a small, elite group of employees working on re-tooling the River Rouge plant for the new Ford Model B. He suspected that it was because he was Jewish.

For four years, Max was unemployed. He marched with union groups and the communists because there was nothing else to do. His family had to sell their house in the Melvindale neighborhood and move into a boarding house, where they occupied two drafty rooms. They sold their Ford Model A that they bought on payments, and pawned Isabel's wedding ring. She took in laundry and Max worked at menial jobs when they came along. His communist leanings deepened — his family and the working man had suffered enough under the yoke of capitalism.

In early 1935, the economy began to improve, and Max heard about a sheet metal job at another, smaller auto company, Republic Motors. The company was building a new car, the Chamberlain. With his background at Ford Motor Company, they hired him, his political leanings unchecked. After all, when he came to America in 1925, there was no union movement at Ford or anywhere else, and in 1935 there still wasn't one of any consequence.

It was early morning and still dark when the alarm clock rang. Jacob Hoffman woke up and fumbled to turn it off. He quietly got up and checked on his son, who slept in a small cot at the foot of the double bed.

Jacob opened the wardrobe, removed his suit, a white shirt, and a nondescript tie, and quietly left the bedroom. He washed, shaved and dressed. From the icebox in the kitchen, he removed the sack lunch Hannah had made the night before. He wished there was a hot cup of coffee and hoped they would have a pot in the engineering office as at Daimler-Benz. He put on his suit coat and was leaving when Max entered the kitchen.

"Wait a moment; I'll walk with you, and make sure you find the employment office. Hopefully, today will be your first day. All dressed up and optimistic, I see."

"Thank you, Uncle. I must confess, I'm a little nervous. My English is not so good."

"Many foreigners work at Republic, and your English is better than most."

The two walked down the stairs to a small foyer that served as the entry to both apartments. Max opened the door, and a rush of warm, humid air engulfed them.

"It's going to be another hot day. Welcome to summertime in Michigan. This way to the right; it's quicker."

The two walked along narrow sidewalks as the sun rose. Other workers came out of their houses, apartments, and flats and soon the two were part of a procession of men and women on their way to another day of work at Republic Motors, where the only reward was a payday envelope on Friday afternoon.

Jacob loosened his collar and tie with the morning warmth. "Where do you think I'll be working?"

"I do not know. But with your experience, I would think the transmission design area. I heard they are having trouble with the new shift gears. They must fix it, and soon, so we can begin production of the new Epoch."

"I'm experienced only in German cars."

"You're experienced. That's all that matters."

"It didn't matter at Daimler. Because I am a Jew, they fired me. Hannah is quite upset about it. Her constitution is not strong like Isabel's."

"Isabel is a force of nature. We lost everything in the Depression. She was hardened by it. But underneath that tough exterior is a decent, kind woman."

"Thank you, again, for taking us in. I hope I did the right thing."

"You did. You saved your family from the Nazis. Your father didn't tell you this because he did not want to upset you, but our oldest brother, Uncle Hans, has been sent to a work camp at Dachau."

"But he worked for the government."

"The previous Weimar government. Lately, he has been quite vocal about the Nazis. Hans was able to smuggle out a letter to your father. More Jews, dissidents, political prisoners, and other undesirables, like homosexuals and Roma, are arriving there every day. They've doubled the size of the prison, and he said they have built other ones, just for our people. So, yes, you did the right thing."

"And my father and mother? Have you heard from them?"

"I received a post yesterday. I didn't tell you because I didn't want to ruin the nice dinner with the children and all. Your father said that they're very worried. He said every month the Nazis pass more anti-Jewish laws and regulations. They even passed one forbidding our people to own cars or have a driver's license. Can you believe? So, your parents stay in their apartment, afraid to go out."

"Can't they emigrate like Hannah and I did?"

"You were lucky. You got one of the last visas. It seems most countries, England, France, the Netherlands, don't want our kind."

"My God! What will become of us?"

"All I can say is that you are safe now."

"Here in America everyone is equal."

"Don't be so naive. You will find that many of your co-workers hate us, too. Along with the Negroes and the Catholics."

"Oh, yes. I read *Mein Kampf.* Henry Ford is the only American who Hitler praises in the book. He calls him a 'single great man'."

"He's not the only one that hates our kind. When I first arrived in America, there was an organization called the Ku Klux Klan."

"That's a strange name, Uncle."

"Indeed. They hold secret meetings wearing white robes and hoods to cover their faces. They burn crosses at night. They mostly hate the Blacks, but Catholics and Jews are on their list as well. In the 1920s their numbers were in the millions across the country, and Detroit was a very popular place for them because of all the immigrants and Blacks who came here for work."

"What happened to them?"

"Their leader, the Grand Dragon…"

"Grand dragon?"

"Yes, nephew, only in America; anyway, he was convicted of the rape and murder of a woman. When that happened the organization lost many members. Don't be fooled; I assure you that the prejudice and the hate continue. Even here in America."

"But you have a good job at Republic Motors, now?"

"When I first came to Detroit, I worked at Ford. But when the Depression came, I lost my job. Isabel thinks it was because I am Jewish. I was lucky to get another job, and I've gotten pretty good at handling sheet metal and using the big presses."

"What about my getting a job at Republic because of my faith?"

Max deflected the question. "Look, here is the employment office. We'll discuss it later. I have another block to go. It is a big plant. Good luck. I'll see you at home tonight."

"Yes. And Max… "

"Yes, Jacob?"

"Thank you, again. And God bless America."

"Indeed… " Max smiled, turned, and walked on.

The sun continued its morning journey as it rose into the bright blue sky.

CHAPTER 22

Jacob entered a large room where several ladies sat behind a large counter. On the walls were motivational posters stating: *"Make Today your BEST day at Republic Motors,"* and *"Nothing will Work unless YOU do."* There were also framed prints of Republic's fleet of automobiles — the Drummond, the Toiler pickup truck, the Zodiac, the Chamberlain, and the soon to arrive, Epoch. Jacob smiled. This place seemed like a good fit. He walked up to the counter.

"May I help you?"

"Yes, I'm Jacob Hoffman. I am here for an interview."

"Let me check the appointments." The matronly woman reached for a clipboard with a sheet of paper that alphabetically listed last names. She found 'Hoffman' with an asterisk by the name.

"Yes, Mr. Hoffman. Have a seat. It'll only be a moment." The clerk went into an office, closed the door, and dialed a number on the desk phone.

"Hello, Mr. Donnelly. Mr. Hoffman is here for his interview."

Donnelly put out the first of many Lucky Strikes. *Let's get this over with,* he thought. Donnelly left his cubicle and reached for and lit another cigarette. He exhaled as he said,

"Good morning, Mr. Hoffman." He extended his hand in a warm handshake. "Mickey Donnelly, welcome to America."

Jacob smiled and took the big Irishman's hand. "Thank you; it is a pleasure to meet you." He felt sure that by the end of the day, he would have a nice office in the technical design department.

"Come this way. Bessie, hold all my calls."

Bessie stared at her boss. He had never told her to hold his calls. "Yes, Mr. Donnelly."

Donnelly ushered Hoffman into his office and motioned for him to sit. "You've had a long journey, haven't you?"

"Yes, very long, but we are grateful to be here in Detroit at last."

"You're staying with your uncle, Max. A good man, a good employee."

"They have been very kind to my family. Their flat is small. I am eager to work so we can get a our own place. He tells me you have jobs here at Republic."

"What is your specialty, your area of expertise, Jacob?"

"I designed a new transmission for the Mercedes S model. It was implemented last year, and I had begun improvements for the 1938 model."

And I have to put this man on the assembly line because of that bigoted asshole, Bullard, he thought.

"Have you heard about our new model, the Epoch?"

"Yes, I have read about it."

"And… "

"German cars are fine automobiles, but they are a little, how do you say, traditional? The Epoch is like nothing I've ever seen. I have read up on it. Very advanced. It gives me the 'goose bumps,' yes?"

Bullard inhaled some fresh smoke. *Fucking Bullard, I need this man figuring out the goddamn transmission problems on this car.*

"Mr. Hoffman, this is how we work here at Republic. You'll start on the floor of the factory. We want you to learn how we produce our cars. Look around. As an engineer, we're open to suggestions. We'd like your perspective as a German engineer on our assembly line. You know, how it works. Eventually, you'll be advanced to the engineering department."

"I am sorry. Eventually?"

"Well, I can't give you an exact date."

"May I ask the pay?"

"Yes, certainly. We'll start you off at $7.50 a day."

Jacob's face registered disappointment and a hint of disgust. "In Stuttgart, I make $25."

"Once you move into engineering, I assure you there will be a good increase."

"I see."

"Mr. Hoffman, consider this your internship. If the work and pay are satisfactory, you can begin tomorrow. However, I think you ought to wear overalls and a light shirt. It can get quite warm on the floor."

"Thank you." He thought for a moment. Perhaps GM or Ford would hire him in engineering. But he wanted to work right away. "It is acceptable. Where will I work in the factory?"

"Let me see." Donnelly moved his finger down a piece of paper that stated, 'Assembly Line Needs.' "Here we are: 'Final assembly-tires.' Your foreman is Jed Koepka. See him tomorrow at eight. There's an unpaid half hour for lunch.

Final assembly is in Plant D. I'm sure Max can help you find it. On your way out, see Bessie. She has forms you'll need to complete."

Jacob mustered a weak, "Thank you."

"Oh, and Jacob, you'll no doubt meet people who want you to join a movement to unionize the factory. You'll avoid them if you ever want to sit at a drafting table working on transmissions."

"Yes, Mr. Donnelly, I understand."

Jacob Hoffman walked out of the employment office an hour later into a hot Detroit summer day. He realized that he did not own any overalls.

CHAPTER 23

"We have oatmeal for breakfast, or cornflakes. Use the milk sparingly. It is expensive." Isabel Hoffman's curt tone permeated the kitchen like the aroma of steaming gefilte fish.

"Thank you. Do you have any tea?" Hannah sat at the table and watched the stern woman add oats to a pot of water.

"Yes, I think so. I'll look."

"I love a cup of tea in the morning."

"We can't afford eggs or the bagels and lox that I'm sure you are accustomed to. We only have those items on Saturday morning at Shabbat."

"You are kind to take us in. And we will pay you. Can I help with anything? I do not want to be any trouble."

"No, this is my kitchen. Why don't you see about the children? Tell them it is time for breakfast."

"Of course. Tomasz has taken to your girls. They have become friends so quickly."

Isabel said nothing as she stirred the porridge and reached for five bowls. She placed a plate of bread on the table.

"Please let me help you. After I was fired from my job, I cleaned apartments for high Nazi officials."

"What did you do in Germany?"

"I was a nurse in a state-run hospital."

"And Jacob was a big shot engineer at Daimler?"

"He was an assistant director, yes, one of the youngest. Then he was fired and worked in a grocery market."

"Well, now you're here, in the land of milk and honey."

"At least there are no Nazis… "

"Please, get the children. I don't want the girls to be late for school."

The breakfast dishes were cleared, and Hannah and Isabel sat at the table.

"I'll pick up some tea; I must shop today anyway." Isabel stared at the tabletop, and refused to meet Hannah's' eyes.

Hannah sipped on a cup of hot water. She didn't know what to do to befriend her distant relation.

"Where do Sarah and Rebecca attend school?"

"The public school, Kosciuszko Elementary. It's full of Poles, but what can you expect? It's free. When we lived in Melvindale, we were among our own kind."

"Are there any private schools nearby?"

"Yes, one, but it is expensive. You can't afford it."

"I need to enroll Tomasz in a school. Will you please provide me the name?"

"I assure you; you won't be able to afford it on your husband's pay."

"Max told Jacob they need engineers at Republic."

"I wouldn't count on it. You're foreigners, and you're Jewish. And they know about Max."

"What about Max?"

"He's active in the union movement, in organizing the workers. He doesn't think they suspect him, but the company has spies. They know, believe me."

Hannah was confused. "Why would Max's activities affect Jacob's employment? He's a well-qualified engineer."

"Because they can. They will. And until there is a union, things will never change."

"I see."

"You lived the nice life in Germany, eh, with a fine apartment, good jobs, money, and an automobile. We have struggled for everything these last six years. We've been in this flat for only six months. And now you are here. You and your big shot husband."

"I'm sorry." Tears welled up in Hannah Hoffman's eyes. "I don't want us to be a burden."

"Well, you are. You take up space and eat food. Your child wanted a second helping of oatmeal and ate two pieces of bread!"

"He was hungry! He's a growing boy. I told you we will pay."

"You know nothing of deprivation, of the struggle of the working class against the bourgeoisie and capitalist pigs, of the total unfairness of the world!"

Hannah drank the last of her cup of hot water and spoke in a flat, emotionless voice.

"My husband was fired from his job because he is Jewish. They spat on him in the street. Because of him, they broke the windows of the food market where he worked for a kind Christian man. I also lost my position because Jews are forbidden to work in a professional capacity. We lost our citizenship; we were state subjects, whatever that's supposed to mean. So, I cleaned the homes of the Nazi filth that passed the laws making it so. One day… ”

Hannah began to cry. She took a deep breath and slowly exhaled.

“One day, one of those Nazi animals raped me in his apartment after I finished cleaning his toilets. I have never spoken of this to Jacob or anyone. Then, they allowed us to leave the country after they took our apartment, all of our possessions, and most of our money. And no, we never owned an automobile. We took public transit. So yes, I think I know a little about suffering.”

Isabel went to the sink and began to wash the empty bowls. “I'll buy you that tea today.”

She said nothing more.

CHAPTER 24

Jacob walked up the stairs and into the second-floor apartment, a bag under his arm. Hannah was on her hands and knees, scrubbing the kitchen floor. She turned as he walked in the door.

"Husband, why are you home? Did they not hire you?"

"Yes, they did. I start tomorrow."

"That's wonderful. In engineering, yes?" His wife got up, kissed Jacob, and hugged him.

"No. On the assembly line."

"What? Why?"

"It's just temporary. They want me to understand how the plant operates, that is all. They want me to make recommendations to improve operations on the factory floor."

"That is good, then. How much will you make?"

"Thirty-seven dollars and fifty cents a week."

"But in Germany, you made three hundred and ten Reichmarks a week. What is that in American dollars?"

"I made one-hundred twenty-five dollars a week at Daimler. But this is America, and it is just temporary."

Hannah's face betrayed her dismay. "We'll have to live here a long time then… "

Jacob hugged his wife and tried to comfort her. "It will be fine, Hannah. Be patient."

"Isabel was right."

"Right about what?"

"She said you would not get your position because Max is trying to get the workers to unionize."

"Max did not mention this. I will talk to him tonight."

Hannah had no words, but her husband's arms comforted her.

"Would you like to see what I bought? Overalls. I'll be working on the final assembly. They were nice. Hannah, I promise; I'll be an engineer very soon. It is just temporary."

Jacob read the *Detroit Free Press* in the easy chair in the living room, though many of the words were strange to him. He heard the front door open; it was 6 PM. He looked up and saw Max enter, eyes blank, face ashen, work clothes dirty. The solid physique of the morning was replaced with a stooped-over, dog-tired body.

"Jacob, you're in my chair, please."

"I'm sorry. Yes, of course, please sit. Are you all right?" Jacob jumped up and moved to the couch, staring at his uncle.

Isabel entered the room with a cold bottle of Stroh's beer.

"He comes home like this every day, exhausted. They have sped up the line, and there are no breaks and only a half-hour for lunch. He works on a stamping machine, repeating the same motion all day. You will see tomorrow."

Max took the beer from his wife, and she saw a bloody rag on his right hand. He took off the soaked bandage exposing a nasty gash.

"What happened!" Isabel gasped, covering her mouth to stop the cry pushing against her lips.

Hannah entered the room and immediately noticed the cut, swollen hand. Without speaking, she quickly turned and left the room.

"A fender got loose from the rubber suction cups. I grabbed for it by the edge of the metal and lost my grip. It fell and sliced my hand."

"Did you go to the infirmary?"

"The foreman wouldn't allow it. There was no one to replace me. He threw me a clean, wet rag and told me to wrap it. After an hour, the bleeding stopped. My blood is on a lot of fenders, I tell you that," he chuckled.

Hannah returned with a pan of very warm water, a washcloth, and a bottle of iodine. "Let me tend to it." She gently moved in front of Isabel, got down on her knees, placed the injured hand in the water, and cleaned the wound. Isabel said nothing.

Max winced as she worked. "You are a good nurse."

She finished washing the cut and unscrewed the bottle of iodine. "This will sting."

"Let me finish my beer first." Max took a deep mouthful of the cold liquid and exhaled. "Now."

Hannah applied the iodine liberally. "You'll need to see a doctor tomorrow."

Max moaned and spoke through clenched teeth. "Can't; I won't miss work. So, Jacob, God bless America, eh?"

CHAPTER 25

"Uncle Max, you should take the day off and see a doctor. That cut must be stitched."

Lunch sacks in hand, the two men walked down Joseph Campeau toward the plant. The morning air was cool, and made the twenty-minute walk pleasant. Throngs of workers filled the sidewalk heading toward the factory.

"I cannot afford to lose a day's wages or pay a doctor to perform some minor surgery."

"It's not minor; it may get infected."

Max ignored the comment. "I like your overalls. Now, you look like a true member of the proletariat. How much are they starting you off at?"

"$7.50 a day. Is that fair?"

"I make $10.00 a day, but my work is more dangerous, as you can see, and I have been working at Republic for two years. So, yes, it is fair for the assembly line."

"Mr. Donnelly told me all new hires worked on the assembly line."

"That is bullshit. You have seven years of experience as an engineer for one of Europe's premier auto companies. I was worried this might happen."

"What might happen?"

"I hoped my work to unionize the workers would be undiscovered, but there is obviously a stool pigeon at our meetings."

"Stool pigeon?" Jacob was confused.

"An informer, a spy. Someone loyal to the company has infiltrated our meetings. Half of the time, I run them. I'm what they call an agitator. They are punishing you because of me by giving you a job on the line, even though they need good engineers."

"Donnelly said something at the end of the interview. He told me to avoid people who want to talk to me about the union movement."

"I guess you had better cross the street then because you're already talking to one. Now, listen carefully. Today will be tough. Tougher than anything you can imagine. Just get through it, and you can have a few beers tonight. Then we will talk about the Union, and why it is important."

"I'm Jed Koepka, the line foreman. You'll stand right here. On the floor there, that's your pneumatic drill; those are your tires, and this bucket contains the nuts. Here is a pair of new gloves. You lose them, you pay for another pair. The car comes along the line. You lift a tire, put it on the front axle, and attach a nut to hold it in place. That fellow there, Lazlo, puts on the other four nuts. The guy after him puts on the rear wheel and a nut. The fellow after him, well, you get the idea. Questions?"

"No, I understand."

"Oh, yeah, you must complete your task in forty-five seconds. If you don't, Lazlo has to attach all the nuts. He won't like that."

"I understand."

"You're a wiry little guy. You sure you can handle this job?"

Jacob Hoffman didn't answer. "What if I need to go to the bathroom?"

"Raise your hand. If I'm not busy, I'll relieve you. If I can't, hold it."

"Are there any rest or water breaks?

"Just lunch, a half-hour. Eat here in the lunchroom or go to the commissary, where a hot lunch is fifty cents. The walk there comes out of your thirty minutes. The assembly line will start moving ten minutes from now."

Jacob looked at the long row of tires extending back into the factory. "There is no conveyor belt. Every time, I must walk further back to get a tire. That takes time away from putting the wheel on the car."

"Every five minutes, another man comes along and moves them forward. At most, you have to go back and get the tenth tire."

"The tenth tire? I see."

"No fraternizing. Don't talk to Lazlo. Stick to your job. Understand?"

"Yes."

"I'll check on you after an hour or so. Oh, one other thing. See that red button. That stops the line. You push it; you better have a good reason."

"Such as?"

"Your hand got ripped off."

Jacob took a deep breath and looked around the vast factory, his new workplace. Though the building was only two years old, it already seemed dilapidated. The large windows were smudged and dirty, a few panes missing, the floors gray-black with oil and metal dust, and overhead fans did little to deal with the rising temperature.

It was nothing like the Mercedes Benz plant in Mannheim, where there were individual assembly areas for each car. The floors were clean and polished; large tables with drawers were stocked with parts; each assembly bay had a sink, and the workers wore gloves. A team of workers assembled a car in one location; conveyor belts brought them the necessary parts or were delivered by teenage boys on delivery carts. The effort was varied for the five men on a team; each worker had a particular skill, but they all possessed an in-depth knowledge of the inner working of the automobile they assembled with pride. There was a competition between the numerous teams up and down the factory floor. It was not about who could assemble a vehicle faster, but which team could make the better product.

While the Daimler factory was like a Mozart symphony, Republic's plant resembled a Gershwin jazz composition: big, brash, and unapologetic. The unfinished cars snaked down the assembly line from the third to the second floor, then to the first, an unending rhythm of movement, shiny metal, and boisterous noise. Each worker, a solo musician, labored alone, repeating the same notes hundreds of times a day.

After an hour, Jacob had placed 80 tires on the front axles and installed the required nut on 70 of them. Lazlo had done the others without complaint.

He had trouble lifting the last half-dozen tires. Rarely had someone shown up to move the tires up to his assigned place on the line. He usually had to walk back fifteen feet to get a tire and roll it to the front. Then, it had to be lifted four feet to the axle. Each inflated tire and steel rim weighed twenty pounds. His arms ached; his physique was that of an academic, not a manual laborer, and not used to such demanding, physical work. He was more accustomed to moving the bar on a slide rule or opening a protractor.

The line slowed down. Lazlo trotted over to Jacob. "Trade places with me."

"Why?"

"You lift the tires; I don't. I can see you are not up to it."

"Thank you, but I'll be all right."

"Fine, let me know if you want to switch. I'm Lazlo Stein, by the way."

"Jacob, Jacob Hoffman."

"A fellow Jew, yes?"

"Yes."

"Shalom. Remember, you let me know."

At lunch time, Jacob could not lift his sandwich to his mouth. Earlier, he had asked for a break, and after waiting forty-five minutes, Koepka relieved him. Jacob pissed in his overalls on the way to the bathroom and finished in the urinal. He cried and then screamed. His parched body, dehydrated from the hot factory, shook. He drank volumes from the water fountain and cursed that he had not brought an empty bottle or jug. He returned to the lunchroom, found a used cup in the trash can and took it back to the assembly line, filled to the brim with water.

Lazlo came up to him. "Here, I have some cake my wife made. Are you ready to switch places?"

"Yes, if you won't get into trouble."

"I've been here four years. They leave me alone. Where are you from?"

"Stuttgart. The Nazis kicked us out."

"You were lucky. I have relatives in Berlin. They can't get a visa. Look, it gets easier. Trust me."

In the afternoon, the monotony set in. Jacob repeated the same action 240 times, and it was only 3:30. To exercise his mind, he re-lived every day of his life that he could remember. They were all better than this day. He thought about his work at Daimler, his office, the aroma of pipe smoke and hot coffee in a fine china cup, the smell of fresh grease and metal from the parts on his shelf, and the sun streaming through the great windows. Then he proceeded to lift a tire and drill a nut onto an axle. Then he did it again. Then again. And again. And again…

At 6:00 PM, Jacob walked out of the factory, ready to drop. Max was outside, waiting for him.

"I think you've earned a few beers, Jacob."

Jacob stared blankly at his uncle. "Yes, it was tougher than anything I have ever known, Max," and dropped into his uncle's arms.

Max held his nephew with his strong biceps. "What do you think of America now, eh, Jacob?"

CHAPTER 26

Friday came.

"Hannah, will you light the candles; it is almost sundown." Isabel's tone was businesslike, but not unkind.

"Certainly. I hope the chicken soup I made tastes all right?"

"I tasted it. It's delicious."

The table set for seven, was covered with a delicate white lace cloth, fine china, crystal, and silverware. In the center were two silver candlesticks and a loaf of challah partially covered with an embroidered cloth adorned with the Star of David.

Hannah clasped her hands and smiled. "Everything looks so lovely, Isabel."

"The men will be home soon. We cannot attend services at the synagogue because of their long work hours. So, we have Shabbat."

"Is there anything else I can do? We didn't practice Shabbat when we were in Germany."

"Funny, you were thrown out of the country because you are Jewish and didn't observe the Sabbath?"

"Yes, I know. We haven't been very faithful. But the Nazis didn't care. They consider us an inferior race, not simply a religion."

Tomasz and the two girls came into the kitchen. Hannah smiled.

"My, doesn't everyone look nice. Rachel, Ana, I love your dresses, and Tomasz, you look very handsome."

"When can I take off this tie?" The boy wore a white shirt, black tie, and a yarmulke.

The front door opened; Max and Jacob entered, worn out and tired. They kissed their wives.

"No Stroh's tonight, Jacob. We will have wine. Let's get cleaned up."

Jacob stared at the table and asked weakly, "What is all this?"

Hannah whispered in his ear, "Shabbat, remember?"

"Oh, yes."

"The bath will revive you. Wear your white shirt and skull cap."

Isabel rolled her eyes, said nothing, and checked on the roast chicken warming in the oven.

As the week wore on, Isabel's icy demeanor had softened only slightly. Hannah tried to befriend her in every way possible since they would likely be guests in her home for a long time.

"Tomasz likes his teacher, Mrs. Grabowski, at the Kosciuszko School."

"Rachel had her last year. Yes, she is good."

"He's made new friends. One Polish boy, one Irish, and even a German boy."

"Welcome to America, the great melting pot."

"He came home today and told me he would no longer speak German. He wants to become an American person!" Hannah let out a short laugh.

Isabel nodded, smiled, but made no response. She continued to monitor the food, all prepared in advance. She opened the bottle of wine and placed it at the head of the table alongside a silver chalice.

"We are ready. We just need the men."

The open window over the sink let in a soft summer breeze, and the sky beyond was turning into a rust red. The candle flames danced on the china and crystal, and created a magical setting.

Max entered the kitchen. "Jacob is coming. We need two bathtubs in this dump."

"Hannah cleaned the house all week, from top to bottom. It is not a dump, Max. Now, let me look at your hand." Isabel reached for it, but Max pulled the hand swaddled in a white bandage away.

"It's fine; look at it later. I just put a fresh dressing on it." The cut was not healing, and he noticed pus around the wound when he had removed his work glove at the plant.

Jacob arrived. He wore a crisp white shirt, black vest, and black slacks. On his head was his father's yarmulke.

Max went to the head of the table, Isabel at the other end.

"Now we can begin. Please, children, come. Jacob, Hannah, please take these seats."

Once everyone was around the table, Max began to sing.

"Peace be unto you, ministering angels, messengers of the Most High, of the Supreme King of Kings, the Holy One, Blessed is He... "

Three prayers of the Shalom Aleichem welcomed the angels into the Hoffman home, requested their blessing, and then bid them farewell. Max repeated each verse three times, and then he poured the wine into the goblet.

"The heaven and earth were finished, and all in their array. On the seventh day, God finished the work that had been undertaken."

He looked down at the chalice.

"Blessed are You, Adoni our God, Sovereign of all, Creator of the fruit of the vine."

With the prayer finished, he sipped the wine and passed it to Jacob.

The ancient tradition continued. After everyone had partaken of the wine, they got up and washed their hands at the sink. No one spoke. They returned to the table where Isabel broke the challah and placed a piece of the bread on each plate passed to her. There was chicken soup, steamed whitefish, roasted chicken and vegetables, and more wine. The conversation was lively, about the old country, the children's schooling, and the Union.

Rachel and Ana cleared the table, and they set out fresh plates, and served apple cake.

Jacob spoke. "Isabel, the meal was truly a feast. Thank you."

"Hannah helped me a great deal." She looked at Hannah. Hannah nodded but said nothing. Isabel reached out for her hand, clasped it and squeezed. She smiled and mouthed, "Thank you."

Hannah smiled back and held back tears.

Max stood and took his Torah from the sideboard. "We finish with a reading from the Holy Book. Today, I read from the book of Deuteronomy:

"Learn then that I, I alone, am God, and learn that there is no god besides me.

It is I who bring both death and life, I who inflict wounds and heal them, and from my hand there is no rescue.

To the heavens, I raise my hand and swear:

As surely as I live forever,

I will sharpen my flashing sword,

and my hand shall lay hold of my quiver.

With vengeance I will repay my foes and requite those who hate me."

Max closed the Holy Book, stood, and looked at Jacob. "To America, to justice."

Jacob stood and raised his glass. "And to your Union."

REPUBLIC MOTORS

1937

CHAPTER 27

1937, Detroit

Fiona Drummond loved her weekly excursions to Hudson's and to the elegant shops up and down Woodward Avenue. Despite her husband's protestations, she insisted on driving downtown herself.

"I don't need Blackburn to drive me on my errands. I can drive myself, and I do know how to change gears on the Drummond."

"You should be drivin' a Zodiac. It's much more luxurious."

The Drummond bears my name and it's quite fine for my purposes and it only has 25,000 miles on it."

"You're a stubborn woman. It must be that red hair. Please, darlin' wife, be careful."

"Always. I need to be around to keep you in line, my dear Angus."

The truck charged down a side street, weaving from one side to the other. The driver was drunk from too many Guinness's from his liquid lunch. The vehicle sped toward Woodward Avenue.

The driver in the Drummond proceeded into the intersection carefully, the backseat full of Easter purchases from Hudson's, Detroit's massive department store.

Fiona Drummond never saw the truck barreling toward her until it was too late.

Angus Drummond climbed to the second floor on the broad, oak staircase, softened by an oriental runner. He stopped at the second landing and caught his labored breath, not helped by multiple scotches. *These stairs will be the death of me yet. I'm not in the shape I was when I boxed. I should have taken the lift.* He turned and walked down the hallway to a pair of ornate oak double doors. Angus gently opened one side to see Fiona in her wheelchair at the window, looking down on the garden. A nurse sat in a comfortable chair near the fireplace, reading to her. She departed through a side door when Angus entered.

"Is that you, Angus?" She put her hand on the right wheel of the chair and turned toward the door. "Where have you been?"

Her face was a tapestry of stitches and bruises, her arms in a cast. The wheelchair spoke for itself. Ever since the accident, Drummond prayed that one day he would check in on his once beautiful wife and she would be fine — that what had happened two weeks earlier had been a bad dream. A terrible dream.

"Jack Bullard came to see me about Wallace."

"He's still spying on the boy, isn't he?"

"Spying is a wee strong way of putting it. More like observin'. To keep the lad safe."

"It's spyin', and he's a grown man, 21 years old, for God's sake. He has a life."

"Such as it is. How are you feelin', me darlin'?"

"I can't walk, and my face screams with pain. And with the medication, I can't have a scotch, so you tell me. And how many have you had this fine afternoon, my love? And why are you not at the office?"

"I took the afternoon off to be with you."

"And here you are at four o'clock, and I'm still where I've been since two."

"I'm sorry, love. Business."

"Business with Jack Bullard? I don't like the man, and I don't trust him."

"He's my oldest friend, and I do. He's keeping the lid on this Union thing."

Fiona looked at her husband, more handsome in her eyes than ever. The auburn-brown hair was turning gray; lines deep across his face, perhaps hardened by the Depression when he almost lost it all if not for his daughter and his family.

"You once told me about working in the steel mill in Bethlehem and all the long hours, the terrible, dangerous conditions. There was no union to stand up for you and the other workers. Why shouldn't your employees have someone or something representing them as well?"

"Republic Motor's is nothing like the steel plant I worked in!" Angus replied with a flash of anger in his voice. "It's a new plant with large windows, good lighting and even fans to cool the air. And I pay my workers much more than I ever made in the steel mill."

"Yes, and it is 1937, Angus, not 1897. And you keep using the Depression as an excuse to keep the wages low. It ended years ago. You pay less than Chrysler, Packard, and others. Olivia told me so."

"She received a fine education at the University of Michigan in Socialism, but not in her major of accounting."

"She sees the numbers. Angus, you made two million dollars last year. You! Not the company. God knows what the company made. What will we do with all that money?"

Angus went over to his wife and got down on his knee; he squeezed her uninjured hand and kissed the stitches on her forehead.

"Darlin', I promised to take you to see Florida's beaches and palm trees, and we'll be doin' it next year."

"I'll not be goin' anywhere. I can't walk, and I look like a freak, my face full of stitches. I'm never leavin' this drafty old castle!"

"It's only been two weeks since the accident."

To him, it was no accident; it was a heinous crime. A drunken delivery driver had ignored a red light as Fiona drove through the intersection in her favorite car, a 1925 Drummond. Her face turned just in time to see the truck ram the driver's side door. The car spun forward and slammed into a light pole, her head snapped back and then forward through the window. The impact from the door crushed her arm, and the firewall of the car smashed against her legs and bruised the spinal cord of several lower vertebrae.

"My sweet husband, I have no feeling in my legs. Mother a' God, I can't even control my bowel movements!" Fiona cried.

Drummond kissed her on the lips. The stitches across her mouth unnerved him. He pulled away to look at her eyes, still beautiful and radiant.

"Your father hired the best reconstructive surgeon in Michigan and a top physical therapist for you. You'll be walkin' and as good as new, in six months."

But he knew it might not be so. The damage to the T-6 spinal cord was significant, though fortunately not total. His father-in-law had told him, through tears only a father could shed, that his darling daughter might never regain feeling in her legs or walk again. The news hardened Angus. Was this God's punishment for his ambition? Was this a jealous God exacting retribution for his father's death and his wife's disfigurement and paralysis, all by way of the automobiles he coveted so much?

"Come, let me wheel you to the elevator. We're going to the living room. And screw them damn doctors. We're going to have a scotch. I have a special single malt to open; it's 20 years old. And we'll be takin' that grand trip next year."

"Angus, don't let what happened to me harden your heart. The man may have been a Union man, but he could have been anybody."

"But he wasn't. He was just comin' from a damned Union meeting."

"Promise me that you'll listen to what they want."

The elevator arrived. Angus pushed Fiona into the mahogany-paneled lift and pressed the button.

"I can't promise that, me love. I won't."

CHAPTER 28

The engine molds kept coming along the overhead conveyor. Tobias' job was to move the crucibles of molten iron, three feet in height, along the track suspended by a heavy block and tackle and align it above the next empty mold. The co-worker on the other side of the line pulled a chain. The pot tilted, and hot liquid iron flowed into the openings above the engine block's encasement. Flames shot out of the mold, the hot against cold, and when full, any excess steaming liquid fell to the floor accompanied by sparks in every direction. The temperature in the confined area reached over one hundred degrees. Fumes attacked the lungs. Some men wore safety goggles, but most did not.

At the end of the shift, Woodson asked the man who had worked beside him why no White people worked in the foundry.

"White boys don't want to work here. Hell, they won't work here! Too hot, too dangerous. Last week, the fella' before you missed gettin' the bucket over the mold. Not by much, but just enough. The hot iron went everywher'. I jumped back to get outta the way. But the shit hit the mold and splattered on his clothes. More run under the conveyor belt to his boots. In a second, they was on fire, then his feet on fire, then his clothes on fire. I ran for a bucket of water, so did others, but it was too late. Time I got the fire out, he was as charred as an overcooked spare-rib. The screams were like nothin' I never heard, the smell worse. And he was a big, strong boy, too. Foreman wasn't happy; he had to shut down the line for the day. So be careful. I don't ever need to see that again."

"Ain't there any other jobs for Black folk at the plant?"

"Yeah, you can clean the washroom toilets or sweep the floors at night when ever'one gone, but that work pay a lot less. How much they payin' you?"

"I don' know if I should say… "

"I tell you what I make then. I been here since Republic start re-hirin' in 1934. I make eight dolla' ever' day."

"They pay me almos' six."

"They always take advantage of the new folk. But you work hard and don't get hurt, you'll get raises. You know how many engine blocks we cast in a day?

"No, but we sho' was busy. I'm pretty damn tired."

"Over 250. That's over 75,000 engines every year."

"That sur' is a lot. My name is George."

"I don't need to know your name. You just Blacky for right now. No one knows anyone. This ain't no social club. Do your job. Let me do mine. We stay alive, and you make more money than pickin' cotton, which I'm sure's what you did."

"Yes, suh."

"All right then…George. I'll see you tomorrow. I'm Amos."

Tobias stood in line at the paymaster's office on Saturday, 3 PM. The week was over. The work at Republic brought back hard memories of the chain gang in youth detention camp —

the heat; the steamy, hot asphalt; the fumes you didn't want to inhale but couldn't avoid; and the foreman, distant and unforgiving. Only two things were different. At work camp, he could relieve himself anytime along the side of the road, and at Republic Motors, you got paid.

He reached the front of the line.

"Name?"

'George. Uh, George Woodson."

The paymaster turned to a rear table with a tray of envelopes arranged alphabetically. He flipped through the "W's."

"Nothing here. You new?"

"Yes, suh."

"Why didn't you say so, boy?"

Before he could answer, the man had gone into a back office and returned shortly.

"Here you are. $31.00." The paymaster counted out three Hamilton's and a Washington.

Tobias had spent Wednesday night figuring out how much money he would make for the week of hard work. He multiplied $5.70 x 6 and looked forward to collecting the princely sum of $34.20. He had only made $5.00 for a whole week picking cotton.

"Suh, beggin' your pardon, but shouldn't it be thirty-four dolla' and twenty cent?"

"Yes, your gross pay is $34.20 less $1.36 for Federal income taxes, $.34 taken out for Social Security, $1.00 for the safety glasses you were issued, and $.50 for two soda pops at the commissary."

"Social Security?"

"Mr. Roosevelt's new government program. When you're old, you won't be penniless. The government will give you a check when you can't work any longer. It's nothin' but socialism, you ask me."

Confused, Woodson could only muster an "I see" in response. He took the four bills, looked at them in amazement, stuffed the money in his pocket, and walked out into a sunny, hot afternoon.

Tobias had brought a change of clothes and showered after work. It was Saturday. During the week, on his way to work from Black Bottom, Tobias passed a unique, strange-looking building prominently situated at the corner of Gratiot Avenue and Mount Elliot Street. It looked like a miniature medieval castle, and below the turrets and parapets were signs that read on both sides:

10¢ - White Castle - 10¢.
Below, in good-sized black letters:
Hamburgers – Buy 'em by the Sack

Ten cent for a hamburger, that be a good deal. He could get several, maybe five or six. He walked in and looked for a 'Colored' section, then reminded himself that he was in the north and sat on a stool at the sparkly, shiny red Formica counter. A nice-looking Black girl wearing a white dress, apron, and a cap that looked like it belonged to a nurse, came up to him and smiled. She wore a name badge.

"What can I get for you today, handsome?"

Tobias blushed. No one had ever called him handsome. He looked at her badge.

"Hello, Miss So… Sonora. Are the hamburgers just ten cent?"

"We call them sliders, and yes, they are. How many you want? You look hungry, sugar."

"Can I get five?"

"Sugar, you can get twenty if you want. But five it is. How 'bout some fries, too?"

"Sure. But make it six, those fries and a Co-Cola."

Sonora smiled. She could tell from his grimy shoes and the time of day that this handsome Black boy probably worked at Republic Motors. That meant he made decent money. And he had sense enough to clean up before leaving the factory.

"Comin' right up. What's your name, since you know mine?"

"George. Yeah, George Woodson. Pleased to meet you, Sonora."

"Pleasure's all mine, George. Where you live?"

"Right now, with Reverend Bradby at the Second Baptist Church parsonage, but I needs to get a place of my own."

"You kiddin', right? I go to Second Baptist every Sunday."

"Maybe I'll see you there tomorrow."

"You will, Georgie, you will."

"I be lookin' forward to that, Sonora. Hey, what's your last name?"

"Lincoln, Sonora Lincoln, George Woodson. Listen, the boss is gone. Lunch is on me."

"Tobias, I'm going to write to your ma and pa tonight and tell them you doin' just fine." Pastor Bradby passed the mashed potatoes.

"Please don't say anything about how hard the work is. Pa'll be wantin' me to come home."

"I'll tell him you're making good money and you are ready to get your own lodgings. After supper, we'll take the bus to Mrs. Perkins' house. She has a room available."

"I'm going to miss these won'erful meals, Mrs. Bradby." Tobias picked up another chicken thigh.

"Thank you, Tobias, but I don't think we can afford you much longer. You eatin' us out a house and home!"

Robert Bradby winked at his wife in acknowledgment.

"Don't fuss at the boy, Althea. He works up an appetite working at the foundry."

"How much does Mrs. Per...?"

"Perkins. Room and board is $13.00 a week, including breakfast and dinner. You can make your own lunch, and that's included, too. There's only a breakfast on Saturday. Sunday there's breakfast early and a nice meal later, around 3 PM. You get your own room and share a bath. Her house is over on Ellery Street. It's a nice place and you can walk to work. You'll save two dollar a week that way."

"Does she cook as good as you, Mrs. Bradby?"

"Honey child, ain't no one cook as good as me."

Officer Samuel Melton couldn't sleep. A killer was at large. It didn't matter that the deceased was a con man, a "grifter," the word Detective Smith had used. And who was Smith to say that justice was served? He wasn't above the law.

Melton got up, showered, dressed in his blue uniform, and ate a slice of butter-less toast, downed with black coffee. Two trolleys later, he was at the station house at the front counter. It was 6:00 AM.

"Kind of early, isn't it, Melton?" The officer behind the tall desk looked at his watch. Only 30 more minutes left on the night shift.

"I need the keys to the evidence room, please."

"What for?"

"To get a piece of evidence, that's what. I'm working a case."

The officer shook his head, reached into a drawer, and tossed a set of keys to the young cop.

"Of course you are."

The newest boxes were at the front, still waiting to be filed and then languish forever in irrelevance. He quickly located the box: "R. Johnson/B. Jones." Melton took it to a side counter and opened it. The bloody jacket was on the top. With the evidence under his arm, it only took 35 minutes to walk to the Greyhound bus station.

He approached the Information Counter. Two Negro men were just opening it up.

"Yes, suh, officer?"

"Does this jacket look familiar to you?"

"Should it?"

"A man who came through this terminal was wearing it last week."

"Terminal? This be a bus station, suh."

"Fine, bus station. Do you recognize this coat?"

"From last week? Does I recognize a coat from last week? You know how many folk come through this place ever' day? Hun'red's."

The attendant stared at the coat. He recognized it right away. It was the coat of the big, friendly, slightly scared

Black boy named Tobias. The attendant could not remember his last name, but he remembered Tobias, who wanted to go to Beale Street.

"Look hard. It's important. See, there's blood on it. The person wearing this jacket committed a murder."

"I sorry, officer, suh, I sure don't be reco'nizing it. Not ever'one stop here at the information counter."

Melton, jaw clenched and eyes narrowed, muttered, "Thanks all the same."

Chapter 29

Max Hoffman angled the fedora low on his forehead. He walked faster, glanced over his shoulder, and looked across the street. Nothing was unusual. After a fifteen-minute walk from his house, he reached 12203 Joseph Campeau. The DAV, Disabled American Veterans Lodge, was a nondescript red brick building among many undistinguished structures that were the backbone of the famous street, named after one of Detroit's earliest and wealthiest landowners.

He knocked on a heavy red door three times, softly, then another time, hard. Felix Joseph, a new member, opened the door. "Max. It's good to see you. You're late; everyone's here." The gatekeeper saw the bandage on Max's hand. "What happened?"

"Cut it on a piece of sheet metal for a fender. Foreman wouldn't let me go to the infirmary; now it's infected. My niece is a nurse. She had to tend to it before I could come. I may lose the whole fucking hand. I'll have to take a day tomorrow and see a doctor."

"Damn, man. Were you followed?"

"I don't think so, Felix. It's not outside I'm worried about. It's who's inside. Anybody new?"

"Two fellas. We checked them out pretty good. I think they're bona fide pro-union. Sent 'em upstairs to the regular meeting. Got a speaker, a socialist, who's talkin' about the history of the labor movement."

"That's good. But we need more than a couple new guys showing up at every meeting. Republic's got thousands of workers. We need more people."

"Come on in a get a beer. I'm sure it'll be a topic of discussion."

Hoffman followed Joseph to the small meeting room. On a table to the side were steins of beer. He grabbed one and sat in a wooden chair at a long banquet table.

A heavy-set man with deep, hard eyes and a short black beard stood up. Rolf Jankowski looked down at his notes. The forty-five-year-old man dyed his beard to look younger. Republic fired older workers, prematurely aged by years on the assembly line. The company preferred to hire young, strong men at lower wages.

He cleared his throat and spoke.

"Hoffman, glad you could join us. Now, we can begin. You have no doubt heard that beginning tomorrow on the first shift, the line will be sped up by ten seconds."

"They sped it up ten seconds just last month! Some workers couldn't handle that, especially on the engine assembly line." Hoffman gulped his beer.

"I know, Max, and another ten seconds will almost be unbearable for most of us. But if we don't adjust, you know the consequences. The foreman will dock your pay and may even fire you. I'll talk about the action we're planning, but first, let's go over the grievances this week. Harry?"

Harry Dunfey, a hefty, younger Irishman with striking red hair and dark green eyes, stood up and read from a wrinkled sheet of paper.

"Let's see. First, one of the Negro employees caught fire in the foundry last week and burned to a crisp. The company had to shut down the line to investigate. They sent everyone home. Forman said it was the crew's fault, so no one got paid for the five hours."

Fists pounded the table, and cries of "Son-of-a-bitch" and "Fucking Republic" echoed in the room.

Dunfey put up his hand for quiet.

"Next, one of our guys wore his union badge to work. They fired him before he got through the door. Outside, a couple a' Bullard's guys beat the bejesus out of him."

More fist-pounding and shouted epithets.

"Okay, then there's this. One of the foremen, Johnny Lawrence, who oversees the radiator assembly line, approached one of our guys. Told him to come by his house Saturday and start painting his garage."

"What's he paying?" one of the seated men asked.

"Not a penny. Told him to paint it or be fired."

"I know that lowlife. He expects guys in his section to do free stuff at his house or bring him a turkey at Thanksgiving. These guys think they're God."

More cursing under sour breaths of draft beer.

"I just heard this in the morning. One of our older workers, Johnny Davidson, couldn't take the monotony of the work any longer, and he went berserk, crazy. Took a wrench to his foreman and fractured the man's skull. They put a strait-jacket on Johnny and took him to the insane asylum."

"A toast to Johnny!"

Everyone drank.

"Last, the boys in the engine assembly plant started howling again at the end of the second shift. It started on the second floor and spread to the first. You could hear the men all the way out to Hamtramck Avenue." Dunfey referred to the growing habit of the factory workers howling to let off their desperation at the monotony of the work. "That's my report. No doubt more happened, but that's what we know about."

Max stood up and raised his heavily bandaged hand.

"A fender assembly came free of the suction cups. I tried to catch it, and the edge of it ripped my hand — a three-inch cut. The foreman wouldn't let me go to the infirmary. He threw me a wet rag and said keep working. I couldn't afford a doctor or to take time off. Now, it's infected. I don't know about you, but I've had enough. When is this shit going to stop? When are we going to strike?"

"Sorry about that, Max. Are you going to be all right?"

"I'll be all right when we stop talking and do something. It's time for the workers, the proletariat, to rise up and revolt!"

"Keep your commie philosophy to yourself, Max! We're Americans first and Union men second. Now, that brings me to new business. We have an action planned next Wednesday after the four o'clock shift ends."

Hoffman was quick to raise his hand. "What kind of action, Jankowski?"

"At the overpass, our members will hand out leaflets. The banner will read: 'Unionism, Not Republic Motor's Empty Promises.' It will announce meetings here and at other locations in Hamtramck to enroll them in the UAW."

A union man asked: "Why there? Why not just outside the factory gates?"

"Too many gates for us to cover. Everyone has to cross that bridge to get home by bus or in automobiles bought with those high-interest company loans."

A man at the other side of the table interjected: "More likely, to walk home a few miles on dog-tired legs."

"Yes, that too. Anyway, we'll strike once we have the membership we need. That's a promise."

Hoffman took a drink of his beer, shaking his head. "Leaflets, we're going to hand out fucking leaflets? Is that it?"

Felix spoke. "Max, we don't have enough members right now to stage a strike. You said it yourself. We need more enrollments. Goddamn, only two new guys showed up tonight."

Another man spoke up. "If the company finds out you joined the Union, you get fired. At the very least, you'll get a beating from Bullard's goons. Guys are scared to join. Their wives won't let them, even if they want to. There are mouths to feed and the rent to pay. Some threaten to leave if their husband's sign up."

Hoffman finished his beer. "I suppose you have a point. We can't rise up and strike if we don't have the people."

"We need to get the women to help us."

"I think I know how to get the wives involved."

"How, Max?"

"I have just the woman, Isabel, my wife. She's talked about forming a Women's Auxiliary. She's been visiting some of the wives and getting them to support the men."

The meeting was over, though upstairs, the melting pot of America learned about the Union movement. Most spoke English, and some didn't. They were the sons of Irish immigrants who had escaped the famine; many English and Scots who yearned for a better life; a few new arrivals from

Germany escaping the cloud of Nazism, and a smattering of Czechs and Slovaks, skilled workers all. White boys from the Upper Peninsula came because of the decline in the lumber industry and from the South because they loved fast cars for running moonshine. Coal miners from Pennsylvania and West Virginia arrived in great numbers to escape their dangerous jobs, only to find ones almost as bad in the auto plant. Lastly, a few Blacks dared to attend, hired by Republic to do the jobs the Whites wouldn't do. They just wanted a small portion of the American dream of life, liberty, and the pursuit of happiness that had escaped them in the Deep South. They listened raptly to the impassioned speeches and applauded, but it ended there. Tomorrow, they'd return to the assembly line, owned by Republic Motors from the neck down. Though they were men, flesh and blood, to Republic Motors, they were nothing more than the cheapest of tools on the assembly line.

Max Hoffman lingered a bit. He, Jankowski, and Dunfey discussed the upcoming action. Dunfey spoke.

"The leaflets in our truck were impounded by the police. Our fool driver was drunk and drove through a traffic light, badly injured a woman driver, and destroyed her automobile. I know the desk sergeant; he's my brother-in-law. He told me."

"Who was the woman?"

"Rumor has it she's Mrs. Angus Drummond."

"Holy Mother 'a God!"

Nothin' we can do about that now. I can get the leaflets back but it will take a handsome bribe."

"We'll fund it from the Union coffers."

"We have to move ahead. To hell with Angus Drummond and his family! The action is on, next Wednesday, at the end of the first shift."

Hoffman said good night and left through the same door into the moonless night. He looked both ways and saw nothing suspicious. Intermittent street lights scalloped uneven illumination on Joseph Campeau Avenue up to Casmere Street. He kept walking, his pace quick.

Two figures emerged from a side alley. They followed him from a distance. Max turned, saw them, and walked faster. They began to run, crossed the street, and gained on Hoffman, already exhausted from a day of work and the lingering infection in his hand. The goons caught up quickly and cornered him. One man pulled out a metal truncheon, the other brass knuckles.

Max turned in time to see the iron rod aim for his head. He ducked. It came down on his neck with a hard thud. He dropped, his hands extended to break the fall. The bandaged hand hit the pavement, and Max screamed from the shooting pain. Then, the sole of a heavily treaded boot stomped on it. The next scream was horrific. The boot came down again, the hand smashed.

"Go to another secret Union meeting, boyo, and we'll be back for that other hand."

CHAPTER 30

"I'm happy you didn't go with Max to the Union meeting tonight." Hannah sat down beside Jacob, who was drawing on a sketch pad.

"I thought about it. Everything he told me about what the workers endure is true. God, I've experienced it. And I'm quite sure there are spies in their ranks. I can't last much longer putting tires onto the cars. I'm all for the Union, and I almost went but I don't want to jeopardize getting into the engineering department."

"If you get promoted to engineering, we'll be able to get an apartment of our own."

"All this has been very hard on you. Be patient a little longer. I'm sure a promotion will happen soon."

Hannah looked at the drawing pad. "What are you sketching?"

"If I have to install the tires, I can make it easier, more efficient. I just need a few parts. Maybe Lazlo can help."

The phone rang. Isabel was out with the children; Hannah got up and answered it.

"Hello?"

She listened intently, her placid face turned to a look of anguish.

"Dear God. Yes, we'll be right there. Goodbye."

Jacob looked up, concerned.

"What is it, Hannah?"

"Max is in hospital. He was beaten by two men. They smashed his hand. I'll leave a note for Isabel. We have to go, now."

"I'm Doctor Rusinski. Mr. Hoffman is being prepped for surgery. I'm an orthopedic specialist, though I've never seen a case like this. There is a three-inch gash in his hand that isn't healing. Someone tried to care for it, but the infection has now spread into his arm. It should have been stitched up long ago."

Hannah looked at the doctor with pleading eyes.

"I know. I saw the arm getting red. I insisted that he go to the hospital, but he refused. I'm a nurse; I've been trying to care for him. I wanted to close the wound, but I had no anesthesia. With the nerves in the hand, it would have been too painful, and I was afraid I'd do more damage than good."

"Under the circumstances I'm sure you did the best you could. I'll clean the wound, sew him up, and I'll prescribe penicillin. The other problem however, is his three broken fingers. The assailants damaged the hand badly."

Jacob studied the face of the doctor. He saw kindness and compassion, and professionalism.

"Will he regain the full use of his hand, doctor?"

"Somewhat. I'll know more when I operate and see what I'm dealing with. If you'll excuse me, I need to scrub up."

"Thank you, doctor."

"Thank the men that assaulted him. A few more days and we'd be amputating."

CHAPTER 31

Wallace Drummond was having the time of his life as Cab Calloway's orchestra played "Minnie the Moocher," and the bandleader was into his "Hi-di-ho" routine strutting from one side of the stage to the other, hands upraised, a baton in one waving to the orchestra. Club Paradise was swinging, and Wallace had never felt so alive. The elegant venue was decorated in white, black, and silver. Black velvet banquettes were separated by faux marble statuary of Roman gods, satyrs, and nudes, which hinted at the wealth and debauchery of the ancient past. Oversize crystal chandeliers hung from a shiny silver tin ceiling.

He poured Jasmine, one of the chorus girls, another glass of champagne, and kissed her. Wallace had never seen anyone so mysterious and beautiful. He liked to call her "Brown Sugar," because of her mulatto skin, a by-product of her mother's brief affair with a White man.

Jasmine Jones, enchanted with this young, rich white boy, knew he was the son of the owner of Republic Motors. Jasmine leaned over and returned his kiss, added a slight flick of her tongue, then kissed his cheek gently, like he was her own little puppy. Although this was just a fling, she wished she were his mistress. Marriage was out of the question; she knew that. But a little blackmail never hurt. She might have his child and demand money for the baby and herself to keep the affair out of the newspapers. She'd think more about that later… it was an enticing option.

"Let's dance, Jasmine."

"Boy, you couldn't keep up with me, sure enough."

"Oh yes, I can," Wallace replied, slightly drunk.

"You think you can dance like Mr. Calloway there?"

"I think I'll need his white tux." He took a swig of his gin martini.

"You need to stay seated and order more champagne, that's what you need to do." Jones cupped her new boyfriend's face and ran her fingers through his hair. She looked him over again. Dressed better than Cary Grant in that poster at the Rialto, he was exceedingly handsome, his twenty-one-year-old body and good looks on the brink of maturing into the man he would soon become. The hair was sandy brown, slicked back with a bit of pomade, his face oval with a strong chin. But it was Wallace's bright blue eyes and wide smile that captured her. The eyes were soft, happy, and that crazy smile full of a future that would be boundless for this heir to an auto fortune.

Her 20 years of life had been difficult. Although born of a short fling, Jasmine's mother, Alvina, loved her. She thought she loved Jasmine's father, but when he started to drink heavily, soft caresses turned to vicious slaps, closed-fist punches, and rough sex. He would sober up, apologize, and promise to be a gentleman, but she knew he would always be the same: a violent drunk.

Jasmine grew up in a family of women, with her mother, grandmother, and two sisters from her momma's other attempts at true love. She graduated high school, and at a tap and ballroom studio, discovered dancing. It was all she ever wanted to do. A man her mother knew owned a club in Paradise Valley, where the rich and well-to-do Negroes of Detroit lived. The nightclub was the Three Sixes, and after a try-out and letting the manager fondle her breasts, she was hired for the chorus. A year later, her talent noticed by the owner of the larger, swankier Club Paradise, she went to work there for fifty dollars and a five-day week. It was good money, but Jasmine knew that by the age of 30, a younger dancer would replace her. She'd figure out her next move in due time. At the moment, her current occupation was Wallace Drummond.

"How old are you, sweetie?"

"How old do I need to be?" Wallace looked for a waiter to order more champagne.

"You sure look old enough for that," she said, nodding at his crotch. "I guess nineteen."

"Please, twenty-one. Am I too old and how old are you?"

"Twenty. Perfect. You gonna marry me?"

"As much as I'd like that, I don't think my family would approve."

"I hear your daddy's rich. Owns Republic Motors."

"He does indeed."

"You gonna work there someday?"

"I work there now. I'm in the factory, and I hate it. But it's all mapped out. I have no choice."

"You got life handed to you on a silver platter, and what, you want to be a painter, a poet, or some shit like that?"

"No, I love cars. I just want to do something else other than make cars. But my father insists."

Drummond polished off the last of his martini and started to dislike the direction of the conversation. He just wanted to get Jasmine in bed. He guessed she was experienced and would be a great sexual partner. She could teach him a lot.

"I didn't know my daddy."

"That might be a good thing. Say, what time do you get off tonight?"

"Midnight. What do you have in mind?"

"A nice little hotel downtown. I'll get us a room."

"Sounds nice. Okay, I guess we can dance now."

CHAPTER 32

Angus Drummond sat in his spacious office in the four-story office building that served as the headquarters of Republic Motors and looked out to his twenty-acre factory complex in Hamtramck. He had bought the tract, vacant but for a few dilapidated warehouse buildings, just outside Detroit, when Republic outgrew its old facilities — the former Maxwell Car Company, that Drummond had expanded two-fold. Over the last fifteen years, he had built a manufacturing behemoth with its own powerhouse, steel foundry, stamping building, three-story assembly line buildings, a glass forge, paint building, cafeteria, infirmary, and a company store offering payday loans at higher than normal interest.

On this bright, cloudless day, his back to Jack Bullard, Angus watched prodigious billows of white smoke belch out of the many smokestacks. This year, Republic would manufacture 180,000 Chamberlain cars, 50,000 of the Zodiac model, 30,000 Toiler pickup trucks, and 18,500 of the reliable but dated Drummond. It would be replaced in 1938 by the Epoch, as soon as the new transmission design was perfected. Now, his mind was on other matters.

"What's the latest on the workers organizing?"

"Their leadership's all in a lather, Angus, particularly since another speed-up went into effect." Jack Bullard stood in front of Drummond's desk; no offer to sit had been proffered. "They want the UAW to be their sole bargaining representative. It's a pot a' potatoes ready to boil over."

Drummond took a drink of his scotch, put out the stub of a fine cigar hard into a crystal ashtray, and turned to his chief of security as he slammed the glass down. His face was taut, turning red. He pounded his fist on his desk. "Republic Motors will never allow the UAW within its factories!"

"You've made that abundantly clear, boss, for quite some time."

"I'll tell you who's behind it all, Jacky boy: a bunch of socialists, and worse, the communists. They have no respect for America. They want Soviet Russia here in the United States of America."

"It's all the Jews fomentin' it; that's who it is. Henry Ford's right, and that's why they'll be no Union over at River Rouge."

Drummond walked around the desk and faced his old friend.

"What is it with you and the Jews, Jacky?"

"They run the country. Run the banks an' Wall Street. It's all part of their international conspiracy to own the world."

"Did I ever tell you about a meeting I had back in the 1920's? It was 1921 or 1922, I can't recall exactly but I remember the encounter like it was yesterday. Two men came to see me. I still remember their names. One was Stone, the other Parker. They didn't have an appointment. They told Mary it was important, so she didn't shoo them away. I offered them a drink and that upset them, them all high and mighty, saying there was prohibition and all, and it was against the law. So, I took them for revenuers, going to arrest me for getting me scotch from Canada. But no, they said they were from a fraternal organization, a secret one, and that a good friend of mine had recommended me for membership." Drummond stared at his security chief.

"What did you say?" Bullard turned, and took a paper cup and filled it from the water cooler.

"I asked them the name of their fraternal group, told them I already belonged to the St. Andrew's Society. One of 'em, Parker it was, came over and whispered in my ear. He said "Ku Klux Klan." He stepped away and said all the finest people in Detroit were members — the mayor, several on the city council, the police chief, others, captains of industry, he called them. Said I'd fit right in with their people. Was it you recommended me to those gombeens, Jacky?"

"I only gave them your name."

"So you're in the Klan?"

"I was; I am. But it's mostly disbanded now."

"I read about that. A fine upstanding leader you had. You want to hear the rest?"

"I don't think I'm havin' a choice."

"I asked them what the price of admission was. They said they'd overlook me drinkin', but I needed to be sure to not hire any, and I use their word, 'niggers' in my factories or for that matter Jews or Catholics. Told me America was for White, God-fearing, Anglo-Saxon Protestants. The rest needed to be sent back to where they came from."

"How did you reply, Angus?"

"I told them that I'd hire whoever I liked. I didn't care about a man's skin color, his religion, his race, or anything else. I only cared about his brains or his brawn. I took a big drink of whisky and I told the gowls to get the hell out of my office. I don't like the socialists and communists, Jacky, but I can live in peace with everyone else. Understood?"

"Understood. So, let me ask you this. Why do the darkies get all the shit jobs at Republic? Tell me that."

"Only Henry Ford and I hire them! Not GM, not lots 'a others. Sure, they take the jobs Whites won't but they make a decent living. And if they didn't work the foundry, we wouldn't have any engines. You heard about the fella burned to death last week. Well, I'm sure a Negro took his place. I didn't make the rules, and I can't help it they're at societies bottom rung. But they're people same as you and me."

"They should be back on the plantation pickin' cotton."

"Jacky, we been friends a long time, and I luv ya, but you're the most prejudiced son-of-a-bitch I've ever known. Ya can't go through life hatin' everyone who's not like you. Remember in the 1850's, your people, the Irish, were hated just for comin' to this country. Think about that."

Bullard said nothing, finished his water and threw the cup in the trash.

"All right; enough of this talk." Angus finished his scotch, his face crimson.

"You want me to leave now that your lecturin's done, boss?"

"No, we've more important things to discuss. What are ya' doin' to stop this Union foolishness?"

"So far, we've, how can I say it, dissuaded many of them from joining up."

"What about in our plant? Union activities are forbidden."

"Even talkin' about the Union ain't allowed. Up on the platforms, I have men can read lips. If we see two workers conversin' and talkin' Union, they get a visit on their way home. We're very persuasive. The fella comes home with a black eye, the wife tells him to stop the Union foolishness."

"You've got people attending their meetings?"

"We're trying. It's not been easy. New people get sent to the big meeting where some radical college professor talks about equality and the workers' movement. But something's up."

"Like what?'

"The 5th Precinct station commander found 5,000 pro-Union leaflets in the truck that hit your wife, and a desk sergeant, related to one of the Union men, gave 'em back. They're gonna hand them out soon."

"When?"

"Not sure, Angus. Even though we have spies in their group, they're not always trusted. We never get access to their executive meetings."

"Well, get access, dammit, and find out what they're planning. I don't want those leaflets handed out from the truck that hit Fiona. I want it stopped!"

"Understood," Mr. Drummond."

"Goddamn those fuckin' communists. They keep stirring up discontent. My workers were happy until they came along.

"Yes, sir, they were."

"How many men do you have in the Service Department?"

"About fifty."

"Well, increase it to seventy-five, a hundred if necessary. I don't care where you find them as long as they can punch like "New York" Tommy O'Brien."

"Or like you, back in the day, Anvil." Bullard smiled.

"Aye. Those were simpler times. Start posting men at each gate at every shift change. The workers will understand the meaning of their presence."

"Yes, sir."

"We're done here." Drummond finished his scotch. He returned in his chair and looked out over his empire.

CHAPTER 33

The silk ropes opened up a new world of pleasure and supplication for Wallace. He lay there, helpless, hands and feet bound to the wood-spindled bed. Jasmine smiled as she slapped him with a bath towel.

"Stop! You're hurting me," Wallace smiled, his manhood at attention. "Get on top and ride me!"

Jasmine Jones laughed. "In due time, my sweet captive." She went over to the radio and turned it on, dialed the knob around until she heard the sound of jazz. She swayed, arms reaching to the ceiling, her feet catching the rhythm and moving to the beat. The young dancer toyed suggestively with her camisole top, momentarily exposing her small, firm breasts; her silk panties showed off her shapely legs.

"Oh, God, I think I'm going to explode! Get on top of me!"

"Patience, my little White boy." Jasmine shook her head, stopped dancing, pulled off her silk drawers, and jumped on top of Wallace. He was in her in an instant. All the foreplay had made her wet. She pretended to be a rodeo cowboy with a lasso, riding him up and down, back and forth. Now, as excited as her young consort, she pulled off her camisole top and threw it across the room.

"Yippee kiy yay!" Jasmine cried out. She rode him harder.

The sight of her swaying, cinnamon body, her hard breasts and taut nipples, and her warm, moist womanhood was too much for Wallace. He screamed as he exploded.

"Oh, my God!" In seconds, it was over, the erotic mood dampened by a pounding on the wall from the adjacent room.

"Hey, people are trying to sleep here!"

Jasmine fell on top of the spent boy and untied him. His arms were around her lithe body instantly, stroking her warm, soft flesh; they both laughed uncontrollably. He looked at the bedside clock: 2:00 AM. He grabbed the brown bag from the nightstand, a half-full bottle of gin, and took a deep drink. Life was great. He fell asleep, the Negro dancer in his arms.

Angus Drummond woke when Fiona nudged him so she could use the toilet. He turned on the light and looked at his Longines watch: 4:00 AM. He threw off the covers and put on his slippers, helped his wife into her wheelchair, took her to the toilet and lifted her petite body onto the commode. He knew she wanted privacy, so he stepped out of the bathroom and waited to hear her voice.

"Angus… "

Once Angus returned Fiona to bed, he went toward the door.

"Where are you going?"

"You know… "

Wallace's bedroom, by his own choosing, was as far from his parents as possible, adjacent to the servant's stair so he could slip in and out from his nightly escapades unnoticed. It was a good-sized room and, at one time, had been used as a morning room by Lord Leith for reading the morning newspapers with breakfast eggs, scones, and tea.

Drummond knocked on the door and opened it without waiting for a response. The bed was made in military precision by Olga, the upstairs maid. He sighed and dropped his head, turned to leave, and then heard the sound of heavy footsteps on the staircase. Drummond returned to the dark bedroom, went to a comfortable chair in the corner, and waited for his delinquent son.

The door opened silently. Wallace tiptoed in and lost his balance from the booze. He managed to fall against the wall, laugh, and covered his mouth to stifle it. He walked gingerly to the nightstand and turned on the lamp.

"Well, I see the prodigal son has returned. Again."

The lamp crashed to the floor when Wallace, startled by the unemotional, husky voice, turned toward his father.

"What, what are you doing in my bedroom?"

"I just wanted to check on you, son. Tuck you in perhaps, laddie?"

"Look, I'm kind of tired."

"And a wee bit drunk."

Wallace managed to get to the bed, fell on it, and passed out.

"We will talk in the morning, at breakfast. Olga will wake you." Drummond removed his son's shoes, pulled the bedspread over him, picked up the lamp, turned off the light, and left.

He returned to the master bedroom, and Fiona tried to roll over unsuccessfully. "Is he home?"

"Yes."

"Is he all right?"

"Yes, in one piece but as full of booze as a Scottish distillery. I told you he's drinking too much."

"The apple doesn't fall far from the tree, my love."

"I'll have a talk with him in the morning."

"Don't be too hard on him. He's young and only having fun."

"And going out with Negro dancing girls. And, I had such grand plans for him."

"Keep those plans. He will mature and grow up. You never had time to be young and carefree."

"I think I'll go to the kitchen and get a glass of milk. Go back to sleep."

Drummond descended the servant's stairs that exited directly to the large scullery maintained by two full-time cooks. He knew the layout by heart, reached for a glass in the cupboard, and opened the refrigerator door. Bottle in hand, the light from the appliance illuminating his effort, he poured the milk, closed the door when done, and sat in the darkness. The glow of an almost full moon invaded the room through high windows above a cluster of sinks. He knew sleep would not come. He closed his eyes as he drank the rich, creamy liquid. He thought about all of his children growing up spoiled, carefree, and spirited. All but Olivia, the serious one, the oldest, his pride and joy. The one who had saved Republic Motors in 1932.

CRASH & DEPRESSION

1929-1932

CHAPTER 34

August 30, 1929
Detroit, Michigan

Olivia Drummond, 22 years old and one year out of the University of Michigan, was petite and pretty with delicate features like her mother. Unlike the matriarch of the Drummond family, she was quiet. Most considered her shy and introverted, a mystery since Angus was the natural-borne salesman and Fiona was always full of spark and wittiness. At least until the accident.

Olivia's alabaster skin and green eyes emphasized her Scottish heritage. Her fiery red hair, unruly and thick, was pulled back tight in a bun at the nape of her neck. With her pale skin and the absence of makeup, she appeared to be unhealthy, but it belied a robust health. Every morning, she rose at five and drove her Zodiac to the Detroit Athletic Club. She swam ten laps in the one-hundred-meter pool, and male members noticed her trim body and shapely legs that made the most of a modest dark blue one-piece swimsuit. Overtures from them were rebuffed; it seemed that the only young man in her life was her younger brother, Wallace, whom she adored and routinely beat at tennis, another sport where she excelled.

The only adornment in Olivia's small office, besides the official company portrait of her father, was her diploma from the University of Michigan in accounting and finance, awarded Magna Cum Laude in 1928. Though her parents had given her first-class tickets and a goodly stipend of cash for a month-long trip to Scotland and the British Isles, she cashed-in the tickets and saved the money. Travel could wait. It was time to make her way in the business world dominated by men. The oldest daughter went straight to work for Republic Motors, and her father took great pride that his firstborn had joined the family enterprise.

Olivia had another passion: playing the stock market. She invested her college graduation money there. In high school, every penny earned and saved was invested into a portfolio of blue-chip shares. By February of 1929, a small fortune of over $100,000 had accumulated.

However, Olivia Drummond knew the stock market's trajectory could not rise forever and she paid close attention to the warning signs. On March 25, 1929, a small crash occurred after the Federal Reserve warned of excessive speculation in the market. Selling became rampant that day. Only after New York's giant National City Bank intervened and provided $25 million in credit did the market right itself.

Unnerved by the slight hiccup in the market, Olivia began to read every report she could get her hands on. She knew about margin buying and detested it. It was usurious lending to people without the proper assets. But it wasn't yet the time to sell. She held steady when the market dipped again in May, though every instinct told her to divest her stocks and reap the rewards. Then, in June, the market rebounded well into August and gained another 20%. Her portfolio increased in value by $25,000. Soon, in the next month or two, she would sell, but first, she had to protect her mother and siblings from the financial house of cards that now was Wall Street. Together, her family owned over 14% of the company, and with her shares, the total was a significant 20% stake in Republic Motors.

Olivia Drummond left her office in Hamtramck at lunchtime Friday and took the rest of the day off. On this eve of the Labor Day weekend, she drove directly to Grosse Pointe Shores toward Manor Druimeanach, the Drummond estate, on the shores of Lake St. Clair.

A few evenings earlier, she had worked late, left her small cubicle, and gone into the office of Archie McLagan, the CFO, to examine the accounts payable and receivables. Being only a junior accountant at Republic with only one year of experience, she was not privy to such figures. Still, as a Drummond, she was not prepared to wait years to see the company's financial inner workings.

She poured over the ledger book under the solitary light of an accountant's desk lamp; the numbers seemed to be in good order. Yet a few numbers jumped off the page at her — the loans that her father had taken out to build his enormous factory complex: the total, over $40 million dollars. Each monthly payment on the debt was over $280,000, offset by only $2,400,000 in revenue. What if sales slowed dramatically and the profits suddenly dried up? There would be no way to make the payments. Her mother, sisters, and even young Wallace would lose it all in a crash.

She drove her Zodiac up the long drive and continued under the porte-cochere into a wide courtyard. Opposite the mansion was the garage that accommodated twenty automobiles, its design reminiscent of Lord Leith's stable where her father had shoveled horse dung as a child. On the other side was the service entrance to the mansion that led directly to the kitchen.

"Hello, Hazel. How's everything here at the castle?" Olivia went up to the long-time cook and hugged her.

"My, my, look who's here. Good afternoon, Miss Olivia! Lawdy, it sure is good to see you."

"It's good to see you too, Hazel. What's cooking?"

"Your daddy wants steak tonight since we startin' the long weekend. Your sisters are here, too."

"I know, I asked them to come."

"What's the occasion?"

"Like you said, it's the Labor Day weekend."

"And it be lunchtime. Can I fix you sumthin'?"

"All right. A salad, maybe?"

"Sure. I'll put some nice slices of chicken on it, too."

"Sounds yummy. Just oil and vinaigrette dressing."

"Your momma's out on the terrace. I'm fixin' her the same. And I'll bring some rolls and tea."

Olivia went out of the grand kitchen, with its polished copper pots hung from hooks, marble countertops, and massive white enamel appliances surrounding the space, into the great gallery that divided the city side of the mansion from the lake side. She turned left into the conservatory and opened a tall, screened French door to the broad terrace shaded from the sun by a canvas awning.

Fiona beamed when she saw her firstborn. "There's my hard-working daughter. How are you, my darling?"

"Fine, mother, just fine." Olivia kissed her mother on the cheek and joined her at the wrought iron dining table.

"Are you staying for lunch? Please say 'Yes,' I see so little of you lately."

"Yes, Hazel's fixing me a salad, too. Where are the twins?"

"I just returned from watching them play tennis. They'll be along. They're going to beat you and Wallace soon."

"And where's that little brother of mine?"

"He's sailing the skiff."

"All by himself?"

"Olivia, he's 13. But don't worry. Two of his school chums are in the boat too and they're all wearing lifejackets."

"Thirteen, already?" Olivia shook her head.

Hazel wheeled out a cart and set four large salads on the table. She placed crystal tumblers on each place setting and poured iced tea into the glasses.

"Darling, you've piqued my interest with this clandestine meeting. Your father won't be home until late. He's obsessed with that new model, the Chamberlain."

"It should sell very well. It's priced to be more affordable than the Zodiac but more aerodynamic than the Drummond."

"I like my Drummond, and I'll not get anything new. So tell me, are you seeing anyone?"

"With the hours I work? Daddy runs a sweatshop. And with all the expansion at the plant, I'm paying bills for the construction of it all day long."

Freya and Jane, in their tennis whites, bounded up from the expansive lawn. The 18-year-old fraternal twins had just started their freshman year at Marygrove College, recognized as the premier four-year college for women in Detroit. It was their mother's alma mater, known then as St. Mary's Academy.

"Hey, Sis, what's shakin'?" Freya said, looking toward the kitchen.

"The stock market. Sit down. I need to talk to both of you, and it's not about boys or anyone that I'm not dating."

"Well, Ollie, if you'd use a little rouge and lipstick and let that pretty red hair down, I'm sure the boys would come a calling."

"Jane, that's not polite," Fiona admonished her youngest daughter, born three minutes after Freya.

"It's what you said this morning at breakfast, Momma."

Fiona blushed. "I believe I'll have a glass of white wine with this lovely salad." She rang the small, engraved service bell. Hazel appeared immediately. "A glass of chilled white wine, please, Hazel." With a nod, Hazel scurried off the porch.

"I know that everyone expects me to marry as I'm the oldest. In good time. I have my lovely apartment in Highland Park, and Roscoe to keep me company," she said, referring to her pet Ragdoll cat. "And don't call me Ollie, Jane."

"So, *Olivia*, what's all the intrigue then?"

"We all own substantial amounts of stock in Republic Motors, gifts from Father. Wallace has a nice share, too, controlled by Momma. I've saved and bought more stock in addition to what Daddy gave me."

"So, we're rich," Freya said, only half interested but on target.

"Not for long. I've been following the stock market since college. It's not sustainable. There's going to be a correction, and soon."

"What do you mean by correction?" Fiona said, sipping her refreshing wine. She had hoped to be toasting an engagement, but this news seemed serious.

"A sell-off, a crash. Prices of stocks will tumble; people who have bought stocks on credit will have their loans called."

"So we're not so rich?" Freya eyed her mother's wine and wished for a cold beer.

"We are today, right now. Collectively, we own twenty percent of a big, very successful automobile company. But when the correction comes, our stock won't be worth the paper it's printed on."

Fiona Drummond choked on her last sip, recovered, finished the glass, and rang the bell again. "When will this happen, darling, and what about your father? He owns thirty-five percent of the company."

"Days, weeks, I don't know, but soon. And Daddy can't sell his shares. It gives him a controlling interest in the company. Even though we have a board of directors, his stock ownership lets him do whatever he wants. Within reason."

Hazel appeared and looked at her employer. "Yes, Ma'am?"

"Bring the bottle, Hazel. It will be a long lunch."

"Hazel, I want a Stroh's and a cold glass. Bring one for Jane, too." Freya's request was not to be debated.

"Freya!"

"Momma, we had beer at the fraternity party last Saturday at Detroit," referring to the University of Detroit located a mile from the women's college.

"We'll discuss that later, girls. Olivia, what are you proposing? You know I've not a head for financial matters. I'm a school teacher."

"I'm asking all of you to give me control of the stock, including Wallace's, Momma."

"What will you do with it?" Fiona looked at her salad; her appetite had waned, but not her thirst.

"Sell it, and soon. The market has maybe a few more weeks in an upward trajectory. I'll sell at the top and then buy gold. It's Roger Babson's advice.

"Who is he?" Freya looked toward the kitchen for the soon-to-be-delivered beer.

"A smart man. A financial expert."

"Won't Daddy find out?"

"Leave Mr. Drummond to me. He won't know."

"You mean we can't tell him?"

"No, it's our family secret. But I assure you, someday, when he can't make the payments, and the bank calls in his millions of dollars in loans on the factory expansions, I'll be there to help out with the gold."

Fiona rang the bell. "I think I need a scotch."

Legal signatures in hand, Olivia toiled over the long weekend to set up one of what would be several shell corporations, this one named Gratiot & Grand Holdings, Incorporated. Its offices were a mailbox at the Grosse Pointe post office. GGH, as she would refer to it, now controlled over fifteen million dollars in Republic stock. On Tuesday, September 3, 1929, the market peaked at 381. It would not reach that mark again until 1952. That day, the debt on stocks purchased on credit topped over six billion dollars. The day before, financial expert Roger Babson wrote: "A crash is coming, and it may be terrific."

Every night, after long hours at work, Olivia Drummond sold the GGH stock to the other recently established shell corporations. Then she started selling the shares daily, grabbed up quickly by greedy investors, anxious to own a piece of a very successful Republic Motors. By September 27, 1929, Olivia had divested all of the family stock, which had increased by another two million dollars. Fortuitously, the stock was sold at a price 75% higher than its value in 1922.

She bought seventeen million dollars in gold and placed it in an unmarked bank account in Zurich, Switzerland.

Unbeknownst to Angus, Olivia Drummond's company, GGH, Inc., with assets of $17,000,000, was now a bulwark against his excessive, albeit necessary, borrowing for his massive plant complex in Hamtramck. In her small junior accountant's cubicle at the company, she shivered at the loans Angus had taken from the Guardian National Bank. She considered borrowing as a necessary evil, but her father's indebtedness and appetite to grow had consumed him and put his company in jeopardy. She could not fathom why he needed to manufacture five different automobiles and compete with General Motors and Ford.

CHAPTER 35

October 29, 1929
Detroit, Michigan

"Mr. Drummond, you have a call from Mr. Madison."

"Thank you. Put him through, Mary." Drummond was eager to receive the latest information on Wall Street from his broker.

"Hello, Angus?"

"Simon, tell me you have better news today. Yesterday was bad enough." Drummond referred to October 28, 1929, Black Monday. The stock market had lost over thirty-eight points, closing at 260.64.

"I'm afraid I can't, Mr. Drummond. It's not good."

"How bad is it?"

"Millions of shares sold; the market is in free fall. It's down another 15 points, and it's only 11 AM."

"Sweet Jesus! What about Republic's stock?"

"Like every other stock, selling at prices that keep falling, if there are any buyers."

"But sales of our automobiles have been fine all summer long once we had that hiccup in March. Hell, the market reached a peak in early September. And Republic's stock was at an all-time high then."

"Not now. Shares of Republic are trading at the values you saw in 1924. But that's still a lot better than most. A month ago, you know that there was a lot of activity with Republic's stock. About 20% of it changed hands just before the crash. Like the seller knew something was going to happen."

"I've been scratching me head over that as well. Hell, I can't keep track of every stockholder, but it caused the value to hold steady because there were plenty of buyers. Truth be told, Simon, the business side with all this stock buying on credit is a wee bit over me head. I'm nothing more than a mechanic; I just know about engines and cars. Anyway, I own over thirty-five percent of the company stock."

"Well, I wouldn't try to sell it now, Angus."

"Simon, what the hell is going on?"

"The market is a house of cards. Too many stocks were bought on margin, as low as ten percent of their value. With stocks falling in value, the margin calls are coming in, and investors can't make the payments. Hell, they didn't have the funds to buy the stock to begin with; it was easy credit extended by their brokers."

"But they tightened up the requirements this year."

Yes, the margin percentage required to buy-in has increased, but there were already millions of shares bought with too little money."

"What about others? How bad is it?"

Angus, I've seen… " Simon Madison choked up.

"Seen what?"

"Men are jumping out of buildings."

"Jesus, Mary, and Joseph! I need to call my banker. Guardian National Bank better not be thinkin' about callin' all me loans on the factory expansions. I've no way to re-pay them."

"You still have twenty-six million dollars in stock, at least that's the value right now. That should be collateral enough."

"Building a factory the size of Hamtramck costs a lot of money. The loans total forty million. And our cash reserves are only $5 million dollars."

"Damn, Angus, I had no idea. I'd be sure to make your payments on those loans. Don't give Guardian any excuses. It won't take much."

"All me money's tied up in stock; stock I can't or shouldn't sell."

"Angus, if you don't mind my asking, what are the monthly repayments to Guardian?"

"A lot, Simon, a lot. Over $280,000 each month."

"I see." Madison's reply was calm but he was shocked by the number.

"One thing's for sure, Simon. This market's as bad as a December nor'easter in Scotland."

The crash was more severe and debilitating than anyone had ever imagined. Guardian National Bank sent a vice president to see Angus Drummond. They needed assurances that their loans were secure and that repayment would be made according to schedule. Angus assured them that his and his family's stock holdings in Republic, over fifty-five million dollars, were all the assurance they needed. What he didn't tell them was that the company's cash reserves might not be able to cover the massive debt.

And it was only 1929. The worst was yet to come.

CHAPTER 36

October, 1930

Archie McLagan was a man of great precision, at least when sober. His desk was a marvel of order — ledger book in the center of the felt desk pad, number two yellow pencils lined up beside it like a setting of fine silverware. To the right, legal pads stacked four high; to the left, an adding machine angled at exactly 45 degrees to his wood and wicker chair.

Since August of 1929, he had kept the door to his office locked. Someone had come into his private sanctuary. He wasn't sure why — nothing had been stolen, but the ledger book was slightly off to the left. Perhaps only two inches, but it had been moved, and opened. He was sure of that. The pencils were also askew.

He unlocked the door to his office at 10:00 AM; as Chief Financial Officer of Republic Motors, he could come and go as he pleased. Hired by Angus Drummond in 1912, he was one of the company's oldest and most respected employees. They had met at the St. Andrew's Club. Archie sat at the bar drinking a gin martini and Angus came in. It was Friday night, the place crowded, and only one stool was available, the one next to McLagan. The two struck up a conversation; Angus immediately recognized the deep Scottish brogue and inquired why a Scotsman was drinking English gin and not the liquid of the motherland, scotch. Archie replied that he liked his liquids clear and untainted by moss and bogs. And he enjoyed the taste of juniper berries. Angus jokingly accused him of being a Limey, and the two almost came to fisticuffs until they both started laughing.

Four rounds of drinks later, McLagan was the new accountant for an upstart company, Drummond Motorcar Corporation.

McLagan went to the credenza behind his desk, where everything seemed to be in order, including a black ledger. He took a small key from his vest pocket and unlocked the door, removed a bottle of gin and a book identical to the one on his desk. It contained the actual numbers on the financial affairs of Republic. The situation wasn't good. Sales were down 35%. This meant that the company was barely breaking even. Cash reserves were down to two and a half million dollars. It would be closer to three million had Archie not lost so much money betting on the ponies at Santa Anita, Belmont, and Monmouth Park. It started as a small diversion but grew, like his fondness for gin, into an addiction.

No worries. The $225,000 he had siphoned from Republic was a loan, only a loan, albeit without interest. In due time, his luck would change and he would pay it all back. And he was sure that 1930 was the worst of the depression. The next year promised to be better, and sales would rebound. But in the meantime, a second set of books needed to be maintained if Angus Drummond wanted to peruse them.

There was a tap on the door. McLagan returned the book and the bottle to its resting place in the credenza just as Angus Drummond entered.

"Archie, how are we this lovely mornin'?"

"Just fine, just fine, Angus," Archie replied, his head pounding from the battle with an empty bottle of gin the night before. He glanced at the credenza. *If I only had a minute before you knocked, I would have had a steadyin' swig.*

"And the company's financial affairs?"

"Sales are down, but only ten percent. And we have over three million in reserves."

"Hmmm, and in good shape with Guardian on the loans?"

"We're making the payments like church collections on Sunday. There's enough money to last another year. By then, things should turn around."

"Aye, let's hope. Archie, you don't look so good."

"I'm fine. Boss, just fine."

"Stayin' off the sauce?"

"Like a Baptist preacher."

"Good day then, my friend."

October, 1931

Things had not turned around. They were worse. Sales dropped another 40%. Despite stopping production on the high-end Zodiac, discontinuing the outdated Drummond model, and reducing the price of the affordable Chamberlain, Republic was bleeding red ink.

Though it was only 9:30 AM, Archie McLagan poured a half-glass of gin. It looked like water, and he was sure his secretary thought so too. But she knew. The office smelled like a bathtub distillery, where the rot gut gin most likely came from as the prohibition era continued. Indeed, like millions, McLagan was a scofflaw, buying quarts at a time from the local pharmacy.

He opened the black ledger, the correct one. Cash reserves were almost depleted, down to less than a million dollars. He owed the company over $500,000. Archie's luck at the track continued to be dismal. In addition, he had taken to betting on other sports like baseball, with a longer duration than the short racing season. The results weren't much different. It only invited heavier betting and greater losses if he had a lucky streak.

The half-million dollars was noted as "other long-term obligations" in the book. When it became apparent the company had no more money to "lend" him, at least money he could hide, Archie resorted to loan sharks. Failure to pay back the Detroit Partnership, as the local Mafia was called, had severe repercussions. The thought of the $50,000 due the mob the next week made him take another drink. He switched the ledger with the bogus one. Angus was coming to his office; he wanted an update on the company's financials.

Angus offered his usual salutation. "Archie, how are we this lovely mornin'?"

"Fine, just fine, Angus."

Drummond looked at the water glass and thought he smelled the aroma of juniper and rubbing alcohol. "Archie, what's in the glass?"

"Water, only water."

His boss picked it up and took a drink, one he quickly spit out. "Archie, that's gin, and its rotten gin to boot. And it's only 9:45. You have a problem?"

"No, boss. None. Well, maybe I'm a little too fond of the sauce these days."

"Why? Are things that bad?"

"No, look for yourself. Cash reserves are holding up. The payments on the loans to Guardian are being made like clockwork. Yes, sales are down another ten percent, but your changes in production are having a positive effect. And in fact, sales of the Chamberlain are up a wee bit this year."

Drummond flipped through the pages in a cursory manner. He didn't want to look like he doubted his friend and trusted financial officer.

"All right. We need to keep holding on. This damned Depression has got to end sooner or later."

"I know, Angus, it will."

"Aye. Thank you, Mr. McLagan."

"Thank you, sir."

"And Archie, stay off of the rot-gut booze. That's an order."

October 12, 1932

Archie picked up the phone.

"McLagan."

"It's me, Archie. The bank called, and they want to see me. Any idea why?"

The chief financial officer took a deep breath. This was bad. "No, Angus, none at all."

"Care to come along, then?"

McLagan hesitated, thinking of an excuse. "Of course I would. But me wife just called. She's taken to bed and wants me to come home. I may need to go to the apothecary to get some medicine."

"I see. Well, give her my best. I'll let you know what they want."

McLagan set the phone down and took another drink of gin. He knew why Guardian had asked for a meeting. He also knew he didn't have to go home to a sick wife. He had to meet "Black Bill" Tocco to repay the $100,000 he had borrowed. Only now with the interest, the amount he owed was $125,000, and he didn't have it. And he knew there would be hell to pay when Angus Drummond and his fearsome temper returned from a very eye-opening meeting.

He finished the glass of gin, poured another, downed it, opened the right hand drawer, and pulled out a .22 caliber pistol. Blurry-eyed, he thought he saw two guns, but he only needed one to do the job. Without thinking further, as no thought would solve his predicament, he inserted the short barrel in his mouth and pulled the trigger. Blood and brain matter splattered the photograph of his wife and children on the credenza, his head ricocheted onto the ledger.

CHAPTER 37

October 13, 1932

"Angus, we appreciate your coming in today." Ernest Kanzler, Chairman of Guardian National Bank, spoke precisely and softly. "Recent events in Chicago are very unsettling, with several major banks collapsing after runs by their depositors. The situation in Detroit isn't much better. Every day, more and more of our customers demand their money. Last week, withdrawals totaled over one and a half million dollars. The Federal Reserve in St. Louis is very concerned with our lack of liquidity and has taken a hard line with us. There'll be no bailouts from the Federal Reserve."

"And what, I'm askin', does that have to do with me?"

"You've missed your last three payments on the $32,570,000 loans for your plant expansions. The monthly payments are over $280,000. In a week, you'll be in arrears by well over one million dollars."

Angus said nothing, and took a deep breath. He felt like he had just taken a hard punch to his midsection.

"What?"

"Mr. Drummond, your company has not been honoring its obligations to the bank. You are almost four months in arrears on your payments. We've discussed the matter with Mr. McLagan, and he assured us payment would be forthcoming. But as of today, we've not seen a dime. "

Angus gathered his thoughts. Only a week earlier, his friend, Archie, assured him the company was in good stead with the bank. *Steady, man, don't let these bastards see you sweat.*

Composed, he spoke. "No need to worry, gentlemen. I'm taking measures to make the payments and get up to date. But let me remind you that since 1929, Republic Motors and every auto manufacturer has seen a 75% drop in sales. I just need a wee bit more time." He knew the company had 20 acres of real estate crammed with mostly idle factory buildings, and parking lots filled with unsold cars. But he knew nothing of the true status of its cash on hand. McLagan had lied to him. He could feel the beads of sweat on his forehead and used his handkerchief to wipe them away.

"How much time, Mr. Drummond?"

"Two months, maybe three." The auto executive continued to maintain his balance.

"By then, you'll owe us nearly to two million dollars, sir. That is just not acceptable."

"What do you propose then, Mr. Kanzler?"

"Thirty days. Under the new guidelines, your loans exceed the amount we can extend to a single borrower."

Angus recovered his footing like a boxer taking a mandatory eight-count. "Ya' made the Goddamn loans five years ago! And did I twist yer arm, Mr. Kanzler?"

Kanzler, taken aback, became defensive. "Perhaps we were a bit too optimistic about the growth prospects for Republic Motors."

"No, ya' weren't! We grew just fine, and then the fucking market crashed. Why? Because you loaned a lot of money to greedy people to buy stocks. And now, if ya' haven't noticed, we're in a bad depression. You want to foreclose on me and own an automobile company? Is that what you want? Well, go right ahead!" The response hit Kanzler like a solid right hook.

"Certainly not, Angus. But we need cash to offset the uncommon amount of withdrawals."

"That sounds like your problem, not mine. I've made every payment for ten years like clockwork. Now, you're threatin' to call in me loans because I'm a wee bit late."

Drummond looked around the richly paneled board room, surrounded by photos of previous chairmen of Guardian National Bank. He shook his head. *These spanners never built or produced anything in their entire lives. All they did was make loans at high-interest rates to people like me. And now I'm fucked!*

"Fine, thirty days it is," Drummond said derisively.

Angus pushed the heavy chair back from the large conference table, got up, and left the room. Another board member, Jamie Ballantine, followed him out as Kanzler shook his head in dismay at the others seated around the large conference table.

Ballantine followed Angus into the men's room.

"Angus, you don't want to alienate the board. Not now. You might have shaken hands, not stormed out."

"See what I'm doin' right now, Jamie? I'm pissin' on those gombeens."

"Angus, we've been friends for years. I'm the one who got you your first loan at Guardian."

"And what, you want me to thank you for that? All those Guardian fools do in there is guard their own arses."

"I'm telling you, be careful of Kanzler. Don't give him any opportunity to foreclose."

"Ya can't get blood out of a turnip; we're not sellin' any cars!"

"Angus, Walter Chrysler came to see Kanzler yesterday. He offered to take on your debt for fifty cents on the dollar. That's over $16,000,000. And he's got it in hard currency. A cash infusion like that would save Guardian."

"That son-of-a-bitch, Walter's been eyein' me company since the Chamberlain outsold his Plymouth model two years ago. Well, thanks for the information. Somehow I'll make the payments, or I'll be workin' for that cocksucker!"

Outside, Drummond lit a cigar. He thought back to 1912, when he had forced Jonathan Maxwell to sell his company for sixty cents on the dollar.

What goes around, comes around, ya greedy fool!

CHAPTER 38

Olivia Drummond heard the sharp report from down the hall. It startled her as she worked to stave off parts suppliers who demanded money. She promised payment to most of them, sweet talked some, and asked others for more time. A few accepted her promises, others filed liens against Republic. She could tell the financial state of Republic had deteriorated, but not the extent. Since the market crash, Archie McLagan, her immediate boss, kept his office locked and held important financial matters close to his vest, insisting that despite the decline in sales, the company had plenty of cash reserves. He told her through slightly slurred words that the company needed to hang on a little longer, and the economy was bound to recover. Olivia was skeptical.

She ran down the corridor to the corner office. The door to McLagan's office was closed. Olivia entered, screamed then covered her mouth, nauseas at the horror before her. His body was slumped over on the desk, covering all but the corner of a black ledger, the back of his head a mass of blood, bone, and brain. The iron stench of gunpowder mingled with the flowing blood and brain and its aroma of death; she held back the rising vomit.

After the police and coroner's people had left, the body removed for an autopsy, Olivia ducked under the ribbon taped across the door by the police: CRIME SCENE—KEEP OUT. She picked up the ledger, the door of the credenza open and noticed a bottle of gin and another book that looked identical to the bloody edition on the desk. Olivia circled the desk, careful not to step in any drying blood and reached into the cabinet for the other book. Within hours, she would know the extent of the financial catastrophe that Republic Motors had become.

It was nearly six o'clock when she climbed the stairs to her father's domain to report on Republic's precarious financial situation.

The Chief Executive Officer of Republic Motors looked at his watch. It was 6:00 PM, four hours since he was told of his friend's suicide. With the awful news, he had sent Mary Campbell home. Although he wished for Archie McLagan's demise after meeting with Kanzler and the board at Guardian, this was not what he had in mind. The man had lied to him but had been a good friend for almost twenty years. He poured more scotch into the Baccarat crystal glass. It was his fifth drink, all doubles. Adding insult to injury, he stared at the piece of paper on his desk, delivered by courier two hours earlier. He tried to focus, and when he blinked, the notice became clear momentarily, but the numbers never changed. He took another drink. "Miserable fuckin' bastards... "

<u>Notice of Impending Foreclosure</u>

Date: October 13, 1932
Republic Motors Corporation
Loan Instruments Totaling $32,570,000.00
Interest due: $1,124,370.00
Late Fees: $22,487.40
Administrative Fees: $5,621.85

TOTAL Due by November 12, 1932: $1,152,479.20

*In the Event of Non-Payment, Foreclosure
Proceedings on the Financial Assets and
Physical Plant of Republic Motors Corporation to
commence in the 36th District Court 421 Madison
Street, Detroit, Michigan November 14, 1932
at 9:00 AM*

Drummond took another pull on the 18-year-old potion; his head spun.

What did that sham do with me money? He told me everything was on the up and up. I'm ruined if I can't find the dough...

He closed his eyes, leaned back in his leather chair and passed out. A minute later, Olivia knocked on his door. There was no answer so she went in, witnessed the lifeless body.

"Daddy, Father! Oh my God!"

Olivia rushed to him; he was breathing heavily. There was no blood but no movement. The office smelled like a whisky warehouse. She silently cursed the empty bottle of Glenlivet on the desk. There was a low moan, and Angus rotated his head, and it dropped against his chest. He lifted it again. "Who's that?"

"Daddy, it's me, Olivia." She went to the sideboard where there were crystal glasses and then to the water cooler, filled the glass, returned to the desk, and made him drink.

Angus took a few sips, and Olivia poured more into his mouth. He began to gag, then bent over and vomited. When he was done heaving, he muttered.

"I'm ruined."

"No, not yet."

After several cups of overheated, bitter coffee from the pot in the small boardroom kitchen, Angus, still drunk, was coherent.

"I got myself scuttered. Archie hoodwinked me, and he was a good friend. Why'd he kill himself?"

Olivia told Angus about the double ledgers, the missing money that totaled over a half-million dollars, the CFO's fraud and embezzlement, and worse, the company's precarious state.

"I've gotten everything arseways with my damn ego, wantin' to be as big as Ford and GM. The company is ruined like all the others that have gone under, like Peerless, Durant, and DeVaux." Drummond sobbed, his body shook.

Olivia wrapped her soft arms around her father's sturdy midsection. "Father, Republic's much bigger than those companies. It's bad, but we're not ruined. And it's not all your fault; McLagan shoulders a lot of the blame. He's fed you and others, including me, rosy reports about the company, and he stole from you. I went back to his office and found racing sheets and betting chits. He was gambling and got in way over his head. I'm sure of it."

"Gambling? Archie? Are you sure?"

"On the racing form, by the horses he picked were numbers 2,000, 5,000, even 10,000. I think those were the amount of the bets he was making."

"Jesus, Mary, and Joseph. And I just thought he was fond of Limey gin, the gombeen."

"Fond is hardly the word for it. There were two bottles on gin in his credenza. One was practically empty. Your mistake; you trusted him too much."

"I know. I was caught totally off guard when the bank told me that we're almost four months behind on the loan payments."

"Dad, I'll find the money. Who's the man at the bank?"

"Kanzler, Ernest Kanzler. He's the big cheese. I've been told he's in bed with Walter Chrysler, who wants to take over the company."

"I'll call for Blackburn to take you home. Give me twenty-four hours. And a new title would help when I go to visit this Mr. Kanzler."

CHAPTER 39

October 15, 1932

"Mr. Kanzler, Miss Drummond is here to see you."

"I'm sorry; did you say Angus Drummond is here to see me?"

"No, sir. It's a Miss Drummond. Olivia Drummond."

"Hmmph. Well, send her in."

Olivia Drummond walked into the impressive office of the Chairman of Guardian National Bank. Her hair was pulled back in a bun, and she had applied some makeup to hide the circles under her eyes from two nights of little sleep. She wore a black business suit and a cream-colored blouse. Her only adornment was a gold chain around her neck and gold earrings. She carried a small brown leather briefcase.

"Miss Drummond, I don't believe we've had the pleasure. Do you work for your father? Angus Drummond is your father, is that correct?"

"Yes, on both counts. I'm the Comptroller of Republic Motors."

"Oh, I've usually dealt with Mr. McLagan, the CFO."

"He passed away two days ago."

"Mr. McLagan? I'm shocked. He was such a pleasant fellow. Did you know him?"

"Yes, I reported to him. His passing is very untimely."

"My sincere condolences. So, how may I help you, Miss Drummond?"

"Today is October 15. I believe a monthly payment on Republic's loan is a little past due. I'm here to ask for some more time."

"I'm sorry, but that's not possible. I gave your father thirty days to get current on his obligations. I'm afraid one month's payment will not suffice. If the account is not fully brought up to date by November the twelfth, the bank will foreclose."

"That won't be necessary, Mr. Kanzler." Olivia reached into her valise. "Here is a copy of a wire transfer from the National Bank of Zurich in the amount of $1,432,480. That covers the four months of past and currently due payments, your usurious late and administrative fees, plus a loan payment for next month. And I included an additional eighty cents so you can buy yourself a good cigar. The money is being sent by international wire from Zurich as we speak. In fact, it is probably already here, so you can disburse it to all your customers who have so little faith in your institution."

Kanzler looked at the draft, speechless.

"Now, Mr. Kanzler, since you were unwilling to give Republic any more time to make repayment, I see no use in discussing whether Republic Motors should deposit an additional fifteen million dollars into Guardian National. But I'm sure the First National Bank of Detroit will appreciate our business."

Kanzler tried to regain his composure on that news. "Miss Drummond, please. I'm sure we can work something out. Your company has always been such a good customer."

"No, thank you. We'll make our future payments on time. And you can tell Walter Chrysler that it will be a cold day in hell when he takes control of Republic Motors. Have a good day."

By the end of business, First National Bank of Detroit had an additional $15 million in working capital, allowing it to survive the 1932 bank runs. In early 1933, First National took over the insolvent Guardian National Bank, received additional cash infusions from General Motors, and became the National Bank of Detroit. The new financial institution worked out generous and extended re-payment terms on the loans to Republic Motors.

A buzzer sounded, interrupting Angus' recollection of less pleasant times. A light lit up on a glass panel above the kitchen counter. Next to the red glow: "Master's Bedroom." There was a light for every main room and bedroom in the mansion, a modern improvement added by Drummond so that servants could be at his or his guests, beck and call.

Fiona, she needs me. He finished the glass of milk, began to climb the rear stairs to the bedroom, and wondered what would have become of Republic Motors if Olivia and his family had not been there to rescue him from Archie McLagan and Guardian National Bank. Now, the challenge was just as great: stop the damn Union. This time, he would be more careful... and less trustful.

UNION FOREVER!

1937

Chapter 40

June, 1937
Final Assembly Building

Jacob Hoffman and Lazlo Stein sat at a table in the lunchroom, off the assembly line, and next to the bathrooms. It afforded them the allotted 30 minutes to eat their sack lunches brought from home. The walk to the cafeteria and back would have consumed nine precious minutes of their half-hour break, and a meal cost over fifty cents. Hoffman laid out his sketches, and Lazlo looked at them with fascination.

"If we can get access to the machine shop and a few parts, we can make our lives a lot easier. See, a simple ramp, eight feet long, to a landing right at the height of the wheel axle. No more lifting tires. I can roll them up."

"I like it. And if we make two of them, I can also do a tire. And if we both put on a tire and fasten the five bolts, we can eliminate the two jobs after us."

"That's not my intention."

"No, but it's a good idea, and maybe you and I will get a raise."

"Where do we get the materials?"

"I'm sure they have what we need in the shop. I know the man there, Stanley. After our shift, I'll ask him to leave the door unlocked to build them. What's this drawing?"

"A simple coiled steel cable to keep the pneumatic drill just above the tire's height. Tie it to the rafters above. No more reaching down to get it off the work bench and lifting it every time to get it to the axle. Saves time and energy." Jacob bit into his cheese sandwich and took a gulp of milk.

"You're a pretty smart engineer, Jacob."

"Common sense, really. Now if I can solve the gear shift ratios on a five-speed transmission, that's engineering."

"You know Donnelly telling you to look around the plant for areas of improvement was a lot of crap, don't you? They don't care about making our lives easier."

"I'm doing this for me, not for Republic. I can't take much more lifting tires and pneumatic drills."

"Try doing it for two years. I once did your job. Got a promotion, I guess, when you got hired. Funny, I never thought about a flexible cable to suspend the drill. I've done a lot of bending down to get to that bitch."

"Do you think we'll get in trouble?"

"For what?

"For changing the way we do our work."

"And getting rid of two more spots on the line. We'll get 'Worker of the Week'."

"May I ask you something?"

"Certainly. We are friends."

"Why do you work here?"

"Where else can I make $45.00 a week?"

"What do you think about the Union?"

Lazlo looked up to the catwalk above. No one was there.

"I'm all for it. I joined, but that's just between you and me."

"Can't you get into trouble?"

"Yes, I could be fired. You should join the movement, Jacob."

"I better not. Donnelly said if I ever wanted to move into the engineering department, I'd stay away from the Union."

"It doesn't matter. Your uncle, Max Hoffman, is a key figure, and you're a Jew and an immigrant. I would not be too optimistic."

"Optimistic is the only thing I can be. Otherwise, I'll go mad." Jacob finished his sandwich.

"We've got a few minutes. Let's get on over to the machine shop. I'll introduce you to Stanley. Tomorrow, we'll get started on your project. Look, my wife put an extra piece of cake in my lunch just for you."

"She's a good woman."

"And you're a good man, Jacob. And you should be in the Union."

CHAPTER 41

The hospital room, painted white but yellowed with age and neglect, seemed harsh because of the morning sunshine that streamed in through one large window. Smells of rubbing alcohol, ammonia disinfectant, and ether floated around the ample room that held three hospital beds. Isabel had just drawn the side curtain to give Max some privacy when Doctor Rusinski walked in.

"Good morning. How's the patient today?"

Max looked down at his lower arm and right hand in the plaster cast. His daughters had written words of encouragement and love on it.

"It itches."

"Can you move your fingers?"

"The broken ones?" Max smiled.

"Yes, the broken ones." Rusinski reached over and felt the tips of the three appendages, waiting hopefully for some movement.

Max grimaced as he concentrated on the task. The fingertips bent upward about half an inch.

"Excellent, Max. You've been practicing."

"I need to if I want to work again."

"I've sent a note to Republic. I told them that your infection resulted from their failure to send you to the infirmary for the cut and your broken fingers to an attack by some riff-raff on the street."

"They were goons from Republic's Service Department. They were after me."

"I understand, but you can't prove that. Anyway, the company won't dare fire you. The personnel department said they would accommodate your physical impairment."

"'Physical impairment?' And what the hell does 'accommodate' mean?"

"With the therapy and your current progress, you'll have partial hand movement."

The curtain rustled and then parted. Hannah and Jacob entered, and Max smiled.

"Well, let's have a party. We can celebrate that the company won't fire me and perhaps I'll partially use my hand one day." His sarcasm permeated the room.

"Mr. Hoffman, I'll leave you with your family. I have rounds to complete; I'll see you tomorrow. Keep moving those fingers, even if it hurts. The cast will be removed by the end of the week, and you'll have more freedom to exercise each finger."

"I'd like to exercise my middle finger at Republic Motors."

The doctor smiled. "Indeed. Have a restful day."

Max looked at Jacob. "I understand congratulations are in order. Isabel tells me you've improved the assembly line and eliminated two jobs. Once in management… "

"They've been reassigned to another area of the line, that's all. I didn't want anyone to lose their jobs. I've had that experience. It was purely for selfish reasons. I was tired of lifting tires with rims. Laszlo helped me build a ramp and string a cable. Pretty simple, really."

"That's why you belong in engineering."

"Soon, I hope."

"Having the Union represent all of us is the best way for that to happen. Listen, and don't breathe this to a soul, but the Union will hand out leaflets this Wednesday at the overpass, at the end of the first shift. I wanted to be there, especially after what just happened, but Jacob, maybe you can take my place, eh?"

Hannah shook her head. "Max, don't ask him to do that."

"Hannah, he knows what life is like on the assembly line. He knows the danger, the boredom, and the working conditions. One day he even pissed in his pants because… "

"Max, is that necessary?" Jacob hung his head. Hannah gave him a confused look.

"Hannah, until the workers are on an equal footing with management, there will be no reform. Jacob will only see a drafting table and a slide rule if he helps us. Right now, he is just expendable labor. Helping the cause is the best way, no, the only way for him to be in an office doing what he was meant to do."

Jacob looked at Hannah.

"Do not fret, wife. With the overtime I'm forced to do, my shift will end after they're done."

"Thank God, Jacob." Hannah's relief trickled down her face in silent tears.

CHAPTER 42

Angus Drummond took a bite of his jam-covered scone and sipped his hot coffee. The morning room was cheerful, its bay windows filled with morning light. The walls were covered in English wallpaper adorned with blooming white and pink dogwood trees in an English park-like setting, replete with swans on a pond. The windows afforded a fine view of Lake St. Claire beyond the deep green lawn, and the reflection of the emergent sun danced on the ripples of water. He wore his tartan morning coat over a crisp white shirt, bow tie, wool slacks, and velvet slippers. Drummond buttered another scone and added marmalade jam as he read the *Detroit Free Press*.

Fiona entered the room in her wheelchair, wrapped in a light green silk bathrobe. Angus thought the scar on her face had diminished, and he marveled at her newfound ability to navigate the mansion in her wheelchair.

Angus put down his newspaper.

"There's my beauty! How are you this fine day, wheelin' around like a race car driver?"

"The pain is not so bad today, but I'm still an ugly freak. Beauty? Are you sippin' already?"

"Just coffee. Come, have some breakfast. I need your sage advice."

Fiona wheeled herself to the table, seated across from her husband. Angus had the dining chair removed so Fiona's wheelchair could easily roll into place at the table. A maid appeared and poured her a glass of orange juice, and Fiona nodded.

"Thank you, Hazel. I'll have two poached eggs, some ham, and toast. Tea as well."

"Right away, Mrs. Drummond." The crisply dressed Black servant left through a door that led directly to the kitchen.

"I see we're gettin' our appetite back. Wonderful." Angus took a drink of coffee.

"The doctor said I need to eat. Once my rehabilitation begins, I'll need a good bit of strength. I'm not spendin' the rest of my life in this iron carriage."

Angus gave her a weak smile. "Of course, you won't."

"So, what sage advice do you need from your *beautiful* wife today?"

"You know. It's Wallace. I thought about your words. That I never had time to be, how did you say it, 'carefree'? So how much time does one allow young Wallace to be carefree? He's never had to work for anything. He lasted two semesters at university and was stopped a coupla' nights ago night for speedin'."

"Oh my. And you said he was drunk."

"That was last night. He was pulled over for the drivin' infraction Wednesday on his way to one of those Negro clubs. I'm guessin' he was still sober then."

Fiona sipped her orange juice and looked away from Angus to admire the morning view.

"He told me that he hates working in the factory."

"He's the assistant plant supervisor, for the love a' Jesus. He doesn't have to do anything or get his hands dirty."

"Maybe that's the problem."

"Liam Henderson runs the show in Plant 4. I just want him to learn how things work and how cars get built. He's going to be takin' over the whole kit and caboodle one day. That's a big task."

"That's your wish. Maybe that's not what he wants to do."

"Well, being a rich playboy is no way to go through life. And I'll cut him off before that happens."

Hazel returned to the room with a tray. Poached eggs sat perfectly on top of two pieces of toast, and there were several slices of ham, the plate garnished with an orange wedge and several strawberries.

"Mister Wallace be in the kitchen looking for tomato juice. I tole him we don't have any. So, he opened a bottle of champagne and poured it and orange juice into a glass."

Drummond frowned. "Hazel, please tell Wallace that if it's not too much trouble, his mother and I would like him to join us at breakfast."

"Yes, sir, Mr. Drummond."

Once Hazel was gone, Fiona looked at Angus, annoyed.

"Seems you have everyone reporting on your son."

"Love, I never told Hazel… "

Wallace waltzed into the room, handsome but bleary-eyed.

"Good morning, Mother." He placed his hand on her shoulder, squeezed it, and kissed her on her forehead. He deftly held the flute of champagne with the splash of juice in the other.

Angus didn't wait for his greeting.

"Would you like to call Commissioner Reilly and apologize for speedin' again, or do you expect me to do it, son?"

"Angus! Must you start?" Fiona put down her fork with a wedge of ham.

"It's all right, Mother."

Wallace gulped some of his morning elixir. He wore the same clothes he had slept in, the shirt partially outside his trousers, the tie well below the unbuttoned collar, his pomaded hair in a tangle, and a stubble of facial hair on his chin.

"And good morning to you, Father. I will personally deliver my regrets to His Excellency for my behavior on the city's thoroughfares, exceeding the woefully low speed limits. Thirty-five miles an hour on Gratiot Avenue. Seriously?"

"They're for your safety and the safety of others."

"Then why did you put a V-8 engine in the Zodiac? It does 90 in a heartbeat."

Angus said nothing and wished his coffee was a Bloody Mary.

Fiona looked at her spouse. "Answer the lad's question."

"It's, well, it's what the buyin' public wants. And it makes no difference. Wallace, you broke the law. Now, it's time you get serious with your life. What are you going to do with it?"

"Father, it doesn't involve making cars. I'm not a mechanic, but I think I'd be pretty good at marketing, advertising, and public relations, and maybe creating great publicity for Republic Motors. I don't want to make cars. I want to sell them."

Angus got up, went to a sideboard, opened its door, and removed a bottle of vodka. He poured some in a glass.

"All right. But you can't market and sell them unless you understand them, by knowin' what's under the hood. So, you must learn all about their makin'. Three months in the plant, especially engine assembly and transmissions. And no more speedin', drivin' drunk and going out with showgirls."

Wallace thought about it for a moment and then put out his hand.

"Deal, Father."

Angus smiled and shook his son's hand.

"See Fiona, my darling, the lad has been thinking of his future, and I think it's a fine plan."

"Yes, Angus, it is. Well done, Wallace."

CHAPTER 43

The hospital room finally emptied. The patient who occupied the other bed suffered from pneumonia; his wife sat close by in resigned silence. The fellow spoke loud Polish between coughing fits, and told her to call out for a doctor. A nurse came and shooed the woman out of the room. No doctor came.

"Isabel, come close." Max motioned with his good hand.

"What, husband? I need to get home soon to make dinner."

"Yes, I know. But Hannah will handle it."

"Well, yes, but… "

"Then let her. I have more important work for you to do."

"And what is that? Spoon feed you your food? You still have one good hand." Isabel crossed her arms.

"Actually, I'm becoming quite able with my left hand. I didn't spill any cereal this morning."

"That's progress, I guess. But you won't ever be able to lift a fender or operate a drill press."

Max ignored the comment; it was typical of his pessimistic wife.

"How's the Women's Auxiliary coming along?"

"Good. About 100 women are signed up."

"I need as many of them as possible at this action on Wednesday. We need them to hand out the leaflets since we won't have enough men to cover all the stairs and approaches."

"I should be able to find some willing to do it. How hard can that be?"

"If Jack Bullard gets wind of it, there will to be a lot of bruised heads and black eyes on Wednesday — maybe worse. This will be the Union's first big demonstration, and Jack Bullard will do everything to stop it."

"Only if he finds out. You said no one gets into your executive meetings."

"We can't be certain. Anyway, if they get wind of what we're doing, there'll be cracked heads for sure."

"And the women will patch the men up as always."

"You know they're scared their husbands will lose their jobs. They don't see beyond a paycheck. Have you been able to convince them otherwise?"

"They are worried, sure. But the ones we signed up support the movement one hundred percent."

"Bullard's men won't spare them for handing out the flyers."

"I suppose I should be worried about that. We may need to form another group. A tougher bunch; women who aren't afraid to mix it up with the Service department or the police."

"That's my girl, always thinking."

"You asked me to take on a big job, and I'm doing it."

"Yes. It's why I asked you to help."

Fritz Joseph wasn't happy that he had to ride two buses and walk six blocks to get to Luci & Ethel's Diner, a greasy spoon located on Bagley Avenue just west of Grand River. But he knew it was unlikely any of his Union brothers would be eating here, far from the Republic Motors plant. The lunch crowd began to arrive around 11:30, and Fritz seated himself at a table in the back, but with a decent view through the large plate glass windows facing Bagley.

A day earlier, he had passed a note to the floor supervisor addressed to Jack Bullard. When his shift ended, he found another note tucked into his jacket with instructions to be at the diner by 11:45 AM the next day. He would have to take two hours of unpaid leave. He was unhappy about that and nervous, too. He had just become a rat.

Fritz watched the black Chamberlain four-door drive up to the diner. A heavy-set man with a toothpick stuck between his lips exited the front passenger side, then held the back door open for Jack Bullard. Fedora low on his forehead, Jack Bullard entered the diner at the appointed time. The goon waited outside, the toothpick rotating around in his mouth, his eyes looking up and down the empty street.

"Mr. Joseph, correct?" Bullard sat down across from his informant.

"Yes. Have a seat; I already ordered. Maybe I can get back to work before two and only lose one hour of pay. Anyway, what I have to tell you won't take long."

A waitress in a pink uniform and white apron appeared and looked at the new guest. "What'll it be, hon?"

"Black coffee, please."

"That all? It's lunchtime."

"That's all. I won't be here long."

"Suit yourself, but the pastrami on rye will blow your wig."

"I'll be blown on another day, then." Bullard turned to Joseph, and tried his best to look pleasant. "So, Joseph, what do you have?"

"Valuable information. What's in it for me?'

"Depends on how valuable I think it is. We already know who all the agitators are. Hoffman, Jankowski, oh, and Dunfey, just to name a few."

The coffee and Fritz's pastrami on rye toast arrived. Bullard ignored the coffee.

Joseph frowned as he spread mustard on his sandwich.

"Yeah, Hoffman. Cuts his hand on the job, and he can't even go to the infirmary. Then he gets it stomped on by two of your people."

"Accidents happen. We can't be lettin' everyone who gets a wee cut go off to hospital. As for him gettin' attacked, well, Hamtramck's a dangerous place, especially for Jews with all the Pollock Catholics livin' there. They hate 'em, they do."

"And what about the man burned to death in the foundry? You shut it down for half a day; no one gets paid."

"Foundry's also a dangerous place. Again, accidents happen. Now, are you done wastin' me time with all your overblown grievances, or do you have some information that will possibly get you a pay raise?"

"Tomorrow's the day."

"What day?" Bullard's face tightened.

"When the Union's goin' to be passing out the leaflets."

"Where?" Bullard's mind raced. *Tomorrow — no time to waste.*

"The overpass."

"What time?"

"After the end of the first shift. 4:00 PM."

"What else?"

"The big shots are comin'. Reuther, Frankensteen, Kennedy… others are going to be there."

"I'll be God-dammed. The big fish. Good information. You done good, Felix."

Bullard stood up, reached into his pocket, and threw a dollar bill on the table.

"Sorry, but I got to go. Lunch is on me."

"That's it, lunch?"

"Oh yeah, I think Republic Motors can reward your loyalty to the company. How about a dollar-a-day raise?"

"How about two? Because of Reuther."

"Buck-fifty." Bullard reached back in his pocket, pulled out a quarter, and tossed it to Joseph.

"For the bus ride back." He put on his hat and walked toward the door.

Felix spoke out. "I want to be a foreman, Bullard."

"Don't push it, Joseph; I'll think about that one."

Joseph looked at his sandwich, devoured it and decided to take the rest of the day off. The corner bar in his neighborhood would be a fine place to get drunk.

Now I know how Judas felt, he thought as he washed down his lunch with the glass of milk.

CHAPTER 44

Billy Hunt, a cub reporter at the *Detroit News*, manned the tip line for the graveyard shift. 6 AM, and mercifully the long night was about to end. The phone rang. Unusual; normally this was the most boring time. Tipsters usually called drunk around 2 AM.

"City desk."

A muffled voice came through on the other end.

"You might want to send a reporter and a photographer to the Republic auto plant today. To the overpass, around four o'clock. The Union's planning an action. Walter Reuther's going to be there. Might get interesting."

The caller hung up. Johnny looked at the receiver. He had gotten anonymous tips before, but nothing like this.

What do I do with this one, he wondered. He scribbled a note on the corner of a yellow legal pad. He walked through the large, harshly lit newsroom occupied by gray metal desks where the reporters of the *Detroit News* lived. Today they would write headlines about Amelia Earhart flying over the Sahara desert, President Roosevelt's latest moves to pack the Supreme Court, and all of the RBI's being hit by the Detroit Tiger's first baseman, Hank Greenberg. He passed the desk of veteran photographer James Kilpatrick, dropped the note, and then headed for breakfast and a day covering nothing important. The message was brief and to the point.

*Take the Graflex to Republic Motors today
At 4 PM, at the overpass.
Hot tip! BH*

At 10:00 AM, Jimmy Kilpatrick arrived at his desk, stowed his brown bag lunch in the bottom drawer, and saw the yellow scrap of paper. *Hmmm, what's this all about?*

Kilpatrick strode over to his boss's office, the assistant editor.

"Bobby, what's going on at Republic Motors?" He dropped the note on his desk.

"Where'd you get this, Jimmy?"

"It was on my desk when I came in."

"BH. That's Billy Hunt. The tip desk. Most never pan out. I know the Union, the UAW, want to get into Republic, but Drummond, the head cheese, says it will never happen. Looks interesting; did you talk to Hunt?"

"No. I just saw the note."

"You got anything else to do?"

"Nothing except a fender bender just reported on Livernois. I'll head over there and then go over to Hamtramck this afternoon."

"Yeah, you do that."

Jack Bullard walked up to a podium in the large meeting room where fifty of his "service department" staff waited. His black eyes surveyed the men under his command. They were former boxers that Bullard knew from his days in the gym; ex-cops who had been on the take all their working lives; and ex-convicts, guilty of "minor" crimes like assault and battery on wives and lovers. Cigarette and cigar smoke formed a small cloud over the men seated in neat rows of wooden chairs. A large aerial photo of Republic Motor's plant hung on the wall.

Bullard's steely presence at the podium in the front of the room quieted the assembled hired guns.

"Boys, listen up. I've come across some information. Today, the rotten Union mogs are goin' to start handin' out propaganda about joining their commie organization. They'll be at the overpass." With a pointer, he slapped the photo in the general area of the railroad crossing. "We're goin' to nip this Union thing in the bud. You've all heard that expression before. We're stopping this business before it gains any traction. Up to now, you boys have done a good job persuading a few bad apples that there are consequences to their stirrin' up trouble. A black eye, swollen knees, a cut here or there. It sent a message home, I tell ya."

"What time, Mr. Bullard?"

"Four o'clock, end of first shift. And I got better news. The head agitator, Reuther, and his cohorts will be in attendance. I want them specially targeted. Flynn, you take Kosinski, Mulrooney, and Adams, more ifn' you need 'em. You know what those Union maggots look like from the papers. Hurt 'em. Hurt 'em bad. The rest of you will go after the chancers givin' out these leaflets."

Bullard passed around a few sample flyers from the truck impounded by the police.

A voice from the back spoke.

"Whaddya mean 'go after,' sir."

"Use your Billy clubs, baseball bats, whatever you've got, and hit them when they try to hand out the leaflets. Anyone who has one in his hand, remove it any way you can. And for what you do, well, only a stepmother would blame you for it. You have my full support and Mr. Drummond's. There'll be no Union at Republic. Least not until the second comin' of the Lord."

"What about the police?"

"You needn't worry about them. The overpass may be public property, but it's strictly out of their jurisdiction. They understand that, if you get me drift," Bullard smiled.

Rolf Jankowski and Harry Dunfey unloaded the boxes containing the leaflets they hoped would spur enrollment in the UAW. The day was overcast, hot, and muggy.

"I wish Hoffman were here," Dunfey said.

Jankowski frowned. "He's a good man, but whatever we do, it isn't enough for him. He wants the workers to revolt and do away with everyone in management. He's read too much Karl Marx. I want a pay raise, decent hours; a coupla breaks a day and a slow assembly line. Drummond can keep his company. Take this box to Hoffman's wife, Isabel, over there at the far stair."

The Union leader looked around the overpass. It was 3:30 PM, and there was no sign of Bullard's men. That was good news. Dunfey came back to the truck.

"I think that's all of the flyers. Boxes at every stair, both sides. I handed boxes to the Women's Auxiliary. Isabel Hoffman's done a good job. There must be fifty gals here. Some are over by Gate A and Gate B, and others outside the fence with first aid kits." Dunfey looked past Jankowski at a figure approaching them with a large camera.

"Hey there, I'm Jimmy Kilpatrick with the *Detroit News*." An introduction wasn't necessary. The brim of Kilpatrick's fedora held a card stating "Press-DN."

Jankowski smiled. His phone call earlier that day had accomplished its intended effect.

"Rolf Jankowski, UAW, Local 174. Nice to meet you."

"I hear the head honcho, Reuther, is coming."

"Should be here any minute."

"What are you doing?"

"Handing out leaflets. Information on how to join the Union."

"Look, I'm no reporter. I just take pictures, but why do you need a Union? Some of you guys probably make more than I do."

"You ever work on an assembly line, Jimmy?'

"Shit, no."

"Well, until you do, you won't understand. What if you had to take the same photograph all day long with a camera weighing fifty pounds in a hundred-degree heat; not be allowed to go and take a piss; have someone break that finger that clicks the shutter because you uttered a small complaint; and worse, be paid less than your fellow picture taker at the *Free Press*?"

"Point taken. I guess I don't know much about making cars."

Jankowski looked beyond the reporter and heard the sound of multiple car engines.

Harry Dunfey waved at the oncoming cars.

"I hope that's Reuther and the others. Rolf, this is goin' to be a big day for the Union."

The cars stopped, and a small brigade of men in suits, fedoras low on their heads and carrying all manner of weaponry, got out. They stood at attention in a long line.

"Hell, its Bullard's army, Harry. Somebody has ratted us out!"

With its shrill, bleating sound, the great whistle announced that the first shift was over. Momentarily, over nine thousand workers would exit the vast Republic Motors factory. Most would funnel up and across the overpass, spanning six train tracks, and then trudge home or catch a bus to distant parts of Hamtramck and Detroit or, if they were fortunate, to their cars, manufactured by Republic Motors. All eight staircases were manned by Union men from the night shift and a smattering of women from the Auxiliary.

Walter Reuther, Richard Frankensteen, J. J. Kennedy, and other union organizers had just arrived from the opposite direction and climbed the overpass. Kilpatrick approached them.

"Gentlemen, a picture, please."

The group, well-dressed in suits, assembled in no particular order with the Republic complex framed behind them.

A flood of factory workers began to exit the plant.

"Quick, son, we'll need to greet our people soon."

Kilpatrick began to snap photos.

Service department goons suddenly appeared from the other side and charged up the stairs at the organizers. There were at least forty of them: big, mean-looking thugs. Kilpatrick yelled at the group. They descended on the Union leaders like locusts on corn. One shoved the photojournalist out of the way. He hit the ground, holding his precious Speed

Graflex over his head. Kilpatrick got up and began to snap pictures.

Frankensteen was the first victim; a burly man pulled his suit coat over his head and punched him in the gut. The Union's second in command, a former football player, fought back. More of Bullard's henchmen surrounded him, and he was knocked to the ground and kicked savagely, pulled up, and beaten again.

Reuther fared no better. Because he didn't resist, he soon found himself tossed down the stairs to the intermediate landing. Bullard's men followed, kicked him repeatedly, and sent his body tumbling down a second flight of stairs. This continued until he landed on the muddy gravel, bloody and unconscious.

Click, click, click. Kilpatrick shot pictures as fast as he could, changed negatives, and stuffed the rigid 4 x 5 film plates in his coat pocket. Bullard's men tried to block him from his task, but he sideswiped them, ran, turned, and kept shooting.

As the workers reached the stairs to the overpass, the Union men and women frantically handed out leaflets, all the more valuable because of the commotion they had caused. What salacious information could spurn such violence? Some auto workers dropped their lunch pails and descended on the service department thugs. Though quickly overcome with truncheons and bats, other employees joined in the struggle of growing violence.

Jacob and Lazlo exited the plant, the uncontrolled brawl displayed before them. The service department men punched anyone with a leaflet that the workers held onto with ferocity. Billy clubs pounded hands, forcing them loose. Hands and fingers, forced open, released the flyers, and they swirled in the air throughout the crowd to be picked up and fought over again. Hands that grasped the papers were bitten until the leaflets were dropped amidst cries and blood. Wads of torn and bloody flyers littered the ground. The last business for anyone who wanted the precious piece of paper was a blow to the back of the neck by Bullard's forces.

"We have to help!" Lazlo's plea brooked no debate. Jacob followed him as he headed for a set of stairs where two women from the auxiliary lay prostrate, stockings ripped, their heads bleeding. They reached into the boxes, grabbed a handful of the flyers, and waved them above their heads, Lazlo yelling: "Union! Union, forever!"

He heard a scream and turned. A Union man had been thrown off the overpass and landed only a few feet away, the drop almost thirty feet. He lay supine, his back likely broken. Lazlo turned away and immediately faced a fist wrapped in brass knuckles. The blow sent him crashing to the ground.

Jacob began to yell. "Join the Union!" A goon with a baseball bat raised it quickly, determined to silence the diminutive man.

A muscular, black arm deflected the bat on its downward trajectory in time to spare Hoffman's life. The weapon dropped, and Tobias Woodson shoved the assailant against the stairs. Stunned, the man looked at the imposing black boy who held him off the ground by the lapels of his jacket. Woodson let go, the man dropped to the ground, got up and ran off.

"You all right, suh?"

"Yes, thank you," Jacob said.

"Gimme some of 'dem papers. I helps you."

Woodson extended his arm and pulled Jacob up. He took up a stack of papers that quickly disappeared from his hands as workers grabbed them.

Jacob Hoffman ran over to Lazlo. Jacob's handkerchief was quickly saturated with the blood that poured from Lazlo's forehead.

"Lazlo, Lazlo! Wake up! Help! I need help!'"

He lay there motionless.

"Lazlo!"

Jacob's friend slowly opened his eyes, and his mouth formed the word "Union." He smiled.

Isabel and another woman were at Lazlo's side in a moment with a medical kit. Jacob looked up in amazement.

"Hannah?"

Jimmy Kilpatrick had all the shots he needed. He ran toward his car, Bullard's men in pursuit. They had smashed other cameras, ripped notepads from other reporter's hands now on the scene, and were determined to eliminate any evidence of the day's violence.

He arrived at his car a minute before his pursuers and hid his precious negatives under the back seat. The goons arrived.

"Give us the plates ifn' you don't want a beatin', paperboy."

"Sure, boys, no problem." Jimmy reached for some unused plates in the front seat. He handed them over, got into the car, and sped away with the story of the year.

Rolf Jankowski's knees throbbed with pain. He raised his head and saw Frankensteen on the ground nearby, motionless.

Other Union brass leaned against railings and staunched their head wounds with the ends of their white shirts; others slowly stood up and rubbed their arms, backs, or shoulders. He crawled to the fence, pulled himself up, and limped over to where the Union leader moaned and began to stir.

"You okay, Mr. Frankensteen?"

He rolled over and blood streamed down his forehead onto the front of his ripped and bloody shirt.

"No, but I'll live. Those boys gave me the worst licking I can ever remember. Please, help me up."

Rolf lifted the injured man under his arms and got him to his feet. He had a perfect view from the top of the overpass. The bodies of the injured littered the ground, some attended to by the Women's Auxiliary. Ambulances and the fire department, red lights flashing, arrived. Firemen extinguished the random, small fires that Bullard's forces had started to incinerate the offending papers. Factory workers waved the leaflets as they stomped out the blazes and gathered the remaining flyers. Cries of "Union forever!" rose with the floating ashes.

CHAPTER 45

Angus Drummond stared at the front page of the *Detroit News*.

Republic Motors Faces Off with UAW

Security Forces Attack Union Members Who Attempted to Hand Out Leaflets
Many hurt, including women, some seriously!

To the left of the lead article, two large photos told the story. One showed Richard Frankensteen, his coat pulled over his head, as several men punched him. The other photo showed a bloodied Union man in a fetal position, clutching a piece of paper and being beaten.

"Tell me, Jacky boy, do you think the public will buy the company press release about loyal factory workers beatin' up on the Union organizers? Factory workers don't wear suits carryin' clubs!" Drummond shook his head, his fury rising with his blood pressure and his rage.

"Boss, you told me to stop it. I did."

"Are ye daft, man? Is this yer way a' stoppin' it? These pictures are goin' to be in every newspaper in the country."

"The boys tol' me they got all the photo plates, but the sneaky bastards switched them on us, I guess… "

"You guess? Well, guess this. His Excellency Frank Murphy, the esteemed guv'nor, called me in the wee early hours. He wanted an explanation. And guess again, Jacky Bullard. When I stopped apologizing' to his majesty, me wife wants to know about all the commotion. 'Angus, why's the Governor of Michigan calling you at 7 AM?' "

"Sorry, Angus, the boys got a little out a' hand. I didn' mean for them to give out such beatin's."

"I heard you threw Reuther down the stairs, poundin' him all the way down, accordin' to Murphy. Sweet Jesus, he's head of the whole shebang!"

"Sendin' a message is all we did."

"What kind of message, Bullard? That we're savages?"

"My boys ain't savages. They're soldiers in the service of our great democracy."

"Jacky, me old friend, let me tell you what Reuther said afterward, and I quote from the paper: 'After the UAW gets through with Jack Bullard and Republic's Service Department, Hamtramck will be a part of the United States, and the workers will be able to enjoy their God-given constitutional rights.'"

"He's a fuckin' communist, probably a Jew. He visited Russia, you know."

"I don' care if he was Vladimir Lenin revoltin' against the goddamn Czar! The guv'nor said Republic Motors violated the Wagner Act and that I'd better prepare meself to go before the National Labor Relations Board!"

"Oh, he's talkin' a lot of bullshit, you ask me."

"Yeah, well, maybe you'd like to take me place then, you stupid gombeen!"

"Now there's no need for usin' ugly names, Angus. We've been friends for many a' year."

"And it's sorely being tested on this sunny mornin'."

"This too shall pass, me friend."

"Maybe, but I'll have to give the workers a bloody raise or slow down the line to keep the lid on the powder keg you've created."

Rolf and Harry placed the front page of the *Detroit News* on Max Hoffman's hospital bed. They smiled as they waited for their friend's reaction. Max pushed aside the breakfast cart and read the headline.

"What they did to our people is better than ten thousand leaflets, Max."

"At the Union Hall, the line of people wantin' to sign up is around the block!" Harry's voice rose in excitement.

Max nodded. "How is Isabel?"

"She was magnificent. Those gals did a bang-up job handing out the leaflets and tending the wounded. Can you believe it? Bullard's goons even attacked the women."

"Was Isabel a target?"

"Yes, but her bag of nails did a man in. She's one of a kind!"

"That she is fellas. That she is."

"Max, Bullard knew we were goin' to hand out the leaflets. His men showed up twenty minutes beforehand. We got a traitor in the leadership."

"With the press we're getting, we should give him a medal."

An icy silence permeated the dining room. Grand in scale, the table could accommodate twenty of Angus and Fiona Drummond's friends and acquaintances. Tonight, as on most nights, it was just the two of them, Angus at the head of the table and Fiona in the first chair to his right. She had said nothing except a few remarks to the maid who served them.

Fiona stirred her soup and took a sip.

Angus spoke. "It's a might chilly in here tonight," trying to break the ice. "The swamp coolers must be workin' overtime considerin' it's well over 80 degrees outside."

"I'm sure your workers are turnin' on their coolers as we speak, Mr. Drummond." The sarcastic comment floated in the air like a zeppelin. Fiona never called Angus by his proper last name unless she was angry with him, and tonight was no exception.

Angus grabbed a jumbo shrimp from the crystal goblet and devoured the crustacean in one bite. "So, what's all this about, me love?"

"Don't be callin' me 'love,' Mr. Drummond. I saw the newspapers. What kind of criminal organization are you running? The Service Department! Indeed. It's nothing more than the hoodlum department. You're beating your own people, your own employees, for the love of heaven!"

"I suspected that's what your stony silence is all about. Bullard's men got carried away. I've already had a stern talk with Jacky about that. It won't happen again."

"A stern talk? You need to fire the man! He's nothing but Black Irish scum."

"Don't say that. He's me best friend and loyal to a fault."

"Loyal men don't get their friends in the pickle you're in now."

"And what kind of pickle is that, pray tell? He sent a message to the workers. A Union will not be tolerated at Republic."

"You think cracking a few heads will stop it? Wallace drove down Joseph Campeau this afternoon. He passed the hall where the Union meets. The line was around the block with men and women waiting to get in. And it wasn't for a mug of warm beer. They're joining the Union and I say, God bless them!"

"They can sign up everyone. I'll fire 'em just as fast and then hire others, the men and women who wait every day outside the plant for a chance to work for my company. They appreciate a good payin' job."

"Angus, what's happened to you? You're not the man I married. Ever since the Depression, you've become as black-hearted as Jack Bullard."

"I almost lost everything I worked for in 1932, and now in 1937, I'm surely not going to lose it to a bunch of socialists and communists runnin' the Union and wantin' to take over me company. I'm still the same man, Fiona, just older and wiser."

"Older, yes. Wiser, I'm not so sure."

CHAPTER 46

After Wednesday's turmoil, Tobias Woodson sat on his bed at Mrs. Perkins's boarding house and read the leaflet. He knew nothing about unions or what it meant; no one had told him anything about the organization or asked him, a Black man, to join. Some of the words muddled together in his head; words he'd never read before. He followed the lines with his finger, sounding them out.

As Tobias carefully re-read the sentences on the leaflet, it became clear. The Union would represent working people just like him. The words demanded a $1.50-a-day pay increase, an end to the speed-ups, and recognition of the United Auto Workers as the member's sole bargaining representative. In addition, there would be a shop steward at each part of the assembly line to represent the men and women on the line, and, most importantly, two bathroom breaks a day. Why would anyone be against that? It didn't matter. The men in the foundry told him there would probably never be a Union at Republic, especially not one Blacks could join.

Tobias walked away from the paymaster's counter Saturday afternoon, and his thoughts were not about the Union. His pocket contained $31.00. That morning, Tobias had asked Mrs. Perkins where to buy some new clothes, some fine clothes, not rough wool or cheap flannel, but smooth cotton. She recommended Hudson's Department Store.

Tobias had someone to impress. Tomorrow was Sunday, and he couldn't wait to see Sonora Lincoln again. It was church day; he had to dress fine. A bus ride later, he was at Woodward and Gratiot looking up at the second largest department store in the world, second only to Macy's in New York City. Mrs. Perkins worried that the store might overwhelm Tobias, but sooner or later he needed to deal with the big city.

The young man walked through one of the revolving doors, another initiation for him. Shoppers passed by, some jostling him. Unnerved, he was ready to leave.

"Good morning, young man. May I be of some assistance?"

"Ma'am?"

"What department are you looking for?"

"I needs to buy some clothes, ma'am."

"Of course. The men's department is on the third floor. The elevators are that way. At the end of the aisle."

"Elevators?"

"Yes, they're lifts that will take you right up to the men's department. Have a nice day."

"Thank you, ma'am." *Lifts?*

Woodson walked down the aisle and display cases contained fine jewelry on one side and perfumes on the other. He had never seen or smelled anything like it; the sparkle of the glass cases, rows of beautiful watches, scents of flowers, lime, and honey. The ornate brass elevator door was open when he reached the end of the aisle, and he walked in with a slight hesitation.

I guess this be the elevator…

"Floor?"

"Three, I think."

"Men's clothes, of course."

The doors closed. It was only him and a uniformed operator. Tobias took a deep breath. He felt the car rise. It stopped at the third floor with a slight lurch.

"Men's apparel."

"Is this the third floor?"

"Yes, it is. Men's clothes."

Tobias exited the small car in amazement. *I gots lots to learn,* he thought.

Surrounded by sights and sounds wholly unfamiliar, he wandered past an endless variety of shirts, ties, coats, shoes, and belts.

"Good morning, fella. What can I do for you?"

"I needs some fine clothes if it ain't too much trouble, suh. This sure is a big store."

"Yes it is. Fine clothes are our specialty. Where would you like to start?"

"I need a nice shirt. Maybe two."

"Right this way. I would guess you are an 18-neck, maybe 36 sleeves. But I'll measure you to be sure. My name is John, by the way."

"Thank you, suh."

"John."

"Thank you, John, suh."

An hour and a half later, Tobias walked onto Woodward Avenue, clutching several bags. He was now the owner of three new shirts, none flannel, but smooth cotton in white, blue, and dark brown. There were two pair of slacks, one was wool and the other cotton; three pair of socks, and several pair of boxer shorts. He added wingtip shoes, a belt, a dark red tie, and a purple paisley tie to complete the ensemble. He spent $19.45 and had enough left to pay for his room and board. And he still had $20.00 saved in the past two weeks.

I can't wait to see Sonora tomorrow, he thought as he headed toward the bus stop. He smiled as he realized that he was getting familiar with his new city.

Tobias arrived at the Second Baptist Church well before the ten o'clock service. He wore the white shirt, purple tie, and navy slacks, set off by his new brown wingtips. Mrs. Perkins was so impressed with Tobias' appearance that she let him use some of her late husband's Aqua Velva aftershave.

The morning was cool. Patchy clouds sparred with the predominant blue sky. He looked around as the congregants began to arrive. By custom or necessity, most walked to church, but others drove or took the bus, such was the renown of the Second Baptist Church and its Pastor and fine orator, Robert Bradby.

Tobias looked down Monroe Street. His heart skipped a beat. Walking with her parents was Sonora, even more beautiful than she was in her White Castle uniform. She wore a peach-colored print dress, a matching wide-brimmed hat, and two-toned medium heels. Her parents were also suitably well-dressed for the week's most important day. The young man froze.

Tobias, boy, don't mess up. Lord, I'm so nervous. What's I gonna say? At that moment, all the days since he had stepped off the bus in Detroit flashed before him. He had a good-paying job, moved into his own place, learned to take the bus, saved money, and navigated through Hudson's Department Store. He took a deep breath and walked toward Sonora. She saw him and waved.

"Good morning, George. My, you do look handsome today. Mother, Father, this is my new friend, George Woodson. George, these are my parents, Otis and Mayrell Lincoln."

The introduction made Tobias realize that he had started his relationship with Sonora in a lie. The thought immediately troubled him, but he put it to the back of his mind, like Memphis.

"Hi, Sonora. You look so pretty. It's a pleasure to meet you, Mr. and Mrs. Lincoln. Oh, Mrs. Lincoln, you look mighty fine too."

"Why, thank you, George. Come. Please sit with us."

"That's awful kind of you."

The foursome walked through a pair of heavy doors under a Gothic arch with a crenelated parapet. It was the only elaboration to the otherwise simple brick structure that housed the sanctuary built in 1926. The church's founding went back to 1836, and as such, it was the oldest Black church in the Midwest.

Two hours later, the foursome waited in line to greet Pastor Bradby and compliment him on another fine sermon. Sonora reached for Tobias' hand and squeezed it, a broad smile on her face.

"Otis, Mayrell, and Sonora. Good morning."

"A fine sermon, Reverend, a fine sermon. And the choir was in top form." Otis Lincoln shook hands and placed his fedora on his head to keep the warming sun out of his eyes.

"Thank you, Otis, thank you. Lovely Sonora. And who is this? Why, Tobias, don't you look sharp today."

Sonora looked at Woodson. "Tobias? Who's Tobias?"

"It be a… my middle name. Pastor knows me as that. It what my Daddy always called me."

Bradby bit his lip and decided to say nothing. He knew a lie when he heard one. "Okay… George."

Sonora looked perplexed.

Beads of sweat formed on Tobias' forehead, a product of the noon heat and his deception.

Mrs. Lincoln ended the awkward moment. "George, please come to the house for dinner. We'd love to hear about working at Republic and your family."

"Say yes… George." Sonora squeezed his hand again.

"Yes, ma'am, I sure would like that."

CHAPTER 47

Hannah Hoffman, the good nurse, insisted that she guide Max Hoffman's wheelchair from his room to the discharge desk. Isabel was happy to oblige, lest she hear more of her husband's complaints about being able to walk out of the hospital on his own two feet. It was his hand, not his foot, which had been crushed by the boot of one of Jack Bullard's thugs.

"Hannah, Isabel tells me you helped at the overpass. You tended to many of the wounded." Max looked up kindly to his chauffeur. The children, Rebecca, Sarah, and Tomasz, joined the entourage of four adults. Tied to the chair's arm, balloons swayed from the air coming from the ceiling registers. Max awkwardly held a bouquet of carnations and daisies in his good hand.

Jacob Hoffman interjected. "Yes, my darling Hannah, this I don't understand. After being so against the Union, what made you have a change of heart and join the Women's Auxiliary?"

"How do they say here in America, 'If you can't beat 'em, join them?' And Isabel told me people might be hurt. She was right. So, I helped."

Max winked at Jacob and smiled. "Jacob, how is your friend Lazlo?"

"Thanks to Hannah's quick work, he'll be fine. Five stitches to the forehead and a concussion. I guess I'll be doing double duty on the line for a few weeks. But I don't mind. Lazlo's a good man."

"A good Union man, nephew. I understand you even gave out the leaflets."

"Caught up in the moment, I guess. Bullard's men reminded me of the Brown Shirts in Germany — Nazi thugs who beat you mercilessly for having a different opinion."

"Or a different religion," Hannah said with a whiff of hatred.

"There's a meeting tomorrow night at the Union Hall. You should come, Jacob." Max looked at Hannah. She rolled her eyes.

"You're determined to lose your job and Jacob's, aren't you, Max? You didn't see what they did to our men, but I did. Like Jacob said, they are just like the Nazis. They can't be stopped."

"Hannah, I won't give up because of a beating. Neither will the Union. We'll call for a strike against Republic and bring them to their knees."

"They'll hire other workers to take your place, and you'll be out of work for good."

"You mean scabs. They can try, but we'll stop it somehow. Jankowski and Dunfey told me we've signed up hundreds of new members. Now is the time to act. Jacob, come to the meeting."

"I suppose I'm in it now up to my neck. I thought I'd be an engineer in a nice private office, but I'm working on the assembly line, going half-mad. What do I have to lose?"

Hannah looked at him. "Your job, that's what."

"Hannah, I have to do something."

"Alright, Jacob, if you insist, go to the meeting," she said. "I'm tired of Jews being pushed around by bullies."

Isabel chimed in. "And the Women's Auxiliary will help. Our time has finally come."

As Max and Jacob walked toward the Union Hall on Joseph Campeau, men and women were lined up down the block.

"What's all that about, Max?"

"Jacob, my God, they're here to join the Union!"

"I suppose I'd better get in that line."

"Even if you might lose your job?"

"If they fire everyone, who'll make the cars?"

"Now you're catching on. I'll see you after the meeting."

Max quickened his pace, excited by so many recruits. He pushed his way through to the front door. Fritz Joseph, the gatekeeper, was absent. He walked up to a table where Rolf Jankowski was busy signing up new members.

"Max, You're back. How's the hand?"

"Much better. I can almost make a fist. Business is good, I see."

"Since four o'clock, it's been a steady stream. We've enrolled two hundred already."

"Where's Joseph? He usually mans the door."

"Haven't seen him. And he wasn't at the overpass either. And one of the guys told me he's also got a new job on the line. It's cushy, with a clipboard doing final assembly checks."

"We might have our rat; how will the Local deal with him and the others that have infiltrated the movement? We have a lot of decisions to make, and we can't have Republic knowing about our every move."

"Sounds like you've been doing a lot of pondering." Rolf looked up and spoke to the next man in line. "Step right up and put your name or your mark here. Two dollars dues." He turned back to Hoffman; the man was an enigma.

"Yes, I had plenty of time thinking in the hospital. We'll need to be better organized for the struggle ahead with all these new members."

"The struggle?"

"Yes, the battle to take control of the company."

Jankowski shook his head. "Go on inside. I'll be there shortly."

"I'll grab a stein for you."

As the new members of Local 174 climbed the stairs to a large meeting room for the orientation on what it meant to be a steadfast "Unionist," the senior members met in a much smaller room on the first floor. There were eighteen men, some wearing bandages and slings from the incident at the overpass. All were in a buoyant mood. They knew that they had enough members to take action against Republic Motors. The dilemma was what kind of action?

The room was warm, but a ceiling fan and cold beer offset the heavy air. This evening, Harry Dunfey was acting chairman. Because the Union was an illegal organization, it had no officers — to elect them would mean immediate expulsion from the company.

"The meeting will come to order." Dunfey banged the gavel a few times, and those assembled turned their attention to him. In his early thirties, Harry was tall, had a shock of red hair, and a face full of freckles. He had worked at Republic since he was seventeen years old. Although he had been offered promotions to foreman, he refused; he never felt superior to his fellow workers, and he never wanted to boss them around. The Union suited him just fine, and the men respected him.

"First, I want to welcome back Max Hoffman tonight. He's been through quite the ordeal having his drinking hand smashed."

Laughter erupted, and Max raised his middle finger from a somewhat disfigured hand and aimed it at Dunfey. In a salute to their injured brother, the men raised their mugs of beer and chanted "Max, Max, Max."

"The next order of business is an important one. With our growing membership, we need to elect officers, a president, a vice president, a secretary, and a treasurer. Oh yes, and a sergeant-at-arms. There will be an action against Republic, and it needs to be carefully planned by those elected leaders."

Heads nodded in agreement. One of the men rose.

"I nominate Max Hoffman as president."

Dunfey shook his head. "Charlie, I haven't asked for nominations yet."

"So, ask. Get on with it."

"Fine then. Do I hear any nominations?'

"Yes, I already said so. Max Hoffman."

Another man rose. "Rolf Jankowski. He's the senior man here. He's the best man and deserves it."

"Alex, there'll be plenty of time for speech makin'. Anyone else?"

No others were nominated, but loud discussions over the best man for the job erupted.

Dunfey banged the gavel. "Order, order." The room quieted. It seemed a good time to take a drink or two of beer.

"Now, if there are no more nominations, let me ask Max and Rolf, if they willing to serve if elected?"

Both nodded. The two men stared at each other; old disagreements over political views and perhaps a dislike of the other slowly rose to the surface.

"Fine, then you each get a coupla minutes to state your case and your plans. Rolf, we start with you."

Rolf took another swig of beer and slowly stood.

"You all know me. My dark hair is almost white. I dye it so I won't lose my job. Many folks think workin' for Republic is a good job compared to other jobs in Detroit. It's not. We're way underpaid, and the company's excuse is that the Depression just ended. Hell, its 1937, and Republic's making more money than ever. We get no piss breaks, a lousy half-hour for lunch, twenty minutes if you count the hike to the commissary. Then there are the foremen who think they're God almighty, and worst of all, the speed-ups so Republic can make more cars and more money."

The men banged on the table and shouted, "Union, Union!"

"If you elect me, I'll form a committee to present our demands to Republic, to Drummond and Bullard. With the membership we now have, they have to listen to us. They have to bargain. One last thing. I don't want to own Republic or be president of it, for that matter. Let the swells run the show. What I want is a fair deal for the workers. So, that's it. I'd be honored to have your vote."

Jankowski sat down to cheers, clapping, and chants of "Rolf, Rolf." Dunfey banged on the gavel. The room quieted.

"Max, the floor is yours."

Max didn't stand but raised his hand, gnarled like an old piece of driftwood. None of the fingers were straight. Seated, everyone could hear his voice.

"What kind of a company refuses to let you go to the infirmary when you have a three-inch gash in your hand? What kind of company has goons stomp on it because you exercised your right of free assembly and attended a meeting? What kind a' company watches their workers faint from the heat of the factory floor or piss in their britches? I'll tell you. It's a company that doesn't care about their workers. They think they own us. We men. We women. We, the means of production. Without us, they are nothing. There are no cars, fat profits, big paychecks, or stock options. No big mansions on Lake St. Clair."

The assembled cheered. "Damn right. Max! Max! Max!"

"My comrade, Rolf, wants to meet with Bullard and Drummond. Talk to them reasonably, he says. Make them see the error of their ways. Well, I have news for Rolf. They won't listen to us. Not now, not ever. It's time for us, the proletariat, the workers of Detroit, of America, to rise up and take over. To seize, manage, and run the means of production equally with management. A fifty-fifty arrangement. Do I want to own Republic? Yes. Some of it. Let me ask you this. If we own the means of production, will we not have control, and will not our lives be better?"

Rolf stood up. "Max, you're a fucking communist!"

The room broke into pandemonium.

Max stood up and shouted above the din of voices.

"Communist? Yes, I am! So what? You want to negotiate. I want to take over the plant! Only then will Republic respect us. Only then will they listen to us!"

"Order! Order!" But there was none. Heated arguments started, beer spilled, knuckles bared, and fights broke out.

Rolf pushed his way to Max. "You fucking Bolshevik! I'm an American! You'll never run this Union!"

"We'll let the others decide. Talk or action!"

CHAPTER 48

The vote was ten to eight. Rolf Jankowski was elected president, and Max Hoffman became vice president by default. The other positions didn't really matter, but Harry agreed to be treasurer. The Union had collected dues from every new member. The war chest now contained over seven thousand dollars. Before, they barely had enough to pay for a keg of beer.

After the vote, the room settled down. Harry poured himself another beer, and passed the gavel to Rolf.

Rolf stood, and addressed the men. "I want to thank those that voted for me for their support. It is, I believe, an endorsement of my proposed sane approach to negotiation with management."

Dunfey broke in. "Rolf, we may not agree with Max wanting the Union to run the company, but Max did have a point. After what happened at the overpass, how can you believe talking with management will do any good?"

"We have to try. If we go on strike and have a picket line outside the factory, it's only a matter of time, days really, until they'll hire scabs and Bullard's men will get them into the plant by force. We'll all be out of work. Is that what you want? Our only option is to negotiate."

"No, that's why Max is right," Dunfey said. "We need to take over the plant, but not how he wants to. At the end of the shift, we simply don't leave. We barricade ourselves inside the factory. We sit down. We shut down the line. Bullard's men can't get in; there will be too many of us holdin' the fort, so to speak, thousands of us, and we stay there until Republic agrees to our demands."

One of the members chimed in. "It would be a strike where we sit down!"

"That it would be, Eddie that it would be."

"Max?"

"It don't go near far enough, but it's better than a lot of useless chit-chat with Drummond. I'm sure however, they'll find a way in, by force if necessary," Max said pessimistically.

Ralph continued the debate. "Max is right. And Bullard's maggots will be armed for sure. They'll find a way in and there will be more cracked heads."

"We don't need to take over every building. If we take over just two plants, say the engine and final assembly building, the workers from other plants can man a picket line. They'll keep them from getting inside. And the women will help, too."

Max spoke up. "Isabel's forming a special group, separate from the Auxiliary, a brigade of tough, hard-core gals. Women fashioned as a military-style unit, who are not afraid to fight. She's calling it the Women's Emergency Brigade. They'd be armed with bats and other weapons. We'll fight fire with fire."

A man named Charlie raised his voice: "My Peggy's sure to join. She's as tough as shoe leather!"

The room erupted in cheers: "To Peggy!"

Jankowski spoke. "Max, tell Isabel no guns, understand?'

Max said nothing, just glared at his nemesis.

Another voice: "But how will we eat?"

"Ah, Tommy O'Halloran, never wantin' to miss a meal. I think I got a solution. There's a vacant restaurant across the street on Conant. We can rent it for a month or two. We got the funds now. The Women's Auxiliary can make sandwiches, soup, and even hot meals."

An hour later, the meeting adjourned. It had been decided. The Union membership would vote for a sit-down strike to start after the four o'clock shift ended on Monday, July 12, in Plant Number 7, the final assembly building, followed by Plant 4, the engine plant. They had four weeks to prepare and would need every day of it, and the plans had to be a well-kept secret.

A week later, the rank and file, now over 5,200 members, voted almost unanimously in favor of the sit-down action. Three weeks were left. Could a new brotherhood of 5,200 men and women keep quiet about an action that was sure to change their lives?

CHAPTER 49

"I need to see the box on the Rivers Johnson murder." Once again, Officer Samuel Melton was at the evidence desk.

"Melton, this is getting to be an obsession with you. You checked it out last week before hours. That's against the regs."

"The regs don't seem to matter a whole hell of a lot with the Memphis PD."

"And what's that supposed to mean? Anyway, all's in it is a bloody coat and two knives."

"And the file. I need to look at the file again."

"This cleared by Smith?" the desk jockey said, referring to the lead detective on the case.

"A… yeah. He's having me work on it."

"Yeah, right. Wait here."

"Where else would I wait?"

"You're a bit of a smart ass, Melton, and you're getting' on my nerves. Be careful."

The box containing the evidence on the murder of Rivers Johnson lay before Sam Melton. He carried it over to a small desk in the corner of the evidence room and removed the bloody jacket from Kaufman's Department Store in Jackson, Mississippi. He vainly searched through the pockets again. Nothing. He looked one more time at the splattered blood, a long trail across the front of the jacket. He removed the two paper bags containing the knives. Melton gently upended the bags until the weapons slid onto the white Formica table. He stared at them. On the older one, he could make out a few smears of blood and the faint outline of a fingerprint.

Damn, he thought to himself. *Of course, fingerprints!*

Melton quickly pulled out the file. It was thin. Four pages — his superior, Lucas Smith's report, his own, an inventory sheet, and the paper noting how many times he had checked out the box. There was no request to run the fingerprints. Smith had no interest in pursuing the murder of a Black man, albeit a thief and a robber.

He went back to the front desk. "Do you have a magnifying glass?"

"Oh, now you're Sherlock Holmes? Melton, you're killing me."

"Do you have one or not?"

"Yeah, I think we got one somewhere." The desk sergeant opened a drawer, reached around, and produced an old, scratched-up relic. Melton grabbed it and hurried back to his small desk, breathing hard. He focused on the handle of old, frayed, dark-brown leather wrapped around the steel bolster. Two rivets held the leather wrapping in place. There were initials on the back of the butt, the end of the knife.

"TW"

Now we're getting somewhere, Melton thought, his heart beating faster.

Upon close examination, he could discern drops of blood and a spray pattern created when the blade slashed Johnson's throat. There were blood smears on the leather, and he could make out more partial fingerprints.

"Eureka," he said softly. He gently touched the end of the blade with his index finger and placed the evidence back in the bag. He folded the opening twice and carried it back to the officer of the watch.

"I need the fingerprints lifted from this piece of evidence. And I need it quick."

"Good evening, Mrs. Perkins. How are you tonight?"

"Why, Pastor Bradby, what a pleasant surprise. Suppers just finished, but I have some cherry pie left over. Would you like a slice?"

"That's very kind of you, but I just finished a meal myself. Say, is Tobias Woodson home?"

"Yes, he was at the table with the other boarders. Boy's eatin' me out of house and home. Had two pieces of pie!"

"He needs his strength. Working at the auto plant's tough."

"I know; some nights, I think he'll fall asleep while gobblin' down his dinner." Mrs. Perkins let out an understanding laugh. "I'm sorry, Reverend, you go right on up. Room number eight."

"Thank you, Mrs. Perkins. I'll see you in church next Sunday."

"You surely will, Pastor, you surely will."

The knock on the door startled Tobias. In the weeks he had lived at Mrs. Perkins's boarding house, only old Rufus Washington, a Ford retiree who now worked as a mechanic at an auto repair shop on Joseph Campeau would rap on Woodson's door, hoping to interest Tobias in a game of checkers.

"Come on in, Rufus."

Bradby slowly opened the door and saw that Tobias was studying his *McGuffey Reader*. "Hello, George."

Tobias looked up, startled by the minister's presence, and confounded by the greeting.

"Pastor Bradby. Hello. Come in, suh."

"Thank you, George."

"Why you call me that? You know my name be Tobias."

"Seems like your name isn't Tobias to everyone. Sonora Lincoln seems to think you're George. Something you want to tell me, son?"

Tobias closed his grammar book, shaking. Should he continue to lie or confess the awful truth he had been hiding since Memphis? He began to choke up. Tears welled in his eyes.

"I guess I do, suh. I guess I do."

Bradby sat down at the foot of Woodson's crisply made bed. He looked around. The room was as neat as a pin. In one corner, a small bookcase held magazines like *Popular Mechanics,* novels like *Treasure Island* and the *Adventures of Huckleberry Finn,* textbooks on basic arithmetic and American history, and his *McGuffey Readers*. Above the bed, Tobias had nailed a simple cross. From the bedroom window was a nice view of the street down below. Bradby knew from past visits to other boarders that several rooms looked down to the gray, ugly alley in the rear. But Tobias had a lovely maple tree along the sidewalk in front of busy St. Antoine Street.

Slowly, as tears flowed, Tobias told the minister everything that had happened, from his friend's lynching in Tallula, the all-night ride to Jackson, his tearful farewell, and that awful day in Memphis.

"Pastor, I so ashamed a' what I did. I done kilt a man."

"In self-defense, I'd say. You said he had a knife to your throat. You said he even cut you."

"But I still kill'd him. Please don' send me back to Memphis. I don't want to go to prison."

"Let me tell you a story, Tobias. My grandmother was a slave. That was an evil injustice like no other. So, she fled her bondage in Alabama. She was a fugitive from justice, but it was intolerant, evil White justice. She found the Underground Railroad, hid by day, and traveled by night, so scared that at any moment, the White posse would find her, take her back to Alabama, whip her, and then lynch her while a fire burned under her feet. She made her way to the free north, to right here in Detroit, married my grandfather, who was also a pastor, and he started Second Baptist. She was guilty, but certainly not in the eyes of God, only to some evil people. I wouldn't make you go back. But you will always have to look over your shoulder. The authorities in Memphis surely won't see it as I do."

"Thank you, thank you so much."

"And I kind of like George. It's a good new name for you in your new city of Detroit. And I do believe Sonora's takin' a shine to you."

"She so fine, she's so nice. What she want with a dumb sharecropper like me?"

"You're not dumb. Just keep adding to that bookshelf. Soon you'll be a foreman at Republic."

"I joined the Union today."

"Good for you. It's a dangerous thing to do, but you'll be fine. I have it on good authority that your Union movement will eventually succeed."

"Who tol' you that?"

"The Lord Almighty, George."

CHAPTER 50

Angus Drummond was tired of all the Union kerfuffle. He hoped his directive to slow down the assembly line would quell any further actions and placate worker resentment. Jack Bullard had assured him that it had the intended effect, though Drummond no longer entirely trusted his head of security. The man seemed out of touch with the pulse of Republic's restless employees.

Right now, he had other problems, ones that involved building automobiles. He picked up the receiver of his Westinghouse telephone and dialed zero, a direct connection to his executive secretary of twenty years.

"Yes, Angus?" After 20 years, Mary Campbell was both his secretary and his confidant. Angus and Mr. Drummond were interchangeable salutations.

"Mary, me dear, I need to talk with Mickey Donnelly." Angus' voice was calm, no emotion registering.

"Right away, sir."

Interesting. Angus rarely concerns himself with hiring matters. There was that time a few months ago; well, it must have to do with the Union troubles. Mary didn't give it any more thought; she dialed Donnelley's extension.

"Mickey, the boss wants to see you."

"What about, Mary?"

"Mickey, ifn' I knew I wouldn't tell you. That's the big man's affair."

"I'll be right there."

Donnelly put down the phone, reached in his shirt pocket, pulled out a Lucky, lit it with a quivering hand, and wondered how bad of an ass-chewing he was in for. That prick Bullard had probably blamed all the Union troubles on his hiring pro-Union men and women.

Donnelly left his office, bounded up three flights of stairs, and walked down a long hallway to the door marked "Executive Offices." It was inaccurate. The only executive office behind that door belonged to Angus Drummond; others of lower positions in management were on the floors below.

"Go right in; Mr. Donnelly, he's expecting you."

"Mary, a hint… "

"Haven't the foggiest, Mickey."

Donnelly took a deep breath and opened the door. Angus Drummond put down a report, got up, and headed to a sideboard where several whisky decanters awaited.

"Och aye, Mickey, come on in. Can I pour you a dram?'"

"As much as I'd like one, sir, I best not. It's only three, and I have a few more interviews lined up. Have to make sure we aren't hirin' Union sympathizers." Donnelly braced for a famous flash of Drummond's temper and the inevitable ass-chewing to follow.

Angus poured a scotch into the crystal glass, put it to his nose but didn't drink, and spoke calmly. "I'm sure that's gettin' a wee bit harder these days. I heard that since the incident at the bridge, the Union's signing up folks by the bushel basket."

"We'll keep that new rabble out of Republic, sir. I promise."

"I didn't ask you up here to talk about the Union."

"Oh." Donnelly exhaled. "Then what, sir?"

"The Epoch or, more specifically, its transmission. The boys can't get it to, well, to mesh. I told you a month ago to find me engineers who knew their business. Steal 'em from Ford, Dodge, Studebaker, I don't care, I tol' ya. Do ya not remember?'

Donnelly suddenly remembered the order from Drummond. After the Jacob Hoffman hire, he had forgotten all about it.

"I do. If you don't mind, sir, I'll have that drink. Gin, straight up."

"If we don't get this new transmission figured out, there'll be no production. We have the Drummond, but it's outdated now. The Chamberlain and Zodiac are fine, but we need a new model, somethin' to set the buyin' publics' hair on fire."

"Yes, sir, but its hard findin' good engineers."

"That's your damn job, isn't it, Donnelly?" He reached for the decanter full of clear liquid and poured three fingers, and held it back from his key employee.

Screw that ass, Bullard. If the boss wants an engineer, I'm going to give him one, Donnelly thought. *I'm not takin' the fall for that shit.*

"Sir, we have your man. He already works for us."

"In engineering?" Drummond was confused.

"No, sir. On the assembly line."

"Sweet Jesus, why, man?"

"Bullard's orders, sir."

"Bullard's orders? I'm getting a wee bit tired of his orders! He's been acting the rogue, and it's gettin' on me nerves. Tell me, who?"

Drummond handed the glass of gin to Donnelly, who nodded and took in a mouthful. "The man's name is Jacob Hoffman. Does the name Hoffman ring a bell?"

"Should it? I have thousands of employees, Donnelly. Hell, I don't even know some of the people downstairs. Maybe I need to keep better track a' things. But this Union business has been an awful distraction."

"To that point, Jacob's uncle is Max Hoffman. He's one of the main Union organizers. Jacob emigrated here just a few months ago from Germany. His family escaped the Nazi regime. He was an engineer and an assistant-director at Daimler-Benz."

"And you put him on the assembly line?"

"Bullard didn't even want me to hire him. Said he was a Jew, related to an agitator who's probably a communist. I didn't listen to him. Jacob Hoffman installs tires in final assembly. He designed some improvements on his own, and we reduced two positions on that line's section."

"Mother Mary, since when does Bullard tell you who to hire?" Drummond imbibed half of his glass, his face getting flushed.

"He has been for some time, Mr. Drummond. Beggin' your pardon, but he thinks he runs the show, so to speak."

Drummond let the remark pass without comment.

"This man improved the line, you say?"

"Right. Now, two fellas get on all the tires instead of four."

Drummond raised his eyebrows. The discussion was getting more interesting by the minute.

"Do you know what my engineers have been working on with the Epoch's transmission?"

"No, sir, should I?"

"No, because it's top-secret. But I'm about to tell you. We are trying to build an automatic transmission."

"Automatic transmission? What's that?" Donnelley sipped on his gin; he was beginning to feel lightheaded.

"One where the car changes gears automatically as the vehicle reaches certain speeds. The driver doesn't have to do a thing. No third pedal and no gear shift. We know GM is working on it. I've got to beat them to it. If I do, we'll sell more Epochs than we can manufacture. So, Mr. Donnelly, send Mr. Hoffman, the director from Daimler, to me. I'll see if he has an interest in working on transmissions."

Donnelly downed the last of his drink and took a deep breath.

"Sir?"

"What?"

"Jacob Hoffman was the director in charge of transmission design at Daimler."

"Sweet Jesus, Donnelly!"

Donnelly decided to deliver the good news personally to Jacob Hoffman. He knew Jed Koepka, the foreman, would be upset to lose a valuable man on his part of the line, especially the worker who had sped up its operations.

As he walked into the final assembly building, the late June heat wave intensified within the factory's thick concrete walls. The open windows just let in more hot air. He looked around the dirty, sweat-soaked bodies and felt a tinge of remorse. He had hired most of these men to work in this small corner of Hades. He shook his head and muttered, "It's a free country, Mickey." Moving through and around the assembly line, he thought, *these boys are making seven, eight dollars a day. They got no reason for complaint.*

Donnelly knew something else. For him, a Union would be a good thing. Pay scales would be uniform; how much a worker made would be determined by the agreement with the Union: by seniority and job function, not by some arbitrary system. No arguments with upper management; the rules would be set. Now, it seemed like all he did was argue for a small increase for the workers — workers he had hired — only to be rebuffed by upper management.

Shiny new Chamberlains rolled off the conveyor belt onto the concrete floor at the end of the assembly line. An engineer in a clean jumpsuit quickly got inside the vehicle, turned the ignition key, and the car came to life. From this point, it would be put through its paces on a test track, then brought to a small shop containing fifty bays and lifted for adjustments and a final inspection. Worker dissatisfaction or not, Republic made a fine automobile.

Donnelly moved up the line to where Jacob Hoffman was rolling tires up his ramp and quickly installed the five lug nuts with the pneumatic drill. He watched him work and realized that Jacob was doing the job of two men, installing the front and then the rear tires immediately. Hoffman worked like a man possessed — a human machine in perpetual motion.

Donnelly went to the column where the red button protruded and pushed it. A horn blared, and the line slowed down and then stopped.

Jed Koepka came out of nowhere shouting, "Who the fuck shut down the line?!" He focused on Hoffman, who looked bewildered. "Hoffman, you better have a good reason for stopping production!"

"I didn't stop anything, Jed."

"No, I did." Donnelly walked over to the line foreman with a smirk on his face. "I need to talk to Mr. Hoffman here; I'll find two men to replace him because he won't be returnin'."

Jacob looked at the man who hired him. He knew he was about to be fired for joining the Union. "Please, Mr. Donnelly, do not fire me. Lots of the boys here are in the Union. I… I was only trying to support my Uncle Max."

"Let's go to my office. We'll discuss your future there."

"You see, I do the work of two men. So what, I'm in the Union? I don't make trouble."

Donnelly smiled as he walked toward the main door, Hoffman followed behind continuing to plead his case.

Jacob bounded up the stairs to the Hoffman apartment. His hand shook as he turned the key in the lock. He could not believe his good fortune.

"Hannah, Hannah, are you here?"

There was no answer.

"Hannah, where are you?"

His petite wife appeared from the long hallway going back to the bedrooms. "I'm here. I was folding clothes in the girl's room. What is it, my husband? Why are you home early?"

"Hannah, my darling, I have great news. I've been promoted to the engineering department!"

"Jacob, finally, such a wonderful thing at last. When?"

"Tomorrow morning. And I'll be working on a top-secret project. I cannot tell even you about it, except it's a totally new type of transmission."

Hannah's eyes sparkled with her husband's announcement. "And how much money, my love?"

"A fortune. $600 a month! Can you believe it? I even met with Mr. Angus Drummond, the president. He asked all about us, he wanted to know about you and Tomasz. I told him what happened in Germany. He seems like a fine man."

"Who won't allow your Union and lets that thug Bullard beat the workers."

"I know, I know, but he was very kind to me."

"Never mind, my darling, now we can move and get our own apartment with a separate bedroom for Tomasz."

"Perhaps a house." Jacob's smile slowly turned to pursed lips. "But, Max… "

"What about Max? He'll be happy for you."

"I'm not so sure. He might even be a little jealous and think that I'm abandoning the cause."

"Nonsense. He knows that you were never an assembly line worker. You are an engineer, one of the best. And you can still support the Union in other ways. Look, Isabel and the children won't be home for a while. There's a bottle of wine in the icebox. Let's celebrate… in the bedroom." Hannah took his hand and kissed Jacob on the lips. "I love you."

The thought of an afternoon interlude made Jacob quickly forget about his uncle. He smiled.

"I'll get the wine."

CHAPTER 51

Fiona Drummond sat in her wheelchair in front of the parallel bars. A handsome young man with impressive biceps bulging from his tee shirt slid his arms under hers to lift her into position at the end of the bars. Today, she would try to walk the eight feet from one end to the other.

"No, let me be. I'll get up on my own, or not at all." Her voice was full of determination. It was the first day of rehabilitation, and she was determined to walk again.

"Yes, ma'am. I'll be next to you just in case."

"In case what?"

"In case you fa… just in case."

Fiona gripped the arms of the hated wheelchair. She had been through oceans of tears, months of depression, and periods of self-loathing, and now the fiery spirit that she had possessed all her life reignited. Slowly, she rose from the confines of the motor-less vehicle. Her arms were fully extended. Now what? She would need to let go of the chair with one hand and quickly grab the bar. She took a deep breath, let go, and tried to grab the rail. But the other arm was too weak. It gave way, and she collapsed into the arms of the therapist.

"Dammit all to hell!"

"Mrs. Drummond, let me get you onto the bar. Then we can begin. I mean, the purpose is to walk a few steps today, and more each time. In time, you'll be able to get out of the wheelchair."

Fiona shook her head and then lowered it. Her eyes moistened. "Oh, all right. Lift me. But by God, I'll not need this bloody seat one day!"

Her attendant smiled. "No. No, you won't."

"Liam, I want you to teach me about engines, transmissions, steering, even how we paint the cars and make the windshields. You have three months. Then I'm going to go into the marketing department to sell the cars."

"I know. Your father told me of the deal you two made. It's a fine plan, since you weren't much use to me in the plant."

"You mean that sweatshop my father calls a factory. No wonder the workers want to unionize."

"Union's bad for business, you know that." Liam put a piece of gum in his mouth, chewing hard.

"Just teach me all you can. I promise I'll show up everyday."

"Fine. We'll start at the foundry. Have you ever been inside there?"

"No, never."

"I assure you it will be an eye-opening experience. Now, here's a manual on the assembly of our V-6 engine. You'll read and study it every night. It's not as much fun as driving a Chamberlain with one under the bonnet, but it's necessary if you're going to sell the cars. You finish that, I have another manual on our new V-8, the one that's going into the new Epoch."

"Where will I work after the foundry?"

"You're not going to work there; it's too dangerous. You'll observe. Then it will be back to Plant 4. This time, you'll report on time and pay attention. At the end of two weeks, you should know all about motors. After that, axles, wheels, shocks, struts."

"Yes, boss."

"Good lad. I'm glad you're getting serious."

"I think I made a deal with the devil."

Chapter 52

Isabel Hoffman was proud of her uniform. She wore her husband's boots from the Great War, with a sock stuffed into each toe so her feet wouldn't slide around and brown flannel pants tucked into the tops of the heavy brogans. The pants were hot and stuck to her sweaty legs, but she wasn't about to wear a dress. Isabel bought a blue denim work shirt with epaulets and brass buttons at Woolworth's, and topped off the martial look with a red beret. The headgear would become the signature of the Emergency Brigade.

At 7:30, plenty of daylight was left for those assembled to practice and drill on the Pershing High School football field. In front of her were over one hundred women dressed similarly in quasi-military style. Some wore red caps, others bandanas like they wore each day on the assembly line. She was impressed by the group. They lined up in regimental order, baseball bats or thick broom-sticks held like rifles. This small army was not to be trifled with.

Isabel climbed up the bandleader's ladder.

"Ladies of the Emergency Brigade, thank you for coming. We drill tonight so we can be ready for a future, the future when our men and women strike for their rights and for a better life for their families. Tonight, we have the honor of having a veteran of the Great War to train us in hand-to-hand combat. He was a master sergeant in the United States

Army and trained thousands of soldiers. After tonight and after several more drills, we will be ready to take our fight to Republic Motors and destroy the capitalist pig owners."

There were a few murmurs, and then cheers. The assembled didn't know that like her husband, Isabel Hoffman was an avowed communist.

The dark gray Drummond Toiler 75 pickup truck sat across the street from the football field, where the view was unobstructed by the grandstands.

"What in the hell is goin' on?" Mike Maloney, one of Jack Bullard's top service department goons, lowered his binoculars and looked at his driver.

"Looks like some sort of military parade. But it's all a bunch of bitches."

"I think I know that woman at the top o' the ladder. She was at the overpass a couple a' weeks ago. Looks like she's the ringleader. I've seen enough. Let's get back and report to Bullard."

"Report what? That they're organizin' a marchin' band?"

"With bats, asshole?"

Charlie, the driver, turned the key in the ignition and quickly accelerated down Seven Mile Road.

Several union men hoisted a new sign above the windows of the retail space. It stated, in bold green letters, Walter's Diner. One of the guys in the paint department had made it. The union men had named the establishment in honor of their leader, Walter Reuther.

"Do you think we did right, namin' the joint after Mr. Reuther?"

"Sure, they're too dumb to connect the bloody dots. And it is a handsome sign that Manny painted for sure. How does the equipment check out?"

"I just got the utilities turned back on. I've checked everything. The water heater is on its last legs, but the stove's good. No gas leaks. One burner's out, Mike said he'll be able to fix it. We cleaned the exhaust grilles. The big mixer is fine. Some of the inspectors that have come by have been pretty nosy. I gave 'em a bunch of crap about the lack of restaurants in the area."

"What about the provisions?"

"Provisions?"

"The food supplies, you dimwit."

"Hey, I'm a brake guy for Chrissakes, not a cook."

"Okay, the food supplies."

"The refrigerators are full, and so is the dry storage room. Joe figures we got enough food for one week."

"And after that?"

"Isn't one week plenty?"

"Not by a long shot. Plan for additional deliveries every couple of days. This strike will last longer than an in-laws visit."

The union leadership had dispensed with further meetings at the DAV meeting hall on Joseph Campeau. They would need to get together almost every other night to plan the sit-down strike, and their comings and goings would be noted by Bullard's men. Harry Dunfey's brother-in-law, Cyrus

McShane, owned a small dive bar in Corktown at the corner of 12th Street and Trumbull. During prohibition, a windowless back room had been used to distill bathtub gin and store beer barrels. The committee decided it was the perfect place to plan a rebellion.

"The first order of business is maintaining order and discipline. I'm concerned about some of our members. They can be hotheads. They'll be cooped up for a few weeks in a factory. It'll be hot, and the men will get bored. Tempers are bound to be short." Rolf Jankowski sucked on his cigarette and blew a copious amount of smoke into the poorly ventilated space. It mixed with the cloud from cigars and pipes. He took a drink of Guinness.

Dunfey spoke. "We'll hold an election. Let the rank and file, not us, vote for a mayor and city council to decide all relevant matters. The men will respect that."

"What the hell do we do if guys break the rules?"

"We'll need to appoint a judge, but the leadership needs to choose him."

"I agree. And we can empty out a couple of the storage lockers used for parts and turn 'em into jail cells if needed."

"Jack, we need to do that. It is an unfortunate but necessary measure."

"And we should create a police force consisting of the union foremen."

"Another necessity, I'm afraid. We can't have company property defaced or damaged."

Jankowski looked down at a piece of paper in front of him. "Next, how do we keep the members occupied? Tommy, can you get hold of chess and checker sets? Even Monopoly games. And cards, lots of packs of cards."

"Sure I can. There's plenty at the VFW hall. Monopoly?"

"All the kids are playing that new game. Families, too; it's very popular. The women's auxiliary can bring some sets from home."

"And we can organize a band so there can be some entertainment."

"Good idea. And we'll need coupla radios to listen to music and the news about the strike."

Max Hoffman slammed his good hand hard on the table. "What are we doing? Setting up a damned country club?! Less than a day after we take over the plant, Bullard's boys will be outside, using any means possible to get in and get us out. That includes tear gas and rifles. We may need guns to fight 'em off 'cause they won't give up at the first rumble."

Jankowski glared at Hoffman. "No guns. This is a peaceful action."

"It's a Goddamn revolt, is what it is, Jankowski! We take over the plant. Do you know what we're doing? We've seized the man's private property! He won't take kindly to that."

Tommy O'Halloran, always the class clown, interjected. "It's our plant; we work here. We're only workin' a little overtime." The comment drew a ripple of laughter.

"Don't kid yourself; we're a bunch of trespassers and expendable to boot. As soon as they're rid of us, they'll bring in the scabs, and our families will look at empty plates during dinner. Drummond and his henchman, Bullard, won't rest until we're thrown out on our collective asses, arrested too, so we'll need guns to win the fight that's coming." Hoffman stormed off to a corner of the room.

"I said no guns, you fucking commie! Men, you elected me president, not Hoffman. We do it my way, or the strike is off!"

The men nodded in agreement. Harry went over to Hoffman, put his hand on his shoulder, and spoke quietly in his ear.

"Max, you've been through a lot. No one wants to see any violence. If someone gets hurt, the blood will be on Bullard's hands. And then we'll let the newspapers do our fighting for us."

Hoffman brushed Dunfey's hand away and retreated to the back of the room with his beer. He mumbled, "Monopoly games, what the hell… "

Tommy decided again to break the palpable tension in the room, thick as the cigar and cigarette smoke. "What about booze, at least beer?"

"I'll think about the beer, but no booze," Jankowski replied. "Maybe brews a few times a week and store the kegs at Walter's Diner. Getting drunk means a fight for sure. The enemy's outside, not inside, and like I said, tempers will get short real quick. Everyone wants this to last a few days only. It's going to take more than that to break Drummond."

Hoffman thought, *Yeah, fucking guns is what it will take.* But he didn't speak.

Charlie spoke. "Maybe we should just picket. All this seems like too much work… "

"It is a lot of work," Rolf responded, "but it sends a much stronger message than a picket line. Now, the next order of business is taking over the plant and gettin' the security people out the door."

The meeting lasted until closing, a good deal of whisky and beer depleted. But the strike was taking on concrete form, becoming a movement to be reckoned with — an unstoppable force.

CHAPTER 53

The Toiler 75 got into the line of cars that waited to get through the security gate at Jack Bullard's compound outside of Port Huron. While the house looked like an imposing lodge constructed from great timber logs, its walls were thick concrete, and guard outposts were tucked into the gable roofs. Behind the house were two sentry towers. When he was home, Bullard had them manned all day long.

A moat with steel pikes below the surface of the piped-in water surrounded the property, and once guests entered past the gate, they walked across a drawbridge to the mansion. Its prominent exterior feature was a 100-foot-long porch populated with groupings of Adirondack chairs. The interiors were more impressive with furniture made by Republic's craftsmen who used the finest leather for the couches and chairs, the same used in the elegant Zodiac automobile. There were majestic fireplaces on either side of a great room. Massive wood beams crisscrossed the ceiling, which drew the eye upward fifteen feet. A twelve-foot bar stood against the far wall. Three taps for each of Michigan's favorite beers — Stroh's, Old Milwaukee, and Pabst, sported mahogany pulls and silver spigots.

Hidden beneath this large and impressive gathering room, a concrete bunker waited in cool, dark silence. The steps leading to it, accessed through a hidden bookcase door, were uneven, every one a different height and width. Bullard practiced ascending and descending them often. Those in pursuit would invariably trip and fall before reaching the bunker. Even if they did reach it, it would avail them nothing. The concrete room, secured with two steel doors, had the best combination locks that money could buy. From the hideout, stockpiled with supplies for a month, Bullard could make his way down a long passageway to a lake, where a four-seat float plane, hidden in a small cove, awaited his quick departure. Jack Bullard was not about to let the Union bastards get him.

"Looks like the boss is havin' a party."

"He better not mind the intrusion. It's a long-ass way out here from Detroit."

"You gonna tell him we found the ladies of the Union formin' a marchin' band?"

"Funny. Something's up."

"You ever been here before?"

"Coupla times, for the Christmas party."

"I didn't get invited."

"Imagine that. Just shut your trap. Let me do the talking."

"Suits me fine."

An attendant in a bowtie and red vest waved the pickup truck toward a field where the cars were parked.

"Welcome, gentlemen. I'll park it for you."

"The hell you will. Just tell me where."

"Oh, sorry, yes, of course. At the end of the row, by the blue Ford."

The Toiler parked, and Bullard's two henchmen approached the moat. Maloney adjusted his fedora and walked toward the door.

"Why didn't you let that kid park the truck?" Charlie was curious.

"Shit, I'd have to give him a tip."

The two enforcers reached the front door.

"Hey, look, it's Eddie."

"Eddie, how they hangin'? What the hell's going on?"

"Fundraiser for that Catholic priest that's on the radio. The one that hates Jews and Roosevelt. For his organization, the… let's see, I got it written down right here. Boss tole me to memorize it, so I wouldn't look stupid."

"You look stupid, Eddie? So, you mean Father Coughlin?" Maloney responded dryly, a bit of sarcasm thrown in.

"Yeah, that's the guy. Here it is; he runs the National Union of Social Justice, whatever that is. He's in there somewhere. Nice guy."

"Yeah, a real peach of a Christian."

"Whadda you two jamokes doin' here?"

"Need to see the boss."

"Geez, he's kinda busy pressin' the flesh. I'm not sure… "

"Eddie, we didn't drive out here for nuthin'. We got important business to discuss with the boss and I'm thirsty."

"Fine. Come right in. Bar's over there." Eddie nodded toward the great room's signature feature and the assembled guests.

It didn't take long to find Jack Bullard. He stood next to Father Charles Coughlin, surrounded by guests listening to an impromptu oration from the Catholic evangelist, whose weekly radio broadcasts reached one in every four households in America. Thirty-million Americans hung on every inflammatory word each Sunday.

"We'll take care of the modern shylocks that have grown fat and happy like every other moneychanger on Wall Street. They are an integral part of the international conspiracy of bankers running the world's finances."

The crowd applauded.

"When we get through with the Jews of America, they'll think the treatment they received in Germany was nothing."

More applause.

"My friends, Jewish persecution only followed after Christians were first persecuted by the Jews and Communists."

More applause.

Mike Maloney nudged his apprentice. "Charlie, go get me an Old Milwaukee."

As the junior enforcer ambled off, Bullard's senior associate walked around to his boss, who was shaking Coughlin's hand.

"Boss, a word, please."

"Maloney, what are you doin' here? I've a fundraiser goin' on. I'm busy."

"This won't take long, boss."

Bullard nodded and excused himself from the priest who began to orate on the great betrayer and liar, Franklin D. Roosevelt. Bullard promised to bring the cleric a glass of red wine.

"Now, Mickey, what's so important that I can't enjoy a social evening?"

"The Union business, boss. Something's afoot."

"Balderdash. The rank and file seem happy enough since Drummond slowed down the assembly line."

"Well, the women aren't. Me and Charlie seem 'em at the football field at Pershing High School doing military drills."

"Really? And that's important?"

"Boss, why would they be doing that?"

"We got a bitch on the inside a' that group. Says it's a bunch of BS. Union's trying to keep the wives happy."

"They were pretty unhappy at the overpass."

"Fine. Point taken. Now if we're done… "

"Listen, boss, what about the new restaurant across from the plant? It's named Walter's."

"Maybe a fella named Walter owns it. 'Bout time the neighborhood got a decent eatin' establishment."

"And there's no meetin's takin' place at the Union Hall on Joseph Campeau. It's very strange."

Bullard shook his head. "Maloney, of course there's no meetin's. There ain't nuthin' to meet about. The Union signed up a bunch of new members, collected lots of money in dues, and now Reuther and his bunch are spendin' it on booze, horse racin', and whores."

"Mr. Bullard, I don't like it. Somethin's not right."

"Mickey, I'm sorry you came out here to tell me this. I told Drummond that since the overpass head beatin' we gave the organizers, there's nuthin' to worry about. Now get a beer and join the festivities. And I'd appreciate a sizeable donation to Father Coughlin's organization."

"Mr. Bullard, with all due respect, I may not like the Union and their kind, but I don't hate the Jews."

"And why not, Mickey? They're ruinin' this country."

"Because my sister-in-law is Jewish."

Bullard stared in disbelief at his senior associate. Maloney turned and headed to the bar, where Charlie picked up the beers.

"Drink your beer, and let's get outta here. I don't care for the smell of these people."

"But we just got here."

"Yeah, and we're just leaving."

CHAPTER 54

July 12, 1937

Lazlo had not expected to be back at work. He still had dizzy spells and felt light-headed when he stood up. But a phone call from Jed Koepka was very convincing: "Come back to work or lose your job." It was not an idle threat. The factory buzzed with the news that two workers had fainted from the heat, and the incident required production to stop. A half-hour later, they were replaced with new workers from the unemployed men and women who assembled daily outside the gates. The timing gave the Union all the ammunition it needed to strike today.

He missed his co-worker, Jacob Hoffman, although he was happy his diminutive friend had been given a proper job that matched his skills. His stomach had the butterflies, and he was slightly nauseous from the lingering concussion. He looked at his watch: 3:53 PM. Things would get interesting in less than ten minutes.

The plans were perfected down to the last detail. At the whistle, men would head for the restrooms or the lunchroom to lay low. Some would do some last-minute maintenance work on the machines along the line, while others would sweep up, watching foremen who were not pro-Union leave. Union men who could not stay for family reasons were allowed to go, promising to be back to walk a picket line later. After fifteen minutes, security personnel would be surrounded and escorted out of the building. The doors to the plant would be shut and barricaded, and newly finished cars coming off the assembly line would be rolled in front of the doors as an added precaution. Holes would be cut with acetylene torches so the nozzles of fire hoses could be inserted to fight the army that was sure to come. Buckets of water with large rags were placed near the windows, providing quick protection from tear gas. Nuts and bolts, heavy car door hinges, and empty milk bottles were piled nearby on the rooftop, projectiles against an attack. The strikers considered the plant their fortress to be protected at all costs. As the coup-de-grâce, a large banner was unfurled from a window on the third floor.

The strike's message would not be lost on anyone:

We SIT Down to STAND Up for Our Rights!

The whistle blared; the moment had come. Lazlo attached the last five nuts to the rear tires of a four-door Chamberlain. He set his drill down and hid under a table as the line stopped. His hands shook, and he realized he could die in the plant, clubbed again by Bullard's army, or shot for trespassing on company property. The risk was great, and the reward uncertain.

Minutes passed. He heard the usual factory noises and loud voices from afar, then shouts of "Union, Union!"

From his lunch box, Lazlo retrieved his journal. With a pencil and a shaky hand, he wrote:

Word came they fired two more Union men today. So it begins. The plant is empty, except for the strikers. There's loud talking and men are shouting: "Union, Union!" The strike is on. Well here we are. The strike has been coming for years. The speed-ups, overbearing foremen, lousy working conditions. You can go just so far you know, even with working men. I'll stick it out with the rest of the boys.

We are right, and when you're right, you can't lose.

The plant was secured with over 1,500 strikers inside the Final Assembly Building, and the previously agreed-upon procedures were now implemented. Long-time workers were assigned to police patrols; a "Fire Squad" was on watch. Others were assigned janitorial duty to keep the factory premises clean.

Rules of behavior were posted:

No Liquor

No Yelling

No Guns

No Damage to Company Property

The workers would enforce the rules.

A handmade calendar was drawn on a chalkboard and placed in a central location by the lunchroom. In crisp, chalked letters, it stated: **"Stick and Stay – They're bound to Pay!"**

By five o'clock, a picket line had formed outside the factory. Hundreds of workers from other shifts, wives, and even children paraded up and down Hamtramck Drive carrying placards:

My Daddy Strikes for Us Little Tykes!

***Give Us a Chance for Better Food
and a Better Life***

Our Dads WILL Win!

Union Labor Marches On

My Daddy is a Union Man!

At 5:00, another whistle blew, signaling the end of the shift in the engine assembly plant. Within a half-hour, the United Auto Workers occupied and controlled that vital facility with an additional 1,700 workers.

Jack Bullard lifted the brass door knocker and let it fall. He repeated the action and then took a step back to take in the enormity of Manor Druimeanach, Angus Drummond's castle. To him, it looked like something out of the movie *Frankenstein*. His friend had indeed done well, and Bullard had benefited from his loyalty to the Scotsman, a loyalty that would be strained by the events Bullard was about to report.

The imposing oak front door, reinforced with iron straps and rivets, opened.

"Mr. Bullard, good evening."

"I need to see the man, a… "

"Cedric."

"Yes, of course. I need to see Mr. Drummond, Cedric."

"Certainly. Come into the study. He is upstairs with Mrs. Drummond."

"Thank you. If you will fetch him, it's important."

"As you wish, sir."

Cedric knocked gently on the door of the upstairs lounge. Angus was sitting, scotch in hand, in a comfortable overstuffed armchair looking out to Lake St. Clair, framed nicely by the pruned elm trees on either side of the rear lawn. Fiona sat upright in the Queen Anne, facing the fireplace. Angus had lifted her feet onto a footstool. It was not the most comfortable position, but was much better than the hated wheelchair. She sipped on a glass of Chardonnay. The scars on her face had softened, but further plastic surgery would be necessary. The painkillers were no longer necessary as there was no pain in her lower body, but there was no feeling either.

"I apologize for the interruption, Mr. Drummond, but Mr. Bullard is downstairs. He says it's important."

"Bullard's here? Now what?"

Fiona sipped her wine and spoke. "Yes, now what? We can't have a quiet evening at home without the likes of him barging in."

"I'll be just a minute, me love. I promise."

"Jacky, what brings you to the lake on such a fine evening?"

"I'm sorry to interrupt you so late in the day."

"Can I get you a drink?"

"If I was a drinkin' man, maybe tonight."

"Has your mother died?"

"That news would be a wee bit easier to tell ya, Angus."

"Then what, man? Out with it."

"The communists, the socialists, the Jews, and other agitators, have taken over the final assembly plant. An hour later, they did the same with the engine plant."

"Taken over? What do you mean, taken over?"

"They're inside and they won't get out."

"You're talkin' about the Union, I presume?'

"Yes, sir, the Union. They locked everyone out after the four o'clock shift. No one can get in, and we can't finish the cars."

Angus' brain reeled, the news beyond comprehension. He glared at Bullard and flung his Baccarat glass full of scotch against the wall, shattering it into a hundred pieces. "It's private property, its Republic's property! They can't just take it over! They can't do that!"

Bullard stepped back and took a breath. "They have, Angus, and they're not leaving. My boys heard them call it a sit-down strike. It's bad, I tell ya."

"Are there pickets outside?"

"Aye, with signs sayin', well, you don't need to know."

"How many are inside?"

"We guess well over a thousand, maybe two. More in the engine assembly."

"That many inside my factory?"

"Yes, inside. My boys saw sparks flying out around the doors. I think they're cutting holes in them for guns."

"Sweet Jesus, Mary, and Joseph!" Angus went to the bar and filled another glass with scotch as he looked out to the lake beyond. He took a sizable swig. "It's my property… who the fuck do they think they're foolin' with? This is America… America." His voice tailed off as he began to comprehend the enormity of the situation,

"This is how revolutions start, Angus. They won't stop until they take over your entire company. Then they'll go after all the other companies and take over the government. It's what happened in Russia. Just say the word, my boys will end this in short order."

Angus stood at the bay window, saying nothing. He shook his head.

"No, Jacky, not this time. This is trespassin'. It's against the law, and the law can deal with it. First, I'll call my good friend, Judge Black, to file an injunction against those gowls. If that doesn't work, I'll call the mayor and have him send in the police."

"All that will take time. Let me bash some heads now."

"No! You did that last time, and we looked a fool and worse."

"So, what do you want the Service Department to do?"

"Nothing for now. Let them have their sit-down. Their arses will get sore soon enough."

CHAPTER 55

Day 2 of the Strike

The Union leadership sat around a large table in the lunchroom. A full day and a half had passed since the final assembly and engine plants had been taken over, and there had been no retaliation from Drummond or Bullard. The men were in good spirits. A 12-piece orchestra had been cobbled together; a basketball court had been created with metal wastebaskets as nets, the bottoms cut out. Checkers and chess tournaments took place on work tables, and daily lectures were given on the Union movement. A movie theatre donated current films, and *Modern Times*, a Charlie Chaplin film, was a big hit. The local actor's guild prepared to stage a rehearsal of a new play, *Our Town,* by Thornton Wilder. At night, a few fortunate strikers slept on seats meant for the cars; others on hard tables.

The diversions did nothing to lessen the suffocating heat; the windows opened only a crack to prevent tear gas canisters from flying in.

"Now what, Jankowski?" Max Hoffman scowled at the leader.

"I think it's time to present our demands to management." Jankowski said, ready for Hoffman's diatribe.

"They won't listen to us," Hoffman replied, skeptical as always.

"Then we won't give the plants back. In two days, we've stopped the production of 1,400 cars. Pretty soon, the other factories will come to a standstill. They'll have nowhere to put the car bodies, the axles, or the transmissions."

"I'll volunteer to go meet that man." Max Hoffman was eager to be at the forefront of the movement. He wanted to see Angus Drummond in person, size him up, and state the Union's demands in no uncertain terms.

"No, Max, we need you here. And, let's face it, you have a reputation. Harry and I will go."

"Then go. Let's get on with it."

"We're here to see Mr. Drummond." Rolf Jankowski looked around the large, paneled reception area. It was as impressive as he had imagined. The gatekeeper, Mary Campbell, looked at the two plainly clothed men in front of her. She knew why they were here, and she sympathized with them in her heart.

"And who may I say is calling?"

"The officers of Local 174, United Auto Workers."

"Do you have an appointment?"

"No, we don't. But I think you know that."

"State your business."

"We will, but only to Mr. Drummond."

"I see. Take a seat, please." Campbell got up and went to her boss's door and went in without knocking.

"Angus, the Union is here to talk to you."

"Aye, here, at last, to fleece me of all me money. I'll not be meetin' with them. I don' recognize the Union."

"Angus… "

"If they don't leave, call security."

"Angus… "

"You heard me. They're nothing but a bunch a socialists and communists wantin' me company."

"Angus, they don't want your company. They want a pay raise."

"If I meet them, then I acknowledge that they're legitimate. That they have the right to bargain for the workers."

"I believe they've already been voted that right. They said they were the officers. Meet with them and see what they want."

"Send them away, Mary Campbell."

"Angus, please meet with them."

"I'm beginnin' to wonder whose side you're on."

"The side of Republic Motors, Mr. Drummond." The executive secretary went to the door, shaking her head, a gesture not lost on her boss.

"And get me Judge Black on the phone!"

Campbell returned to her desk and looked up at the strikers.

"I'm sorry. Mr. Drummond is presently occupied."

"You mean he won't meet with us."

"Correct. I'm sorry. I know what you are doing is dangerous. And… " Mary motioned for Jankowski to move closer to her. She whispered. "And I support you one hundred percent."

"Thank you. We'll just leave this here. It's a list of grievances and our proposal for ending the sit-down."

"I'll leave it on his desk after he leaves. Good luck.'

"Thank you, maam."

CHAPTER 56

Day 8 of the Strike

"You wanted to see me, Father?" Olivia Drummond took a seat across from her father without asking permission. Angus sat at his large mahogany desk, a gift from the First Minister of Scotland to recognize the success of their native son. A half-full glass of brown liquid did not escape her gaze. She said nothing.

"How bad is it?"

"How bad is what?"

"Dammit, you know. The losses."

"There's a decent inventory at the dealerships and at the plant. The problem is no one, well, almost no one, is buying your cars. It's a sympathy protest, I think."

"For that riff-raff? Sweet Jesus!"

"The way the papers portray it, it's David against Goliath. And they're not riff-raff. They're Americans, and they want a raise."

"I have been made well aware of that fact, young lady."

"Miss Drummond, please. I'm the Comptroller."

"Another fact I continue to be made aware of. So, we're in good shape, even though this damn sit-in is, what, in its seventh day?"

"Eighth. And I didn't say we're in good shape. Cash reserves are dwindling. We should be selling over a thousand units a day. We're selling maybe a hundred. The strike is headline news in the papers all across the country."

"They're not units, my dear. They're automobiles. Motor cars."

"Mr. Drummond, each automobile sells for $927.00, and every sale, or unit, as we accountants refer to them, covers $560.00 in production cost and $225.00 in profit, the rest goes to the dealers. Instead of bringing in $800,000 daily, we're bringing in less than $80,000. In other words, you're losing $720,000 daily."

Angus smirked. "Well, at least we aren't payin' the strikers."

"Yes, there is that." Olivia was silent, mulling over her next comment, then spoke. "Father, please put an end to the strike. At least meet with them."

Her father ignored the plea.

"What happened to Mr. Drummond?" Angus took a hefty mouthful of scotch. He had heard the figures loud and clear. He rose, went to the window, and looked down on the picket line and the words on the large banner hanging on the factory. It was a personal affront to him:

We SIT down to STAND up for our RIGHTS!

"Mr. Drummond, what happened to the injunction order that was issued by Judge Black?"

"Since he owns over $200,000 in Republic stock, the law says he has to recuse himself. The injunction's invalid."

"You knew he owned the stock. It's why you asked him to issue the injunction in the first place."

"Is that so?'

"Now, what are you going to do?"

"Shut the whole place down. Then I won't have to pay anybody. And I'll call the mayor. He owes me a favor. Several I believe. It's time for the police."

"Daddy, don't do that." Olivia got up and went toward the door.

"This match is not over. The ball's not on the slates yet, Miss Drummond."

Olivia walked out and slammed the door shut. Angus finished his scotch, picked up the phone, and dialed. It rang twice.

"Bullard."

"Jacky, get the men ready. In a few days, I'm going to end this."

"What about the police?"

"They'll be there if you need reinforcements."

"Aye, Anvil, aye."

Tobias Woodson was lost without the daily ritual of going to work. Angus Drummond had shut down all production at Republic partly as revenge, but mostly to conserve cash.

Mrs. Perkins took note of her boarder after the second day.

"Boy, what you doin' in your room all day?"

"Can't work, Mrs. P. Plant be closed."

"Temporarily. Once the strike be over, you'll be back workin' and eatin' like a horse. You in the Union, son?"

"Yessum, I joined coupla' weeks ago."

"Then you best get down there and picket. The more folks show up and show… what's that word? I know… solidarity, the sooner the boss man listens to your demands."

"That's a good idea, Mrs. P."

"Sho' it is. And I gots lots of 'em."

That afternoon, Tobias joined the picket line. He was one of only two Blacks in it.

A few days later, he went downstairs and informed Mrs. P. that he would not be home for a while. He would get into the factory and join the protesters until the strike ended. He, along with 1,500 others, would sit down for their rights.

None of the Southern boys knew what to make of this uppity Black who had climbed through an open window to join their cause. The Union leaders eyed him suspiciously for a day and interrogated the boy to ensure he wasn't a spy. They finally accepted him, and over the passage of days, he became one of the leaders, respected by the White boys from Dixie, too.

CHAPTER 57

Day 11 of the Strike, 4:00 PM

Boredom set in. One could only take so many lectures on the benefits of unionization when, as yet, no concessions had been realized. The factories were still hot, though the windows had been opened as the fear of a tear gas attack had subsided.

The strikers had lost two weeks of pay. Union funds were being spent at a record pace. Walter's Diner was going through enough food for an army, though local farmers, sympathetic to the striker's plight, donated food in great quantity. Every day, 500 pounds of meat, 100 pounds of potatoes, 300 loaves of bread, and 120 quarts of milk were consumed.

Rolf and Harry were engaged in a game of chess in the lunchroom.

"What are you going to do?" Dunfey looked at his opponent.

"Continue to beat you at chess." Jankowski smiled and reached across the board with his bishop and knocked over Dunfey's queen. "Checkmate. Admit it, Harry, I've beat ya' again."

"I meant about the strike, Rolf."

"How much money is in the Union coffers?"

"As of this morning, $15,600. At the rate we're spending, we'll be out of cash in two weeks."

"I think that's all the time we need. By my calculation, Mr. Drummond has lost much more than what it has cost the Union. No one's buying his cars, and several dealerships have been forced to close. Sit-down strikes are happening everywhere. Even the milk delivery boys have unionized. We're having an effect."

"That don't help us. Rolf, the men are restless. They want to go home. And the wives have no money for rent or food. "

"Start making deliveries to the neediest households. Basic goods."

"The strikers inside are already costing us a pretty penny in groceries."

"Send in less; two meals a day from now on."

"Well, it's almost five; the Women's Auxiliary will be along soon with tonight's dinner. I'll let them know and I'll tell Isabel Hoffman to relay the message about food for the families."

"Drummond's got to make a move soon, and then things will get tough."

The lights above flickered, and then went out. Only the fading afternoon light through the high clearstory windows illuminated the space.

"Now, ain't that a coincidence?" Dunfey got up and flicked the light switch off and on. Nothing. He went to the water fountain. Water flowed out, but it quickly turned to a trickle. "What were you sayin' about things getting tough, Rolf?"

One pair of doors in the final assembly plant had not been locked shut and secured with a new car behind it — the rear doors on Conant Street. Across from the Diner, the unobstructed doors were required for the daily food deliveries. Bullard noted this as he watched the meals brought in every day since the strike began. At four-thirty, his men arrived, carrying clubs, tear gas, and a battering ram. Some carried handguns in shoulder holsters. They planned to swarm the plant and evict the occupants by any means of force necessary. The police would follow behind, if needed, with Billy clubs and guns to disperse the picketers and secure the perimeter. The strike would summarily end.

Isabel Hoffman pushed a cart of fried chicken and mashed potatoes across Conant; other carts followed. She stopped in her tracks. The rear doors were surrounded by men from the Service Department. They bludgeoned the few picketers guarding the doors, and others scattered like mice. They were ready to use the battering ram.

Nodding toward an unsecured part of the plant exterior, Isabel responded quickly. "Ladies, take the food to the windows over there. Quickly now. Sally, go back to the Diner and call for help. We need the Emergency Brigade in force right away!"

Jankowski and Dunfey heard the first blows to the back doors as Max Hoffman entered the room.

"What the hell's going on?"

"The battle has begun, Max. Sound the alarm."

Air horns placed strategically throughout the plant were grabbed up by strike leaders. Max grabbed the one in the lunchroom and went outside into the main plant. The shrill sound woke men napping and startled others playing cards or performing their daily tasks. In confusion and disorder, the strikers scrambled to their assigned positions.

Jankowski and Dunfey followed and looked toward the doors, straining to stay shut.

"We've got to get a car behind that door."

"How? The completed autos are on the opposite side of the plant."

"Harry, get a couple of dozen men with tire irons, anything to keep the Service Department out. I'll get a car. Max, get to the windows and shut them!"

Hoffman ran between the maze of conveyor belts, machinery, and racks of car parts to a window facing Conant and looked out. About fifty of Bullard's men were massed; more were coming. Some fought with the picketers who had re-grouped to keep them away from the doors. A tear gas canister crashed through the glass and exploded nearby. His left hand covered his eyes and wiped away tears while reaching out with his feet to find the cylinder. With a quick glance, he looked for a water bucket, but the flood of tears and searing pain in his eyes slammed them shut. He lifted his shirt to form a mask over his mouth and felt the smoking container roll against his foot. His hand felt the metal below his boot; he grabbed the canister and threw it back outside. Another flew through the same open window. Max dove after it and tossed it back. Eyes burning and gagging with noxious fumes, he felt along the wall and closed the windows.

Jankowski had marshaled a couple of men who were now rolling a new Chamberlain toward the rear entrance as the Service Department forces continued to pound the door. Finally, it gave way, and Bullard's men pushed their way inside. Max ran back to the strikers who tried to contain the invasion with their makeshift weaponry. Hubcaps had been fashioned into shields in the machine shop, and they deflected swinging baseball bats. Heavy iron truncheons made of various car parts — struts, ball joints, coiled springs slipped onto arms, tire irons, and sacks full of bolts, swung indiscriminately at the arms and bodies of Bullard's thugs as they tried to get entry into the plant.

Jankowski and a handful of strikers rolled the car toward the doors, forcing the fighting to the side. They pressed hard and the car was against the doors. They pushed harder, forcing it shut. The superior numbers of the strikers soon overcame the invaders entering the building. Those who made it inside were un-ceremoniously neutralized and dragged to the makeshift jail cells that had once been parts lockers.

On Conant Street, Isabel and the women were frantically handing food through windows, a choking haze of tear gas making every movement almost impossible. They continued anyway. She realized it might be the last time the men would be fed for a good while. But she wanted to be elsewhere, with the women of her Emergency Brigade.

"Jane, keep getting food through the windows! I'll be back soon with help."

"You got it, boss."

Isabel turned, headed back to the rear doors and saw it was shut. Good news, but now the Bullard's thugs were taking out their frustration on the demonstrators, thrashing them. The picketers fought back as best they could with the thin wood standards of their signs. Heads were bloodied; screams were constant, along with the dull thud of a truncheon on flesh. But the number of Union picketers was growing; they eagerly joined the fight as they arrived from other locations throughout the besieged complex. Some of Bullard's men re-grouped and picked up the battering ram again. Others began throwing more tear gas into the plant, most quickly doused in buckets of water; some hurled back onto Conant, the fumes gagging anyone in proximity.

Isabel looked in the direction of Hamtramck Drive. There was no sign of the Emergency Brigade. Sirens were now audible in the distance, growing louder. *Where the hell are the women,* she thought. She heard shouting above and glanced up to the roof of the plant. Strikers were pointing toward the sound, yelling, "Police! Lots of 'em!" Reinforcements were now less than a quarter mile away.

The commander of the Emergency Brigade felt sickened by the ominous news. Once the police arrived, the battle would be lost, the plant surely retaken, the strike a miserable failure.

A Union sound truck arrived from up Hamtramck Drive. Ray Reuther was at the microphone, and he urged the picketers to stay strong and fight back. Isabel looked in that direction, and behind it was the Emergency Brigade, four hundred women strong, all wearing red berets or bandanas and red arm bands with "EB" in white letters on their sleeves. The women carried bats, brass knuckles, and bags of nails. They were singing *Solidarity Forever.*

They have taken untold millions that they never toiled to earn. But without our brain and muscle, not a single wheel can turn. We can break their haughty power and gain our freedom when we learn that the Union makes us strong!

Isabel frantically waved her arms and shouted: "Over here, women! Over here!"

But it was too late. The women of the Brigade slowed and then stopped too far from the battle to help, as black and white squad cars and vans filled the street and uniforms streamed out and surrounded Hoffman, the mass of picketers, and the Service Department thugs. Soon, the police were five deep, and they were joined by Bullard's forces that had bashed as many heads as they could. A stalemate ensued as the armed forces waited on further orders from Jack Bullard and Commissioner Reilly.

A gauzy haze of tear gas smoke tinted to orange with the aura of the slowly descending sun. Isabel pushed through the crowd and got through the police cordon on her hands and knees, crawling until she reached the sound truck and Ray Reuther.

"What do we do, Ray?"

"Isabel, it's good to see you. I guess we wait and let them make the next move."

CHAPTER 58

Jacob Hoffman worked his slide rule with the confidence of performing years of accurate calculations, a cup of hot coffee in a china cup on his desk. Although the second-floor engineering department had a premier view of the picket line marching back and forth along Conant Street and Hamtramck Drive, his thoughts were on other matters — the conundrum of designing an automatic transmission. Since he had reported for work at his new job, he had worked twelve hours a day, six days a week. Hannah was annoyed, but her displeasure was assuaged by the first week's paycheck: $127.75. The sum was his entire monthly paycheck on the assembly line.

Deep worry lines crossed Jacob's forehead, and a few wooden pencils showed bite marks of frustration. Jacob was befuddled. He knew there was no way a version of a manual transmission, even an advanced one, its gears attached to two or three connecting rods, fastened to a gear shift lever that moved the gears back and forth, could ever be "automatic." A human hand had to move the gear shift up, over, and back. That was a simple fact.

At University, he had learned of another type of gearing system developed back in the 15th century for astronomical clocks called epicyclical gearing, and crudely improved in 1650 by a French architect, Desargues, as a means of raising the water of the Seine River in a grist mill near Paris. Hoffman had worked to develop such a gear system, known in the

20th century and at Daimler, as a "Planetary Gear System." He made good progress on its further development when the Nazis intervened and stopped his further investigations. Now, in America, he could pursue the system that seemed like an unsolvable puzzle. It was a puzzle, all right, but one that Jacob was determined to solve.

"Hey, Hoffman, get over here. Take a look at what's going on." Tom Nelson knew the rumor that Jacob worked on the assembly line. He was eager to see Hoffman's reaction to the scene outside.

Jacob reluctantly got up and went to the window. He was treated with smug disdain as the only Union member in the department and the only Jew, and was usually ignored by his fellow engineers. He was shocked at the scene below.

"My God, there's smoke. Bullard's Service Department thugs and the police are attacking the picketers and trying to break into the factory."

"It's Mr. Drummond's factory, not those strikers, Hebe boy. It's about time Jack Bullard's men started bashin' some heads. They're just a bunch of commie's and Jews."

"No, Tom, they're a bunch of hard-working men and women who make the cars you design. If it wasn't for them, your designs, as mediocre as they are, would be just a set of blueprints." Jacob returned to his desk, and Tom followed, ready to pick a fight.

"Up yours, Hoffman. What's their beef anyway? They make a good living down in the plant."

Jacob turned and faced Nelson. "You ever worked in the plant, Nelson"?

"Hell, no!"

"Then you have no idea what you're talking about."

Jacob reached into his back pocket for his wallet and removed his Union membership card. He held it out. "I believe I do, Tom. Union forever, my friend."

Nelson shook his head, turned to go, and then looked down at Jacob's desk, the papers full of formulas and numbers and a unique model of a group of gears interconnected, which he had never seen before.

"What the hell is all this?" waving his hand over Jacob's desk.

"It's the future of the automobile, Nelson, the future of the automobile." Jacob resumed his calculations and picked up the cup of coffee, now cold.

Hoffman's stomach rumbled; he was hungry. He had skipped lunch, fully engrossed in the task before him. He went down the rear stairs to the first-floor cafeteria just as it was about to close and bought a turkey sandwich, potato chips, several chocolate chip cookies, and a Coke. He had to solve the puzzle. Maybe then the strike could end. He wasn't sure how the two were connected, but he felt the two might be intertwined.

He worked into the night. The machine shop had built two prototypes of planetary gears. Unlike the conventional gear shift of individual ribbed wheels, these gears consisted of three circular outside "planets" in a carrier that revolved around a larger central "sun" gear. All four were held in place by an outside "ring" gear. They all worked along one single rod, or shaft, from the engine. In this arrangement, multiple combinations of gear-shifting patterns were possible.

As Jacob fiddled with the arrangement of gears on one unit, the greased assembly slipped from his hands and fell directly onto the other planetary gear assembly lying on his desk. They almost meshed together.

Jacob looked down in wonder. *Maybe that's it...*

As he worked on the two mockups together, he found that the integrated gears connected as one assembly would now produce many variations. But he only needed four forward movements, a reverse gear, and one other in a fixed position that he called "Park." Six total. If calibrated in the correct gear ratios, the connected planetary gears together would make that job easy.

Now, Jacob needed to figure out how the assembly could shift gears without the driver having to do anything.

Hoffman rubbed his temples, then his eyes. He got up, and went to the windows and looked down onto Conant Street. The police were gathered in force, ready to storm the final assembly building.

"Oh no, dear God. No."

CHAPTER 59

Day 11 of the Strike, 6:30 PM

The green Zodiac convertible coupe pulled up to the array of parked police cars and a large command truck. Jack Bullard got out and quickly entered the bulky unmarked conveyance. Commissioner Conan Reilly looked up from the Republic Motors Hamtramck complex map. His eyes narrowed, and a slight scowl betrayed his feelings. He didn't like Jack Bullard and his Service Department. To him, they were just a vigilante, rogue police force, although he had to admit, he had no interest in maintaining order at a company that employed over 20,000 workers.

"Bullard, what are you doing here?"

"The Service Department is taking back the company's property. Maybe I should be askin' you the same."

"Your boss requested we take back his plant, since it appears you've been unsuccessful in that task."

"Temporary setback. We'll be prevailin' eventually."

"Looks like you could use some help right now."

"Always appreciate any support from Detroit's finest, Commissioner."

"Then let's formulate a plan. Whisky?"

"Just coffee."

Max, Rolf, Harry, and other strike committee members finished their fried chicken and washed it down with milk.

"What are we going to do without water?"

"There may not be water to drink, but there's plenty of water in the fire hoses. I turned one on, and there's sufficient pressure. It must be on a different system."

"Of course. I didn't think of that. Detroit has a separate system of water lines for fighting fires. We probably can't drink it, but we can wash in it."

"And we can aim it at the police."

"Tommy, take a couple of guys and bring some hoses from the other side of the plant over here, and position 'em by the rear doors."

"How many?"

"I think two should do it."

'Think they'll attack again?"

"You can bet on it. If they can't retake the plant, Drummond has to deal with us, which is something he doesn't want to do. So we have to win this battle."

"We still have our home-made ammunition and the fire hoses. I like our chances."

Day 11 of the Strike, 9:00 PM

Jankowski manned the rear door with a hundred strikers ready for battle. Another hundred waited in reserve. They had all been hand-picked, the biggest and toughest of the lot. Tobias Woodson, a visible figure because of his size and his race, kneeled. Scared stiff, he clutched a steel pipe. He spoke to another striker, huddled next to him.

"I never thought being in the Union be so dangerous."

"Neither did I."

Harry Dunfey oversaw the perimeter with its filled water buckets and stacked wet rags. The windows were shut, and the hot evening and immobile fans made the plant a hothouse. Minimal lighting was provided by kerosene lanterns aided by the police floodlights out in the street; the combination cast eerie shadows against the high concrete walls and conveyor lines inside the building. A striker was posted every ten feet along the exterior walls, buckets of bolts nearby.

Max Hoffman looked down from the roof at a blue army amassed against the strikers. Under his command were over two hundred men along the wall, extending to Hamtramck Drive. Pails full of makeshift ammunition and stacks of soda and milk bottles were ready. He stared at the area in front of the critical doors. There was no battering ram, but a couple of police in heavy vests attached something to the doors. He froze as he realized what they were doing and ran for the stairs to warn Rolf.

The rear doors were now heavily fortified by a shiny black four-door Chamberlain and parts wagons stacked two high. Rolf Jankowski turned away to bend over and tie the laces of his boots. It was the last thing he remembered.

A loud explosion shook the factory. The blast threw Jankowski ten feet, and shrapnel sprayed his back. He landed unconscious on his stomach, and the back of his blue shirt blossomed red. The men who kept watch on the doors weren't as lucky. The blast blew them back into a tangle of bodies and blood. Those who could, rose like drunkards swaying and feeling their bodies for injury. Gashes, large and small, bled freely from their heads, stained T-shirts, sweaty arms, and soiled hands.

As the smoke cleared, a mob of suits and blue uniforms scurried over the barricade like ants from a disturbed hill. The going was treacherous, and the invaders fell over one another, the crush of reinforcements pushed behind them, knocking over those in front like dominoes. The strikers quickly dispatched the few that got through, furious at the callow use of a bomb. But many others were filling the breech.

Moaning in and out of consciousness, Jankowski was carried back to the lunchroom. Next in seniority at the back doors, Lazlo Stein took over and issued his first order.

"Soak 'em, boys. Give 'em a bath!"

A stream of water slammed into the three dozen or so goons and police who stood on top of the Chamberlain and on the carts. The high pressure knocked them off their feet. Those behind began to retreat.

Max looked down on the melee of confusion. Police and Service Department personnel were backing up from the entry while those not engaged in the effort to storm the plant fought with the picketers along the perimeter of the building. The Union picketers, warned by the sound truck, quickly ran away from the building when they heard the command.

"Let 'em have it, boys! Bombs away!"

The men on the roof let fly a barrage of bolts, bottles, and car door hinges onto the phalanx of police and thugs. It reminded Rolf of medieval warriors pouring vats of hot oil on invaders trying to storm a castle. Police and goons screamed and fell. Others covered their heads as they ran past those less fortunate, their heads cracked open, and faces gashed apart by the lethal projectiles. Inside the plant, the strikers had covered tear gas containers with heavy cloths to stanch the spread of the toxic fumes. Despite the effort, the men coughed violently, half-blind, and some vomited. Dunfey gave the word.

"Send the poison back to 'em, men!"

Windows all along the street smashed as the canisters flew out of the plant, and their noxious stench and smoke filled the air. At that moment, the wind shifted, and the fumes drifted toward the police cordon. The strategic retreat turned into a rout. The police and the now depleted ranks of the Service Department took refuge behind the line of police cars.

From the Union sound car, Ray Reuther, who had been directing the resistance outside the factory and delivering intelligence to those inside, shouted into the microphone: "They're retreating! Union forever!"

In the police command truck, Jack Bullard glared at Conan Reilly.

"That bomb pissed them off a wee bit don' ya think, Commissioner?"

"It got us in, didn't it?"

"And wet. I got to admit it; those boys have grown some brass balls since the overpass. Any more bright ideas?"

"We'll re-group, and this time, we'll have guns drawn. That'll send the proper message."

"You hope."

At nine o'clock, Jacob Hoffman heard the explosion and ran to the window as a large plume of smoke rose from the rear doors. He feared for his uncle, Max, Isabel, and his friend, Lazlo. How could a strike turn into a bloody war?

Back to his desk, he said a silent prayer: *Haskiveninu Adoni Eloheinu. I pray, Holy One, for peace.*

Deep into calculations that he believed could finally solve the enigma of an automatic transmission, dusk gave way to a moonless night illuminated by floodlights, lampposts, small fires, sirens, and police car headlights aimed at the rear door. Stooped, exhausted, and afraid, he packed his valise with his research and the planetary gear mockups. Perhaps after a beer and dinner, he'd spread his work on the dining room table and work more formulas. He went home along Conant, in front of the final assembly plant, to witness the war between management and workers more closely. His memory was flooded with images of Nazi Germany and the SA, the Sturmabteilung or Brown Shirts, Hitler's private army of thugs. The routine roundups by the SA, who broke up socialist and communist rallies with truncheons, fists, and polished jack-boots unleashed on Christians and Jews alike, would never leave the reservoir of his mind.

Picketers on the ground moaned, heads and bodies were bloodied. The army of police and goons re-grouped 50 yards from the rear doors, protected by a barrier of squad cars. Domed lights swathed the adjacent buildings in a wash of sinister red light, while a voice from a loudspeaker rumbled into the air, but the message shrieked inaudibly. Smoke still hovered over the rear entrance to the plant, wafting up to strikers poised on the roof, chanting, "Union forever, Union forever!"

Jacob stepped on a picket sign, his heart filled with admiration for these determined warriors. He couldn't help but smile at the optimistic words on the placard:

Be Wise... Organize!

Briefcase in hand, he walked toward the picketers. He wanted to join them, congratulate them, and hug them. He could tell that the assembly building was breached but still belonged to the Union. The strike would go on. Perhaps he would see Lazlo or Max. As he got closer, in the no-man's land that had opened between the Union supporters and the police, he spotted the sound car and Isabel. She spoke to its occupant, the voice that echoed over Conant Street.

He quickened his pace toward her and glanced down at his briefcase. It contained critical calculations, drawings, the important mockup, and his notes. The consequences would be disastrous if the satchel got into the wrong hands. He pondered for a moment and realized that his work was not only quite valuable to himself and certainly to Republic Motors but perhaps to the workers huddled in the factory in front of him.

You're not an assembly-line worker anymore, Jacob. You're an engineer. This is not your fight. But perhaps what you're doing can help.

Jacob Hoffman turned back down Conant Street, past the command truck, empty tear gas canisters, and the picket signs lying on the ground. He reached down and retrieved one he had stepped on, tucked it under his arm, and walked home. *Be wise, indeed...*

"Come to bed, husband. It is midnight." Hannah's usually deferential tone had an edge to it. Her husband was obsessed with this crazy transmission design; lately, he had no time for Tomasz or her. And the strike was sure to end in defeat, and Max, Isabel, and the two girls she had grown so fond of, would be out in the street, or perhaps living with them, resentful of their nephew's new-found success and prosperity.

Jacob entered the small bedroom. Tomasz was sound asleep, not wakened by his mother's call.

"Soon, I almost have it solved."

"So Drummond can make more millions selling his new car model with the fancy transmission?"

"Shhhh… you'll wake the boy. Go to sleep."

Three AM. Jacob had made a pot of coffee, now almost gone. His head pounded, but the proper gear ratios and the changing of the various planetary gears, with the number of teeth on the gears adjusted, and fixed in size and relationship to one another, was complete. The six planetary gears performed in unison and provided first, second, third, plus a fourth — an overdrive gear, reverse, and the park position. Now, he only had to figure out where and how to provide enough power to change the gears.

He vaguely remembered reading a technical journal about a Canadian inventor, Alfred Munro, who, in 1923, had patented an automatic transmission design with interlocking gears that changed with the force of compressed air. Its problem was it didn't provide enough air power to cause the gears to shift. Hoffman excelled in hydraulics class at the technical university and knew water or any liquid for that matter, with enough pressure applied, created a very powerful force. Perhaps some form of lubricant, oil, or a heavy viscous fluid fed into the gearbox would do the trick. But how could the liquid get to it and change the gears?

Jacob was exhausted. He would need help on this next piece of the puzzle. And the only person he knew who was smart enough to help solve it was Tom Nelson.

CHAPTER 60

Day 11 of the Strike, 10:30 PM

Jimmy O'Donnell had been a police officer for exactly two months. Mostly, he wrote out parking tickets. The highlight of his young career had been a drunk and disorderly arrest of a rowdy baseball fan after the second-place Tigers had lost to the last-place St. Louis Browns.

Now he was in a war, a war with his fellow citizens. He had two cousins who worked for Republic Motors. His daddy worked there briefly in the 1920's. But on orders from his sergeant, he drew his service revolver and moved slowly toward the final assembly plant. He looked up to the roof, strikers ready with their arsenal of makeshift weaponry. Jimmy had been standing next to another officer when the man's nose was ripped in two by the edge of a car door hinge. He trembled in fear.

"All right, boys, on the double quick. Let's get into that plant!"

As the police crossed no-man's land, the strikers hurled rocks and bottles from the open first-floor windows. Then, a cascade of metal rained down from above. A coiled spring hit Jimmy's arm. His gun discharged. He panicked, looked up to the roof, and kept firing. This was all the incentive the rest of the police force required, furious at the bloodshed that had already been inflicted on Detroit's finest. A barrage of gunfire rang out; bullets hit strikers and picketers, glass windows disintegrated. There was no let-up. The police kept firing, some at point-blank range, as they moved closer to the opening in the building. As bodies dropped before them, they continued to push forward, determined to finally occupy the plant.

Isabel witnessed all this from the sound truck. Incensed, she grabbed the microphone from Reuther and climbed onto the car's hood.

"Cowards! Cowards! Shooting unarmed, defenseless men!"

She looked back at the Women's Brigade and waved them forward.

"Women of Detroit! This is your fight now. Defend your job, your husband's job, and your children's future!"

Though dressed and armed for battle, the women of the Brigade were reluctant to get between the police and the picketers and certainly not into the withering line of fire.

Isabel saw that the women weren't moving. She turned and addressed them again.

"Women of the Brigade, break through the police lines now, and stand beside your husbands, brothers, uncles, and sweethearts!"

No one moved. Then through the smoke and haze, Isabel saw a woman walk forward. A policeman grabbed her by the arm. She turned, kicked him in the groin, and kept walking toward the plant. Slowly, one woman and then another, and then more women followed. All four hundred marched into no man's land. They began to sing *Hold the Fort*. As they reached the open area between the police and the picketers, the Brigade turned their backs to the police and faced the plant, daring the men in blue to shoot them in the back.

This was a war but not one the police were going to fight against women, armed or not. The firing stopped. Shaking their heads, guns lowered, the police retreated behind the line of black and whites and slowly began to leave. The strikers in the plant and on the roof cheered. Atop the loudspeaker truck, Isabel smiled, and just as the batteries died, she cried one more time into the microphone.

"Union forever! Union forever!"

Jack Bullard watched as defeat spread over Conant.

"Fucking bitch!"

He reached under his suit coat, pulled out his .38 magnum, and aimed. That bloody night's last shot hit Isabel Hoffman just above the heart. She dropped like a rock, falling off the car hard onto the street. From the roof, he heard a scream, "Isabel!"

Bullard turned and headed for his car.

CHAPTER 61

Day 12 of the Strike, Early AM

Jacob had gone to bed at four, and Hannah woke him at six to make him breakfast, their daily ritual of eggs, bagels, and talk. As the strike continued with no end in sight, Rachel and Ana had moved in with Jacob and Hannah, who was now the de facto head of both houses, washing clothes, cooking, cleaning, and getting all three children ready for school with lunches and checked homework. Max was holed up in the factory, and Isabel was a full-time general in the Women's Brigade. She came home to their flat only to bathe and grab a bite to eat.

With two hours of sleep, Jacob showered, dressed, kissed his annoyed wife, and headed to the engineering offices of Republic Motors, his briefcase heavy with a potential breakthrough design for an automatic transmission. He was not surprised that Isabel hadn't come home from the previous night's battles; he imagined her tending to the wounded or helping with breakfast at Walter's Diner. Through her hard exterior and sometimes icy demeanor, Jacob had grown to respect his sister-in-law for her tenacity and resolve. She was indeed a force of nature.

"Good day, Tom."

"Jacob." Nelson's tone was frosty.

"Look, I want to apologize."

"For what?"

"My comments yesterday. You're a good man, a smart engineer. Let me buy you lunch today."

"All right. I never turn down a free meal."

The men sat down at a corner table in the cafeteria reserved for middle and upper management. Jacob's tray contained a hearty meal of meat loaf, mashed potatoes and gravy, and peas. He picked his favorite drink, Coca-Cola, and three chocolate chip cookies, which he believed were the best on earth. Tom Nelson chose the chicken pot pie, a salad, and a slice of blueberry pie.

"So I don't get it. You're an engineer, but you worked on the assembly line?"

"Yes, for four months."

"Why?"

"A few reasons, as I have been told. I'm a foreigner, I'm Jewish, and my uncle is inside the final assembly building right now as one of the Union leaders."

"Damn."

"Yes, damn."

"Was it hard?" Tom's chair legs squeaked against the floor as he moved closer to Jacob. His eyes betrayed his disbelief with a squint.

"Harder than anything you can imagine. Every day, I installed 500 to 600 hundred tires. No bathroom breaks. You couldn't afford to eat at the commissary. You only had thirty minutes if you did; no, twenty because of the walk there and back. But you were already too tired to go there. The plant is hot, the air stinks with metal and grease, and the smell of unwashed, sweating bodies. But I survived."

"How much did you make, if you don't mind me asking?"

"Not at all, $7.50 a day."

"A day? Shit, I make $25 a day."

Jacob smiled; he now made $5.00 more than Nelson but said nothing.

"What happened? How'd you get into the engineering department?"

"In Germany, before the Nazis invited me to leave, I was an assistant director at Daimler-Benz, in charge of transmission design. When Mr. Drummond heard of this, I got, how do you say, a promotion. He wants a design for an automatic transmission, and soon."

"It can't be done. The guys and I have been trying to crack that nut for months."

"Hard nut to crack. I think I have the right nutcracker, but I need your help. What do you know about hydraulics?"

"A good bit. My favorite class in college. I designed a new radiator for the Chamberlain."

"What college? I attended Technical University in Berlin."

"The University of Detroit, of course. It's the best engineering school in the country for mechanical engineering. Every car company in Detroit hires us as soon as we graduate. And we've got a good football team, too."

"Good. I need your knowledge on the subject for the design I'm working on."

"Look, I'm sorry about my comment yesterday about your people… "

"No need to apologize. My people are used to it. Just help me crack the nut."

"Sure thing, Jacob. I'm all in."

The two engineers spent the remainder of their lunch hour reviewing Jacob's notes and theories. For the most part, Nelson nodded his head in agreement.

"Tom, we have to get this done right away. There's no time to waste."

"All right, Jacob."

The secretary for the engineering department hurried into the cafeteria, and looked around. She saw Jacob and went to his table.

"Mr. Hoffman, I'm sorry, but I have some bad news."

"Bad news? What?"

"Your sister-in-law, Isabel Hoffman, was shot last night."

"Shot?"

"She's in critical condition at Detroit Receiving Hospital. Your wife called. She's there now and wants you to come."

CHAPTER 62

Day 13 of the Strike

"The governor will see you now."

"I thank you."

Angus Drummond had never been to Lansing, only Ann Arbor, where Olivia had matriculated at the University of Michigan. He looked around the small reception area; he imagined a larger welcoming room for the high office of the governor. The state capitol building, completed in 1879, was impressive overall, although beginning to show signs of age. Could the U.S. Capitol in Washington, D.C. be any grander than this building? Then it occurred to him; he had never been there, or for that matter, to any place in the United States other than New York City, Bethlehem, Pennsylvania, and Detroit.

Fiona and I will travel when this Union business is finished, he thought as he was ushered into Frank Murphy's ceremonial office. Hat in hand, he had come to ask for help.

"Angus, come in. Please sit down. I haven't seen you since I was the mayor of Detroit." Murphy got up from his desk, walked around, and shook hands. He was tall, with an angular face, bushy eyebrows and receding hairline. His expression was neutral, despite his anger about the event's two days before.

"Guv'nor, I should have thrown me hat into this room before enterin'."

"Oh, and why is that?"

"It's a mess in Hamtramck, for sure."

"That it is. Let's see, I have the report right here. Sixteen of the strikers were wounded, mostly with bullets, and eleven police hurt, some severely. Several were hit by two-pound door hinges. Very ingenious, I must say."

"I'm sorry for all the trouble, but the police were provoked."

"And your Service Department is completely innocent?"

"They were only trying to evict the trespassers from my factory."

"How's the woman that was shot exercising her right of free speech?"

"Oh, you heard about that?"

"I did. Rumor has it your head of security, what's his name, ah, here it is, Bullard, targeted her."

"There's no proof a' that. Anyway, she's in intensive care. It's serious; she may not make it. Frank... I'm so sorr... "

"Angus, do you know who just called me about this whole tragic business? The President."

"Mr. Roosevelt."

"Yes, that president, who's my dear friend. He told me to restore order and convince you to negotiate with the Union."

"I came here for the same reason, Guv'nor. You need to uphold the law and call in the National Guard. Restore order is what you need to do."

"And you'll sit down with the UAW?"

"You know I can't do that."

"Angus, those workers are my supporters."

"They're agitators, socialists, and communists, is what they are."

"A few maybe, the others are Democrats, and they voted for me. I helped FDR become the first Democrat in decades to win the state of Michigan, and he wants you to recognize the Union and get those people back to work."

"Vice President Garner doesn't see it that way. I talked to him meself just the other day."

"The vice president doesn't count for shit, Angus, and you know it. All right. I'll send in the National Guard to restore order. The next move is up to you."

Blackburn drove the four-door black Zodiac down the two-lane macadam road that connected Lansing with Detroit.

Angus Drummond pondered his meeting with Governor Frank Murphy while sitting in the rich, leather-upholstered back seat replete with polished walnut trim.

The President of the United States wants me to negotiate with the UAW and get the strikers back to work. Negotiate hell! I voted for the man in '32, after being a staunch Republican from the day I became a citizen of this country. Now he wants me to talk to a bunch a' communists. Maybe that Catholic priest, Coughlin, is right about Roosevelt. He's a socialist and can't be trusted.

Angus reached for a crystal glass in the console behind his driver, removed the cover of a small ice bucket and added several cubes to the glass. He poured an inch of scotch, swirled the ice with his finger, and took a drink. His attention turned to the rural countryside outside the window. White clapboard farmhouses and red barns in disrepair were interspersed with fields of alfalfa, corn, and cherry and apple orchards. He passed another farm with a Toiler 75 pickup truck parked on the gravel drive beside a tractor. Another property featured a dusty, old 1917 Drummond, and he smiled. *Still running my friend; good for you.*

They passed through small towns bustling with activity — Webberville, Parkers Corner, and Brighton. At noontime, the streets were full of women as they shopped for groceries or bolts of cloth to make work shirts and simple dresses for Sunday church. Men stopped at grain stores for feed and seed. On the outskirts of the town, cows and pigs were being auctioned in a small arena. He took another drink and realized he had seen so little of his home state. It was beautiful in its simplicity. He thought back to the meeting.

Well, Angus, you're in some kinda predicament. The president's against you; the guv'nor's against you. The Service Department and the Detroit police can't get rid a' the rats who've overrun the plant. Let's hope the National Guard will roust them, and this strike will end. But I'll not meet with those chancers at the UAW. Never...

CHAPTER 63

Day 15 of the Strike - Night

The quiet of the late night was broken by the ominous sound of diesel engines coming down East Grand Boulevard. Olive-green trucks carrying soldiers and pulling 37-inch howitzers and machine guns mounted on caissons chugged down the thoroughfare. Those awakened by the racket witnessed a small army pass by their front doors. Over fifty trucks carrying 1,200 National Guardsmen with weapons, ammunition, tents, food rations, and a myriad of army supplies headed for the Republic Motors Hamtramck factories. In short order, the complex would be surrounded. Later in the morning, another 2,500 soldiers would arrive.

Sleeping picketers woke at the army's arrival and informed the strikers inside. Surely, this meant the end of the standoff. It was one thing to hurl milk bottles at the police but quite another to take on the United States Army with their cannons and machine guns.

A handful of the men in the plant, including Harry and Lazlo, came outside to size up the new threat firsthand. Young men in khaki uniforms and helmets, left over from the Great War, jumped out of the trucks. The cannons and machine guns were unhitched. Sergeants and lieutenants barked commands. The troops dispersed as the soldiers lined up five deep in precision formation. Gun batteries of six men wheeled the howitzers and machine guns into position. It was only a matter of time before the National Guard would occupy the plant.

"Well, Lazlo, it's been nice knowin' ya. Maybe I can get a job pickin' up garbage 'cause I won't be workin' for Republic Motors come the mornin'."

"Come on, Harry, we can beat these fellas. Look, I got a bag of washers in my hand." He laughed and, as they turned to go back into the factory, was dumbstruck by what he saw.

Day 16 of the Strike – Day

Angus Drummond opened the door to his office in a fury.

"Miss Campbell, get me the goddamn guv'nor on the phone! Now!" He stormed back into his office and slammed the cherry-wood door. The upper panel with his name affixed in gold letters on the milky glass shattered; the broken shards fell to the floor in a hundred pieces. Drummond ignored the minor disaster, reached for the scotch decanter on the sideboard, and capped the bottle when he realized it was only nine o'clock in the morning. He stormed back to the closed door and yelled through the opening. "And get me some coffee!"

"What the hell are ya' doin', guv'nor?"

"And good morning to you, Mr. Drummond. I'm not sure I understand?"

"The National Guard. They've surrounded my factories."

"Wonderful. Then order has been restored."

"They're pointing their bloody rifles and cannons in the opposite direction away from the plant, and they're sitting on their arses doing nuthin'!"

"Exactly. Order has been restored."

""'You're supposed to kick out the chancers and snakes occupyin' me property. You're supposed to enforce the law! What about the new court order issued by Judge Gadola forbiddin' picketing at the plant? And this particular magistrate doesn't own any Republic stock."

"I'm considering it, Angus, but sometimes the law is wrong. Did you know my grandfather was hung by the English because he fought for Irish independence? And my daddy was imprisoned by the British simply for wanting a little freedom and a better life? The way I see it, Angus, your strikers want the same thing that my kinfolk did."

"They're goin' about it all wrong. They can strike but not take over me property. I know the Wagner Act like the back of me hand."

"Don't bullshit me, Angus. If they were just pickets, you'd hire scabs in a heartbeat. The men inside your plant are risking everything, and I've decided to protect them and their right to strike for the time being."

"How ya doing that?"

"The National Guard, for starters; no one will mess with them. And I've signed an executive order requiring you to turn on the plant's electricity and water. And you'll allow food deliveries twice a day."

"You can't do that, guv'nor."

"I signed the orders this morning. So don't play games with me, Angus. It's time to negotiate with the UAW."

"I'll not meet with that gaggle a' agitators."

"Fine, I'm not going to act on the injunction then. As far as I'm concerned, the picketers can stay forever."

The governor hung up.

Drummond slumped back in his chair, almost defeated.

CHAPTER 64

Day 17 of the Strike

Isabel Hoffman lay unconscious in intensive care, her breathing shallow, but steady. Max Hoffman had left his fellow strikers to be at her bedside and hold her limp hand; there was no response to his words or his touch. He seethed with a deep rage at the wanton act of violence against his wife. He had seen her drop the microphone in her hands and fall from the hood of the car. He followed what seemed to be the trajectory of the shot, toward the police cars and the command center vehicle. He saw Jack Bullard pat his jacket pocket and get into in his Zodiac convertible, and drive away. Max was certain the man had shot his wife.

Jacob and Hannah sat by the window in uncomfortable upright chairs. Hannah looked down at her aunt-in-law, her torso bandaged from her shoulder to her waist. With a stethoscope she listened to the heartbeat.

"Isabel's heartbeat is strong. That's a good sign," Her words were meant to encourage hope, but for Max there was little; he only heard her struggles for breath and saw the face he knew so well, a ghostly pallor of white.

Jacob's mind re-lived the strike's violence. He looked compassionately at Isabel, and gently touched her shoulder. A bottle of saline dripped fluids into her body. There was nothing more any of the room's occupants could do but wait. He felt helpless. Would she die for nothing? Surely not.

His mind went back to his own dilemma. A hundred theories invaded his thoughts on ways to solve the enigma of shifting gears without human intervention. Then he nodded and smiled slightly. "I have to get back to my office."

Max glared at his nephew. "Your office? Fuck your office. You care more about your damn job than your family?"

"Husband, you cannot go. You must stay here." Hannah's voice rose in anger.

"I'm sorry; I'll explain later. Trust me; what I'm doing will help Isabel. It will help all of us." Jacob left the room, the smile still pasted on his face.

Chapter 65

Day 22 of the Strike

Max, Rolf, and Harry sat in the plant lunchroom finishing a dinner of vegetable soup with a slice of cornbread.

"How's Isabel?"

"She's out of intensive care. Her first question was how are we holding up here in the factory?"

"She's a pistol. So, Harry, just how are we holding up?"

"The union coffers are about empty; the men sorely want to go home; we're not headline news anymore, and that judge levied a $15,000,000 fine against the Union. Other than that, things are just peachy."

"I'm sure that Drummond's hurtin' just as bad." Max's voice contained no emotion other than resignation.

"How are we going to break this stalemate? I'm tired of soup for dinner, cold showers, and missing my wife and kids. At the beginning, we had fried chicken and all the fixin's." Harry looked at his two close friends.

"I don't know, but we've got to hang on. We can't quit now after twenty-two days." Rolf rubbed his back against the chair; it was still a landscape of scabs and stitches that itched like red ant bites.

Jacob Hoffman, Tom Nelson, and two other engineers, Stanislaus, an émigré from Poland, and Edward, a local Detroit boy, looked over drawings, calculations, and additional mockups built by the department's machine shop.

"We've been working day and night, and we aren't close to a workable solution." Tom's frustration was palatable.

"We're going in the right direction, Tommy. We're close; don't be so pessimistic. I've come up with a way to distribute the hydraulic fluid to the individual gears. Individual tubes won't work; they will become brittle if they don't disconnect from the transmission first. I'm designing a metal casing, a diaphragm with separate channels that send the fluid directly to each of the gear bands that Stanislaus designed."

"A diaphragm?"

"Yes, Tom. They have mazes here in America, right?"

"Like corn field mazes?"

"Yes. In Berlin, there was a maze of tall hedges at the Tiergarten Park. I loved getting lost in it as a kid."

"What's your point?"

"I'm trying to design a diaphragm that surrounds the epicyclical gears with individual paths to the bands. It would be just like a maze, with multiple routes for the hydraulic fluid to get to specific gears and it would be powered by a pump. The fluid would go into the diaphragm at high pressure into the bands, causing them to rotate and change the gears as necessary, from stop to top speed. Gravity would send the fluid to a basin below the assembly and the pump would recirculate it."

"It's certainly worth a shot. But we need to get the fluid coupling assembly perfected so the excessive torque from the engine can be controlled." Nelson ran over the impediments in his head. Its complexity seemed so impossible to build.

Edward looked up from his calculations. "I've got the shop doing a mockup of a torque converter now. I'm close, Jacob. Maybe by tomorrow."

Jacob nodded. "Good, then I think it is time I report to Mr. Drummond on our progress. Put everything that's on the table into a box. He'll want to see all of it. "

"My dear guv'nor, will you enforce the injunction or not?" Angus Drummond's voice was full of frustration and anger, but it sounded like a plea for help.

"Angus, as governor, it is my duty to enforce the law, but in this case, I will ignore it. The men have every right to picket as established in the Wagner Act which as Federal law trumps the opinion of one local appellate judge."

"But they're not picketin'. They're a bunch of trespassers loiterin' in my plant. I can't produce any automobiles. In another month, I'll be bankrupt!" Drummond looked over to his sideboard, then his watch. It was only two o'clock. He took a drink of iced tea.

"Then Angus, I suggest you end the strike. Let me be the go-between if you don't want to meet face to face. I'm coming to Detroit tomorrow to meet with John L. Lewis of the CIO and Walter Reuther. I'll get their demands, and then I'll pay you a visit."

"I'll not be available."

"Yes, you will."

"No I won't."

"Then good day, Angus." Governor Murphy hung up.

Drummond turned from his desk and looked out to his massive complex of buildings, smokestacks absent their usual billowing white smoke. He stood up and watched the picketers walking back and forth and the National Guard beyond, doing nothing to stop the quiet procession. Powerless because of the governor's decision, he rubbed his throbbing temples and swiped the telephone from the desktop. It slammed onto the floor.

"To hell with the tea, I need a fuckin' drink."

Drummond retrieved the sturdy phone off of the floor, swiveled his chair back under the desk, and buzzed Mary Campbell.

"Mary, tell Ms. Drummond I'd like to see her."

"As a matter of fact, Angus, she's been waiting to see you along with Wallace, for ten minutes. I'll send them in straightaway."

The office door, its glass panel replaced, opened, and Olivia, dressed in a gray pinstripe suit, white blouse, and a small gold cross on a gold chain around the neck, entered with a sheath of manila folders. Behind her, Wallace followed in a grease-stained set of overalls over a somewhat clean white shirt.

"Och aye, if it ain't me two strong-headed children! To what do I owe the pleasure?"

"Father, I'm here… we're here to ask you to end the strike."

Angus shook his head. "I should have known."

"We're almost broke. Our reserve funds are about gone. You've sold less than 2,000 units… "

"They're motor cars."

"Two thousand automobiles when we should have sold 20,000. There's no inventory left, and several dealerships have closed. I have the figures right here." She dropped a folder onto the desk.

"And if I give those communist bastards a raise, it'll cost me at least ten million! I've done the sums, too, Miss Drummond."

"Father, it won't be that much. But if the strike continues, I won't come to your rescue. I haven't seventeen million dollars in Swiss gold bars to save you."

"Who says I need savin'?"

Wallace chimed in. "Dad, the bad publicity is killing us."

Drummond looked at his son in his dirty overalls. "Well, at least you're finally learnin' about what's under the hood."

"Yeah, it's an engine, and it's pretty swell, too," he said sarcastically.

"Have ya been stayin' out of the clubs?"

"Yes, sir. Been really busy learning about 'what's under the bonnet'. Dad, please end the strike and begin production of the Epoch, and we'll sell the hell out of that new model."

The intercom buzzed. "Mr. Drummond, I'm sorry to interrupt, but Jacob Hoffman is here to see you. He says it's important."

"Who's that?"

"The nice young engineer you recently hired. You know, to work on transmissions."

"Och, aye, send him in!" Drummond looked up at his two offspring. "I'll keep your concerns in mind, children. Now I've got to tend to business."

As the two Drummond children walked to the door, Olivia turned. "Father, Momma wants the strike to be over, too." In the reception area, she took note of Jacob Hoffman as he entered Drummond's sanctuary. *Handsome man.*

CHAPTER 66

"Young Mr. Hoffman, it's Jacob, yes?" Drummond held up the decanter of scotch and offered it to his employee.

He shook his head. "No, thank you; I'm fine. And yes, sir, it is Jacob." Hoffman's voice quivered in the presence of the titan of industry.

"How's the progress on the automatic transmission, lad?"

"Mr. Drummond, I've come here to resign."

"What? Ya can't quit. I knew the design of an automatic transmission would be tough — as tough as anything, but ya can't just up and leave without finishin' the task."

"It is finished, sir, well, almost finished."

"Good, then a promotion and a raise are in order. So, you see, no reason to leave; you've a bright future here at Republic." Drummond poured himself a shot of scotch, neat.

"No, I'm quitting if you don't immediately end the strike. If you don't, I'll take the design to General Motors. You need to sit down with the Union and end it. If you do, I'll stay, a loyal employee and you'll have your functioning automatic transmission in a month. By the time the factory has re-tooled in four months, the automatic transmission will be ready for full production, too. "

"You've got some stones, boy! I employed you to design that transmission. I own your notes, your calculations, mockups, every-thing! Hell, I own you!"

"Mr. Drummond, You don't own me and you can't get to the calculations and notes unless the strike is settled."

"Are you blackmailing me, laddie?"

"You may see it that way. I look at it as merely a business proposition. I'm giving you a choice. Beat GM to the automatic transmission design, or keep the strike going. Only you can make that decision for the future of Republic Motors."

"Where the hell is the design, the notes, all of it?"

"I don't have them. I just dropped a box off at the final assembly building. Max Hoffman, my uncle, has put it under lock and key in the safe. I'm the only one he'll give it to, and only if you end the strike. And then I'll be glad to complete the design details, all of which are up here in my head, and you can begin production of the Epoch, charge whatever you want for the car, and give the men and women in the plants a decent wage increase, and the other benefits they're entitled to." Hoffman crossed his arms; legs spread, and faced Drummond across the desk.

Stunned and silent, Drummond's mind went back thirty-five years earlier when he had taken the same stance in front of Mr. Vickers, demanding a commission on bicycle sales. He scowled, refilled his glass, took a deep pull, sighed deeply, was silent for a minute, nodded, and finally spoke.

"And how much is a decent increase?"

"I don't know, two dollars a day. Another dollar the year after, and another the year after that."

"$2.00! And the rest?"

"You recognize the UAW as the sole bargaining entity for the workers and give them a few other minimal benefits, such as being permitted to use the bathroom. You'll pay for all the medical bills for my sister-in-law who was shot, Isabel Hoffman, and those of the strikers who were wounded."

"She's your sister-in-law, eh?"

"She is. She's a strong woman. She'll survive."

"Stones, you got 'em all right, Mr. Hoffman. Bullard warned me about your people."

As soon as the comment came out, Drummond regretted it.

"And what kind of people is that, Mr. Drummond?"

"I apologize. I've nuthin' against you or your people. I'll consider you're…offer. But don't get your hopes up. And finish that design unless you want to be back on the assembly line lifting tires."

Jacob turned to leave. "Good day, sir."

As Hoffman walked out, Angus went over to the window and looked down on his idle empire.

Olivia was chatting with Mary Campbell when Jacob Hoffman came out of the big office. He looked defeated. She said goodbye and proceeded to walk alongside the young engineer.

"Excuse me, Mr. Hoffman, I'm Olivia Drummond, the comptroller."

"His daughter?"

"Yes."

"He's a hard man."

"Stubborn might be a more apt word. What did you talk about, if I may ask?"

"I offered him a deal. He won't take it."

"What kind of deal?"

"I've designed the automatic transmission he wants so badly for the Epoch. I told him I would give him the design if and when he ends the strike and gives into the Union demands."

"My, my. That's quite bold. He didn't fire you for insubordination?"

"No worse. He told me I'd be back on the assembly line."

"Let me talk to him. How soon can this transmission be ready?"

"It can go into production in four months along with the new assembly line for the Epoch that they're working on in Building 6."

"Thank you, Mr. Hoffman."

"Call me Jacob."

"Yes, Jacob." Olivia shook his hand, and then for no reason, let her hand linger in his. She smiled at him. He nodded and looked down, avoiding her gaze.

Angus Drummond slumped back into his leather chair. He stared at his desk, shuffled papers and picked up Olivia's report. He read, flipped pages, moved his finger down columns of figures, looked at charts, and read more. Finished, he put the report down.

Where's that damn list of demands from the Union?

He found it under week old *Wall Street Journals,* flipped open the first page and began to read.

Working Conditions at Republic Motors Hamtramck Plant

He finished reading and shook his head. *I had no idea.*

Drummond turned the page and reacted to the next heading:

United Auto Workers Offer

Offer? More like demands.

He picked up the phone. "Mary, get Ms. Drummond back here."

"Yes, sir."

"Father, you have to take the offer from Mr. Hoffman."

"Do you not know how to knock? And it's not an offer, its blackmail."

Olivia had returned to her father's office. "Call it what ever you will, you need that transmission, and the strike needs to end."

"I read your report. I also read the Union's grievances and demands. I guess they have a point."

"A point?" Olivia stared hard at her father.

"All this time I've been obsessed with not losing everything like I almost did in 1932. Now, I guess I need to see it as giving my workers a wee bit better life and sharing in the success of this company. Anyway, I'm tired of it all. I'm a beaten man."

"Daddy, you're not beaten. You've maybe come to your senses, that's all."

"Is that it? Well, you go sit down with those mogs from the Union, and settle the strike. And don't give away the whole shebang in the process."

"I won't, Daddy. I won't."

CHAPTER 67

Day 23 of the Strike Morning

"Mr. Max, I hear the strike be over. Is that right? Can I go home now?" Tobias looked intently at Hoffman. He wanted so much for the news to be true. Woodson longed to see Sonora and for some of Mrs. Perkins home cooking.

"It's just Max, George, not mister. I'm no better than you. We're all Union members. And yes, the strike is over. Mr. Drummond came to the bargaining table; he's offered us a $1.50 a day raise, plus other benefits."

"Lawdy, Mister… I mean Max, you mean I gonna make seven dollar plus more a week?"

"Nine if you work Saturday, and I'm sure Mr. Drummond will want to produce as many cars as he can, now that he has to pay us so much more."

"So, I can leave now?"

"Not yet. The Union is planning a victory parade. In an hour we'll all march out together. And I talked to the other leaders. We want you to carry the UAW flag, and lead the parade, along with the boys carrying the Stars and Stripes and the State flag, of course. It's quite an honor."

"Me. Why me, suh?"

"You fought like hell at the barricade, for starters. And, you're the only Negro that sat down with all us White boys.

But that was our fault. The Union hasn't supported your people enough. Blacks get the worst jobs in the plant. Well, that's gonna change now that the Union has a say in it. And everyone seeing you carrying the UAW banner is the first step."

"Then I be happy to do it. Thank you."

"Thank you, George Woodson. And I'll ask the Executive Committee to recommend you for a promotion. Time you got out of that foundry. Where would you like to work?"

"I sure would like to build the engines, Max."

"Let me see what I can do. Now, let's get lined up. We've got a victory parade to stage."

Tobias beamed as he carried the Union flag to the cheers of thousands. Mrs. Perkins and Pastor Bradby broke through the throng and ran up to him to congratulate him. He was happy to see them, but his heart soared when Sonora Lincoln ran out and kissed him.

"I'm so proud of you, George."

"Tomorrow be Saturday. Are we going to the movie show?"

"Like always. I'll see you at the White Castle."

CHAPTER 68

Day 23 of the Strike Late Afternoon

Angus Drummond pushed Fiona's wheelchair down the stone path toward the dock on Lake St. Clair. They went through the topiary garden, past a gurgling fountain, the sound soothing in the late afternoon quiet. Angus wheeled his wife of thirty-two years across a broad swath of lawn, finally arriving at the jetty. The late summer day was unusually cool and bespoke an early fall; a brisk breeze drifted across the lake.

"What's this trek all about, Angus? We've not sat out on the dock in ages, since we had the sailboat."

"I wanted to get away from the house, all the servants, and have a quiet moment with me bride."

"We could have done that in your study."

"I need your perspective on a few things, and it's a lovely evening."

The two reached the dock, and he wheeled his wife to a bench at the end of it. He set the brakes and sat down next to Fiona.

"See, me love, how peaceful this is. We own all this, and never come outside to enjoy it."

"Yes, Angus, it is a beautiful property."

Lake St. Clair, a deep purple, entertained several sailboats as they skidded across the water. The couple looked south along the shoreline where white sand beaches were interspersed with pines and silver oaks. A red-orange and blue sky framed the idyllic picture. Drummond gazed over the water, saying nothing.

"This must be serious. What has Wallace done now?"

"Surprisingly, nothing. He's taking the task of learning about the making of cars seriously. He showed up in overalls yesterday, grease under his nails."

"I told you he'd be fine. So, then, what is it my love?"

"What's happened to me, Fiona? Why have I become so blind to the conditions in the world and of my workers? I feel like an angry fool. As a boy, I detested Lord Leith, my parent's employer. Hell, I've become just like him."

"Maybe you felt like you were carrying the whole world on your shoulders all alone, and you can't see it on top of you."

"Bullard shot that woman; her name's Isabel Hoffman. The police report came in today. Her husband is one of the leaders in the Union."

"I won't rub it in and say, 'I told you so'."

"There's a warrant out for his arrest."

"I know he was your friend, but I'm not at all sorry about that."

"Hoffman's nephew, Jacob, is one of my best new engineers, came and saw me today. He's promised he'd solve the riddle of the automatic transmission within a month."

"Well, that's good news. Why have I not heard of him?"

"Bullard made him work on the assembly line."

"Again, 'I told you so.'"

"I need to listen to you more."

"Yes, you do. Anything else?"

"I've told Olivia to sit down with the Union and end the strike.

"Angus, that's the best news!"

Looking back, I don't know why I was so against them people to begin with. But I was scared a' losin' everything I worked for, just like in 1932."

"Yes, but Olivia and your family saved you."

"This time she said she couldn't. But Mr. Hoffman may have. He's Jewish, you know. Bullard always accused those people of fomentin' the rebellion. Well, he's the one doin' the fomentin.'"

"With a little help from my husband."

"Yes, that's true. Guilty as charged. So, I'm getting rid of Bullard and the Service Department. He'll be arrested soon."

"What about the Union, the UAW?"

"I'm going to let them in and give the workers a raise and some other benefits." He reached for her hand and held it.

"I guess you've finally lowered the world to where you can see it again. This is happy news to be sure."

"You know, at lunch, I went into the factory. I met Max Hoffman, Mrs. Hoffman's husband. Nice enough man. Bitter, but that's understandable. He told me he was a Communist, but he thanked me for agreeing to meet and said he appreciated working for Republic. I also met Harry Dunfey, I think that's his name, an Irishman, and a Pollack, Rolf, I forgot his moniker. Good, hard-working Americans. And they've all worked for me for years. We talked for awhile. I must admit, their grievances were justified."

"Just ordinary folks wanting a piece of the dream and a better future." Fiona squeezed her husband's hand.

"I can't remember how long it's been since I've walked through the plants. The strikers hadn't destroyed a thing. Floors were spotless, no trash anywhere. Oh, a coupla' seat cushions were ruined being slept on for twenty-one days. But the plant was a crushing, brutal place, not somewhere I'd want to work every day. It was hot, downright oppressive, even unsafe."

"I see you have the world turned to a view of Hamtramck now."

Drummond smiled, reached into his pocket, and pulled out a silver flask. He twisted the small cap open and took a sip, then offered the chalice to his wife. She nodded and smiled, and took a swig.

"So, that's everything you wanted to tell me, my love?"

"No. The other reason I wanted to come to the dock is tell you its too small."

"Why on earth do we need a bigger one?"

"I went down to see a man at Zug Island, a Mr. Pessano, who owns Great Lakes Engineering Works. I'm going to have him build us a nice boat."

"We already own a sailboat."

"All right, a yacht."

"A yacht?" Fiona grabbed the flask and took another drink.

"Yes, one-hundred-ninety feet in length. You and I are goin' on vacation. For a goodly while."

"Husband, you never cease to be full of surprises. Can such a vessel cross the ocean?"

"We're not going to Scotland, me love; I told you months ago, we're going to Florida."

"And who'll run the company?'

"Olivia Drummond, the new vice president of operations. And I'm makin' Wallace the new vice president of sales and marketing."

"My, my, so much news. Can we go back to the house now? It's getting chilly and I'd better call for more appointments at the therapy center. I'll be needing my sea legs."

"Yes, me love, as soon as you kiss me."

And she did.

AFTERMATH

Late 1937

Chapter 69

The sentries had been posted on the roof batteries and watch towers since the night in Hamtramck when Jack Bullard shot Isabel Hoffman. Now they were gone, terminated by Republic Motors. Bullard hoped they would stay out of loyalty to him, but his goons and thugs knew nothing of that attribute. It wouldn't take long for them to slither back into the back alleys and dark crevices of Detroit — the gambling houses, the gin joints, and dens of inequity with which they were more than familiar.

Alone, except for Flynn, his first lieutenant and pilot, Bullard felt like a prisoner in his own house, which, in fact, he was. It was entirely possible the Detroit Police didn't know about the Port Huron retreat. He could stay there for a while, weeks maybe, until the police got wise. The only address he ever listed was an apartment in Corktown, the one he kept for secret meetings and rendezvous with ladies of the night.

However, it was more likely that the cops had been tipped off. Some rat in the disbanded Service Department would roll on him, if not now, soon. The phone rang.

"Hello." Bullard did not identify himself. He listened. "The cops are on their way, eh. Me bags are packed. Thanks for the heads up. I owe you." Bullard hung up.

"What's up, boss?" Flynn asked.

"Time to go. The boys in blue are on their way. We have maybe five minutes. Come on."

Bullard went to his office. He used a small key to open a lower desk drawer, remove several stacks of money, a brown envelope full of forged documents and passports, his gun, and a can of Zippo lighter fluid. He stuffed all of it in a valise, got up, and went to the bookcase. He removed a King James Bible from the shelf and pressed a button inside the hollow. The panel of books swung open. Flynn followed Bullard through the narrow opening, and they descended the purposely uneven staircase.

"Be careful, Flynn; remember I told you the steps are uneven."

"I've noticed. You might've installed handrails."

"Now that would be defeatin' the whole purpose, wouldn't it?"

They reached the basement. Bullard dialed the combination lock back and forth, and the lock dropped open an inch.

"It's a shame I won't live here anymore. It's all fuckin' Drummond's fault, givin' in to that Union scum. The man has no balls, I tell ya."

Flynn looked around. It was an entire apartment, complete with a pool table.

"You could live down here for months, and the police wouldn't even know you were here, boss."

"Right, but I'm a wee bit claustrophobic."

The two men walked briskly past a warren of rooms, storage vaults, and ventilation units until they reached another door. Bullard opened it, and the cool night air enveloped him. In the distance, he heard sirens.

"Hurry, we've no time to waste."

Bullard's seaplane was hidden about a hundred yards away in a small, densely wooded cove.

"Follow me."

"I'm right behind ya, boss."

Commissioner Conan Reilly sat in the lead car, one of six squad cars sent to arrest Jack Bullard. He couldn't wait to put that arrogant son of a bitch in irons. He'd watched as the man pulled out a massive gun and shot the woman standing on the hood of the car. It was one thing to fire in self-defense but another to commit pre-meditated murder. It had taken a few days to locate a trusted lieutenant named Maloney. He seemed to relish the opportunity to turn on his boss, and knew the location of Bullard's remote compound. He had been there only four weeks earlier for a fancy party and happily gave Reilly the remote address. The convoy sped toward the lodge. Hopefully, they wouldn't arrive too late.

Bullard and Flynn climbed through the small door into the plane.

"Start the engines. Let's get the hell outta here!"

"Willow Run, boss?"

"No, not Willow Run. Too dangerous. They might be waitin' for us there."

"Then where? I need the coordinates."

"We're going to Blind River, Ontario, on the big lake in Canada just east of the Upper Peninsula; the coordinates are under the visor. Land there."

One and a half hours later, they landed into a strong headwind along the shores of Lake Michigan. Flynn taxied the plane to the brown sand beach, big waves rolling over the small plane's pontoons.

"With the strong headwinds, boss, we're gonna have to find some gasoline to get back to Detroit," the pilot yelled back to Bullard back in the passenger compartment where his employer had tried to get some shuteye.

"That won't be necessary." Bullard reached in his valise and pulled out the .38 Magnum. He aimed it at the back of Flynn's head. The report shattered the quiet of the rural night as the cranium exploded and the windshield disintegrated into a million bloody pieces.

Bullard returned the gun back to the bag, and retrieved the lighter fluid. Backing up through the small cabin, valise and suitcase in one hand, he squeezed the accelerant on the seats made from Kapok, a highly inflammable material, then on the cabin carpet. He climbed down the short ladder onto the pontoon, put down his bags, and took out the gun. He aimed at the opposite float below the water line and fired. Bubbles appeared. Bullard took out his Zippo lighter, flicked it, and tossed it into the cabin. He threw his belongings onto the sandy shore, jumped off the funeral pyre, and dispatched several more bullets into the second pontoon. A slow flame erupted, and it grew until the fuselage was an inferno. With all his strength, he pushed the plane away from the shore. The seiche slowly took it out into the vastness of Lake Michigan. As he walked toward a small cabin where he had stored an old Ford, he heard an explosion and the sky lit up. It didn't matter. There was no one living within two miles of the cabin.

One hour later, Jack Bullard boarded a train in Blind River to Sudbury, Ontario, then onto Toronto, where he would catch a non-stop flight to Havana, Cuba. It was perfect because he hated the winters in Detroit. He might even break his abstinence and try a mojito at the El Floridita bar.

CHAPTER 70

Saturday was the day Tobias treasured most. Sonora had to work, but her shift ended at 3:00 PM. He always showed up at 2:30, ate a half-dozen sliders with fries, and after his girlfriend changed into street clothes, they took the bus downtown to one of the grand motion picture palaces. The theatres had air-conditioning, and Tobias cherished the cool auditorium and held Sonora's hand. He didn't care for most of the films she picked, except for *Captains Courageous.*

After the show, they ate at a cafeteria, one of the few restaurants downtown that welcomed all races, and then walked home to Hamtramck. On Sunday, "George" Woodson would attend church with Sonora and her family, who had grown fond of him. But Sonora's father had one reservation. He wanted George to have a high school diploma and confided his concern to Pastor Bradby, who mentioned it to Tobias. The young man was both saddened and angered by the news. Pastor Bradby told him that he could earn his high school diploma by attending night school. Tobias didn't think his dog-tired body could take an evening of history, math, and English, but he decided to sign up at Central High School. It would be difficult, but he wanted to make something of himself. He wanted to marry Sonora; he would tell her his new plans, and ask her to marry him. He still didn't know how to tell her his dark secret, the killing in Memphis. He just didn't know.

"Sonora, I have something to tell you."

She put down her fork and squeezed his hand. "George, you sound so serious. Is everything all right?"

"Oh, it be fine. I'm going to go to night school and get my high school diploma. I don'ts just want to work on the assembly line, I want to be somebody."

"Oh, that's wonderful, George. I'll be happy to tutor you if you need help."

"I'll be needin' help stayin' awake in class."

"Won't it be easier now that you're in the engine assembly building rather than in the foundry?"

"Has to be. Nothin' worse than the foundry. I gonna get a five dolla' a week raise workin' in assembly, plus seven dollar and more a week with the Union raise."

"I have something to tell you too, George Woodson. I got a new job."

"No White Castle? I'll sure miss those hamburgers!"

Sonora laughed and kissed him on the cheek. "I only took that job because I couldn't find any other work. I'm going to be a switchboard operator at the Bell Telephone Company. I'm getting a raise, too."

"That be wonderful. That be a great job." Tobias ate some of his food, too nervous to ask her the next, most important question.

"Is there something else, George?"

"Yes. Sonora, I love you."

"Oh, George! I love you too!" Sonora kissed her boyfriend, this time a quick kiss on the lips.

"Sonora, is it all right if I ask your daddy's okay to marry you? We can have a good life. I don' have no ring to give you, but I'm savin' for one, and I'll take good care of you."

"Oh yes, George, ask him. I know he'll say 'yes'."

"You think so?"

"I know it. And George, I'm saying 'yes' too."

Tobias kissed Sonora and said nothing more. He didn't want to ruin the moment with a confession.

CHAPTER 71

"Melton, there's a letter here for you." The desk sergeant's voice was curt and to the point. He was tired of Officer Samuel Melton inquiring every day about the mail. But he knew Melton had waited over a month for this day to arrive.

"Finally!"

"The wheels of justice turn slowly, my boy."

Melton grabbed the legal-sized envelope. The return address said "Tennessee Bureau of Investigation." He was surprised that there wasn't more bulk to the package. Melton hoped for a thick rap sheet. He had rejected Detective Smith's theory that what happened was an act of random violence committed in self-defense. A murderer didn't become one overnight. A life of crime and malfeasance usually preceded the ultimate act of violence. And Rivers Johnson was murdered, plain and simple.

"I need a letter opener, Sarge."

"Geesus, Melton, it's not a piece of evidence. It's the results of the fingerprint analysis."

"Which might become admissible in a court of law. The letter opener… "

The desk sergeant reached into one drawer, then another, and came up with the requested item. "Don't you carry a pen knife, Melton?"

He ignored the question, slid the blade across the top of the brown envelope, and reached inside the single piece of paper. He squinted as he read it, and then smiled.

"What's it say, Dick Tracy?"

"It says the prints match those of a juvenile offender in Mississippi who spent six months in a work-release program for theft of candy at a five and dime."

"Sounds like a vicious, violent criminal, Melton."

"Kiss my ass, Sarge. It was a chain gang. And all killers start out small."

"What's the perp's name?"

"Woodson, Tobias Woodson. TW. That matches the initials on the knife. I got him, Sarge; he's the killer. Now I just need to get Smith's OK to go to Detroit to find him."

"How do you know he went to Detroit?"

"Just a hunch, but I bet I'm right."

"Detroit's a big place, and if he didn't get a job in the factories, you would be looking for a needle in a haystack."

Detective Lucas Smith sat by the window at a greasy spoon diner on Beale, enjoying the house specialty — spareribs with a side of sweet potato casserole and cole slaw. He always sat there so he could keep an eye on the street. Besides being the home of the Blues, Beale Street was infamous for its purse snatchers, pickpockets, muggers, prostitutes, and doped-up petty thieves committing some minor crime. Most days making an arrest was like catching fish in a barrel.

Timmy Barnes, the latest rookie assigned to Smith to learn "real" police work, finished a plate of fried chicken and mashed potatoes. Unlike Smith's previous charge, Samuel Melton, Barnes had no noble illusions about his new career.

He wanted to catch "perps" and would have no hesitation bending the rules now and then to arrive at the desired outcome.

"Barnes, do you know why I always sit by the window?"

"To keep an eye out for the bad guys?"

"You're a smart one, Barnes. You'll go far. Even though we're off duty, we're never really off duty. In addition, if anyone wants to come in here and demand that the owner, Joe, empty the cash register, we'll be able to block his escape."

"Got it."

"How was the fried chicken? Whoa, now, what's this?"

"Good. What's what?"

"Across the street. If it isn't my old buddy, Bluffton Jones. Looks like he's running his game on some poor hayseed."

"Who's he?"

"Someone I'd like to talk to. He knows something about a killing that happened a while back. One he was involved in."

"I was gonna get some pie, but this sounds like a lot more fun."

The two got up, a dollar bill left on the table, the meal always on the house, and quickly crossed the street as Jones led a country boy clad in overalls, carrying a cardboard suitcase, into the Monarch Club. Smith and Barnes followed behind and spotted the two at the bar where Bluffton was trying to get the bartender's attention.

"Well, hello, Bluff. How are things at the Chamber of Commerce?"

"Who you? I'm buying my friend a beer here." He didn't turn to face Smith but continued to wave his hand toward the bartender.

"It's been a few years, Bluff. I collared you for purse snatching, right here on Beale."

Back still to the detective, he said: "I remember that. I did my 90 days, so leave me alone."

"Oh, we have lots to talk about. How's your buddy, Rivers Johnson?"

Bluffton's head snapped at the name. He turned. "Ain't seen him in a coon's age. Now, I tole you, leave me alone."

"No, I'm afraid further discussions at the station are in order to jog your poor memory."

The hayseed, confused, spoke. "Is I in trouble? The man say he buy me a beer. He be the welcoming committee from the city."

Smith tossed a quarter on the bar. "Beer's on the city, boy. Welcome to Memphis. If you're smart, get on a bus quick and leave. Now, Bluff, you come on."

"I ain't leavin'."

"Officer, this man needs some persuading."

"Right, Detective." The rookie cop quickly grabbed Jones' arm and put him in a Half-Nelson. "Do as the detective asks, Mr. Jones, or I'll break your arm."

At the stationhouse, Sam Melton smiled at his good fortune: his boss walked down the hallway toward the interrogation room.

"Detective, I need to talk to you. I found Johnson's killer."

"Is that so, Melton? Well, then, come with me."

Melton followed Smith to a steel door, and they entered. Another cop was in there, one whom Melton did not know.

"Melton, this is Bluffton Jones." Smith nodded toward the table in the center of the windowless interrogation room. Jones was handcuffed to it. "He's going to tell us all about how Rivers Johnson got his throat cut. Maybe then, you'll stop your foolish pursuit of his killer."

"But I've found his killer, Detective."

"Really, Melton? Just shut up and let Mr. Jones tell us what really happened."

Smith sat down at the table, across from Jones, who was sweating heavily.

"Bluff, what happened when Rivers Johnson got his throat cut?"

Jones tried to free himself from the handcuffs, one end locked onto a metal bar attached to the sturdy steel table. He squirmed in his seat.

"I don' know what choo talkin' about."

"Barnes… "

The young officer needed no instructions. He grabbed Jones by the neck and slammed his head on the stainless-steel top. Melton recoiled in disgust.

Jones screamed. "Al'right, al'right. I tell you!"

"We're all ears, Bluffton."

"If I say, what in it fo' me?"

"Depends. Tell us."

Barnes grabbed Jones' neck again.

"Fine. I tell you! Rivers and me, we be doin' our thing on guys we see at the bus station. People, country bumpkins, we can ask for money."

"You mean rob."

"Yeah, al'right, rob, anyway we see this big Black boy go up and talk to the man at the info'mation booth. Then, he head toward Beale. As good a mark as any. We follow him, talk him up, introduce ourselves, and he say he headed to Detroit."

Melton leaned forward when he heard Detroit.

"Detroit?"

Bluff turned his head toward Melton. "Yeah. Ever'body wants to go to Detroit."

"Did the boy give you his name?" Melton warmed to the interrogation

"Yeah."

"And… "

"I don's remember."

Detective Smith nodded toward Barnes, who was quickly at Jones' neck. He squeezed with two fingers and his thumb, and applied a vice-grip against the carotid artery. The punk screamed in pain, and his bound hands tried to gain a hopeless freedom.

"Was Tobias! I don's remember his last name!"

Melton, sickened by Barnes' unorthodox methods, blurted out: "Was it Woodson?"

"Melton, never give the perp the answer to the Goddamn question! Well, Bluff, was it?"

"Yeah, that be it."

Melton nodded and smiled.

Smith interrupted. "Go on."

"We buy the boy beers, he gets juiced after four, maybe mo', and we tell him all 'bout the Peabody. Ever'one want to see the ducks at the Peabody. Country boy would be impressed. So, we takes him there."

"Yeah, so you see the ducks. Then you take him out into the back alley and jump his ass."

"Sumthin' like that. We offer to walk him to the bus station, but he say 'No.' So, we grab his arms and take him through the kitchen into the alley to persuade him just a little. Rivers put a blade to his throat."

"A little?"

"Yeah. So, Rivers tells me to punch him, I don'ts want to, but I do. Boy doubles over… "

Bluff shook his head and got quiet.

"Keep going."

"Rivers gets him upright and sticks the tip of the switch into the nigga boy's neck and cut him, but jus' a little."

"Again a little? Just a little?" Smith looked down at the concrete floor shaking his head in disbelief.

"Well, after the stick, his body be shakin' like Ma Rainey dancin' at the Palace, the blood run down his neck. I punch him again, and he say he gots money in his boot, let him go. Rivers take the knife away and the boy… " Bluffton's mouth was dry.

"The boy what?"

"Boy reach down into his boot and pull out a blade. Swings it wildly, scared, like he not knowin' how to use it. But he get lucky, leastways for hisself. Knife hits the mark, cuts right through Rivers throat, clean as cuttin' a stick o' warm butter. Rivers drops to the ground, blood ever'where, and I run. That's all there is. I din't do nothin' wrong. I din't kill him. So can I go?"

"Satisfied, Melton?"

"I guess you're not going to let me go to Detroit and arrest this Woodson for manslaughter."

"It was self-defense! At best it's misdemeanor man, and, no, I'm not letting you go anywhere near Detroit. That scumbag Rivers had it coming to him."

"I don't think police work is for me, Detective, leastways not your kind. I'm going to turn in my resignation tomorrow."

"That's probably the smart move, Officer. And what are you going to do?"

"Law school, maybe."

Lucas Smith shook his head and walked away. "Perfect… a fucking lawyer."

CHAPTER 72

Streamers and balloons decorated the door of the second-floor flat on Charest Street. Isabel's daughters used poster paint to make a sign of bright pink and green: "Welcome Home Momma." Max assisted his wife up the stairs, Jacob behind with a wheelchair, and Hannah with the three children in tow. Inside, on the table in the kitchen, Hannah had made a layer cake, and in the refrigerator there was ice cream.

"Max, I can climb up these stairs myself; I don't need your help."

"Fine, woman, but you're just out of the hospital." Isabel continued to climb and stopped midway, breathing heavily.

"Perhaps I could use a little assistance. I'll never be better!"

Max lifted her and completed the ascent. "You will; it will just take time."

"I need to get back to work with the Union. You told me that I'll get paid now as head of the Women's Auxiliary."

"Soon enough. I've been promoted to foreman and got a raise to go along with the contract that the Union agreed to last week. So I'll be bringing home $22.50 more every week. We're going to celebrate."

"We'll need that extra money to hire a housekeeper. I can barely catch my breath."

"Always the pessimist, this wife of mine!"

"Isabel, I'll be happy to come by and lend a hand as often as you need me." Hannah patted Isabel's hand.

"You'll be too busy decorating that big house in Palmer Park. I'll be fine."

Jacob chimed in. "I have an idea. Why don't all of you come and live with us until you're fit, Isabel? We have four bedrooms, two and a half baths, plenty of room, and a large backyard for the children."

Hannah gave Jacob a look that could turn him into a block of salt. *I'm not having Isabel living under my roof,* she thought. *She'll nitpick my cleaning and complain about every little thing.*

Before Jacob could pull back the offer, Isabel responded.

"I'm not moving. My house may not be as grand as yours, but it's mine, and that's where I'll stay. And thank you, Hannah, for offering to help. That's very kind of you."

Jacob took the brick of ice cream from the icebox and Hannah began to cut the cake. The wheelchair opened, and Isabel sat at one end of the table.

"Such foolishness, all because I'm home from that awful hospital." Isabel took a piece of cake without reluctance, sliced a wedge of ice cream, and took a hearty bite.

"Hush, woman. The strike is over, I got a new job, and Jacob's been promoted to head of the engineering department."

"Not quite, Max. I'm only in charge of the transmission group, and if I don't work out the last details of the new Hydra-Glide transmission, I'll be back on the assembly line."

"What's wrong with the assembly line, Mr. Big Shot Engineer?" Isabel shot a look at Jacob, jealous of his new position.

"I'm sorry, Isabel, I didn't mean it that way," Jacob said with genuine contrition.

"Wife, it's all right. I'm proud of my nephew. He's working where he belongs, using that brain of his. But I do have one question. What was in that box you gave me to put into the factory safe? We only keep diamond-tipped drill bits and the like in there. And then suddenly the strike was over, and you came and got the box."

"Let's just say it was a bargaining chip to help end the stand-off."

Hannah interjected. "He's being too modest. Jacob put his job on the line to get the strike settled. That box contained all the information about the new transmission he's been working on day and night. If Drummond didn't settle the strike, Jacob was going to take all of it to General Motors."

Max, in the middle of taking a bite of cake, stopped, and looked at Jacob. "Is that true, Jacob?"

"I was bluffing. I wasn't going to take it to GM."

"What if Drummond hadn't agreed to end the strike?"

"Honestly, I don't know what I would have done, Max. But it turned out all right, didn't it?"

Max stared at his piece of cake.

"So, he settled the strike only to make more money, not to give the workers what they deserve?"

"Max, it was probably a little of both. Drummond's a good man, but he's a capitalist to the core. And he agreed to fifty cents more a day than the Union expected. He gave the workers more, a lot more."

"But still… "

"Max, he's set up a group in the engineering department devoted to improving the working conditions in the plant. By this time next year, the factories will have rooftop chillers to cool the buildings."

"I guess things will never change. It will always be the working man eking out a living while the fat capitalists live off the sweat of our toil."

"Max, the Union won! Celebrate that! And God bless America."

"I guess you're right, nephew. God bless America, indeed."

"Enough of the business talk," Hannah said softly. "If you want to know why we moved, aside from having imposed on you for six months, it's because we will need more room." She looked lovingly at her husband. "Jacob, my love, I'm expecting. And the doctor heard two heartbeats. It's twins."

CHAPTER 73

November 1937

With three months in the plant behind him, Wallace Drummond relished his new position as vice president of marketing and sales. Like his father, he was a natural-born salesman. But Republic was behind the times, and Wallace knew their marketing was downright stodgy, a holdover from the bicycle shop days. For years, Republic had done no more than advertise in *Life* magazine and the *Saturday Evening Post*. The ads were dull, in black and white, with too many words about the car's technical capabilities, allowing for only small pictures of the automobiles. Angus Drummond hadn't even permitted attractive models to stand alongside his vehicles. This was all about to change. Young Wallace determined that 1938 would be a big year for the company; the strike settled, and the new Epoch unveiled. He only needed to convince his conservative father and frugal sister, his new boss, about his plans.

All the hard work and long hours had given Wallace Drummond an itch that a backscratcher couldn't fix. He wanted to see Jasmine Jones. At first, he'd considered her as a one-night stand, a roll in the hay. And maybe she still was, but he loved her lust for life. He realized that because she was mixed-race, her choices were limited, but he saw that she was ambitious and determined to accomplish something in life. She had an air about her; Wallace couldn't put a finger on it. He decided it was class. That was it. Jasmine Jones was a class act.

Wallace drove his new dark-blue Zodiac down Mack Avenue at a careful forty-five miles an hour toward Paradise Valley, just north and east of downtown Detroit. It was a far cry from the stately homes and manicured lawns of the three Grosse Pointe neighborhoods. Simple, modest frame houses without indoor plumbing and lacking good maintenance epitomized the neighborhood. He drove down bustling Hastings Street, and arrived at Club Paradise. He tipped the valet a handsome $5.00, ensuring that his vehicle would be parked prominently at the front door. Both the car and its occupant attracted stares and nods of approval. While white folk generally didn't come to this part of the city, those who liked jazz and Black music did, and their financial support was welcome.

The head waiter greeted him like a long-lost son. "Mr. Drummond, suh, where you been? It's been a month a' Sunday's since we seen you in here."

"A month of Saturday's, Presley, my good fellow. Do you have my usual table?" Drummond slipped $5.00 into the head waiter's hand.

"Been so long since you visited, it ain't your table no mo'. But you in luck; it's free. You come to see Duke Ellington tonight?" "He here as a favor to the boss-man with a smaller group, just an eight-piece orchestra."

"I'm sure that's all he'll need. Say is Jasmine working tonight?"

Presley smiled. "Mr. Drummond, you don't care 'bout no jazz. Just so happens, she is. You wanna see her?"

"Is Roosevelt the president?" Wallace slipped Presley another fiver.

"My, my, my, look who's here. Where you been, rich White boy?"

"You won't believe this but I'm actually working. And hard. Please sit down; I missed you. I'll order champagne, the good stuff."

"Good stuff is all I drink." Jasmine sat down and gave Wallace a peck on the cheek.

Weeks had gone by. She had written off Wallace Drummond as just another white boy who wanted to get some exotic pussy. Yes, he was devastatingly handsome, but he was young, shallow, and she thought, confused. Tonight, though, he looked more mature, more focused. What did he want that he hadn't already gotten from her? Maybe more of it. This time she wouldn't give in so easily.

"Presley, bring us some Dom Perignon, '27."

"Right away, Mr. Drummond."

Jasmine's eyes sparkled. Was there possibly a future with this scion of a major auto company?

"I guess you haven't become a painter or a poet, huh, Wally? They can't afford that good French bubbly."

"My Dad settled the strike. We're in business again. I'm in charge of marketing and sales. Let's celebrate!"

"And you have time for me now. I'm impressed."

"I told you… I missed you."

"And the only time I ever see you is here in Black Bottom. You miss me so much, take me out to where your kind go. Or you ashamed of being seen with a colored girl?"

"Not at all. Personally, I could give a rat's ass what people think. So, you want a proper date? Yeah, I can understand that."

"I'm off Thursday night. You gonna be workin' late?"

"I normally would, but I'm going to take you to dinner."

"To the all you can eat buffet on Woodward?"

"Funny. Let's see… how about the London Chop House?"

"They let Negro folk in?"

"They will if you're with me."

"OK. Pick me up here. You don't need to see where I live."

"Got it. 7:00 o'clock. Afterward, I'll take you to my place. My parents are out of town. Since the strike, my dad's been taking time off. He deserves it."

"And where would your place be?"

"Grosse Pointe Shores."

"Damn, sweet boy!" Jasmine kissed Wallace on the lips.

CHAPTER 74

November 30, 1937

Wallace had set up three easels in the company's executive conference room. The title board read:

Republic Motors – A Marketing Vision For the Future

Angus and Olivia Drummond sat at the conference table, intrigued.

"I guess you've finally taken a shine to the automobile business, laddie." Angus took a sip of scotch.

"I'm excited about the new job. After the bad press with the strike, we need to make some bold moves."

"A newspaper's news is only good for a day. People forget; it's been three months since I ended the strike. But I understand your point, and I am eager to hear your ideas," Angus said.

Olivia said nothing. She suspected her younger brother's vision would cost a lot of money. But it would be unfair to quash his new enthusiasm for hard work, and for setting Republic Motors on a forward, positive course. Her comments would wait until the presentation was over.

"Okay. All right, first — advertising." He took out another board. From now on, all our print ads will be in color in *Life*, the *Saturday Evening Post*, and that new magazine, *Look*. There will be fewer words and a large photo of our automobiles with handsome models, a man and a woman, the potential buyers. Readers will identify with them, and the research I've done shows that more and more women are having a say in the purchase of the family car. And many women are learning to drive. The ads will run in every issue, and we'll design separate, distinctive ads for the Zodiac, Chamberlain, and the new Epoch to distinguish them as individual brands. They'll be no mention of Republic Motors."

"I see." Angus pondered the concept of individual branding. He hadn't thought of that approach. A point for Wallace.

"What about the Drummond, Wallace?" Olivia was curious as she jotted down $500,000 on a yellow notepad.

"It's time to discontinue it, don't you agree, Dad?"

"It's the first automobile I ever produced, and it breaks my heart to say so, but we'll need that assembly line to manufacture the Epoch. Hopefully, it will outsell the Drummond two to one."

"It will, Father. Epoch's a great car. And everyone will order it with the Hydra-Glide transmission. It's revolutionary. Can you imagine no more shifting gears?"

"I did, my son, and my best engineer, Jacob Hoffman, made it a reality."

Olivia thought back to that fateful meeting with her father when she nodded to the handsome young man and talked to him afterwards. She would need to see him again soon to get his 'perspective' on working conditions on the factory floor.

"Next, we will totally redesign our display for the Auto Show. And yes, Dad, we'll have models, beautiful girls in stunning gowns to open doors, lift the hood, and answer questions. And the cars will rotate on platforms. I'm also working with Liam and the design department to create a 'concept car,' an automobile of the future, unlike anything anyone has ever seen. It will show that we are looking beyond today."

Olivia, impressed, said nothing. So far, Wallace had probably spent another million or more dollars.

"Go on, son. You have my attention."

"All right. In 1939, New York will stage the biggest, grandest, World's Fair ever, just outside of the city in Flushing Meadows. The theme is "A World of Tomorrow," and Republic will have a pavilion there, along with the other big companies, Ford, GM, and Chrysler."

Olivia wrote down $5,000,000 under the other numbers she had already notated.

"Aye, and you had better make our pavilion grander than all the others, especially fucking Chrysler!"

"Exactly, Dad."

Angus finished his glass of whisky, went to the sideboard and poured another. Olivia raised her eyebrow and Wallace shook his head.

"We don't want to be Johnny-come-lately to the party. What ideas do you have in mind?"

"I'm working on some concepts with the architect. Maybe a ride along a track in one of our convertibles around a giant city of the future."

Olivia wrote down two million dollars.

"Capital! Who's the architect? Albert Kahn? He designed all of our buildings at the Hamtramck plant." Drummond's relationship with Detroit's most renowned architect dated back to 1915.

"No, someone new. Eliel Saarinen. He designed a private school in Birmingham, Cranbrook, and is the dean of the School of Architecture there. I want a new perspective, plus it's not an industrial building. But I have another commission for Mr. Kahn."

"Oh? Tell us, please."

"I want to build a company showroom and sales offices away from the plant, on Woodward Avenue. I've already contacted Mr. Kahn to design it. Interested buyers will be able to get special discounts on our cars there. Perhaps you can visit the sales floor every so often and personally meet and greet our customers. It would be great publicity for the company."

"I do miss the interaction with the buyin' public. I think that's a superb idea."

Olivia added another million and a half dollars to her list.

"Anything else?"

"That's it for the moment on marketing."

"Well done, lad." The buttons almost popped off Drummond's vest, he was so proud of his son.

"Father, I've done some quick calculations. All of what your head of sales is proposing will cost the company over $10,000,000 or more."

Angus rubbed his beard and frowned. "The strike has left us broke, Wallace. Can you pare back some of your ambitious ideas?"

Before he could reply, Olivia spoke.

"Father, we'll find the money. Wallace, we need to implement your plans. They're big and they're bold and I'm behind them one hundred percent."

"And how, Miss Drummond, will you find the money?"

"We still have gold in Zurich. After we righted the ship in 1935, there was still three million dollars left. And in 1934, the Treasury took us off the gold standard and the price shot up from $20 and ounce to $35, and our gold increased proportionately to over five million."

"I remember. Personally I was against leaving the gold standard." He took a sip of his refill.

"That's why I was your comptroller. I also fibbed a bit. I wanted the strike to end, so I told you all of our reserves were gone. But just as in 1932, I wasn't about to let that happen. 1935 and 1936 were fairly profitable for us after I repaid the loans. You know that. This year was set to be big, but the profits we accrued were offset by the loss of business during the strike. We still have a good deal in reserve, and it's invested in gold, just like in 1929. And, if the company needs to, we'll borrow the money. As much as I hate it, once in a while we may need to resort to that."

Angus stared at his offspring and frowned. "I'm going to have to watch you, young lady. You could fleece me worse than Archie McLagan."

"Yes, but what would I do with the money? I don't bet on the ponies, and I live with a cat." She looked at her brother, smiled, and shrugged.

"You better keep her around, Dad."

"Aye. Well, then, I think we're done here. Proceed, Wallace. And, Miss Drummond?"

"Yes, Mr. Drummond?"

"Don't ever fib to me again. I'm still the boss."

"Yes, Daddy."

CHAPTER 75

December 1, 1937

"Mr. Drummond, the doctor will see you now."

"Good. I'm a busy man, and he's kept me waiting for more time than I'm accustomed to."

"I'm sorry. It gets very busy during the holidays."

"Angus, have you cut out the drinking?"

"Aye. A wee bit, doc."

"I don't believe you. I have the results back from the urine tests. You're in generally good health… "

"There you go. I'll toast to that."

"Your urine is deep yellow. Your eyes are yellow. Are you nauseas, tired?"

"Sometimes. And I've been very busy."

"It's the booze. I told you to cut back, and cut back a lot."

"I know, but it was a stressful year with the Union shenanigans, the strike and all. All right, I probably overdid it. But we Scots, we can hold our whisky."

"No, you can't. Angus, your liver is enlarged. I'm quite sure you have liver disease. If you don't stop drinking, and I mean today, you'll be dead in a year."

"But I've a company to run, and I'm building a yacht for Fiona and me to travel."

"If you want to do those things, you quit now."

"Damn, I love my drink."

"I know. Too much. Be back here in three months and we'll take another look."

Angus walked out into the cold December day. He felt a sharp abdominal pain and a bit of nausea.

"Damn physicians. Well, I'll quit tomorrow."

CHAPTER 76

December 2, 1937

The London Chop House, located downtown in the Murphy Building at 155 West Congress was Detroit's newest and already its finest restaurant.

Tonight, Wallace had Blackburn take over the driving duties and chauffeur him and Jasmine in the stretch black Zodiac limousine, usually reserved by his father for special occasions. The young scion considered this just such a night.

As requested, Wallace picked up Jasmine Jones in front of the Paradise Club at 7:00 PM, amidst the stares of passersby and the valet who had just come on duty. Jasmine, dressed in a silk black dress that terminated well above her knees, and complemented by high heels that displayed her dancer's legs. Around her neck, a solitary string of pearls contrasted against her rich, cinnamon skin.

"Miss Jasmine, you a knockout for sure tonight! And who's that pickin' you up in that mighty fine chariot?"

"He's my boyfriend. And thank you for the compliment, Curtis."

Blackburn got out of the Zodiac and proceeded around the vehicle, the chrome and the body shined to perfection; he tipped his hat as he opened the rear door.

"Madam." He did his best to show no emotion.

"Why, thank you…?"

"Blackburn. At your service."

Jasmine slid into the black leather rear seat. Wallace waited with a glass of champagne.

"You make a nice entrance, Wally."

"So do you. I guess Wally's better than White boy." He leaned over to kiss Jasmine, and she willingly pursed her lips. The kiss was long and passionate, tongue to tongue.

"Damn, girl, keep that up, and we'll all be saluting this flagpole."

"Just my way of saying thank you for the nice date. You sure make a girl feel special." Jasmine took hold of Wallace's hand and held onto it.

"Blackburn, to the London Chop House."

"Yes, Mr. Drummond."

"Reservation for two. The name is Drummond. I requested Booth 2 at 7:30."

"Good evening, Mr. Drummond. Of course. Right this way."

Wallace and Jasmine drank champagne, martinis with olives, fine French wines, and laughed between bites of food and good conversation. Though from two different worlds, they seemed to have a symbiotic relationship. How? Only the god's knew.

After an elegant dinner — French lamb chops with Major Grey's chutney, and an iceberg lettuce wedge with bleu cheese dressing for Jasmine, and filet mignon with mushrooms, and O'Brien potatoes for Wallace, they finished with dessert — a coconut snowball for her and cheese cake topped with berries for him.

There had been a few awkward stares and hushed comments, but for the most part, the other diners ignored the mixed-race couple and enjoyed their own food. Rules of civility applied in this upscale establishment. The staff had been suitably discreet; they seemed to bend over backwards for this unique, albeit handsome couple.

"Jasmine, I have a proposition for you."

"A proposition? You propositioned me long ago, Wally."

"Very funny. I want you to come to work for me."

"What? You want me to be your secretary, like your own personal Stepin Fetchit?"

"No, nothing like that. I want you to be a model for us at the auto shows. You'll stand by one of our cars set on a revolving platform. You'll open doors to show off the interiors, sit in the car, and pretend to drive it. You'll even open the hood. A big mirror above the car will show off the motor. Of course, you'll need to study up on the cars and know something about them. The patrons are sure to ask questions. Republic will provide your entire wardrobe, and the clothes will be from the finest designer houses in New York."

"Baby, I'm just happy to shop at Hudson's once in a while. But tell me more."

"Well, there's lots of travel. You'll stay in the best hotels. The auto show goes to all the big cities — New York, Chicago, Los Angeles, Atlanta, St. Louis, and Washington. And the best part is I'll be there with you, not every night, but as much as possible. I'm in charge of the show, and I'll be responsible for all the arrangements, the set-up, tear down, and lunches and business dinners. "

"That your Negro girlfriend can't attend."

"I'm sorry, I didn't make society's rules. You're here with me tonight, right? And I'll take you to nice places on the road, too."

"What's this job pay, Wally?"

"I'll double your salary to $100 a week, plus travel expenses. All meals, hotels, transportation, and the clothes that you can keep are covered. Please say 'Yes.' "

"Yes."

That night, in a suite at the Statler Hotel overlooking Grand Circus Park, the couple made crazy, exhausting, uninhibited love. Like it or not, Wallace Drummond was in love with Jasmine Jones.

CHAPTER 77

December 3, 1937

Fiona Drummond hated physical therapy, not because she didn't have the desire to walk again, but because she seemed to make so little progress. At every session, she dragged her legs; they had almost no feeling and certainly no strength. After twelve sessions, she had reconciled herself to life in a wheelchair. There were worse things. Her mind was sharp, and she was otherwise healthy. Her upper body, arms, and lungs were strong from moving about in the wheelchair. She had seen the rare photos of the president, Mr. Roosevelt in one. But like him, she hated to be seen in the contraption. His reasoning might be political; hers was vanity. She decided that she needed to get beyond that. The year 1938 promised to be better than the awful year of the strike, and better than all the years of the Great Depression. There were holiday parties to give and social events to attend. And since Angus had admitted that he was wrong about the Union and given his workers better compensation and benefits, she loved him more than ever.

"Blackburn, the tree is crooked."

"Yes, Ma'am, I see that now. Mr. Jackson, help me right the fir. I think we need to move it a little to the left."

"Aye, sir."

The Drummond's chauffeur and the gardener, Bram Jackson, did their best to wrestle with the fifteen-foot Scotch pine tree, the centerpiece of the elaborate Christmas décor at Manor Druimeanach. Situated in the Great Room, a large parlor that Lord Leith had once used for official receptions, Fiona directed the decorating of the Drummond home. Though it was her least favorite room in the great house, too large and cavernous for just one or two people, it was perfect for a large family gathering or the annual Christmas party on December 23, and the great tree that the servants would decorate over the next two days, fit in it handsomely.

There would be additional trees in the morning room, the library, the dining room, the upstairs hallways, and even out on the back patio, where the family would watch a great bonfire on New Year's Eve. In addition, garlands with pinecones and berries would festoon the banister up to the second floor. Now, if there were only grandchildren to add to the festivities.

This year, though, promised to be especially joyful. Six months pregnant, Freya would travel from Philadelphia with her husband, Paul, a banker, educated at Wharton, and an ambitious man in the best sense of the word. The Drummonds were pleased with their daughter's choice, although he was a Catholic. And Jane would travel from New York with her fiancé, Michael. He was in his second year of medical school at Columbia, another fine choice and a Presbyterian to boot.

Fiona finished her second glass of Chardonnay. She had become quite fond of wine at lunch and afterward. With the busy work of decorating, she had barely touched her cold salmon and asparagus, but the second glass was de rigueur.

"Blackburn, I need to check on the trees upstairs. If you give it a good blow or two with the hammer to the wood support on the right side of the stand, the tree should be good."

"Yes, Mrs. Drummond. Ma'am, may I have a word?" The senior houseman went over to his mistress and wheeled her off to a window alcove, out of earshot of the others scurrying about.

"What is it, Blackburn?"

"I don't know how to tell you this, but it's been weighin' on me all mornin'."

"Tell me."

"Mister Wallace… "

"What now?"

"I chauffeured him and a lovely lass to a restaurant last night."

"Allright. So?"

"The lady was a Negro. Oh, she was very nice mind you. Very lovely, if I say so meself. But… "

"I see. But what?"

"He seems quite taken with the lass. They were kissin' on the way to the hotel… "

"The hotel?"

"The Statler Hilton. He told me to go there."

"That's quite enough. Thank you, Blackburn. You may get back to the tree."

Blackburn left Fiona by the window with her thoughts and returned to the task at hand.

"All right Jackson, you heard the lady. Get the hammer."

Fiona wheeled around and headed for the elevator, off the grand foyer and across from the great staircase being decorated by several maids and Cedric, the houseman.

I'll need to check on the banister decorations, too, Fiona thought as she pressed the call button for the lift. The richly appointed conveyance descended from the third level. It was being used by the staff to get boxes of decorations stored on the rarely used floor. The house contained thirty-seven rooms, and now, only three people lived there. The household staff outnumbered the occupants three to one.

The lift arrived, lighting up the number "1" above the carved wooden door with a small window. With effort, Fiona opened the door and then wheeled her chair closer to pull back the accordion metal gate while her wheelchair kept the main door open. She rolled into the small chamber, turned the chair 180 degrees and shut the gate, the main door closing freely, the latch engaged. She pressed "2" on the call pad. The elevator began to rise. The exit would also be a challenge, and require her to rotate her chair sharply 90-degrees to avoid the staircase six feet in front of her while she got clear of the lift-door that required opening.

The elevator stopped. Fiona pulled back the metal accordion gate, turned the main door handle and pushed her chair against it. The door seemed heavier, more cumbersome and somehow required more effort to open. The effort made her a little dizzy. With all the strength in her arms, she gripped the wheels and pushed them forward. The chair lurched out of the elevator past the heavy door. Her hands were again upon the wheels, one to pull forward, the other back to make the turn. But her right hand missed the wheel and the chair rolled forward to the very edge of the stairs.

Fiona screamed as she rolled off the landing, let go of the wheels, and held out her arms to thwart the imminent disaster. The wheelchair dipped forward 45 degrees; Fiona flew out and landed hard on the first three steps, jarring her back as her head hit the last riser. Momentum carried her body forward onto the intermediate landing. She came to rest inches away from the hard plaster wall and the high oak base.

The wheelchair became airborne, absent the weight of its occupant. Her head sideways, semi-conscious, she dreamily watched it fly through the air, and then land hard onto her lower back.

Cedric and the maids rushed up the wide stairs. Fiona's supine body lay beneath the broken wheelchair, motionless.

CHAPTER 78

Angus Drummond rushed down the spotlessly clean, linoleum tiled hallway of Mercy Hospital, only to stop momentarily at the nurse's station.

"Fiona Drummond, room number, quickly."

The on-duty nurse lifted her eyes from a chart. "Room 530, down this hall. It's the third door on the left." She looked at the sturdy, well-dressed man and felt pity for him. The occupant of Room 530 had been unconscious and unresponsive since she arrived.

Fiona's mother and father stood by her bed alongside Olivia. Wallace was on his way to Mercy, considered Detroit's best private hospital. Her eyes were closed. A solitary bottle above her head let intravenous fluid make its way down the thin tube into her arm.

"John, please tell me everything's all right with Fiona." Angus looked anxiously at Dr. John Stewart.

"We don't know, son. She's been unconscious since the ambulance brought her here. The good news is nothing is broken. That's a small miracle."

"Cedric told me the wheelchair fell down the short flight at the top of the stairs, and then it landed on her back. Sweet Jesus! I've told him time and again to never let her use the elevator on her own."

"Don't be too harsh on your people," said Dr. Stewart. "You know my daughter is quite an independent soul. And we both know she can navigate that wheel chair better than most."

Angus went to her bedside and squeezed her hand. "Fiona, it's me, Angus. Wake up darlin', please wake up." He kissed her on the lips. "Fiona, please wake up. I canna live without you!" He squeezed her hand again.

He felt a slight reaction from her. Not a squeeze, but a slight movement, a small, reflexive response. Then she did it again, only stronger. Her head moved toward his voice.

"Fiona, Fiona! Wake up!"

She mouthed the whisper of a word. "Angus…"

"Yes, my darlin', I'm here. Please wake up."

"Where am I?" The voice was barely audible.

"In hospital. Mercy Hospital."

"Why?"

"Angus, I'm sure she's suffered a concussion from the fall. She's disoriented." Her father knew the symptoms of a hard fall, especially one to the head.

Olivia went to the bed and kissed her mother's cheek. "Momma, it's me, Olivia. You're going to be fine."

"Olivia? Why am I here?"

Angus smiled and kissed his wife again. "You had a bad fall, but nothing is broken."

"Then why do my legs hurt?"

Angus looked at his father-in-law, shook his head, and said nothing.

"Darlin', you've been paralyzed from the waist down for almost a year. Is it your head that hurts? Maybe your arm?"

Fiona opened her eyes and looked at Angus. Tears ran down her face. "There's feeling in my legs, Angus! I can feel my legs!"

Angus looked at Dr. Stewart. "Is she delirious?"

Fiona raised her arm up and gently slapped Angus. "No, husband, I can feel sensation in my legs. They hurt! They're tingling and look, I can move them." She lifted her legs off the bed an inch, perhaps two.

Dr. Stewart looked at his daughter, amazed. "Well, I'll be dammed."

CHAPTER 79

December 23, 1937

"You look very handsome, my husband."

"I have to look good for the boss; and it is a holiday party." Jacob opened a drawer of the new dresser in their comfortable bedroom and took out his father's yarmulke.

"You're going to wear that? I'm quite sure it is a Christmas party. It's December 23, after all." She walked to her closet. He followed her to the door.

"Being here in the United States and seeing all the prejudice, not just against our people, but the Blacks and others, I'm more proud than ever of my race and my faith. And don't get me started about what's going on in Germany." Jacob kissed the yarmulke and placed it on his head, then turned and lifted his starched white shirt placed on the bed by Hannah.

Hannah picked out a simple black dress from the generous wardrobe. "I don't know why we were invited to this party. Drummond knows you're Jewish."

"Mr. Drummond did not invite me. His daughter did."

"His daughter?"

"Yes, she's the new vice president of operations, and I report to her."

"Really? Is she pretty?"

"Hannah, she's my boss. She's attractive but a bit buttoned up, and wears her hair in a bun. Businesslike, if you know what I mean."

"Is she a good boss?"

"I wasn't going to tell you this until tomorrow night when we have Max, Isabel, and the girls over for Shabbat in our home, but now that the Hydra-Glide transmission is in production for the Epoch, Olivia, that's my bosses name, has named me the head of engineering for the entire company."

"Oh, Jacob, that's wonderful. I'm so proud of you."

Jacob nodded, walked over to his wife smiled, and kissed her.

"I'll be making $1,000 a month. Maybe we can buy a Chamberlain?"

"Oh, my goodness, so much money. Maybe we can buy this house! I love Palmer Park and Tomasz loves his new school."

"Yes, and to think less that a year ago I was putting tires on autos on the assembly line. It makes my head spin."

"But how do the others in the department feel about working for you?"

"Because I'm Jewish?"

"Well yes, that, and that you've only been in engineering for five months."

"When they found out that I bargained to end the strike with the new transmission design, I believe they felt empowered by what we do, that their work has real consequences. So, yes, they respect me and have, I think, accepted me. I've named Tom Nelson as my second in command. He got a nice raise too."

"So, what does this Miss Olivia have planned for you? Will I ever see you for dinner again?"

"A nice bit of steady work. I'll even have Saturdays off. She wants me to look at the entire production process in the factory, the assembly line, the machines, and of course, the workers. The settlement with the UAW will cost Republic a lot of money. She is determined to increase efficiency and produce more cars with less effort. And less cost."

"And fewer people. Your work will eliminate jobs." Hannah frowned as shook her head.

"Unfortunately, that may be true. But with retirements, and normal attrition, people quitting to work somewhere else, I hope it will be minimal. And if the Epoch is a success, we will have to add a third shift, which means hiring more people. That's the plan."

Jacob looked at his watch. "Are you ready? The cab should be here shortly."

"I have no idea where Grosse Point Shores is."

"It's light years away from our old lodgings in Hamtramck, I can tell you that."

CHAPTER 80

December 23, 1937

The porch railing of the parsonage was strung with a set of big colored lights. The front door was adorned with a simple wreath with red berries and a red bow. Snow had begun to fall and added to the holiday scene, though the evening was bitter cold.

Sonora Lincoln, her parents, Otis and Mayrell, and George Woodson entered the small but comfortable house on Beaubien Street. Reverend Bradby and his wife were having a few of the more faithful congregants of Second Baptist Church over for punch and a Christmas buffet.

They entered a small foyer; a stair to the second floor was immediately in front of them, the parlor to the left was adorned with a Christmas tree, and the dining room on the right had a large table that was set with platters, bowls and casseroles of traditional fare from the South and the North. A large country ham festooned with cranberries and oranges served as the centerpiece. Women in their finest holiday attire passed through the doorway between the two rooms with more dishes and platters of food. On the wall between the kitchen and dining room hung a reproduction of Christ praying in the garden before His crucifixion. It seemed a little severe on this soon-to-be-celebrated feast day of His joyful birth.

The four guests were welcomed by the warmth of the house as a small fire burned in the parlor fireplace. Aromas of cinnamon, cloves, and collards permeated the house full of visitors, who greeted one another with laughter and hugs. George had never seen anything like it, nor had he seen so many well-dressed, well-spoken Black people. Christmas for him had been a simple affair in his parents' small cabin. Each person received a handmade gift, and dinner usually consisted of whatever fowl his daddy had been able to shoot, but there was always warm cornbread and apple pie.

The old Ford pickup truck made its way along Beaubien Street, slipping and sliding.

"Lawd a'mighty, Thurgood be careful on these icy streets. I didn' come all the way from Mississippi to get in a wreck."

"Hush, woman, I needs to find a place to park." Thurgood Woodson looked through the streaky glass for an empty spot.

"You sure we in the right place? Detroit is a mighty big city." Leonie Woodson clutched onto her big purse as if it were about to be grabbed by a purse snatcher.

"I lived here long enough. This here is the place."

"You think Tobias be surprised to see us?"

"Oh, he be surprised all right! He probably be amazed the ol' pickup made it. Took us four days, but we here at last."

"I can't believe my baby boy getting married. Pastor Bradby said she was a peach of a girl." Leonie reached for a handkerchief from her purse and dabbed at happy tears.

"There's Otis and Mayrell! And Sonora and George. What a handsome couple. Merry Christmas to you all." Althea

Bradby greeted the arriving guests with cheek kisses and hugs.

"Thank you for having us, Miss Althea. This place sure bring back good memories." Tobias hugged the hostess.

"George, you look so handsome. I know your favorite room be right over there. I made your favorite dish for you tonight, too."

"Thank you ma'am. You the best cook."

"I am, but Mayrell gives me a run for my money whenever we have church suppers."

"I'm no competition, Althea, but I try."

There was a knock on the door, and then Leonie and Thurgood walked in. Tobias turned and went immediately to his mother, his eyes welled up.

"Momma, Daddy, what are you doing here?" Tobias hugged his mother for a long time, exchanging kisses on the cheek, and then he went to his father with a great bear hug.

"We had to come and meet your girlfriend. And we missed you awful, son. My, this house smell good."

"Please listen up, everyone." Pastor Bradby commanded the parlor with his stentorian tenor voice. "Otis Lincoln would like to make an announcement. Please, everyone, give him your undivided attention."

"Thank you, Pastor. Ladies and gentlemen, a fine young man came to see me last week. His name is George Woodson."

Leonie looked at her husband and whispered, "He say George?"

Lincoln continued. "He's somewhat new to Detroit, having been raised in Tallula, Mississippi. He is the grandson of former slaves, and his parents, Leonie and Thurgood, have driven all the way from Mississippi to be here tonight."

The assembled clapped and cheered, and those closest to the visitors shook their hands.

As the room quieted, Otis continued. "George worked in the fields picking cotton. But he wanted a better life, so he came north, to Detroit. Thanks to Pastor Bradby, he works at Republic Motors, and recently got a promotion. Last week, he asked my permission to marry my only daughter, Sonora. I wholeheartedly gave it. And so, I am pleased to announce the engagement of my darling daughter to Mr. George Tobias Woodson."

The guests clapped and cheered again. Tobias was flustered by all the sudden attention and the hands that reached out to shake his. There were pats on the back and kisses for Sonora, who beamed as she stood close to her fiancé. She looked at him, but he did not seem happy, and tears welled up in his eyes. He looked toward his parents and their confused expressions. His father mouthed "George?" The handshakes continued until Tobias threw up his hands and ran from the room.

The falling snow and the cold air on the back porch soothed Tobias from the smothering affections inside the warm house. He was living a lie, and it could not go on. Sonora followed him out.

"George, what's the matter?"

"You don'ts want to marry me, Sonora."

"And why not, my knight in shining armor."

"I'm not a good person."

"Yes, you are. You're the most kind, wonderful, sweet man I've ever known."

"I done kilt a man in Memphis, Sonora, and my real name is Tobias."

"I know."

"You know?"

"Pastor told me. He knew you asked me to marry you, but he also knew that fact was too hard for you to bear, or you to tell me. He thought I needed to know. George, what you did was in self-defense. The man had a knife at your throat. He even cut you."

"You don't think worse of me?'

"No, George, I'm proud of you. I cannot wait to be Mrs. George Woodson."

"The law may come for me one day."

"It's been nine months. I would think they'd have come for you by now. And if, someday, they do, I'll be by your side and we'll handle it. I love you, George."

"But my real name is Tobias."

"No. To me, you'll always be my George. Let's go back inside. It's cold out here. And I think you might want to introduce me to your parents and explain a few things to them."

"Ladies and gentlemen, please excuse the groom. He is simply overcome with emotion." Reverend Bradby received everyone's immediate attention. "The nuptials, as I have been informed by Mr. Lincoln, will take place around the corner at Second Baptist on June 11, 1938. I look forward to binding these two fine young people in holy matrimony. Afterward, they will have a honeymoon trip to Idlewild, Michigan, where Mrs. Bradby and I have a small cabin. We have enjoyed many summers there with our folk and would be honored for Sonora and George to enjoy it."

The assembled guests clapped and cheered once again, and after Sonora kissed Tobias, he walked over to his parents, tears in his eyes. He felt the grip of fear and guilt that had haunted and consumed him leave his body. It was if his soul could finally breathe; finally look for the good in life, and in love. He was home in the Motor City.

CHAPTER 81

The snow had abated slightly, as a steady stream of automobiles and limousines passed under the stone entry with its massive iron gates. Their prominent feature was the Drummond family crest above the center — a goshawk perched above a simple ancient crown with the words "Gang Warily" meaning "Go Carefully" inscribed in a round circular belt. Once beyond the gates, two Scots guards dressed in wool waistcoats, tartan kilts, and Glengarry bonnets tended to small fires on either side of the narrow roadway. The vehicles proceeded down the long, paved drive until they were directed by the valets with flashlights to park on the expanse of the front lawn of Manor Druimeanach. The attendant's beams of light pierced the falling snow, creating a magical scene. Carolers sang traditional Christmas songs by the front entrance, the limestone archway decorated with a garland of holly and berries.

Cedric, the first houseman, greeted the guests in full Scottish evening wear, complete with a kilt and sparran leather pouch. He ushered them into the Great Room, where the magnificent Scotch pine glowed with colored lights and tinsel and a garland of wide ribbon in the Clan Drummond tartan of red and green squares looped over the branches. A fire in the massive fireplace warmed and lit the room. Candles glimmered everywhere; the staff, dressed in black dresses with white aprons, and tuxedos, walked about the room with flutes of champagne and glasses of the finest Scotch whisky.

Jacob and Hannah Hoffman checked their coats at a special table setup for the occasion.

"Husband, this is too much. I'm so nervous."

"Don't be. You've attended functions at Daimler that were as fancy as this. Come. I see Olivia Drummond. Let me introduce you."

Jacob took a glass of champagne for his wife and a scotch for himself, and they made their way through the crowd. Olivia stood off to the side, sipping a scotch, observing the affair that would to cost Republic many thousands of dollars.

"Olivia!"

"Jacob, I'm so glad you could come."

"Thank you for asking us, even though we do not celebrate. Let me introduce my wife, Hannah."

"Hannah, so nice to meet you. Despite what your husband says, we can all celebrate peace on earth and goodwill towards others. I know you have had an eventful year and escaped the intolerance in Germany."

"Intolerance isn't a strong enough word, Olivia. Let me thank you for the new position you gave Jacob. He is very excited about it."

"He richly deserves it."

Angus Drummond relieved himself in the bathroom. The urine was dark yellow in color. Since the unpleasant doctor's visit, he had continued to drink, but only two cocktails every evening with Fiona. He didn't dare tell her about his condition, and if he drank club soda, inquiries would be made. And the symptoms had worsened. He felt fatigued as the day wore on. Then there was the nausea. That awful feeling came over him, and he quickly bent over and vomited.

"Steady, boyo, you've a party to attend," he whispered. He took a linen towel from the stack by the sink, wet it, and cooled his face. Then he poured mouthwash, provided for the guests, into a small paper cup and rinsed. He took a deep breath, flushed, and left the small, elegant restroom.

He made his way through the crowd, took a scotch off a tray that passed by, and stopped when he saw the Hoffman's.

Why are they here? They don't celebrate the birth of our Savior. I didn't invite them. He stared, frowned slightly, but only for an instant. *Oh, rubbish, Angus, it's Christmas.* He took a breath, nodded, and went up to the couple, with a broad smile.

"Well, here's my young engineer. Jacob, I'm delighted, so nice to see you."

"Thank you for having us. Mr. Drummond, allow me to introduce my wife, Hannah."

"The pleasure's all mine, Hannah. You should be very proud of your husband. He invented the automatic transmission. And he is a quite persuasive individual, I might add."

"It's a pleasure to meet you, Mr. Drummond."

"Call me Angus, please. Welcome to our home. Jacob tells me you were a nurse in Germany?"

"Yes, until the Nazis fired me."

"I see. How terrible. I'd like you to meet my wife, Fiona. She's had some health issues because of a car accident earlier this year."

"I'm so sorry to hear that."

"Speaking of Fiona, I haven't seen her."

Beyond the Great Room, the guests parted. Fiona entered in her wheelchair, pushed by Hazel through the expanding pathway. Fiona wore a deep emerald green satin gown, a solitary diamond on a gold chain hung around her neck, and a diamond tiara crowned her fading red hair. She looked radiant. A gold-tipped walking stick straddled her lap. Hazel guided the chair to where Angus stood as the guests heartedly applauded.

"Merry Christmas, my love." He bent down and kissed his wife on the cheek. She returned the gesture, kissing him on the lips.

"Hazel… "

She pulled the wheelchair back several feet. Fiona took the cane and set it solidly on the floor, gripped it firmly in her right hand, and moved her feet off the footrests. Her left arm pushed against the arm of the chair, and she slowly rose until she stood erect. She began to walk toward her husband, the cane her steady companion. When she reached him after a half-dozen steps, she placed her free hand in his and kissed him again.

"Fiona, this… this is the best present." Tears welled in Angus' eyes.

"I've been to therapy everyday since I was released from hospital. I told you I could feel my legs."

A cheer rose from the assembled guests. A waiter came by with an empty tray to pick up used glasses and plates. Angus looked at his drink, finished it and gave the empty glass to the waiter.

"Done then!"

"What, Angus?"

"Never mind. We'll talk later. Fiona, this is Jacob Hoffman my chief engineer, and his wife, Hannah. She's a nurse. "

"Mr. Hoffman. Ah, yes. Jacob and Hannah, we are so glad to have you here at our home. And Hannah, you're a nurse?"

"Yes, ma'am, that's correct."

"I'm going to have some surgery to improve this lovely face of mine, and there's more rehabilitation in my future, I'm afraid. I might need some assistance in the New Year. Might you be available?"

"Mrs. Drummond, yes, a least until the babies are born."

Fiona smiled and took Hannah's hand. "Did you say babies?"

"Yes, we're expecting twins."

"Congratulations, we're very happy for you both. We have four wonderful children. Speaking of them, Angus, is Wallace here?"

"I've not seen him. I certainly hope he comes. Republic's World's Fair pavilion model was delivered today, and I had it brought directly here for the party. It's a grand building. We're going to have a ride with cars around an enormous city of the future. It was Wallace's idea."

"The building is almost as grand as your yacht. I see you had a model of it made as well. It's not a boat; it's a ship. You show-off!"

"Me love, it will be our home next summer as we travel to Florida and leave Olivia and Jacob to run the show."

Angus took a glass of champagne off a brass tray and handed it to Fiona as the crowd quieted once more, parting for the newest arrivals. There were gasps and hushed words.

Wallace Drummond entered the great hall, Jasmine Jones on his arm. Dressed in a white lame' gown, her hair up, secured with silver brooches, and a fine silver chain hung around her neck. She was stunning, beautiful. Angus looked at Fiona and shook his head, a frown instantly on his face. He started to speak, but his wife had the first word.

"Angus… remember your manners. White, black, or green, it doesn't matter. We're all God's children." She took her husband's hand and squeezed it.

He freed himself from Fiona's grasp as she looked at her son beaming at his date. She worried about what harsh words were in store for them.

Angus walked up to Jasmine.

"Father, this is our newest employee, Jasmine Jones. I've hired her to show off our cars at the auto shows."

"Capital! Delighted! But I'm afraid no one will pay any attention to my automobiles when you are up on that platform, Miss Jones. May I get you a glass of scotch?"

"Mr. Drummond, I'm a champagne kind of a girl."

"Then champagne it is!"

THE END

AUTHOR'S NOTES

The events depicted in the section "Union Forever!" are based on two actual events:

The Battle of the Overpass, as it came to be known, took place on May 26, 1937, at the Ford Motor Company River Rouge plant. The overpass was a steel structure of multiple staircases used by the auto workers to cross over the railroad tracks that served the massive complex. The fledging Union, the United Auto Workers, planned to give out leaflets entitled "Unionism — Not Fordism." The flyers demanded an $8.00 per day wage and a six-hour workday. Walter Reuther, head of the UAW, and other top Union brass were assaulted and severely beaten by employees of Ford's Service Department which was headed by Harry Bennett, the inspiration for Jack Bullard's character. The events depicted in the book are close to the actual reality of the incident.

The General Motors sit-down strike at the Chevrolet plant complex in Flint, Michigan took place from December 30, 1936 to February 11, 1937, a span of 43 days, longer than the 23 days depicted in the novel. It was the first major sit-down strike in American history. Its success firmly established the United Auto Workers as the official bargaining entity of the workers, and its membership grew from 30,000 to 500,000 members in the year after the strike. Again, many of the events depicted in the novel occurred, especially the "Battle of the Bulls Running" where the police retreated and ran after being repelled by the strikers who had taken over the plant. Sit-down strikes soon became illegal, but this first one in 1936-37 became known as "The strike heard round the world."

Other Commentary

Isabel Hoffman's character is based on Genora Johnson Dollinger, a socialist and Union activist who was active in the UAW, and who at 23, organized the first Woman's Auxiliary and later, the Emergency Brigade, whose members did indeed carry baseball bats and brass knuckles. Later, as a result of her UAW union activities, Genora was severely beaten with a lead pipe while she was asleep in her home in Detroit. Johnson is known today as the "Joan of Arc of Labor." She died in 1995.

The main character, Angus Drummond, is based upon many of the early automobile pioneers who started out in the bicycle business. Republic Motors is based on the Dodge Brothers company, and their plant was located in Hamtramck. Drummond is also based on Andrew Carnegie, who, though he became a magnate in the steel industry, immigrated to the United States from Scotland in 1848. His first job as a bobbin boy paid $1.20 a week.

Tobias Woodson represents the thousands of African Americans who made their way north during what became known as the "Great Black Migration," expecting to find good-paying jobs and equality. Instead, most found few job opportunities because of the color of their skin. Ford Motor Company was an exception, and Ford hired many Blacks, though in menial or dangerous positions. In addition, discrimination in many subtle forms existed in the north. The Black population of Detroit lived in two neighborhoods: Black Bottom (named not for the color of the resident's skin but because of the black soil which was farmed there in the

1800's), or Paradise Valley, where more prosperous Blacks lived. These neighborhoods are now gone, replaced by the I-75 freeway or upscale residential developments (e.g., Lafayette Park).

Jacob Hoffman represents the small number of Jewish people who were allowed to immigrate to the United States under its restrictive immigration laws in the 1930s. Though 110,000 Jewish refugees escaped to the United States from Nazi-occupied territory between 1933 and 1941, hundreds of thousands more applied to immigrate and were unsuccessful. The United States was not alone, however, in these policies. In the period from 1935 to 1939, few European countries accepted Jews from Germany. Once the lucky few arrived, they were still subject to discrimination (e.g., Henry Ford and the anti-Jewish articles in the *Dearborn Independent*, Father Charles Coughlin's anti-Semitic speeches, and the existence of the Ku Klux Klan.)

The automatic transmission was developed and perfected by General Motors and made its debut in 1937 in the Oldsmobile as the "Hydra-Matic Transmission."

The description of places, buildings, customs, events, costs of things, news of the day, and people (other than the main characters) are accurate and the result of extensive research. Dates have been changed slightly to better integrate with the story. For example, The London Chop House did not open until 1938.

Acknowledgements

Many thanks again to the staff and researchers at Wikipedia. Their articles are thorough and in-depth.

Thanks to Doug Barnes for his outstanding article on the Wright Brothers Cycle Company. Thanks to Susan Rosenthal for her in-depth interview with Genora Johnson Dollinger.

Thanks to the BBC Press for its comprehensive article on the GM Chevrolet sit-down strike. It was more comprehensive than any American article, but was only one of many I researched.

About the Author

R. J. Linteau is the author of three previous novels and two screenplays. In his former life he was an architect and real-estate developer. He lives in Marietta, Georgia with his wife of 41 years. They enjoy international travel and spending time in Key West, Florida.

Please email your comments to
RJLinteau.author@gmail.com.

I would love to hear from you.